The Collected Works of

Langston Hughes

Volume 7

The Early Simple Stories

Projected Volumes in the Collected Works

The Poems: 1921–1940

The Poems: 1941–1950

The Poems: 1951–1967

The Novels: *Not without Laughter*
  and *Tambourines to Glory*

The Plays to 1942: *Mulatto* to *The Sun Do Move*

The Gospel Plays, Operas, and Other
  Late Dramatic Work

The Early Simple Stories

The Later Simple Stories

Essays on Art, Race, Politics, and World Affairs

Fight for Freedom and Other Writings on Civil Rights

Works for Children and Young Adults: Poetry,
  Fiction, and Other Writing

Works for Children and Young Adults: Biographies

Autobiography: *The Big Sea*

Autobiography: *I Wonder as I Wander*

The Short Stories

The Translations

An Annotated Bibliography of the
  Works of Langston Hughes

The Collected Works of
Langston Hughes

Volume 7

The Early Simple Stories

Edited with an Introduction
by Donna Akiba Sullivan Harper

University of Missouri Press
Columbia and London

Copyright © 2002 by Ramona Bass and Arnold Rampersad, Administrators of the Estate of
    Langston Hughes
Introduction copyright © 2002 by Donna Akiba Sullivan Harper
Chronology copyright © 2001 by Arnold Rampersad
University of Missouri Press, Columbia, Missouri 65201
Printed and bound in the United States of America
All rights reserved
5 4 3 2 1   06 05 04 03 02

Library of Congress Cataloging-in-Publication Data

Hughes, Langston, 1902–1967
    [Works. 2001]
    The collected works of Langston Hughes / edited with an introduction by
Donna Akiba Sullivan Harper
        p.   cm.
    Includes bibliographical references and indexes.
    ISBN 0–8262-1370-7 (v. 7 : alk. paper)
    1. African Americans—Literary collections.   I. Harper, Donna Akiba Sullivan.
II. Title.
PS3515 .U274   2001
818'.5209—dc21   00066601

⊗™This paper meets the requirements of the
American National Standard for Permanence of Paper
for Printed Library Materials, Z39.48, 1984.

Designer: Kristie Lee
Typesetter: Bookcomp, Inc.
Printer and binder: Thomson-Shore, Inc.
Typefaces: Galliard, Optima

Contents

Acknowledgments

The University of Missouri Press is grateful for assistance from the following individuals and institutions in locating and making available copies of the original editions used in the preparation of this edition: Anne Barker and June DeWeese, Ellis Library, University of Missouri–Columbia; Teresa Gipson, Miller Nichols Library, University of Missouri–Kansas City; Ruth Carruth and Patricia C. Willis, Beinecke Rare Book and Manuscript Library, Yale University; Ann Pathega, Washington University.

The *Collected Works* would not have been possible without the support and assistance of Patricia Powell, Chris Byrne, and Wendy Schmalz of Harold Ober Associates, representing the estate of Langston Hughes, and of Arnold Rampersad and Ramona Bass, co-executors of the estate of Langston Hughes.

Akiba Harper thanks God, whose grace enables her to do whatever she has accomplished.

The University of Missouri Press offers its grateful acknowledgment to Eugene Davidson for his generous assistance in the publication of this volume of *The Collected Works of Langston Hughes*.

Chronology
By Arnold Rampersad

1902   James Langston Hughes is born February 1 in Joplin, Missouri, to James Nathaniel Hughes, a stenographer for a mining company, and Carrie Mercer Langston Hughes, a former government clerk.

1903   After his father immigrates to Mexico, Langston's mother takes him to Lawrence, Kansas, the home of Mary Langston, her twice-widowed mother. Mary Langston's first husband, Lewis Sheridan Leary, died fighting alongside John Brown at Harpers Ferry. Her second, Hughes's grandfather, was Charles Langston, a former abolitionist, Republican politician, and businessman.

1907   After a failed attempt at a reconciliation in Mexico, Langston and his mother return to Lawrence.

1909   Langston starts school in Topeka, Kansas, where he lives for a while with his mother before returning to his grandmother's home in Lawrence.

1915   Following Mary Langston's death, Hughes leaves Lawrence for Lincoln, Illinois, where his mother lives with her second husband, Homer Clark, and Homer Clark's young son by another union, Gwyn "Kit" Clark.

1916   Langston, elected class poet, graduates from the eighth grade. Moves to Cleveland, Ohio, and starts at Central High School there.

1918   Publishes early poems and short stories in his school's monthly magazine.

1919   Spends the summer in Toluca, Mexico, with his father.

1920   Graduates from Central High as class poet and editor of the school annual. Returns to Mexico to live with his father.

1921   In June, Hughes publishes "The Negro Speaks of Rivers" in *Crisis* magazine. In September, sponsored by his father, he enrolls at Columbia University in New York. Meets W. E. B. Du Bois, Jessie Fauset, and Countee Cullen.

1922   Unhappy at Columbia, Hughes withdraws from school and breaks with his father.

1923   Sailing in June to western Africa on the crew of a freighter, he visits Senegal, the Gold Coast, Nigeria, the Congo, and other countries.

1924   Spends several months in Paris working in the kitchen of a nightclub.

1925   Lives in Washington for a year with his mother. His poem "The Weary Blues" wins first prize in a contest sponsored by *Opportunity* magazine, which leads to a book contract with Knopf through Carl Van Vechten. Becomes friends with several other young artists of the Harlem Renaissance, including Zora Neale Hurston, Wallace Thurman, and Arna Bontemps.

1926   In January his first book, *The Weary Blues*, appears. He enrolls at historically black Lincoln University, Pennsylvania. In June, the *Nation* weekly magazine publishes his landmark essay "The Negro Artist and the Racial Mountain."

1927   Knopf publishes his second book of verse, *Fine Clothes to the Jew*, which is condemned in the black press. Hughes meets his powerful patron Mrs. Charlotte Osgood Mason. Travels in the South with Hurston, who is also taken up by Mrs. Mason.

1929   Hughes graduates from Lincoln University.

1930   Publishes his first novel, *Not without Laughter* (Knopf). Visits Cuba and meets fellow poet Nicolás Guillén. Hughes is dismissed by Mrs. Mason in a painful break made worse by false charges of dishonesty leveled by Hurston over their play *Mule Bone*.

1931   Demoralized, he travels to Haiti. Publishes work in the communist magazine *New Masses*. Supported by the Rosenwald Foundation, he tours the South taking his poetry to the people. In Alabama, he visits some of the Scottsboro Boys in prison. His brief collection of poems *Dear Lovely Death* is privately printed in Amenia, New York. Hughes and the illustrator Prentiss Taylor publish a verse pamphlet, *The Negro Mother*.

1932   With Taylor, he publishes *Scottsboro Limited*, a short play and four poems. From Knopf comes *The Dream Keeper*, a book of previously published poems selected for young people. Later, Macmillan brings out *Popo and Fifina*, a children's story about Haiti written with Arna Bontemps, his closest friend. In June, Hughes sails to Russia in a band of twenty-two young African

Americans to make a film about race relations in the United States. After the project collapses, he lives for a year in the Soviet Union. Publishes his most radical verse, including "Good Morning Revolution" and "Goodbye Christ."

1933   Returns home at midyear via China and Japan. Supported by a patron, Noël Sullivan of San Francisco, Hughes spends a year in Carmel writing short stories.

1934   Knopf publishes his first short story collection, *The Ways of White Folks*. After labor unrest in California threatens his safety, he leaves for Mexico following news of his father's death.

1935   Spends several months in Mexico, mainly translating short stories by local leftist writers. Lives for some time with the photographer Henri Cartier-Bresson. Returning almost destitute to the United States, he joins his mother in Oberlin, Ohio. Visits New York for the Broadway production of his play *Mulatto* and clashes with its producer over changes in the script. Unhappy, he writes the poem "Let America Be America Again."

1936   Wins a Guggenheim Foundation fellowship for work on a novel but soon turns mainly to writing plays in association with the Karamu Theater in Cleveland. Karamu stages his farce *Little Ham* and his historical drama about Haiti, *Troubled Island*.

1937   Karamu stages *Joy to My Soul*, another comedy. In July, he visits Paris for the League of American Writers. He then travels to Spain, where he spends the rest of the year reporting on the civil war for the *Baltimore Afro-American*.

1938   In New York, Hughes founds the radical Harlem Suitcase Theater, which stages his agitprop play *Don't You Want to Be Free?* The leftist International Workers Order publishes *A New Song*, a pamphlet of radical verse. Karamu stages his play *Front Porch*. His mother dies.

1939   In Hollywood he writes the script for the movie *Way Down South*, which is criticized for stereotyping black life. Hughes goes for an extended stay in Carmel, California, again as the guest of Noël Sullivan.

1940   His autobiography *The Big Sea* appears (Knopf). He is picketed by a religious group for his poem "Goodbye Christ," which he publicly renounces.

1941   With a Rosenwald Fund fellowship for playwriting, he leaves California for Chicago, where he founds the Skyloft Players. Moves on to New York in December.

1942   Knopf publishes his book of verse *Shakespeare in Harlem*. The Skyloft Players stage his play *The Sun Do Move*. In the summer he resides at the Yaddo writers' and artists' colony, New York. Hughes also works as a writer in support of the war effort. In November he starts "Here to Yonder," a weekly column in the Chicago *Defender* newspaper.

1943   "Here to Yonder" introduces Jesse B. Semple, or Simple, a comic Harlem character who quickly becomes its most popular feature. Hughes publishes *Jim Crow's Last Stand* (Negro Publication Society of America), a pamphlet of verse about the struggle for civil rights.

1944   Comes under surveillance by the FBI because of his former radicalism.

1945   With Mercer Cook, translates and later publishes *Masters of the Dew* (Reynal and Hitchcock), a novel by Jacques Roumain of Haiti.

1947   His work as librettist with Kurt Weill and Elmer Rice on the Broadway musical play *Street Scene* brings Hughes a financial windfall. He vacations in Jamaica. Knopf publishes *Fields of Wonder,* his only book composed mainly of lyric poems on nonracial topics.

1948   Hughes is denounced (erroneously) as a communist in the U.S. Senate. He buys a townhouse in Harlem and moves in with his longtime friends Toy and Emerson Harper.

1949   Doubleday publishes *Poetry of the Negro, 1746–1949,* an anthology edited with Arna Bontemps. Also published are *One-Way Ticket* (Knopf), a book of poems, and *Cuba Libre: Poems of Nicolás Guillén* (Anderson and Ritchie), translated by Hughes and Ben Frederic Carruthers. Hughes teaches for three months at the University of Chicago Lab School for children. His opera about Haiti with William Grant Still, *Troubled Island,* is presented in New York.

1950   Another opera, *The Barrier,* with music by Jan Meyerowitz, is hailed in New York but later fails on Broadway. Simon and Schuster publishes *Simple Speaks His Mind,* the first of five books based on his newspaper columns.

1951   Hughes's book of poems about life in Harlem, *Montage of a Dream Deferred,* appears (Henry Holt).

1952   His second collection of short stories, *Laughing to Keep from Crying,* is published by Henry Holt. In its "First Book" series for children, Franklin Watts publishes Hughes's *The First Book of Negroes.*

1953 In March, forced to testify before Senator Joseph McCarthy's subcommittee on subversive activities, Hughes is exonerated after repudiating his past radicalism. *Simple Takes a Wife* appears.

1954 Mainly for young readers, he publishes *Famous American Negroes* (Dodd, Mead) and *The First Book of Rhythms.*

1955 Publishes *The First Book of Jazz* and finishes *Famous Negro Music Makers* (Dodd, Mead). In November, Simon and Schuster publishes *The Sweet Flypaper of Life,* a narrative of Harlem with photographs by Roy DeCarava.

1956 Hughes's second volume of autobiography, *I Wonder as I Wander* (Rinehart), appears, as well as *A Pictorial History of the Negro* (Crown), coedited with Milton Meltzer, and *The First Book of the West Indies.*

1957 *Esther,* an opera with composer Jan Meyerowitz, has its premiere in Illinois. Rinehart publishes *Simple Stakes a Claim* as a novel. Hughes's musical play *Simply Heavenly,* based on his Simple character, runs for several weeks off and then on Broadway. Hughes translates and publishes *Selected Poems of Gabriela Mistral* (Indiana University Press).

1958 *The Langston Hughes Reader* (George Braziller) appears, as well as *The Book of Negro Folklore* (Dodd, Mead), coedited with Arna Bontemps, and another juvenile, *Famous Negro Heroes of America* (Dodd, Mead). John Day publishes a short novel, *Tambourines to Glory,* based on a Hughes gospel musical play.

1959 Hughes's *Selected Poems* published (Knopf).

1960 *The First Book of Africa* appears, along with *An African Treasury: Articles, Essays, Stories, Poems by Black Africans,* edited by Hughes (Crown).

1961 Inducted into the National Institute of Arts and Letters. Knopf publishes his book-length poem *Ask Your Mama: 12 Moods for Jazz. The Best of Simple,* drawn from the columns, appears (Hill and Wang). Hughes writes his gospel musical plays *Black Nativity* and *The Prodigal Son.* He visits Africa again.

1962 Begins a weekly column for the *New York Post.* Attends a writers' conference in Uganda. Publishes *Fight for Freedom: The Story of the NAACP,* commissioned by the organization.

1963 His third collection of short stories, *Something in Common,* appears from Hill and Wang. Indiana University Press publishes

Five Plays by Langston Hughes, edited by Webster Smalley, as well as Hughes's anthology *Poems from Black Africa, Ethiopia, and Other Countries.*

1964   His musical play *Jericho–Jim Crow,* a tribute to the civil rights movement, is staged in Greenwich Village. Indiana University Press brings out his anthology *New Negro Poets: U.S.A.,* with a foreword by Gwendolyn Brooks.

1965   With novelists Paule Marshall and William Melvin Kelley, Hughes visits Europe for the U.S. State Department. His gospel play *The Prodigal Son* and his cantata with music by David Amram, *Let Us Remember,* are staged.

1966   After twenty-three years, Hughes ends his depiction of Simple in his Chicago *Defender* column. Publishes *The Book of Negro Humor* (Dodd, Mead). In a visit sponsored by the U.S. government, he is honored in Dakar, Senegal, at the First World Festival of Negro Arts.

1967   His *The Best Short Stories by Negro Writers: An Anthology from 1899 to the Present* (Little, Brown) includes the first published story by Alice Walker. On May 22, Hughes dies at New York Polyclinic Hospital in Manhattan from complications following prostate surgery. Later that year, two books appear: *The Panther and the Lash: Poems of Our Times* (Knopf) and, with Milton Meltzer, *Black Magic: A Pictorial History of the Negro in American Entertainment* (Prentice Hall).

The Collected Works of

Langston Hughes

Volume 7

The Early Simple Stories

Introduction

Often labeled the "Poet Laureate of the Negro people," Langston Hughes remained deeply committed to the African American people throughout his lifetime. Using poetry, short fiction, plays, and several other genres of literature, he expressed, "without fear or shame,"[1] the dreams and frustrations, the accomplishments and failures, the laughter and tears of ordinary black folks. He never hesitated to use black vernacular English, but he carefully imbued such dialect with dignity, depth, and insight. Although he often spoke in the language of the common black people, he warmly invited any who might not consider themselves to be a part of the black masses to "listen fluently," as Simple says, to both the cadences and the messages of their words.

The universal and widely celebrated character we now call Simple originated as an occasional feature in a newspaper column Langston Hughes began writing for the (then weekly) *Chicago Defender* on November 21, 1942. The third most widely read black newspaper of that decade, the *Defender* provided Hughes with a ready and extensive audience of black readers, including subscribers nationwide and abroad. Contributing a column to the *Defender* resolved for Hughes the long-standing dilemma of audience, a troublesome issue for most black writers. Hughes did not need to consider the tastes and knowledge of white readers as he chose his subject matter, inserted his allusions, or selected his dialect. Only after Simple became the subject of a book did Hughes edit and revise the slang and the references to help his uninitiated readers appreciate the nuances of the conversations. His subject matter, however, never deviated. An excerpt from the first of Hughes's weekly *Defender* columns helps to establish the scope of Hughes's vision and prefigures the use of the Simple character, who would not appear until February 13, 1943.

"Guns, Not Shovels"

The cat was taking his first physical, standing in line in front of me at the hospital where our draft board had sent us. He was talking and he didn't

---

1. The phrase is from "The Negro Artist and the Racial Mountain," Hughes's noted 1926 essay for the *Nation,* in which he declared the bold aims of New Negro artists.

care who heard him. (Chalk up one point for the democracies—at least a man can talk, even a colored man.) He said, "I know they gonna send all us cats to a labor battalion. I'm a truck driver, and I know they gonna make me a truck driver in the army."

"How do you know," I asked.

"All the guys I know from Harlem," he said, "have gone right straight to labor battalions. Look at the pictures you see of colored soldiers in the papers, always working, building roads, unloading ships, that's all. Labor battalions! I want to be a fighter!"

"I know a fellow who's gone to Officers School," I said. "And another one learning to fight paratroopers."

"I don't know none," he said. "And besides, if they don't hurry and take this blood test, I'm liable to lose my job. This Italian I work for don't care whether the draft board calls you or not, you better be to work on time. He ain't been in this country but six or seven years and owns a whole fleet of trucks, and best I can do is drive one of 'em for him. Foreigners can get ahead in this country. I can't."

"Some colored folks get ahead some," I said.

"You have to be a genius to do it," he argued.

Another man in the line spoke up, older, dark brownskin, quiet. "Between Hitler and the Japanese," the other man said, "these white folks are liable to change their minds. They're beginning to find out they need us colored people."

It was that third fellow who took the conversation all the way from the here of Manhattan Island to the yonder of Hitler, the Japanese, and the arena of struggle—that far-off yonder—including Africa, India and China, Gandhi and Chiang Kai-Shek—that yonder that, in spite of all, is changing our world in Harlem, on State street, and maybe even in Mississippi.

There was no chance to talk any more for the line moved on. He went in to the little room where the doctors were, had his blood drawn, and hurried off. I do not know his name. Probably our paths will never cross again. But I hope, since he wants to be a fighter, Uncle Sam will give him a gun, not a shovel or a truck. A gun would probably help his morale a little—now badly bent by the color line.[2]

Hughes has introduced ordinary people, folks who do not know the exceptional blacks who were among Hughes's own friends and acquaintances. Such ordinary people who face and overcome racism in their daily work are actually heroes, Hughes had argued in "The Need for Heroes"

2. From "Why and Wherefore," *Chicago Defender,* November 21, 1942; rpt. in its entirety in *Langston Hughes and the* Chicago Defender: *Essays on Race, Politics, and Culture, 1942–62,* ed. Christopher C. De Santis (Urbana: University of Illinois Press, 1995), 221–23.

in 1941.[3] Thus, even in his first column for the *Defender*, Hughes fore-shadowed the techniques he would use throughout the Simple stories.

As does "Guns, Not Shovels," the Simple columns, created in the dynamic and turbulent 1940s, focus on current events and conditions. World War II, Jim Crow racial policies in the South, restrictive housing covenants in the urban North, restricted opportunities for employment (even in the armed forces), high prices in black neighborhood stores, and the professional and private activities of black athletes and entertainers all figure prominently in the earliest Simple stories.

The anonymous fellow in "Guns, Not Shovels" proves his assertions about the ways black men are used in the military by pointing to "the pictures you see of colored soldiers in the papers." As he appeared in the *Defender*, Simple frequently links his comments to specific current events. In fact, Jesse B. Semple in his earliest form actually read the column Langston Hughes contributed to the *Defender*. An avid reader of the news, the character introduced on February 13, 1943, was at first called Hughes's "Simple Minded Friend." He always had an opinion, and he never minded sharing it, even to challenge what the presumably more savvy and better educated columnist had written.

Admittedly the Simple character and the bar buddy with whom he held forth regularly both voiced the opinions of their creator, Langston Hughes. Yet these characters exceeded and amplified what Hughes could say in his own voice or in the voice of a single poetic speaker. From the earliest columns, Hughes received letters from readers who claimed to know Simple or to know someone who felt or spoke the same way. Years of consistent presentation permitted growing numbers of faithful readers to "know" Simple. He became so real to some readers that they mailed gifts to him or to Joyce.

The original foil for Simple was Langston Hughes himself, and the dialogue was often dominated by Hughes in his well-intentioned desire to share a global vision with his associates who suffered a more parochial perspective. However, the responses of readers helped the author to surrender the dominant role to his Simple Minded Friend. As Hughes withdrew his own editorial voice, the bar buddy with whom Simple conversed became an anonymous foil. Not until he needed to list his

3. "The Need for Heroes," *Crisis* 48 (June 1941): 184–85, 206; rpt. in *The Collected Works of Langston Hughes, Volume 10*, Fight for Freedom *and Other Writings on Civil Rights*, ed. Christopher C. De Santis (Columbia: University of Missouri Press, 2001), 223–29.

characters for the play *Simply Heavenly* (1957) did Hughes name the foil Ananias Boyd. Such naming confuses the foil with another character, Ezra Boyd, who is a roomer in Simple's building. Ezra Boyd is *not* the foil, because Simple occasionally speaks *to* his bar buddy about Boyd. Yet, by the time of the publication of the fourth volume of Simple stories, *Simple's Uncle Sam,* in 1965, the foil is occasionally called Boyd. Thus, some critics refer to the usually unnamed foil as Boyd.

Readers truly delighted in having a champion for their own views, even if their views were challenged and even scoffed at by the increasingly anonymous bar buddy. Simple's significance as a voice for the masses becomes crystal clear when he speaks about the Harlem Riots of 1943 (see the story "Ways and Means"). While the preponderance of documentation for that period reveals black politicians and leaders of African American organizations speaking about the need for the residents of Harlem to be calm, Simple unapologetically acknowledges that he did smash windows. While the so-called black leaders attributed the unrest to outside agitators, Simple attributes the unrest to long-standing friction between the police and the residents of Harlem, against the background of blatant racism exhibited toward black soldiers in uniform. Smashing store windows expressed Simple's long-standing frustration about high prices in Harlem stores. Most important, Simple did not loot the stores; he only wanted justice. The bar buddy was conveniently out of town during the riot, but he challenges Simple's actions and represents the opinions of the many blacks who remained inside their homes and who disapproved of the riots. Thus, the conversations represent a range of black opinions on the riots. Significantly, however, unlike other literature from the period, the Simple stories give a voice to one member of the masses who intentionally participated in the Harlem Riots of 1943.

Simple's subjects are not always serious political matters. He also discusses the problems he has with his landlady, with his boss, and with his female companions. Simple holds a steady job—except when he is laid off. Nevertheless, he never seems to have enough money, especially to buy the beer he enjoys drinking each evening after work. His bar buddy, Boyd, generally has a little extra money and often lends money to Simple—or at least buys his beer. Varying economic conditions are represented in these two main characters, again helping uninitiated readers to recognize that neither man represents "THE Negro."[4]

---

4. In "Coffee Break," a later story to be included in the next volume of *The Collected Works,* Simple complains because his boss talks about "THE Negro" and fails to recognize the "50–11 different kinds of Negroes in the U.S.A."

The stories never diverged from their focus on black people, but because the focus was sharp and clear, they became accessible to a wide international readership. When the stories from the *Defender* were revised and edited for the first volume of stories, *Simple Speaks His Mind,* white readers could observe black life almost as if they had become flies on the wall. Rather than hearing a black voice directed to white readers— as with the powerful essays of James Baldwin—nonblack readers actually eavesdropped on a conversation between black men written to be read in the black press. Readers perceived the honesty, and the stories were translated and grew popular all over the world. As Langston Hughes had predicted, his "writing as well as he knew how"[5] about these memorable and universal black characters opened their stories to the world.

While many of Langston Hughes's poetic images linger with us, the fictional character Jesse B. Semple became his greatest sustained creation. More than any other body of his work, the Simple stories demonstrate Hughes's appreciation for the masses. Hughes wrote all of his newspaper columns, including the Simple episodes, for a mass black audience, and he continued to write the Simple stories because of the praise and support he received from that mass black readership. Simultaneously, the Simple stories also represent those blacks whose education and travel had afforded them a more expansive view of the world. Conversing regularly and as friends, Jesse B. Semple and Ananias Boyd brought to readers the conflicting views of blacks and exposed many of the hypocrisies of America's platitudes. "America never was America to me" took on far deeper meaning during the twenty-two years of Simple's creation and development.[6]

The success of the stories is reflected in their longevity. Langston Hughes spent several frustrating years combining, expanding, and revising the newspaper episodes to convert the stories into his first book-length collection.[7] The fruit of his revising and polishing, *Simple Speaks His Mind,* was published by Simon and Schuster in 1950. One of Hughes's most successful publications, that volume led to a second collection in 1953, also published by Simon and Schuster: *Simple Takes a*

5. Hughes states in his second volume of autobiography, *I Wonder as I Wander,* "I wanted to write seriously and as well as I knew how about the Negro people, and make that kind of writing earn for me a living" (New York: Hill and Wang, 1964), 5.

6. "America never was America to me": A parenthetical stanza in "Let America Be America Again," a poem Hughes first published in 1936.

7. Those curious about the details of those arduous years of effort and revision should consult my *Not So Simple: The "Simple" Stories by Langston Hughes* (Columbia: University of Missouri Press, 1995).

Wife. As the title suggests, the domestic scene dominates the second volume. Many of its episodes were edited so that they flow almost seamlessly, as Simple recalls his first wife, Isabel, along with other women with whom he has spent significant amounts of time. Joyce Lane, the respectable, socially conscious, and budget-restricted young woman he has grown to love, becomes his second wife by the end of the volume.

This volume of *The Works of Langston Hughes* brings back to print these first two volumes of Simple stories, both of which have been out of print for decades. Although *The Best of Simple* (1960) selected some of the episodes from these two volumes, the actual books in their entirety restore the full context of Simple's repertoire. A second volume will recapture two later collections of the stories, *Simple Stakes a Claim* (1957) and *Simple's Uncle Sam* (1965), along with some stories Hughes did not previously collect.

The important challenge for twenty-first-century readers of Simple is to acknowledge the context of his origination. Emphasis on racial discrimination has been scoffed at by contemporary pundits, white and black. Indeed, achievements by and opportunities for blacks in the twenty-first century are now almost so commonplace as to escape mention on the news or at the dinner table. Some observers resent any news that someone is still being heralded as "the first black" to achieve some goal. Thus, when a black person in the twenty-first century complains about racial discrimination, a frequent response highlights a lack of ambition or failure of preparation on the part of the one who feels that race has held him or her back. By contrast, in the 1940s and 1950s, the historical context for these Simple stories, major universities in the South were still racially segregated. Black voters in the South were legally disenfranchised. Even the Red Cross separated blood donated by blacks so that it would not be transfused into whites. Twenty-first-century readers must understand that Simple's complaints about racial discrimination reflect historically documented realities. Readers unfamiliar with the rocky passages of Americans descended from Africans might consult a comprehensive history, such as *From Slavery to Freedom* by award-winning historian John Hope Franklin (with assistance in the most recent editions from Alfred A. Moss). Those more familiar with the historical details might consult Franklin's reflections in *The Color Line: Legacy for the Twenty-First Century* on the changes of the past decades and the ongoing problems faced by blacks.[8] Even without undertaking additional

8. John Hope Franklin and Alfred A. Moss, *From Slavery to Freedom: A History of African Americans,* 8th ed. (New York: Knopf, 2000); John Hope Franklin, *The*

reading assignments, contemporary readers must accept that these early Simple stories reflect racist realities for blacks in the United States, but they do so from the perspective Hughes valued: everyday heroism. Simple achieves victory in the face of oppression; he never becomes blind to the problems surrounding him, but he never surrenders to the power of oppression.

Simple left his boyhood home in the Commonwealth of Virginia, moved to Baltimore, where he worked for a while, and finally settled in Harlem. Simple sought a greater measure of freedom and opportunity than he could achieve in the South. Most important, he sought to be surrounded by other black folk who could help him to gain a sense of empowerment. These things he finds and celebrates in one of the earliest stories in *Simple Speaks His Mind*, "A Toast to Harlem." He later embraces his young cousin Franklin D. Roosevelt Brown, who "always did want to come North" (see "They Come and They Go"). With his own restricted budget and rented room, Simple shares what he has so that he might extend opportunity to his ambitious young cousin. Thus, the Simple stories also embody both hope and generosity, even in the midst of meager resources.

Since the Simple stories are not always included in the selections anthologized to represent Langston Hughes, these stories may be completely new to some readers. As they did for their initial readers in 1950, the stories should unfold easily in this volume to reveal Jesse B. Semple, Joyce Lane, the bar buddy Ananias Boyd, the good-time gal Zarita, and the other occasional characters. The details of the historical events and the identities of the actual individuals mentioned are not unraveled in detailed footnotes. Better than ponderous notes would be the occasion to use the questions generated by this volume to do what Simple and Boyd did: talk. The volume captures conversations—imagined, but very much like real ones heard throughout the 1940s and 1950s in Harlem. Perhaps this volume can also stimulate genuine conversations, so that the newest generation of readers can ask the baby boomers and senior citizens about Jackie Robinson, Cab Calloway, and the Un-American Committee. Perhaps this volume can encourage us all to ask each other in the twenty-first century whether the Simple characters who still see the fallacies in our democracy will continue to express themselves—and whether the so-called sophisticated will listen.

Color Line: Legacy for the Twenty-First Century (Columbia: University of Missouri Press, 1993).

A Note on the Text

For this edition of the first two volumes of Simple stories, we have used the first editions of *Simple Speaks His Mind* and *Simple Takes a Wife,* published by Simon and Schuster in 1950 and 1953, respectively. All spellings, capitalization, punctuation, and word compounding have been retained as they originally appeared, although obvious typographical errors have been corrected.

Simple Speaks His Mind

(1950)

To Zell and Garnett

The author and publishers of *Simple Speaks His Mind* are grateful to the *Chicago Defender,* where these stories originated, the *New Republic,* and *Phylon,* for permission to reprint material in this book.

Contents

Part One

Summer Time

Feet Live Their Own Life

"If you want to know about my life," said Simple as he blew the foam from the top of the newly filled glass the bartender put before him, "don't look at my face, don't look at my hands. Look at my feet and see if you can tell how long I been standing on them."

"I cannot see your feet through your shoes," I said.

"You do not need to see through my shoes," said Simple. "Can't you tell by the shoes I wear—not pointed, not rocking-chair, not French-toed, not nothing but big, long, broad, and flat—that I been standing on these feet a long time and carrying some heavy burdens? They ain't flat from standing at no bar, neither, because I always sets at a bar. Can't you tell that? You know I do not hang out in a bar unless it has stools, don't you?"

"That I have observed," I said, "but I did not connect it with your past life."

"Everything I do is connected up with my past life," said Simple. "From Virginia to Joyce, from my wife to Zarita, from my mother's milk to this glass of beer, everything is connected up."

"I trust you will connect up with that dollar I just loaned you when you get paid," I said. "And who is Virginia? You never told me about her."

"Virginia is where I was borned," said Simple. "I *would* be borned in a state named after a woman. From that day on, women never give me no peace."

"You, I fear, are boasting. If the women were running after you as much as you run after them, you would not be able to sit here on this bar stool in peace. I don't see any women coming to call you out to go home, as some of these fellows' wives do around here."

"Joyce better not come in no bar looking for me," said Simple. "That is why me and my wife busted up—one reason. I do not like to be called out of no bar by a female. It's a man's perogative to just set and drink sometimes."

"How do you connect that prerogative with your past?" I asked.

"When I was a wee small child," said Simple, "I had no place to set and think in, being as how I was raised up with three brothers, two sisters, seven cousins, one married aunt, a common-law uncle, and the minister's grandchild—and the house only had four rooms. I never had no place just to set and think. Neither to set and drink—not even much my milk before some hongry child snatched it out of my hand. I were not the youngest, neither a girl, nor the cutest. I don't know why, but I don't think nobody liked me much. Which is why I was afraid to like anybody for a long time myself. When I did like somebody, I was full-grown and then I picked out the wrong woman because I had no practice in liking anybody before that. We did not get along."

"Is that when you took to drink?"

"Drink took to me," said Simple. "Whiskey just naturally likes me but beer likes me better. By the time I got married I had got to the point where a cold bottle was almost as good as a warm bed, especially when the bottle could not talk and the bed-warmer could. I do not like a woman to talk to me too much—I mean about me. Which is why I like Joyce. Joyce most in generally talks about herself."

"I am still looking at your feet," I said, "and I swear they do not reveal your life to me. Your feet are no open book."

"You have eyes but you see not," said Simple. "These feet have stood on every rock from the Rock of Ages to 135th and Lenox. These feet have supported everything from a cotton bale to a hongry woman. These feet have walked ten thousand miles working for white folks and another ten thousand keeping up with colored. These feet have stood at altars, crap tables, free lunches, bars, graves, kitchen doors, betting windows, hospital clinics, WPA desks, social security railings, and in all kinds of lines from soup lines to the draft. If I just had four feet, I could have stood in more places longer. As it is, I done wore out seven hundred pairs of shoes, eighty-nine tennis shoes, twelve summer sandals, also six loafers. The socks that these feet have bought could build a knitting mill. The corns I've cut away would dull a German razor. The bunions I forgot would make you ache from now till Judgment Day. If anybody was to write the history of my life, they should start with my feet."

"Your feet are not all that extraordinary," I said. "Besides, everything you are saying is general. Tell me specifically some one thing your feet have done that makes them different from any other feet in the world, just one."

"Do you see that window in that white man's store across the street?" asked Simple. "Well, this right foot of mine broke out that window in the Harlem riots right smack in the middle. Didn't no other foot in the world break that window but mine. And this left foot carried me off running as soon as my right foot came down. Nobody else's feet saved me from the cops that night but these *two* feet right here. Don't tell me these feet ain't had a life of their own."

"For shame," I said, "going around kicking out windows. Why?"

"Why?" said Simple. "You have to ask my great-great-grandpa why. He must of been simple—else why did he let them capture him in Africa and sell him for a slave to breed my great-grandpa in slavery to breed my grandpa in slavery to breed my pa to breed me to look at that window and say, 'It ain't mine! Bam-mmm-mm-m!' and kick it out?"

"This bar glass is not yours either," I said. "Why don't you smash it?"

"It's got my beer in it," said Simple.

Just then Zarita came in wearing her Thursday-night rabbitskin coat. She didn't stop at the bar, being dressed up, but went straight back to a booth. Simple's hand went up, his beer went down, and the glass back to its wet spot on the bar.

"Excuse me a minute," he said, sliding off the stool.

Just to give him pause, the dozens, that old verbal game of maligning a friend's female relatives, came to mind.

"Wait," I said. "You have told me about what to ask your great-great-grandpa. But I want to know what to ask your great-great-grand*ma*."

"I don't play the dozens that far back," said Simple, following Zarita into the smoky juke-box blue of the back room.

2

Landladies

The next time I saw him, he was hot under the collar, but only incidentally about Zarita. Before the bartender had even put the glasses down he groaned, "I do not understand landladies."

"Now what?" I asked. "A landlady is a woman, isn't she? And, according to your declarations, you know how to handle women."

"I know how to handle women who act like ladies, but my landlady ain't no lady. Sometimes I even wish I was living with my wife again so I could have my own place and not have no landladies," said Simple.

"Landladies are practically always landladies," I said.

"But in New York they are landladies *plus!*" declared Simple.

"For instance?"

"For a instant, my landlady said to me one night when I come in, said, 'Third Floor Rear?'"

"I said, 'Yes'm.'"

"She says, 'You pays no attention to my notices I puts up, does you?'"

"I said, 'No'm.'"

"She says, 'I know you don't. You had company in your room after ten o'clock last night in spite of my rule.'"

" 'No, ma'am. That was in the room next to mine.'"

" 'Yes, but you was in there with your company, Mr. Simple.' Zarita can't keep her voice down when she goes calling. 'You and you-all's company and Mr. Boyd's was raising sand. I heard you way down here.'"

" 'What you heard was the Fourth Floor Back snoring, madam. We went out of here at ten-thirty and I didn't come back till two and I come back alone.'"

" 'Four this morning, you mean! And you slammed the door!'"

" 'Madam, you sure can hear good that late.'"

" 'I am not deaf. I also was raised in a decent home. And I would like you to respect my place.'"

" 'Yes, ma'am,' I said, because I owed her a half week's rent and I did not want to argue right then, although I was mad. But when I went upstairs and saw that sign over them little old pink towels she hangs there in the bathroom, Lord knows for what, I got madder. Sign says:

GUEST TOWELS—ROOMERS DO NOT USE

"But when even a guest of mine uses them, she jumps salty. So for what are they there? Then I saw that other little old sign up over the sink:

WASH FACE ONLY IN BOWL—NO SOX

And a sign over the tub says:

DO NOT WASH CLOTHES IN HEAR

Another sign out in the hall says:

TURN OUT LIGHT—COSTS MONEY

As if it wasn't money I'm paying for my rent! And there's still and yet another sign in my room which states:

NO COOKING, DRINKING, NO ROWDYISMS

As if I can cook without a stove or be rowdy by myself. And then right over my bed:

NO CO. AFTER 10

Just like a man can get along in this world alone. But it were part Zarita's fault talking so loud. Anyhow when I saw all them signs I got madder than I had ever been before, and I tore them all down.

"Landladies must think roomers is uncivilized and don't know how to behave themselves. Well, I do. I was also raised in a decent home. My mama made us respect our home. And I have never been known yet to wash my socks in no face bowl. So I tore them signs down.

"The next evening when I come in from work, before I even hit the steps, the landlady yells from the parlor, 'Third Floor Rear?'

"I said, 'Yes, this is the Third Floor Rear.'

"She says, 'Does you know who tore my signs down in the bathroom and in the hall? Also your room?'

"I said, 'I tore your signs down, madam. I have been looking at them signs for three months, so I know 'em by heart.'

"She says, 'You will put them back, or else move.'

"I said, 'I not only tore them signs down, I also tore them *up!*'

"She says, 'When you have paid me my rent, you move.'

"I said, 'I will move now.'

"She said, 'You will not take your trunk now.'

"I said, 'What's to keep me?'

"She said, 'Your room door is locked.'

"I said, 'Lady, I got a date tonight. I got to get in to change my clothes.'

"She says, 'You'll get in when you pay your rent.'

"So I had to take the money for my date that night—that I was intending to take out Joyce—and pay up my room rent. The next week I didn't have enough to move, so I am still there."

"Did you put back the signs?" I asked.

"Sure," said Simple. "I even writ a new sign for her which says:

DON'T NOBODY NO TIME TEAR DOWN THESE SIGNS—ELSE MOVE"

3

Simple Prays a Prayer

It was a hot night. Simple was sitting on his landlady's stoop reading a newspaper by streetlight. When he saw me coming, he threw the paper down.

"Good evening," I said.

"Good evening nothing," he answered. "It's too hot to be any good evening. Besides, this paper's full of nothing but atom bombs and bad news, wars and rumors of wars, airplane crashes, murders, fightings, wife-whippings, and killings from the Balkans to Brooklyn. Do you know one thing? If I was a praying man, I would pray a prayer for this world right now."

"What kind of prayer would you pray, friend?"

"I would pray a don't-want-to-have-no-more-wars prayer, and it would go like this: 'Lord,' I would say, I would ask Him, 'Lord, kindly please, take the blood off of my hands and off of my brothers' hands, and make us shake hands *clean* and not be afraid. Neither let me nor them have no knives behind our backs, Lord, nor up our sleeves, nor no bombs piled out yonder in a desert. Let's forget about bygones. Too many mens and womens are dead. The fault is mine and theirs, too. So teach us *all* to do right, Lord, *please,* and to get along together with that atom bomb on this earth—because I do not want it to fall on me—nor Thee—nor anybody living. Amen!'"

"I didn't know you could pray like that," I said.

"It ain't much," said Simple, "but that girl friend of mine, Joyce, drug me to church last Sunday where the man was preaching and praying about peace, so I don't see why I shouldn't make myself up a prayer, too. I figure God will listen to me as well as the next one."

"You certainly don't have to be a minister to pray," I said, "and you have composed a good prayer. But now it's up to you to help God bring it into being, since God is created in your image."

"I thought it was the other way around," said Simple.

"However that may be," I said, "according to the Bible, God can bring things about on this earth only through man. You are a man, so you must help God make a good world."

"I am willing to help Him," said Simple, "but I do not know much what to do. The folks who run this world are going to run it in the ground in spite of all, throwing people out of work and then saying, 'Peace, it's wonderful!' Peace ain't wonderful when folks ain't got no job."

"Certainly a good job is essential to one's well-being," I said.

"It is essential to me," said Simple, "if I do not want to live off of Joyce. And I do *not* want to live off of no woman. A woman will take advantage of you, if you live off of her."

"If a woman loves you, she does not mind sharing with you," I said. "Share and share alike."

"Until times get hard!" said Simple. "But when there is not much to share, *loving* is one thing, and *sharing* is another. Often they parts company. I know because I have both loved and shared. As long as I shared *mine,* all was well, but when my wife started sharing, skippy!

"My wife said, 'Baby, when is you going to work?'

"I said, 'When I find a job.'

"She said, 'Well, it better be soon because I'm giving out.'

"And, man, I felt bad. You know how long and how hard it took to get on WPA. Many a good man lost his woman in them dark days when that stuff about 'I can't give you anything but love' didn't go far. Now it looks like love is all I am going to have to share again. Do you reckon depression days is coming back?"

"I don't know," I said. "I am not a sociologist."

"You's colleged," said Simple. "Anyhow, it looks like every time I gets a little start, something happens. I was doing right well pulling down that *fine* defense check all during the war, then all of a sudden the war had to jump up and end!"

"If you wanted the war to continue just on your account, you are certainly looking at things from a selfish viewpoint."

"Selfish!" said Simple. "You may *think* I am selfish when the facts is *I am just hongry* if I didn't have a job. It looks like in peace time nobody works as much or gets paid as much as in a war. Is that clear?"

"Clear, but not right," I said.

"Of course, it's not right to be out of work and hongry," said Simple, "just like it's not right to want to fight. That's why I prayed my prayer. I prayed for white folks, too, even though a lot of them don't believe in religion. If they did, they couldn't act the way they do.

"Last Sunday morning when I was laying in bed drowsing and resting, I turned on the radio on my dresser and got a church—by accident. I was trying to get the Duke[1] on records, but I turned into the wrong station. I got some white man preaching a sermon. He was talking about peace on earth, good will to men, and all such things, and he said Christ was born to bring this peace he was talking about. He said mankind has sinned! But that we have got to get ready for the Second Coming of Christ— because Christ will be back! That is what started me to wondering."

"Wondering what?" I asked.

"Wondering what all these prejudiced white folks would do if Christ did come back. I always thought Christ believed in folks' treating people right."

"He did," I said.

"Well, if He did," said Simple, "what will all these white folks do who believe in Jim Crow? Jesus said, 'Love one another,' didn't He? But they don't love me, do they?"

"Some do not," I said.

"Jesus said, 'Do unto others as you would have others do unto you.' But they don't do that way unto me, do they?"

"I suppose not," I said.

"You know not," said Simple. "They Jim Crow me and lynch me any time they want to. Suppose I was to do unto them as they does unto me? Suppose I was to lynch and Jim Crow white folks, where would I be? Huh?"

"In jail."

"You can bet your boots I would! But these are *Christian* white folks that does such things to me. At least, they call themselves Christians in my home. They got more churches down South than they got up North. They read more Bibles and sing more hymns. I hope when Christ comes back, He comes back down South. My folks need Him down there to tell them Ku Kluxers where to head in. But I'll bet you if Christ does come back, not only in the South but all over America, there would be such another running and shutting and slamming of white folks' doors in His face as you never saw! And I'll bet the Southerners couldn't get inside their Jim Crow churches fast enough to lock the gates and keep Christ out. Christ said, 'Such as ye do unto the least of these, ye do it unto me.' And Christ *knows* what these white folks have been doing to old colored me all these years."

"Of course, He knows," I said. "When Christ was here on earth, He fought for the poor and the oppressed. But some people called Him an agitator. They cursed Him and reviled Him and sent soldiers to lock Him up. They killed Him on the cross."

"At Calvary," said Simple, "way back in B.C. I know the Bible, too. My Aunt Lucy read it to me. She read how He drove the money-changers out of the Temple. Also how He changed the loaves and fishes into many and fed the poor—which made the rulers in their high places mad because they didn't want the poor to eat. Well, when Christ comes back this time, I hope He comes back *mad* His own self. I hope He drives the Jim Crowers out of their high places, every living last one of them from Washington to Texas! I hope He smites white folks down!"

"You don't mean *all* white folks, do you?"

"No," said Simple. "I hope He lets Mrs. Roosevelt alone."

4

Conversation on the Corner

It was the summer the young men in Harlem stopped wearing their hair straightened, oiled or conked, and started having it cut short, leaving it natural, standing up about an inch or two in front in a kind of brush. When Simple took off his hat to fan his brow, I saw by the light of the neon sign outside the Wishing Well Bar that he had gotten a new haircut.

"What happened to your head?" I asked.

"Cut short," said Simple. "My baby likes to run her fingers through it. This gives her a better chance."

"As much as you hang out on this corner," I said, "I don't see when she has much of a chance."

"You know Joyce is a working woman," said Simple, "also decent. She won't come to see me, so I goes to see her early. I already paid my nightly call."

"I understand that you work also and it's midnight now. When do you sleep?"

"In between times," Simple answered, lighting a butt and taking a long draw. "Sleep don't worry me. I just hate to go back to my little old furnished room alone. How about you? What're you doing up so late?"

"Observing life for literary purposes. Gathering material, contemplating how people play so desperately when the stakes are so little."

"What you mean by all that language?" asked Simple.

"I mean there are very few people of substance out late at night—mostly hustlers. And all the hustlers around here hustle for such *small* change."

"They will not hustle off of me," said Simple. "No, sir! Somebody is always trying to take disadvantage of me. The other night I went to a poker game and lost Twelve Bucks. They was playing partners, dealing seconds, stripping the deck and palming, so all I could do was lose. I could not win—so I prefer to drink it up."

"At least you'll have it *in* you," I said. "But why do you imbibe practically every night?"

"Because I like it. I also drink because I don't have anything better to do."

"Why don't you read a book," I asked, "go to a show or a dance?"

"I do not read a book because I don't understand books, daddy-o. I do not go to the show because you see nothing but white folks on the screen. And I do not go to a dance because if I do, I get in trouble with Joyce, who is one girl friend I respect."

"Trouble with Joyce?"

"Yes," said Simple, leaning on the mailbox so no one could mail a letter. "Joyce thinks every time I put my arms around a woman to dance with her, I am hugging the woman! Now, how can you dance with a woman without hugging her? I see Joyce enough as it is. I drink because I am lonesome."

"Lonesome? How can you be lonesome when you've got plenty of friends, also girl friends?"

"I'm lonesome inside myself."

"How do you explain that?"

"I do not know," said Simple, "but that is why I drink. I don't do nobody no harm, do I? You don't see me out here hustling off nobody, do you? I am not mugging and cheating and robbing, am I?"

"You're not."

"So I don't see why I shouldn't take a beer now and then."

"*When* did you say?"

"Now," said Simple.

"You said 'now and then,' which is putting it mildly."

"I meant *now*," said Simple, "*right now* since I have met up with you, old buddy, and I know you will buy a beer."

"I saw Zarita in that bar," I said, "and if we go in there, you will have to buy her more than a beer."

"No, I won't! I'm off that dame. She talks too loud—come near getting me put out of my room. Besides, she will drink you up coming and going and not try to pay you back in no way. She is one of them hustlers you was talking about always out in the street at blip-A.M."

"Most of these people where you hang out are hustlers."

"All but you and me. I came out here hoping to run across you to borrow a fin until payday."

"I regret to say that I don't have anything to lend."

"Too bad—because I was going to buy you a drink."

"Then lose the rest in a game?"

"I was not," said Simple. "You see that cat inside the bar with that long fingernail, don't you? Well, he uses that nail to mark cards with. Every time I get in a game, there is somebody dealing with a *long* fingernail.

It ain't safe! I am tired of trickeration.[2] Also I have had too many hypes[3] laid down on me. Now I am hep."

"I'm glad to hear that," I said. "It's about time you settled down anyhow and married Joyce."

"Right. I would marry her," said Simple, "except that that girl insists that I get a divorce first. But my wife won't pay for it. And looks like I can't get that much dough ahead myself—in my line of work, I can't grow no long fingernails because they would break off before night."

"Oh, so you would like to be a hustler, too."

"Only until I pay for my divorce from Isabel," said Simple.

"If you hadn't quit your wife, you wouldn't need a divorce," I said. "If I had a wife, *I* would stay with her."

"You have never been married, pal, so you do not know how hard it is sometimes to stay with a wife."

"Elucidate," I said, "while we go in the bar and have a beer."

"A wife you have to take with a grain of salt," Simple explained. "But sometimes the salt runs out."

"What do you mean by that parable?"

"Don't take serious everything a wife says. I did. For instant, I believed her when my wife said, 'Baby, I don't mind you going out. I know a man has to get out sometimes and he don't want his wife running with him everywhere he goes.'

"So I went out. I didn't take her. She got mad. I should have taken that with a grain of salt. Also take money. My wife said, 'A man is due to have his own spending change.' So every week I kept Five Dollars out of my salary. When that ran out 'long toward the end of the week, and I would ask Isabel for a quarter or so, she'd say, 'What did you do with that Five Dollars?'

"I'd say, 'I spent it.'

" 'Spent it on what?' she'd say.

" 'I drunk it up.'

" 'What did you do that for?' she'd yell. 'Why didn't you have your clothes pressed, or spend it on some good books?'

" 'I didn't want any good books.'

" 'Why didn't you send some of it to your old aunt?'

" 'Next time I will *tell* you that I sent it *all* to my old aunt.'

" 'Then you intend to lie to me?' says my wife.

" 'Anything to keep down an argument,' I says.

" 'You do not trust me,' Isabel hollers. Then she starts to quarrel. So you see how it is. A woman will get you going and coming. You can't outargue a woman. She even had the nerve to tell me, 'Why don't you buy your beer by the case and set up home here and drink it with me?'

"I said, 'Baby, I cannot set up here at home and look into your face each and every night.'

"She said, 'You took me for better or worse. Do I look worse to you now?'

"I said, 'You do not look any worse, baby, but neither does you look any better as time goes on.'

"She said, 'If you would buy me some clothes, maybe I could look like something.'

"I said, 'Honey, we ain't got our furniture paid for yet.'

"She said, 'So you care more for an old kitchen stove than you does for me?'

"I said, 'A man has to eat, and a woman can't cook on the floor.'

" 'All you got me for is to cook,' Isabel said. 'If I had knowed that, I could of stayed home with my mother.'

" 'I must admit,' I said, 'your mother cooks better than you.'

" 'Huh! I can't do nothing with them stringy old round steaks you bring home for us to eat,' she says.

" 'My money won't stretch to no T-bones,' I says. 'Anyhow, baby, no matter how tough the steak may be, you can always stick a fork in the gravy.'

"I just said that for a joke, but somehow it made her mad. She flew off the handle. I flew off the handle, too, and we had one of the biggest quarrels you ever saw. Our first battle royal—but it were not our last. Every time night fell from then on we quarreled—and night falls every night in Baltimore."

"Night does," I said.

"The first of the month falls every month, too, North or South. And them white folks who sends bills never forgets to send them—the phone bill, the furniture bill, the water bill, the gas bill, insurance, house rent. They also never forget you got their furniture in the house—and they will come and take it out if you do not pay the bill. Not only was my nose kept to the grindstone when I was married, but my bohunkus[4] also. It were depression, too. They cut my wages down once at the foundry. They cut my wages down again. Then they cut my wages *out,* also the job. My old lady had to go cook for some rich white folks. *And don't you know Isabel wouldn't bring me home a thing to eat!* Neither would she open a can when she got home.

"I said, 'Baby, what is the matter with you? Don't you know I have to eat, too?'

"She said, 'You know what is the matter with me. Ever since I have been with you, I have been treated like a dog for convenience. Who is paying for this furniture? Me! Who keeps up the house rent? Me! Who pays that little dime insurance of yourn? Me! And if you was to die, I would not benefit but Three Hundred Dollars. It looks like you can't even get on WPA. But you better get on something, Jess. In fact, take over or take off.'

"Then it were that I took off," said Simple.

"And ever since you've been a free man."

"Free?" said Simple. "I would have been free if I hadn't run into some old Baltimore friend boy here in Harlem who wrote and told my wife where I was at. So for the last year now she's been writing me that if I wasn't going to even give her a divorce, to at least buy her a fur coat this winter."

"Why didn't you give her a divorce when you left?" I asked.

"You can't buy no divorce on WPA. And when the war came, she was working in a war plant making just as much money as me," said Simple. "She could get her own divorce. But no! She still wanted me to pay for it. I told her to send me the money then and I would pay for it. But she wrote back and said I would never spend none of her money on Joyce. Baltimore womens is evil."

"Evidently she does not trust you."

"I would not trust myself with Three Hundred Dollars," said Simple.

"So you are just going to keep on being married then. You can't get loose if neither one of you is willing to pay for the divorce."

"I've been trying to get Joyce to pay for it," explained Simple. "Only thing is, Joyce says I will have to marry her *first*. She says she will not pay for no divorce for another woman unless I am hers beforehand."

"That would be bigamy," I said, "married to two women at once."

"It would be worse than that," said Simple. "Married to one woman is bad enough. But if I am married to two, it would be hell!"

"Legally it would be bigamy."

"Is bigamy worse than hell?"

"I have had no experience with either," I said. "But if you go in for bigamy, you will end up in the arms of justice."

"Any old arms are better than none," said Simple.

5

Family Tree

"Anybody can look at me and tell I am part Indian," said Simple.

"I see you almost every day," I said, "and I did not know it until now."

"I have Indian blood but I do not show it much," said Simple. "My uncle's cousin's great-grandma were a Cherokee. I only shows mine when I lose my temper—then my Indian blood boils. I am quick-tempered just like a Indian. If somebody does something to me, I always fights back. In fact, when I get mad, I am the toughest Negro God's got. It's my Indian blood. When I were a young man, I used to play baseball and steal bases just like Jackie.[5] If the empire would rule me out, I would get mad and hit the empire. I had to stop playing. That Indian temper. Nowadays, though, it's mostly womens that riles me up, especially landladies, waitresses, and girl friends. To tell the truth, I believe in a woman keeping her place. Womens is beside themselves these days. They want to rule the roost."

"You have old-fashioned ideas about sex," I said. "In fact, your line of thought is based on outmoded economics."

"What?"

"In the days when women were dependent upon men for a living, you could be the boss. But now women make their own living. Some of them make more money than you do."

"True," said Simple. "During the war they got into that habit. But boss I am still due to be."

"So you think. But you can't always put your authority into effect."

"I can try," said Simple. "I can say, 'Do this!' And if she does something else, I can raise my voice, if not my hand."

"You can be sued for raising your voice," I stated, "and arrested for raising your hand."

"And she can be annihilated when I return from being arrested," said Simple. "That's my Indian blood!"

"You must believe in a woman being a squaw."

"She better not look like no squaw," said Simple. "I want a woman to look sharp when she goes out with me. No moccasins. I wants high-heel shoes and nylons, cute legs—and short dresses. But I also do not want her to talk back to me. As I said, I am the man. *Mine* is the word, and she is due to hush."

"Indians customarily expect their women to be quiet," I said.

"I do not expect mine to be *too* quiet," said Simple. "I want 'em to sweet-talk me—'Sweet baby, this,' and 'Baby, that,' and 'Baby, you's right, darling,' when they talk to me."

"In other words, you want them both old-fashioned and modern at the same time," I said. "The convolutions of your hypothesis are sometimes beyond cognizance."

"Cog hell!" said Simple. "I just do not like no old loud back-talking chick. That's the Indian in me. My grandpa on my father's side were like that, too, an Indian. He was married five times and he really ruled his roost."

"There are a mighty lot of Indians up your family tree," I said. "Did your granddad look like one?"

"Only his nose. He was dark brownskin otherwise. In fact, he were black. And the womens! Man! They was crazy about Grandpa. Every time he walked down the street, they stuck their heads out the windows and kept 'em turned South—which was where the beer parlor was."

"So your grandpa was a drinking man, too. That must be whom you take after."

"I also am named after him," said Simple. "Grandpa's name was Jess, too. So I am Jesse B. Semple."

"What does the *B* stand for?"

"Nothing. I just put it there myself since they didn't give me no initial when I was born. I am really Jess Semple—which the kids changed around into a nickname when I were in school. In fact, they used to tease me when I were small, calling me 'Simple Simon.' But I was right handy with my fists, and after I beat the 'Simon' out of a few of them, they let me alone. But my friends still call me 'Simple.'"

"In reality, you are Jesse Semple," I said, "colored."

"Part Indian," insisted Simple, reaching for his beer.

"Jess is certainly not an Indian name."

"No, it ain't," said Simple, "but we did have a Hiawatha in our family. She died."

"*She?*" I said. "Hiawatha was no *she*."

"She was a *she* in our family. And she had long coal-black hair just like a Creole. You know, I started to marry a Creole one time when I was coach-boy on the L. & N. down to New Orleans. Them Louisiana girls are bee-oou-te-ful! Man, I mean!"

"Why didn't you marry her, fellow?"

"They are more dangerous than a Indian," said Simple, "also I do not want no pretty woman. First thing you know, you fall in love with her—then you got to kill somebody about her. She'll make you so jealous, you'll bust! A pretty woman will get a man in trouble. Me and my Indian blood, quick-tempered as I is. No! I do not crave a pretty woman."

"Joyce is certainly not bad-looking," I said. "You hang around her all the time."

"She is far from a Creole. Besides, she appreciates me," said Simple. "Joyce knows I got Indian blood which makes my temper bad. But we take each other as we is. I respect her and she respects me."

"That's the way it should be with the whole world," I said. "Therefore, you and Joyce are setting a fine example in these days of trials and tribulations. Everybody should take each other as they are, white, black, Indians, Creole. Then there would be no prejudice, nations would get along."

"Some folks do not see it like that," said Simple. "For instant, my landlady—and my wife. Isabel could never get along with me. That is why we are not together today."

"I'm not talking personally," I said, "so why bring in your wife?"

"Getting along *starts* with persons, don't it?" asked Simple. "You *must* include my wife. That woman got my Indian blood so riled up one day I thought I would explode."

"I still say, I'm not talking personally."

"Then stop talking," exploded Simple, "because with me it is personal. Facts, I cannot even talk about my wife if I don't get personal. That's how it is if you're part Indian—everything is personal. *Heap much personal.*"

6

A Toast to Harlem

Quiet can seem unduly loud at times. Since nobody at the bar was saying a word during a lull in the bright blues-blare of the Wishing Well's usually overworked juke box, I addressed my friend Simple.

"Since you told me last night you are an Indian, explain to me how it is you find yourself living in a furnished room in Harlem, my brave buck, instead of on a reservation?"

"I am a colored Indian," said Simple.

"In other words, a Negro."

"A Black Foot Indian, daddy-o, not a red one. Anyhow, Harlem is the place I always did want to be. And if it wasn't for landladies, I would be happy. That's a fact! I love Harlem."

"What is it you love about Harlem?"

"It's so full of Negroes," said Simple. "I feel like I got protection."

"From what?"

"From white folks," said Simple. "Furthermore, I like Harlem because it belongs to me."

"Harlem does not belong to you. You don't own the houses in Harlem. They belong to white folks."

"I might not own 'em," said Simple, "but I live in 'em. It would take an atom bomb to get me out."

"Or a depression," I said.

"I would not move for no depression. No, I would not go back down South, not even to Baltimore. I am in Harlem to stay! You say the houses ain't mine. Well, the sidewalk is—and don't nobody push me off. The cops don't even say, 'Move on,' hardly no more. They learned something from them Harlem riots. They used to beat your head right in public, but now they only beat it after they get you down to the stationhouse. And they don't beat it then if they think you know a colored congressman."

"Harlem has a few Negro leaders," I said.

"Elected by my *own* vote," said Simple. "Here I ain't scared to vote— that's another thing I like about Harlem. I also like it because we've got subways and it does not take all day to get downtown, neither are you Jim Crowed on the way. Why, Negroes is running some of these subway trains. This morning I rode the A Train down to 34th Street. There were a Negro driving it, making ninety miles a hour. That cat *were really driving* that train! Every time he flew by one of them local stations looks like he was saying, 'Look at me! This train is mine!' That cat were gone, ole man. Which is another reason why I like Harlem! Sometimes I run into Duke Ellington on 125th Street and I say, 'What you know there, Duke?' Duke says, 'Solid, ole man.' He does not know me from Adam, but he speaks. One day I saw Lena Horne coming out of the Hotel Theresa and I said, 'Huba! Huba!' Lena smiled. Folks is friendly in Harlem. I feel like I got the world in a jug and the stopper in my hand! So drink a toast to Harlem!"

Simple lifted his glass of beer:

> *"Here's to Harlem!*
> *They say Heaven is Paradise.*
> *If Harlem ain't Heaven,*
> *Then a mouse ain't mice!"*

"Heaven is a state of mind," I commented.

"It sure is *mine*," said Simple, draining his glass. "From Central Park to 179th, from river to river, Harlem is mine! Lots of white folks is scared to come up here, too, after dark."

"That is nothing to be proud of," I said.

"I am sorry white folks is scared to come to Harlem, but I am scared to go around some of *them*. Why, for instant, in my home town once before I came North to live, I was walking down the street when a white woman jumped out of her door and said, 'Boy, get away from here because I am scared of you.'

"I said, 'Why?'

"She said, 'Because you are black.'

"I said, 'Lady, I am scared of you because you are white.' I went on down the street, but I kept wishing I was blacker—so I could of scared that lady to death. So help me, I did. Imagine somebody talking about they is scared of me because I am black! I got more reason to be scared of white folks than they have of me."

"Right," I said.

"The white race drug me over here from Africa, slaved me, freed me, lynched me, starved me during the depression, Jim Crowed me during the war—then they come talking about they is scared of me! Which is why I am glad I have got one spot to call my own where I hold sway— Harlem. Harlem, where I can thumb my nose at the world!"

"You talk just like a Negro nationalist," I said.

"What's that?"

"Someone who wants Negroes to be on top."

"When everybody else keeps me on the *bottom,* I don't see why I shouldn't want to be on top. I will, too, someday."

"That's the spirit that causes wars," I said.

"I would not mind a war if I could win it. White folks fight, lynch, and enjoy themselves."

"There you go," I said. "That old *race-against-race* jargon. There'll never be peace that way. The world tomorrow ought to be a world where everybody gets along together. The least we can do is extend a friendly hand."

"Every time I extend my hand I get put back in my place. You know them poetries about the black cat that tried to be friendly with the white one:

> *The black cat said to the white cat,*
> *'Let's sport around the town.'*
> *The white cat said to the black cat,*
> *'You better set your black self down!'*"

"Unfriendliness of that nature should not exist," I said. "Folks ought to live like neighbors."

"You're talking about what ought to be. But as long as what *is* is— and Georgia is Georgia—I will take Harlem for mine. At least, if trouble comes, I will have *my own window* to shoot from."

"I refuse to argue with you any more," I said. "What Harlem ought to hold out to the world from its windows is a friendly hand, not a belligerent attitude."

"It will not be my attitude I will have out my window," said Simple.

7

Simple and His Sins

Just as the street lights were coming on one warm Sunday evening in midsummer, I ran into my friend of the bar stools between Paddy's and the Wishing Well. He was wiping his brow.

"Man, I came near getting my wires crossed this afternoon," he said, "and all by accident. I told Joyce I would meet her in the park, so I was setting out there on a bench with my portable radio just bugging myself with Dizzy Gillespie, when who should come blaséing along but Zarita."

"How did she look by daylight?" I asked.

"She looked fine from the bottom up, but beat from the top down," said Simple.

"You kept your eyes down, I presume."

"No, I didn't neither," said Simple. "I looked Zarita dead in the eye and I said, 'Woman, what you doing out here in the broad-open daytime with your head looking like Zip?'[6]

"Zarita said, 'Don't look at my hair, Jess, please. I ain't been to the beauty shop this week.'

" 'Then you ought to go,' I said. 'Besides, how are you going to get your rest staying up all night? Last thing I saw last night was you—and now you're out here in the park and it ain't hardly noon.'

" 'I could ask you the same thing,' said Zarita, 'but I ain't that concerned about your business. And I don't have to answer your questions.'

" 'You didn't mind answering them last night when I was buying you all them drinks,' I said.

" 'To be a gentleman,' said Zarita, 'you speaks too often about the money you spend. I'll bet you if your girl friend ever saw you setting up in the bar having a ball every A.M. she would lay you low.'

" 'Joyce knows all about me,' I said, 'and I would thank you to keep her name out of this. Joyce is a lady.'

" 'What do you think I am?' yells Zarita.

" 'You ain't even an imitation,' I said, 'coming out in the street with your head looking like a hurrah's nest!' "

"Why were you so hard on Zarita?" I asked. "I thought she was a friend of yours."

"She ain't nothing but a night-time friend," said Simple, "and I do not like to see her in the day. You would not like to see her neither if you had seen her this noon. I often wonders what makes some women look so bad early in the day after they have looked so sweet at night. Can you tell me?"

"You can answer that yourself."

"Well, for one thing, a woman is half make-up," said Simple, "and the other half is clothes. They got no business coming out in the morning before they fix themselves up. I said, 'Zarita, go on home and put on some face, also oil your meriney.'[7]

" 'I can see through you,' she hollered. 'You just scared somebody will spy you talking to me out here in the broad daylight and go tell that female friend of yourn. Well, you ain't gonna drive me off with your insulting remarks. This is a public park. I aims to set right here on this bench with you, Jess Simple, and listen to that radio until the Dodgers come on. I follows Jackie.'

" 'You will have to follow Jackie on somebody else's radio,' I said. 'I will not be seen setting in the park with no uncombed woman. Neither do I know you that well, Zarita, for you to set down here with me.'

" 'I set on a bar stool with you,' says Zarita.

" 'Not on the same stool,' I says. 'Woman, unhand me and lemme go.'

"Don't you know I had trouble getting away from that girl. Zarita pitched a boogie[8] right there in the park and she has got a voice like a steam calliope. I cut out and went up to Joyce's house.

"When I rung Joyce's bell, she comes to the door in her wrapper and says, 'Baby, I thought you was going to set in the park until I got dressed.'

"I said, 'Joyce, you took too long. Let's go to a nice air-cooled movie instead of setting in the park listening to the ball game today. I hear Jackie's twisted his ankle, anyhow.' And I put that radio down and took that woman the other way, so she would not run into Zarita."

"Your sins will find you out," I said.

"I don't care nothing about my sins finding me out," said Simple, "just so Joyce don't find out about my sins—especially when their hair ain't combed."

8

Temptation

"When the Lord said, 'Let there be light,' and there was light, what I want to know is where was us colored people?"

"What do you mean, 'Where were we colored people?' " I said.

"We must *not* of been there," said Simple, "because we are still dark. Either He did not include me or else I were not there."

"The Lord was not referring to people when He said, 'Let there be light.' He was referring to the elements, the atmosphere, the air."

"He must have included some people," said Simple, "because white people are light, in fact, *white,* whilst I am dark. How come? I say, we were not there."

"Then where do you think we were?"

"Late as usual," said Simple, "old C. P. Time. We must have been down the road a piece and did not get back on time."

"There was no C. P. Time in those days," I said. "In fact, no people were created—so there couldn't be any Colored People's Time. The Lord God had not yet breathed the breath of life into anyone."

"No?" said Simple.

"No," said I, "because it wasn't until Genesis 2 and 7 that God 'formed man of the dust of the earth and breathed into his nostrils the breath of life and man became a living soul.' His name was Adam. Then He took one of Adam's ribs and made a woman."

"Then trouble began," said Simple. "Thank God, they was both white."

"How do you know Adam and Eve were white?" I asked.

"When I was a kid I seen them on the Sunday school cards," said Simple. "Ever since I been seeing a Sunday school card, they was white. That is why I want to know where was us Negroes when the Lord said, 'Let there be light'?"

"Oh, man, you have a color complex so bad you want to trace it back to the Bible."

"No, I don't. I just want to know how come Adam and Eve was white. If they had started out black, this world might not be in the fix it is today. Eve might not of paid that serpent no attention. I never did know a Negro yet that liked a snake."

"That snake is a symbol," I said, "a symbol of temptation and sin. And that symbol would be the same, no matter what the race."

"I am not talking about no symbol," said Simple. "I am talking about the day when Eve took that apple and Adam et. From then on the human race has been in trouble. There ain't a colored woman living what would take no apple from a snake—and she better not give no snake-apples to her husband!"

"Adam and Eve are symbols, too," I said.

"You are simple yourself," said Simple. "But I just wish we colored folks had been somewhere around at the start. I do not know where we was when Eden was a garden, but we sure didn't get in on none of the crops. If we had, we would not be so poor today. White folks started out ahead and they are still ahead. Look at me!"

"I am looking," I said.

"Made in the image of God," said Simple, "but I never did see anybody like me on a Sunday school card."

"Probably nobody looked like you in Biblical days," I said. "The American Negro did not exist in B.C. You're a product of Caucasia and Africa, Harlem and Dixie. You've been conditioned entirely by our environment, our modern times."

"Times have been hard," said Simple, "but still I am a child of God."

"In the cosmic sense, we are all children of God."

"I have been baptized," said Simple, "also anointed with oil. When I were a child I come through at the mourners' bench. I was converted. I have listened to Daddy Grace and et with Father Divine, moaned with Elder Lawson and prayed with Adam Powell. Also I have been to the Episcopalians with Joyce. But if a snake were to come up to me and offer *me* an apple, I would say, 'Varmint, be on your way! No fruit today! Bud, you got the wrong stud now, so get along somehow, be off down the road because you're lower than a toad!' Then that serpent would respect me as a wise man—and this world would not be where it is—all on account of an apple. That apple has turned into an atom now."

"To hear you talk, if you had been in the Garden of Eden, the world would still be a Paradise," I said. "Man would not have fallen into sin."

"Not *this* man," said Simple. "I would have stayed in that garden making grape wine, singing like Crosby, and feeling fine! I would not be scuffling out in this rough world, neither would I be in Harlem. If I was Adam I would just stay in Eden in that garden with no rent to pay, no landladies to dodge, no time clock to punch—and *my* picture on a Sunday school card. I'd be a *real gone guy*—even if I didn't have but one name—Adam—and no initials."

"You would be *real gone* all right. But you were not there. So, my dear fellow, I trust you will not let your rather late arrival on our contemporary stage distort your perspective."

"No," said Simple.

9

Wooing the Muse

"Hey, now!" said Simple one hot Monday evening. "Man, I had a *fine* weekend."

"What did you do?"

"Me and Joyce went to Orchard Beach."

"Good bathing?"

"I don't know. I didn't take a bath. I don't take to cold water."

"What did you do then, just lie in the sun?"

"I did not," said Simple. "I don't like violent rays tampering with my complexion. I just laid back in the shade while Joyce sported on the beach wetting her toes to show off her pretty white bathing suit."

"In other words, you relaxed."

"Relaxed is right," said Simple. "I had myself a great big nice cool quart of beer so I just laid back in the shade and relaxed. I also wrote myself some poetries."

"Poetry!" I said.

"Yes," said Simple. "Want to hear it?"

"Indeed I do."

"I will read you Number One. Here it is:

> *Sitting under the trees*
> *With the birds and the bees*
> *Watching the girls go by.*

How do you like it?"

"Is that all?"

"That's enough!" said Simple.

"You ought to have another rhyme," I said. "*By* ought to rhyme with *sky* or something."

"I was not looking at no sky, as I told you in the poem. I was looking at the girls."

"Well, anyhow, what else did you write?"

"This next one is a killer," said Simple. "It's serious. I got to thinking about how if I didn't have to ride Jim Crow, I might go down home for my vacation. And I looked around me out yonder at Orchard Beach and almost everybody on that beach, besides me and Joyce, was foreigners—New York foreigners. They was speaking Italian, German, Yiddish, Spanish, Puerto Rican, and everything but English. So I got to thinking how any one of them foreigners could visit my home state down South and ride anywhere they want to on the trains—except with me. So I wrote this poem which I will now read it to you. Listen:

> *I wonder how it can be*
> *That Greeks, Germans, Jews,*
> *Italians, Mexicans,*
> *And everybody but me*
> *Down South can ride in the trains,*
> *Streetcars and busses*
> *Without any fusses.*
>
> *But when I come along—*
> *Pure American—*
> *They got a sign up*
> *For me to ride behind:*
>
> *COLORED*
>
> *My folks and my folks' folkses*
> *And their folkses before*
> *Have been here 300 years or more—*
> *Yet any foreigner from Polish to Dutch*
> *Rides anywhere he wants to*
> *And is not subject to such*
> *Treatments as my fellow-men give me*
> *In this Land of the Free.*
>
> *Dixie, you ought to get wise*
> *And be civilized!*
> *And take down that COLORED sign*
> *For Americans to ride behind!*

Signed, *Jesse B. Semple*. How do you like that?"

"Did you write it yourself, or did Joyce help you?"

"Every word of it I writ myself," said Simple. "Joyce wanted me to change *folkses* and say *peoples,* but I did not have an eraser. It would have been longer, too, but Joyce made me stop and go with her to get some hot dogs."

"It's long enough," I said.

"It's not as long as Jim Crow," said Simple.

"You didn't write any nature poems at all?" I asked.

"What do you mean, nature poems?"

"I mean about the great out-of-doors—the flowers, the birds, the trees, the country."

"To tell the truth, I never was much on country," said Simple. "I had enough of it when I was down home. Besides, in the country flies bother you, bees sting you, mosquitoes bite you, and snakes hide in the grass. No, I do not like the country—except a riverbank to fish near town."

"It's better than staying in the city," I said, "and spending your money around these Harlem bars."

"At least I am welcome in these bars—run by white folks though they are," said Simple, "but I do not know no place in the country where I am welcome. If you're driving, every little roadhouse you stop at, they look at you like you was a varmint and say, 'We don't serve colored.' I tell you I do not want no parts of the country in this country."

"You do not go to the country to drink," I said.

"What am I gonna do, hibernate?"

"You could lie in a hammock and read a book, then go in the house and eat chicken."

"I do not know anybody in the country around here, and you know these summer resort places up North don't admit colored. Besides, the last time I was laying out in a hammock reading the funnies in the country down in Virginia, it were in the cool of evening and, man, a snake as long as you are tall come whipping through the grass, grabbed a frog right in front of my eyes, and started to choking it down."

"What did you do?"

"Mighty near fell out of that hammock!" said Simple. "If that snake had not been so near, I would've fell out. As it were, I stepped down quick on the other side and went to find myself a stone."

"Did you kill it?"

"My nerves were bad and my aim was off. I hit the frog instead of the snake. I knocked that frog right out of his mouth."

"What did the snake do?"

"Runned and hid his self in the grass. I was scared to go outdoors all the rest of the time I was in the country."

"You are that scared of a snake?" I said.

"As scared of a snake as a Russian was of a Nazi. I would go to as much trouble to kill one as Stalin did to kill Hitler. Besides, that poor little frog were not bothering that snake. Frogs eat mosquitoes and mosquitoes eat me. So I am for letting that frog live and not be et. But a snake would chaw on my leg as quick as he would a frog, so I am for letting a snake die. Anything that bites me must die—snakes, bedbugs, bees, mosquitoes, or bears. I don't even much like for a woman to bite me, though I would not go so far as to kill her. But of all the things that bites, two is worst—a mad dog and a snake. But I would take the dog. I never could understand how in the Bible Eve got near enough to a snake to take an apple."

"Snakes did not bite in those days," I said. "That was the Age of Innocence."

"It was only after Eve got hold of the apple that everything got wrong, huh? Snakes started to bite, women to fight, men to paying, and Christians to praying," said Simple. "It were awful after Eve approached that snake and accepted that apple! It takes a woman to do a fool thing like that."

"Adam ate it, too, didn't he?"

"A woman can make a fool out of a man," said Simple. "But don't let's start talking about women. We have talked about enough unpleasant things for one night. Will you kindly invite me into the bar to have a beer? This sidewalk is hot to my feet. And as a thank-you for a drink, the next time I write a poem, I will give you a copy. But it won't be about the country, neither about nature."

"As much beer as you drink, it will probably be about a bar," I said. "When are you going to wake up, fellow, get wise to yourself, settle down, marry Joyce, and stop gallivanting all over Harlem every night? You're old enough to know better."

"I might be old enough to know better, but I am not old enough to *do* better," said Simple. "Come on in the bar and I will say you a toast I made up the last time somebody told me just what you are saying now about doing better. . . . That's right, bartender, two beers for two steers. . . . Thank you! . . . Pay for them, chum! . . . Now, here goes. Listen fluently:

> When I get to be ninety-one
> And my running days is done,
> Then I will do better.
>
> When I get to be ninety-two
> And just CAN'T do,
> I'll do better.
>
> When I get to be ninety-three
> If the womens don't love me,
> Then I must do better.

When I get to be ninety-four
And can't jive no more,
I'll have to do better.

When I get to be ninety-five,
More dead than alive,
It'll be necessary to do better.

When I get to be ninety-six
And don't know no more tricks,
I reckon I'll do better.

When I get to be ninety-seven
And on my way to Heaven,
I'll try and do better.

When I get to be ninety-eight
And see Saint Peter at the gate,
I know I'll do better.

When I get to be ninety-nine,
Remembering it were fine,
Then I'll do better.

But even when I'm a hundred and one,
If I'm still having fun,
I'll start all over again
Just like I begun—
Because what could be better?"

10

Summer Ain't Simple

"It's summer time," said Simple late one Saturday evening, "but the living ain't easy—no raise in wages and everything still sky-high. Also Joyce mad. I tell you, it ain't easy."

"What's Joyce mad about?"

"Because I don't keep my eyes on her. I was walking down the street with that woman the other night and I just *had* to look back two or three times at what went by. One chick was long, tall, looked like a million dollars—chocolate, man! Another one was high yellow and mellow with her hair blowing back over her ears and her toes sticking out of her shoes pink as the inside of a sugar melon. Man, I could not prevent myself from turning around. Joyce snaps, 'I hate to walk down the street with a man that is always embarrassing me.'

"I said, 'Baby, why is it you do not put pink polish on your toenails, too?'

"Joyce said, 'You are not looking at no toenails. You are looking at limbs.'

"I said, 'If you mean *legs*, baby, I did kinder pass inspection.'

" 'You uncouth men embarrass me,' said Joyce. 'If I wasn't almost home, I would not walk another step with you. I know you want to stop in Paddy's Bar, anyhow. I never did go in the back room of a bar until I started going with you, Jess Semple.' Getting all formal now. 'I do not want to go in a bar tonight. I want me some ice cream to take home.'

"So I had to buy Joyce some ice cream—all because she was mad. I also had to buy enough for her landlady and her landlady's sister—which meant a whole quart. Boy, it takes money to live in the summer time! All the uptown movies are too hot, so she has to go to a downtown movie what's air-cooled. Half a day's pay gone right there. And when she gets home, her room is too stuffy, so she keeps hinting she wishes somebody would buy her a little electric fan.

" 'It seems funny,' Joyce says, 'nobody ever thinks of giving nobody nothing 'less'n it's Christmas.'

"Aw, man, I'm telling you, summer can really become a drag. I am off Saturdays and Sundays, July and August, whilst Joyce is only off Sundays.

But I dare not go to no beach on Saturday without her because she will swear I am laying out there in the sun with some other girl—which I am."

"How does Joyce know you have been to the beach unless you tell her?" I asked.

"I tans quickly. Also, it's hard to get all that sand out of my hair. Joyce can always tell when I have been on the beach."

"But how can she tell you've been with somebody else?"

"I reckon she can see it in my eyes," said Simple. "But a woman ought to know summer ain't no time for a man to keep his eyes on nobody *but* her—with all these fine chicks walking around in frilly dresses and nothing much on underneath."

"Doesn't Joyce dress rather diaphanously?"

"Joyce better not dress like that and let me catch her! You think I want her sashaying up and down the street for every man to whistle at with the sun shining through her skirt like Zarita? Joyce better wear a petticoat."

"You're certainly old-fashioned," I said.

"I may be old-fashioned, but I know what I like."

"In somebody else, yes. You just said you can't keep your eyes off those other girls, which is why you can't keep your eyes *on* Joyce."

"There're times when any man's mind wanders. I'm telling you, it's hard to do right in July. And when comes August, I ain't gonna have a penny saved up for my vacation. I'm gonna have to borrow from Joyce. My papa warn't rich nor my mama good-looking. It's summer time, but the living ain't easy! Facts is, I do not know where I'm going to eat my Sunday dinner. I hate to have my week ends spoiled."

"What do you mean, spoiled?"

"That Joyce has gone over to Jersey to spend Sunday with her foster aunt's cousin's niece whose baby is being christened and Joyce is going to be its godmama. They ask me did I want to be the godpapa, but I said, 'Naw!,' which sounded kinder short-answered. So I thought I better say something nice. So I told 'em, 'As pretty as that little girl is, it will take a better godpapa than me to keep her straight when she grows up. Mens will be running after her like cats after catnip. You pick out some better man for her godpapa.' The way Joyce batted her eyes, I must not of said the right thing. Anyhow, Joyce has gone to Jersey for the cermonials and I have to eat out tomorrow."

"What is so bad about that?"

Simple looked at me in amazement.

"Ain't you ever et in a Harlem restaurant?"

"Certainly, at Bell's or Mrs. Frazier's or Frank's."

"I am not talking about them high-toned places," said Simple, "where they take your week's salary. I am talking about just a plain ordinary restaurant where they wipe the counter off with a dishrag, and where most people eat at."

"I have eaten in such restaurants," I said.

"Then you ought to know what I'm talking about. I went in a nice cheap-looking little place on Seventh Avenue this noon time thinking I would have me a good breakfast. The waitress frowns like I was in the wrong place and comes up and says, 'What do you want?' as if the joint wasn't public.

"I says, 'Gimme some ham and eggs, baby, please.'

"She says, 'Breakfast is *been* over!'

"I says, 'I cannot get no ham and eggs?'

"She says, 'The cook ain't bothering with no breakfast orders now, I told you. It's after noon.'

"I said, 'You ain't told me nothing like that. Anyhow, what have you got for lunch?'

"She puts down an old beat-up menu. I say, 'Gimme side pork and cabbage.'

"She says, 'We don't have that.'

"I say, 'It is writ on here.'

"She says, 'We generally has that on Thursdays and we do not have it today.'

" 'What can I get then for lunch,' I says, 'that you have got?'

" 'Pork chops, fried liver, pot roast, and hog maw,' she says.

"I said, 'Gimme some pot roast.'

"She goes off and in about ten minutes she comes back and says, 'The pot roast ain't ready yet.'

" 'Then gimme the hog maw,' I says, 'because I do not like a lot of fried stuff in the summer.'

" 'The hog maw ain't quite done.'

" 'I can't get breakfast, neither can I get lunch! What have you got?' I says.

" 'I can give you pork chops, fried liver . . .'

" 'You can't give me nothing,' I remarks and walks out. I tried another place further down the street around the corner. Two large fat ladies was sitting on their haunches behind the counter. I sets, but neither one of 'em moves.

"Finally one says, 'You wait on him, Essie. I waited on the last customer.'

"The other one says, 'Aw, go see what that man wants, sis! I'm tired.'

"I said, 'Don't none of you-all move. I will move.' So I moved out.

"I went into a big place on 125th Street. A fine Creole-looking old gal come up and put down a glass of water and a menu card. I hadn't hardly got the card in my hand when she says, 'Make up your mind, daddy. I ain't got all day to stand here.'

" 'Don't stand then,' I said. 'Set down! I'm gone!'

"So I took the subway like I had some sense and went downtown on Broadway where at least you can get some polite service at the Automat. What do you suppose makes them act that way in Harlem restaurants? They look like they are mad when you come in, then they bark at you like a dog, and do not have half of the things they put on the menu. Now, why is that?"

"No doubt because most of them are poor restaurants with untrained personnel."

"Person—hell!" said Simple.

11

A Word from "Town & Country"

"Have you seen Watermelon Joe?" asked Simple, looking around the bar.

"No, I have not," I said. "Why?"

"He owes me a quarter."

"Do you expect to get it back?"

"No."

"Then why did you lend it to him?" I asked.

"From some people you expect to get nothing back," explained Simple, "but you does for them right on."

"Why?" I pursued the question.

"Why do you do for a dog? Why do you do for a woman?"

"Surely you do not put women and dogs in the same class?" I asked.

"Sometimes both of them are b——," Simple began.

"Shsss-ss-s! That is not a polite word," I said. "It will get you in the doghouse with the ladies, and there are ladies in this bar."

"The word for a lady dog *is* a polite word," Simple said. "I have seen it in *Town & Country*, which my boss's wife reads."

"Harlem does not read *Town & Country*," I said. "Colored people think *bitch* is a bad word, not a female hound."

"But I were using it in its good way to mean a woman and a hound," said Simple.

"In polite company, you do not use it for a female unless you mean it to be a hound," I said.

"I do not mean it to be a hound now," said Simple. "I mean it to be a woman who acts like a hound."

"Then you are using it in its profane sense," I said, "and you are insulting womankind."

"My mother was a woman," said Simple indignantly, "and I would not insult her."

"But you would insult *my* mother," I said, "if you applied that term to womankind."

"I do not even know your mother," said Simple.

"Well, I would appreciate it if you did not talk about her now," I said, "in the same breath with female hounds."

"You must be drunk," said Simple. "I did not mention your mother."

"You just got through mentioning my mother," I said, "so how can you say that?"

"I did not say she was that word I saw in *Town & Country*," said Simple.

"You'd better not," I said.

"But women in general are," said Simple.

"My mother is a woman."

"I mean, not including *your mother and mine*," said Simple.

"You're still making it rather broad," I said. "I also know some other women whom I highly respect."

"I will leave them out," said Simple. "But you know what I mean. Women is women. When you do for them, it is just about the same as doing for Watermelon Joe. You do not expect to get anything back."

"What do you want back?" I asked. "The little bit of money you spend?"

"No," said Simple. "I want love, respect, attention, 'Here is your slippers, daddy,' when I come home. Not, 'Where is that pound of butter I told you to bring?' And I say, 'Aw, woman, I just forgot.' Then she says, 'It is funny you can remember your Cousin Josephine's birthday and send her a card which costs a quarter and you cannot remember to get a pound of butter for your own home. No, you neglect what is nearest to you. I am your wife! Remember?'

"Then I say, 'Of course, you are my wife, Isabel, and I did not forget you. I just forgot the butter. Do you want to make something out of it?'

" 'Yes,' she says, 'I want to make something out of it. You don't work no harder than me and yet you expects me to do the shopping, cooking, cleaning, and wash your filthy clothes, too, when I come home. Yes, I think you should remember that butter! You getting ready to go down to that old bar right now and eyeball them loose womens.' Only she didn't say *womens*. She said that word that was in *Town & Country*. And all I could think of to say back, 'It's a lie! You are the only (word that's in *Town & Country*) that I have gazed at all day—and you hurt my eyes.'

"Then it were on! That is why we did not stay together. A woman is evil. And when a man is tired, sometimes the only word he can think of to say is the one that white folks use for dogs. I don't know why we can't use it, too."

"Because it is disrespectful to women," I said, "that is why."

"But that is what they is," said Simple.

"Be careful! My mother is a woman," I said.

"I am *not* talking about *your* mother, neither about *my* mother," said Simple. "I am just talking about women."

"Your mother was not a man, was she?"

"I do not play the dozens when I am drinking," said Simple.

12

Matter for a Book

"I saw Jackie yesterday," said Simple as blue Monday drew to a close.

"What Jackie?" I asked, feigning ignorance.

"There ain't but one," said Simple.

"How was he doing?"

"Making home runs and hitting all balls."

"Jackie does not *always* hit," I said.

"I did not see him miss," said Simple.

"You are a Negrophile," I said.

"A which?" said Simple.

"Too much of a race man."

"That's a lie," said Simple. "When my race does wrong, I say, NO. But when they do right, I give 'em credit."

"Credit in moderation is O.K. But overenthusiasm is as bad as not enough. Jackie Robinson is a good ballplayer—but there are other good ballplayers on the Dodgers, too."

"None as dark as Jackie," said Simple. "That is why I like him. He is two shades darker than me! Nobody can say he is a Cuban or some kind of foreigner. He is pure-D Negro—and I am proud of it."

"I am proud, too," I said. "But you are mistaken as to his complexion—Jackie Robinson is not as dark as you. You are what I would call a very dark brownskin."

"I am a light black," said Simple. "When I were a child, Mama said I were chocolate, also my hair was straight. But that was my Indian blood."

"They say folks grow darker as they get older," I said.

"Then there would be no way for age to show on me any more," said Simple. "But to get back to Jackie—I did not mean to holler so loud when he stole them two bases yesterday, but I just could not help myself. I were so proud he were black, I couldn't keep my mouth shut. And as long as Jackie stays colored, I am going to holler when he's up at bat."

"Well, holler. Nobody is stopping you," I said. "But if Jackie were not good you would stop hollering. I bet you that."

"I holler because I am a race man," said Simple.

"In other words, you are cheering yourself then," I said.

"And anybody connected with me! I want my race to hit home all the time."

"That's a very laudable desire," I said. "And I hope you are doing your part to help your race go on, up, and ever forward. I trust you are trying just as hard as Jackie."

"I am," said Simple. "I'm *cheering*."

"Figures in the sports field like Jackie and Joe rate plenty of cheering. But sometimes I wish the public were equally aware of the men of our race in the cultural fields. You, for instance, have you ever bought a book by a Negro writer?"

"Joyce is the one who likes to read," said Simple. "That girl reads a book a week, sometimes two—and I don't mean comic books neither. I don't go in for reading much myself, but Joyce is cultural. The other night when I stopped by, she was reading a book about some vixens and—"

"Frank Yerby's *The Vixens*, I guess."

"That were it," said Simple. "Man, that story is real gone! Joyce says a colored man wrote it."

"That's right, Frank Yerby is colored."

"And Joyce says he wrote a book before that about the wolves of Harlem," continued Simple.

"What she probably said was not *wolves* at all. You have your animals and places mixed up. His first best seller was *The Foxes of Harrow*, not *The Wolves of Harlem*."

"Say not so," said Simple. "It is good when a colored man writes a book."

"Not necessarily," I said. "Colored books can be bad, too. But it just happens that both of Yerby's books were best sellers, and they made a movie of *The Foxes of Harrow*."

"That is real great," said Simple.

"In fact, we've had other books by Negroes on the best-seller list, among them, Richard Wright's *Black Boy* and Willard Motley's *Knock on Any Door*. The race is rising," I said.

"All but me," said Simple. "I ain't got nowhere and I'm colored. In fact, of late I have gone back. My finances have been cut and my wages are lower while everything else is higher. My landlady is mad because she can't get a raise in rent so the hot water is cold and she put a ten-watt bulb in the bathroom so I can't even see to shave. This morning I paid seventy cents for two little old dried-up slivers of bacon and one cockeyed egg. It took me till noon to get my appetite back. Then it cost me a dollar for lunch. If I hadn't et dinner with Joyce this evening I would have been tee-totally broke."

"It is not food alone that keeps you broke," I said pointedly.

"If you mean licker, I am not able to hardly drink more than a drop. I am not Jackie Robinson—up in the money. But say, since that writer fellow made all that money out of *The Foxes of Harry,* maybe I could write *me* a book and call it *The Wolves of Harlem* by Jesse Semple."

"What would you put in your book?"

"Chapter Number One. I would start out on Lenox Avenue. Then I would bring in the wolves. I would show how if prices keep high as they is and wages go down, not a living wolf will be able to howl this time next year. They can do no more than go to work and come back weak, man, weak."

"What will you put in Chapter Two?" I asked.

"That will be a killer," said Simple. "In Chapter Number Two, I will put the plot."

"What is the plot?"

"That I will not tell," said Simple, "you are liable to steal it."

"What is your love interest, then? Your romance? In a novel you have to have romance."

"Who has got time for romance, as high as meat stays?" objected Simple. "Romance costs money. I will not put no romance in my book. I will put beefsteaks, pork chops, spare ribs, pigs' feet, and ham in *my* story."

"Then all your hero will do is eat like a wolf," I said, "which is not very edifying."

"*Satisfying,* though," said Simple.

13

Surprise

"There are lots of curs in the human race," said Simple. "Some very sweet—but curs right on."

"Referring, for example, to what?" I asked.

"To women right now," said Simple, "for example, Vivian."

"She did do Johnny rather badly, didn't she?"

"Moved out, left him, and didn't even leave him a note," said Simple. "And he had been taking care of her like a queen all these years. He hadn't no more than been out of work two weeks till she was up and gone with another huck. Women cannot stand for a man to get out of work. My wife was like that."

"Love and hunger do not mix," I said, "except in books, where, of course, people are faithful until death, job or no job."

"Books have nothing to do with life," said Simple; "they are like movies. In movies gangsters always come to a bad ending. In life, they live on Park Avenue and eat at the Waldorf. But you are changing my subject. I am talking about curs, not books. Did you hear what that sweet little cur-hussy of a Lauretta did to Rudolph?"

"Rudolph? I thought he was in the army."

"He come back from occupying Japan this morning and is occupying a jail tonight," said Simple.

"No!"

"Yes, he is. And he had not been home in three years. His mistake was not to let his wife know he was coming. A soldier should always let his old lady know when he plans to return to the fold."

"He no doubt wished to surprise her," I said.

"He surprised his own self," said Simple. "Order me another beer so I can tell you what happened as Zarita told it to me. Fellow, it were awful!"

"Give the man a beer," I said. "Now, go on."

"A week end is the wrong time to come home anyhow," said Simple. "So many people do not work on Saturdays nowadays. Lucky it were not me! I tried to make time with Lauretta myself while Rudolph were in Tokyo, but she liked that old conk-headed boy that works in the dye plant—you know, light black Freddy. You saw them both in here last night drinking Scotch. Well, seems like yesterday being Friday and Freddy did not have to work no more till Monday, he went home with Lauretta and were laying up there in her apartment this morning when Rudolph got in."

"No!" I said.

"Yes, he were," said Simple. "Rudolph took a taxi from the station because he had too many Japanese swords, Chinese gongs, and Hawaiian grass skirts to come in the subway—all of which he bought for presents for his wife. He got to Harlem about ten A.M. Seems like Lauretta had gone to the A & P store to purchase some grits. Before she left out, she told Freddy, 'Honey, just you stay in bed till I get back and I will squeeze you some nice fresh orange juice. You hear, Freddy, honey? Then you can bathe yourself while I fix breakfast.'

"Freddy said, 'Ummm-mm-hum!' and turned over to sleep some more.

"Whilst Lauretta were gone, Rudolph arrived on his furlough, put his key in the lock, and started to set his stuff down in the hall. Well, sir, Freddy heard them grass skirts rustling and he thought it were Lauretta with her paper bags from the store. So he calls out, 'Baby, bring me a nice cooo-oo-o-ool glass of water before you squeeze that orange juice.'

"What did Freddy say that for—and her husband right there in the hall? Rudolph sweated blood, also tears. But he did not say a thing. He just eased his pistol out of his bag, tiptoed into his bedroom, aimed that gun at his bed, and said, 'Who wants a nice cooo-oo-o-ool glass of water, huh?'

"Freddy were too petrified to reply when he noticed it were Lauretta's husband. In fact, he were speechless. Rudolph made him get up out of *his* bed, take off *his* pajamas, and jump buck naked in the closet, where he locked him up. Then Rudolph himself put them pajamas on—after hiding his grass skirts and his gear so Lauretta would not see. Then he got in his *own* bed for the first time in three years and turned his back like as if he were asleep. In a few minutes the hall door opened and in come Lauretta.

" 'Freddy, baby,' she called, 'wake up now. I'll have your orange juice in a minute, darling.'

" 'Um-m-hum-m-m . . . ,' said Rudolph, pretending to be Freddy half asleep.

"It were a long minute to him, I reckon. And even longer to Freddy, locked in that closet. But finally Lauretta came from the kitchen with the orange juice, ice just a-tinkling. Rudolph had his back turned and his arm stretched out in them same striped pajamas as Freddy had had on.

" 'Wake up, Freddy, baby, and turn over and drink this nice cold juice,' Lauretta said. When he did not move, Lauretta shook his shoulder in the bed very sweet-like. 'Wake up, honey, here!'

"Honey turned—but it were not the man she had left there a-tall! Not Freddy—but her husband!

"I cannot tell you what happened to Lauretta—except that the least she did was to faint. And the orange juice spoiled her counterpane. Rudolph were too much of a gentleman to shoot her. But he whipped her with everything at hand, including a grass skirt. He did not kill Freddy neither. But Freddy will not go to the dye works for some time because both of his eyes is closed. And Rudolph is in jail the first day he come back home.

"Zarita says she told Lauretta to bathe her face in witch hazel to take the bruises off. I hope that helps because Lauretta is a right sweet girl, even if she did act like a little old cur-fice dog while Rudolph was in Tokyo. But Rudolph really ought to of let her know he was coming home. A surprise like that is not pleasant for all concerned."

14

Vacation

"What's on the rail for the lizard this morning?" my friend Simple demanded about 1 A.M. at 125th and Lenox.

"Where have you been all week?" I countered, looking at the dark circles under his eyes.

"On my vacation *at last*," said Simple.

"You look it! You appear utterly fatigued."

"A vacation will tire a man out worse than work," said Simple.

"Where did you go?"

"Saratoga—after the season was over and the rates is down."

"What did you do up there?"

"Got bug-eyed."

"You mean drank liquor?" I inquired.

"I did not drink water," said Simple.

"I thought people went to Saratoga Springs to drink water."

"Some do, some don't," said Simple, "depending on if you are thirsty or not. There is no water on Congress Street, nothing but bars—Jimmie's, Goldie's, Hilltop House. Man, I had myself a ball. I was wild and frantic as a Halloween pumpkin, drinking cool keggie and knocking myself out. I met some fine chicks, too! The first night I was there one big fat mellow dame, looking all sweet and sweetened, started making admiration over me. I would not tell you a word of lie, she wanted to latch on to me for life."

"Where was Joyce?"

"You know I did not take Joyce with me on no vacation," said Simple. "I left her in Harlem. Her vacation and mine does not come at the same time anyhow, and we do not go the same places. Joyce is a quiet girl. But this old girl I met in Saratoga—oh, boy! We was sitting at the bar. She started jitterbugging right on the stool, so I introduced myself. She said, 'Baby, play that piece again,' which I did. Then she said, 'Play "The Hucklebuck" about six times,' which I also did."

"So that's where your money went," I said, "right over the bar and down the juke box?"

"That's where it went," said Simple, "but it were worth it. This old gal looked like chocolate icing on a wagon-wheel cake, partner. And I met another one looked like lemon meringue on a Sunday pie. Between the two of them I had a ball! But I come back to Harlem a week early because my money ran out. When I got home, first thing I did was go see Joyce.

"She said, 'Baby, how come you back so soon?'

"I said, 'Sugar, I wanted to see you'—and don't you know, Joyce believed me! Womens is simple.

"Joyce said, 'You sure do look tired.'

"I said, 'It's from just a-wearying for you, honey. I can't stay away from you a week at a time no more without it worries me.'

"Joyce said, 'I thought you would come back here looking all spruce and spry from drinking that sulphur water, baby.'

"But I told her, 'That water did not agree with me. Neither did that Saratoga food. Honey, you know the best thing about a vacation is coming home. When are you going to make some biscuits?'

"Man, don't you know Joyce went right out in the kitchen and made me some bread! I was hongry, too. Funny how fast your money can run out on a vacation."

"Especially when you're spending it on *two* women," I said. "You have got to learn to change your character and budget *both* your money and your pleasure."

"God gave me this character," said Simple. "In His own good time He will change it. You know that old saying:

> *A bobtail dog*
> *Can't walk a log.*
> *Neither can a elephant*
> *Hop like a frog.*

My character is *my* character! It cannot change."

"It's certainly true that nobody can make a silk purse out of a sow's ear," I said.

"Who wants to?" asked Simple.

Part Two

Winter Time

15

Letting Off Steam

"Winter time in Harlem sure is a blip," Simple complained. "I have already drunk four beers and one whiskey and I am not warm yet."

"Your blood must be thin," I said.

"Thin, nothing! It's just cold out there. I do not like cold, never did, and never will, no place, no time."

"Well, what are you doing out in this weather if you're so cold-natured? Why didn't you stay home?"

"Man, this bar is the warmest place I know. At least they keep the steam up here."

"You mean to tell me you haven't got any steam in your room?"

"There's a radiator in my room," said Simple, "but my landlady don't send up no steam. I beat on the radiator pipes to let her know I was home—and freezing."

"What happened?"

"Nothing. She just beat back on the pipes at me! I tell you, winter is a worriation."

"I don't like the cold, either," I said. "But mortal man can do very little about the weather. Of course, one could be rich and go to Florida."

"You couldn't give me Florida and all that Jim Crow on a silver platter! But if these womens keep after me, I am liable to have to go somewhere."

"What's the matter now?" I asked.

"My wife writ me from Baltimore that if I don't buy her that divorce she's been wanting for seven years, she is going to get herself a new fur coat and charge it to me. She says I better pay for it or else! And Joyce has been hinting around lately that she needs a silver fox—and she ain't even married to me yet. Here I am going around wearing my prewar Chesterfield and can't get a new coat for myself. I ain't even got no rubbers for this snow."

"You love Joyce, don't you? So I know you wouldn't want to see her freeze."

"Freeze, nothing," said Simple. "If Joyce would put on some long underwear and drop them skirts down some more and wrap up her neck, she would be warm without a fur coat. Also, if she would stop wearing open-worked shoes. Women don't wear enough clothes."

"Do you want your best girl to look like somebody's grandma?"

"I don't want her to catch pneumonia," said Simple, "but I *ain't* gonna buy her no fur coat."

"A fur coat would have made a nice gift for Christmas. By the way, what did you give Joyce?"

"A genuine pressure-cooker-roasting-oven to cook chickens, since I like them. It cost me fifteen dollars, too. But when I was back in the kitchen Christmas Eve mixing drinks she came in and gave me one of them cold-roll-your-eyes looks and said real sweet-like, 'It's just what I wanted—except that I've got too many cooking utensils now to be just rooming—and that cute little fur jacket I showed you last week would've looked so nice on me.'"

"What did Joyce give you for Christmas?" I asked.

"A carton of *her* favorite brand of cigarettes. Ain't that just like a woman? Then she comes wanting a fur coat."

"Well, even dogs have fur coats. I see in the papers where a downtown store is advertising fur wrappers especially for dogs, priced up to Two Thousand Dollars. If someone would pay that much for a fur coat for a dog, it looks as though you might consider one for Joyce."

"Man, the rich peoples that buy them expensive dog-jackets have paid Two Thousand Bucks for their dog in the first place. To have a fur coat like that, the dog is bound to be a thoroughbred-pedigreedy-canine dog. They ain't buying fur wrap-arounds for no mutt. They got their investment to protect. But Joyce ain't cost me nothing. Money couldn't buy that girl. I met her on a Negro Actors' Guild public boat ride when the moon were shining over Bear Mountain. She just floated into my life—free. And took up with me for the sake of love."

"So you would value a dog more than the woman who is your friend?"

"I do not have a dog, and if I did, as sure as my name is Jess Semple, I would not buy it no fur coat—a dog has its own fur. And unless Joyce raises herself some foxes, she will not get any, neither. I won't buy a human nor a dog a fur coat this winter."

"Why don't you just say you *can't* buy a fur coat?"

"You have hit the nail on the head. I have just cash enough for *one* more beer. You have that glass on me."

"No, thanks."

"Then I will have a *bottle* on you," said Simple, "before I go out in the cold. The Lord should have fixed it so humans can grow fur in the winter time—instead of buying it. . . . Hey, Bud, a bottle of Bud!"

16

Jealousy

"That Joyce," said Simple, "is not a drinking woman—for which I love her. But if she wasn't my girl friend, I swear she would make me madder than she do sometimes."

"What's come off between you and Joyce now?" I asked.

"She has upset me," said Simple.

"How?"

"One night last week when we come out of the subway, it was sleeting too hard to walk and we could not get a cab for love nor money. So Joyce condescends to stop in the Whistle and Rest with me and have a beer. If I had known what was in there, I would of kept on to Paddy's, where they don't have nothing but a juke box."

"What was in there?"

"A trio," said Simple. "They was humming and strumming up a breeze with the bass just a-thumping, piano trilling, and electric guitar vibrating with every string overcharged. They was playing off-bop. Now, I do not care much for music, and Joyce does not care much for beer. So after I had done had from four to six and she had had two, I said, 'Let's go.' Joyce said, 'No, baby! I want to stay awhile more.'

"Now that were the first time I have ever heard Joyce say she wants to set in a bar.

"I said, 'What ails you?'

"Joyce said, 'I *love* his piano playing.'

"I said, 'You sure it ain't the piano *player* you love?' He were a slickheaded cat that looked like a shmoo and had a part in his teeth.

"Joyce said, 'Don't insinuate.'

"I said, 'Before you sin, *you* better wait. It looks like to me that piano player is eying you mighty hard. He'd best keep his eyes on them keys, else I will close one and black the other, also be-bop his chops.'

"Joyce says, 'Huh! It is about time you got a little jealous of me, Jess. Sometimes I think you take me for granted. But I *do* like that man's music.'

"'Are you sure it's his music you like?' I says. 'As flirtatious as you is this evening, your middle name ought to be Frisky.'

" 'Don't put me in no class with Zarita,' says Joyce right out of the clear skies. 'I am no bar-stool hussy'—which kinder took me back because I did not know Joyce had any information about Zarita. A man can't do nothing even once without Harlem and his brother knowing it. Somebody has been talking, or else Joyce is getting too well acquainted with some of my friends—like you.''

"I never mention your personal affairs to anyone," I said, "least of all to Joyce, whom I scarcely know except through your introduction."

"Well, anyhow," said Simple, "I did not wish to argue. I says to her, 'I ignore that remark.'

"Joyce says, 'I ignore you.' And turned her back to me and cupped her ear to the music.

" 'Don't rile me, woman,' I says. 'Come out of here and lemme take you home. You know we have to work in the morning.'

" 'Work does not cross your mind,' says Joyce, turning around, 'when you're setting up drinking beer all by yourself—so you say—at Paddy's. I do not see why you have to mention work to *me* when I am enjoying *myself*. The way that man plays "Stardust" sends me. I swear it do. Sends me. Sends me!'

" 'Be yourself, Joyce,' I said. 'Put your coat around your shoulders. Are you high? We are going home.'

"I took Joyce out of there. And by Saturday, to tell the truth, I had forgot all about it. Come the weekend, I says, 'Let's walk a little, honey. Which movie do you want to see?'

"Joyce says, 'I do not want to see a picture, daddy. They are all alike. Let's go to the Whistle and Rest Bar.'

" 'O.K.,' I said, because I knowed every Friday they change the music behind that bar. They had done switched to a great big old corn-fed blues man who looked like Ingagi, hollered like a mountain-jack, and almost tore a guitar apart. He were singing:

> *Where you goin', Mr. Spider,*
> *Walking up the wall?*
> *Spider said, I'm goin'*
> *To get my ashes hauled.*

The joint were jumping—rocking, rolling, whooping, hollering, and stomping. It was a far cry from "Stardust" to that spider walking up the wall.

"When I took Joyce in and she did not see her light-dark shmoo with the conked crown curved over the piano smearing riffs, she said, 'Is this the same place we was at last time?'

"I said, 'Sure, baby! What's the matter? Don't you like blues?'

"Joyce said, 'You know I never did like blues. I am from the North.'

" 'North what?' I said. 'Carolina?'

" 'I thought this was a refined cocktail lounge,' says Joyce, turning up her nose. 'But I see I was in error. It's a low dive. Let's go on downtown and catch John Garfield after all.'

" 'No, no, no. No *after all* for me,' I said. 'Here we are—and here we stay right in this bar till *I* get ready to go. . . . Waiter, a beer! . . . Anyhow, I do not see why *you* would want to see John Garfield. Garfield does not conk his hair. Neither is he light black. Neither does he play "Stardust." '

" 'You are acting just like a Negro,' says Joyce.

" 'It's my Indian blood,' I admitted."

17

Banquet in Honor

"Well, sir, I went to a banquet the other night," said Simple, "and I have never seen nothing like it. The chicken was good, but the best thing of all was the speech."

"That's unusual," I said. "Banquet speeches are seldom good."

"This one were a killer," said Simple. "In fact, it almost killed the folks who gave the function."

"Who gave it?"

"Some women's club that a big fat lady what goes to Joyce's dancing class belongs to. Her name is Mrs. Sadie Maxwell-Reeves and she lives so high up on Sugar Hill that people in her neighborhood don't even have roomers. They keep the whole house for themselves. Well, this Mrs. Maxwell-Reeves sold Joyce a deuce of Three-Dollar ducats to this banquet her club was throwing for an old gentleman who is famous around Harlem for being an intellect for years, also very smart as well as honest, and a kind of all-around artist-writer-speaker and what-not. His picture's in the *Amsterdam News* this week. I cannot recall his name, but I never will forget his speech."

"Tell me about it, man, and do not keep me in suspense," I said.

"Well, Joyce says the reason that club gave the banquet is because the poor old soul is so old he is about on his last legs and, although he is great, nobody has paid him much mind in Harlem before. So this club thought instead of having a dance this year they would show some intelligence and honor him. They did. But he bit their hand, although he ate their chicken."

"I beg you, get to the point, please."

"It seems like this old man has always played the race game straight and has never writ no Amos and Andy books nor no songs like 'That's Why Darkies Are Born' nor painted no kinky-headed pictures as long as he has been an artist—for which I give him credit. But it also seems like he did not make any money because the white folks wouldn't buy his stuff and the Negroes didn't pay him no mind because he wasn't already famous.

"Anyhow, they say he will be greater when he's dead than he is alive—and he's mighty near dead now. Poor old soul! The club give that banquet to catch some of his glory before he passes on. He gloried them, all right! In the first place, he ate like a horse. I was setting just the third table from him and I could see. Mrs. Maxwell-Reeves sort of likes Joyce because Joyce helps her with her high kicks, so she give us a good table up near the speaking. She knows Joyce is a fiend for culture, too. Facts, some womens—including Joyce—are about culture like I am about beer—they love it.

"Well, when we got almost through with the dessert, which was ice cream, the toastmistress hit on a cup with a spoon and the program was off. Some great big dame with a high voice and her hands clasped on her bosoms—which were fine—sung 'O Carry Me Homey.' "

" 'O Caro Nome,' " I said.

"Yes," said Simple. "Anyhow, hard as I try, daddy-o, I really do not like concert singers. They are always singing in some foreign language. I leaned over the table and asked Joyce what the song meant, but she snaps, 'It is not important what it means. Just listen to that high C above X.' I listened fluently, but it was Dutch to me.

"I said, 'Joyce, what *is* she saying?'

"Joyce said, 'Please don't show your ignorance here.'

"I said, 'I am trying to hide it. But what in God's name is she singing about?'

"Joyce said, 'It's in Italian. Shsss-ss-s! For my sake, kindly act like you've got some culture, even if you ain't.'

"I said, 'I don't see why culture can't be in English.'

"Joyce said, 'Don't embarrass me. You ought to be ashamed.'

"I said, 'I am not ashamed, neither am I Italian, and I do not understand their language.' We would have had a quarrel right then and there had not that woman got through and set down. Then a man from the Urban League, a lady from the Daughter Elks, and a gentleman librarian all got up and paid tributes to the guest of honor. And he bowed and smiled and frowned and et because he could not eat fast, his teeth being about gone, so he still had a chicken wing in his hand when the program started. Finally came the great moment.

" 'Shsss-ss-s-ssh!' says Joyce.

" 'I ain't said a word,' I said, 'except that *I sure wish I could smoke in here.*'

" 'Hush,' says Joyce, 'this is a cultural event and no smoking is allowed. We are going to hear the guest of honor.'

"You should have seen Mrs. Sadie Maxwell-Reeves. She rose to her full heights. She is built like a pyramid upside down anyhow. But her head was all done fresh and shining with a hair-rocker roached up high in front, and a advertised-in-*Ebony* snood down the back, also a small bunch of green feathers behind her ear and genuine diamonds on her hand. Man, she had bosom-glasses that pulled out and snapped back when she read her notes. But she did not need to read no notes, she were so full of her subject.

"If words was flowers and he was dead, that old man could not have had more boquets put on him if he'd had a funeral at Delaney's where big shots get laid out. Roses, jonquils, pea-lilies, forget-me-nots, pansies, dogwoods, African daisies, also hydrangeas fell all over his head out of that lady toastmistress's mouth. He were sprayed with the perfume of eloquence. He were welcomed and rewelcomed to that Three-Dollar Banquet and given the red plush carpet. Before that lady got through, I clean forgot I wanted to smoke. I were spellbound, smothered in it myself.

"Then she said, 'It is my pride, friends, my pleasure, nay, my honor— without further words, allow me to present this distinguished guest, our honoreeeee—the Honorable Dr. So-and-So-and-So.' I did not hear his name for the applause.

"Well, sir! That old man got up and he did not smile. It looked like he cast a wicked eye right on me, and he did like a snake charmer to Joyce, because nobody could move our heads. He did not even clear his throat before he said, 'You think you are honoring me, ladies and gentlemen of the Athenyannie Arts Club, when you invited me here tonight? You are *not* honoring me a damn bit! I said, not a bit.'

"You could have heard a pin drop. Mens glued to their seats. Joyce, too.

" 'The way you could have honored me if you had wanted to, ladies and gentlemen, all these years, would have been to buy a piece of my music and play it, or a book of mine and read it, but you didn't. Else you could have booed off the screen a few of them Uncle Toms thereon and told the manager of the Hamilton you'd never come back to see another picture in his theater until he put a story of mine in it, or some other decent hard-working Negro. But you didn't do no such a thing. You didn't even buy one of my watercolors. You let me starve until I am mighty nigh blue-black in the face—and not a one of you from Sugar Hill to Central Park ever offered me a pig's foot. Then when the *New York Times* said I was a genius last month, here you come now giving a banquet for me when I'm old enough to fall over in my grave—if I was able to walk to the edge of it—which I'm not.

" 'Now, to tell you the truth, I don't want no damned banquet. I don't want no honoring where *you* eat as much as me, and enjoy yourselves more, besides making some money for your treasury. If you want to honor me, give some young boy or girl who's coming along trying to create arts and write and compose and sing and act and paint and dance and make something out of the beauties of the Negro race—give that child some help. Buy what they're making! Support what they're doing! Put out some cash—but don't come giving me, who's old enough to die and too near blind to create anything any more anyhow, a great big banquet that *you* eat up in honor of your *own* stomachs as much as in honor of me—who's toothless and can't eat. You hear me, I ain't honored!'

"That's what that old man said, and sat down. You could have heard a pin drop if ary one had dropped, but nary one dropped. Well, then Mrs. Maxwell-Reeves got up and tried to calm the waters. But she made matters worse, and that feather behind her ear was shaking like a leaf. She pulled at her glasses but she could not get them on.

"She said, 'Doctor, we know you are a great man, but, to tell the truth, we have been kinder vague about just what you have done.'

"The old man said, 'I ain't done nothing but eat at banquets all my life, and I am great just because I am honored by you tonight. Is that clear?'

"The lady said, 'That's beautiful and so gracious. Thanks. It sounds so much like Father Divine.'

"The old man said, 'Father Divine is a genius at saying the unsayable. That is why he is great and because he also gives free potatoes with his gospel—and potatoes are just as important to the spirit as words. In fact, more so. I know.'

" 'Do you really think so, Doctor?'

" 'Indeed, or I wouldn't have come here at all tonight. I ate in spite of the occasion. I still need a potato and some meat—not honor.'

" 'We are proud to give you both,' said Mrs. Sadie Maxwell-Reeves.

" 'Compliment returned,' said the old man. 'The tickets you sold to this affair on the strength of *my* name are feeding us all.'

"Mrs. Sadie Maxwell-Reeves came near blushing, but she couldn't quite make it, being brownskin. I don't know what I did, but everybody turned and looked at me.

"I said, 'Joyce, I got to go have a smoke.'

"Joyce said, 'This is so embarrassing! You laughing out loud! Oh!'

"I said, 'It's the best Six Dollars' worth of banquet I ever had.' (Because I paid for them tickets although Joyce bought them.) I said, 'If you ever want to take me to another banquet in honor, I will go, though I don't reckon there will be another one this good.'

" 'You have a low sense of humor, Mr. Semple,' said Joyce, all formal and everything like she does when she's mad. 'Shut up so I can hear the benediction.'

"Reverend Patterson Smythe prayed. Then it were over. I beat it on out of there and had my smoke whilst I was waiting for Joyce, because she looked mad. On the way home I stopped at the Wonder Bar and had two drinks, but Joyce would not even come in the back room. She waited in the cab. She said I were not the least bit cultural. Still and yet, I thought that old man made sense. I told Joyce, just like he said, 'It is more important to eat than to be honored, ain't it?'

"Joyce said, 'Yes, but when you are doing both at the same time, you can at least be polite. I mean not only the Doctor, but *you*. It's an honor to be invited to things like that. And Mrs. Maxwell-Reeves did not invite you there to laugh.'

"I said, 'I didn't know I was laughing.'

" 'Everybody else knew it,' she said when we got to her door. 'You was heard all over the hall. I was embarrassed not only for you, *but for myself*. I would like you to know that I am not built like you. I cannot just drink and forget.'

" 'No matter how many drinks I drink,' I said, 'I will not forget this.' Then I laughed again—which were my error! I did not even get a good-night kiss—Joyce slammed the vestibule door dead in my face. So I went home to my Third Floor Rear—*and laughed some more*. If I wasn't honored, I sure was tickled, and, at least, I ain't stingy like them Sugar-Hillers. They wouldn't buy none of his art when he could still enjoy the benefits. But me, I'd buy that old man a beer *any time*."

18

After Hours

"Bartender!" Simple cried in a loud voice as though he were going to treat everyone in the place. "Once around the bar." Then pointing to ourselves, "This far—from my buddy to me."

By the time the beers were drawn, Simple had begun to recount a story.

"You know," he began, "I was way down under in Harlem the other night, way, way down on Lenox Avenue." I could see it was a serious story because he forgot his beer, allowing his glass to remain on the bar.

"It was so cold I went into a barbecue place thinking I might take an order of spareribs and coleslaw to Joyce if I had enough change—and at the same time get warm. Man, the juke box was playing up a breeze, flashing colored lights, and the joint was full of young kids and girls not buying nothing much but drinking Pepsis and jiving around the juke box. I looked at them kids and I felt sorry. I can see now why these girls wear open-worked shoes in zero weather because them cheap soles are so thin they couldn't keep their feet warm anyhow, so they'd just as well be open-worked.

"And the boys," continued Simple, "with them army-store raincoats on and last spring's imitation camel's hairs—which would not keep nobody warm—because they ain't had the money this winter to buy an overcoat. They was just jiving and jitterbugging quietly-like, till the woman hollered, 'Stop!' because there was a big sign up:

NO DANCING POSITIVELY

"They also had a sign up:

DON'T ASK FOR CREDIT—HE'S DEAD

"I reckon that is why those kids could not eat much, on account of credit being dead. But they had to move to keep warm because it was kinder cold in that place, the only heat being from that thing where the barbecue turns and that was not much. It were a Greek place or some kind of foreigner's, but at least they had colored help. The foreigner just set behind the cash register and took the money.

"While I was setting there waiting for the woman to wrap up my sandwich and coleslaw for Joyce, a half-dozen little old teen-age boys come in and stood around listening to the juke box, singing with the records and rubbing their ears to get warm. By and by a quarrel started amongst them and before you could say 'Hush,' one of them let a blackjack a foot long slide out of his sleeve and another one drew a knife. They all started cussing and damning.

"The woman behind the counter said, 'Somebody ought to call the Law,' which kinder riled me the wrong way because after all, they was nothing but kids.

"So I said, 'Madam, the cops could only lock them kids up. The cops could not make their papa's kitchenette big enough for them to invite their young friends to come home and have fun in and not have to look for it in the streets. I bet where these boys live there are forty-eleven names in the doorbell, the house is so crowded. Also some roomer has the spare bed.'

"The woman said, 'I reckon you right. There are about that many names in the bell where I live, too. But I just don't want these boys to fight in here, that's all. They make me nervous.'

"The boys didn't fight. They finally put up their weapons, and I took my sandwich and coleslaw and went on up the street. Zero outside, man! And cold enough to freeze a brass monkey! But all the way to Joyce's I kept thinking about them kids that didn't have no place to go in the evening but to that juke-box joint with a sign up:

NO DANCING POSITIVELY

"I said to myself, 'If I ever have a kid, I will have a juke box *at home* and his friends can come in and dance as much as they want.' "

"A victrola would be more appropriate for the home," I said.

"A juke box is more sociable," declared Simple, "then they wouldn't get into the habit of wanting to be out in the streets so much and later when they got grown start to running around to bars and after-hour joints."

"Like you," I said.

"Yes, like me," said Simple. "I almost got caught in a raid the other night. But the cops phoned first that they was coming. The raid were just a polite hint to the houseman to keep their graft up to date and let the Law have theirs on time. I guess the reason cops are so hard on after-hour spots, and them folks who run them have to pay off so steep to stay open, is because they serve such bad bodacious licker."

"There must be some after-hour spots that serve good liquor."

"They are few and far between," said Simple. "Just because it was cold outside, I went into one of them gyp joints night before last and I have not got over my hangover yet. In fact, it is just like one of them prohibition hang-overs—the kind of licker that hits you in the head like a baseball bat, cracks your skull inside, and mighty near blinds you besides. If the licker ain't bad, then it's like up at Mamie Lou's last Saturday— cut so much it wouldn't even make you high, let alone leave you with a hang-over. In these after-hour joints, either they gyp you or try to kill you, one.

"At that place I went the other night, Mojo Mike's King Kong Palace, basement floor, last apartment, down the hall off Lenox, the guy sold me a half pint of pure white mule mixed with blue lightning. I thought my tonsils would explode.

"I said, 'What *is* this? It looks like water and tastes like fire.'

"He said, 'That is some of this new atomic licker. It will make you Nagasaki, then go up in smoke. For Thirty-Five Cents you can solid blow your top, I mean anatomize your wig.'

"I said, 'It's too big a bargain for me.' But since I'd paid for it, naturally, I drunk it. And, boy, what a hang-over!"

"I don't sympathize with you," I said.

"I do not expect you to," said Simple. "I guess you have never over-sported *yourself*—therefore you cannot understand. If you don't under-stand, you cannot sympathize. It is just like somebody who never had the toothache and don't know what it is."

"I've had a toothache," I said.

"Then you can sympathize with me when I have the toothache. But you cannot sympathize with me if I have a hang-over."

"The wise thing to do," I said, "would be to avoid bootleg liquor and stay out of after-hour joints."

"Then where would a human go after the bars close?"

"Home," I said.

"That would be too simple," said Simple. "A man can *always* go home."

"It would be better for your health, your reputation, and your pocket-book if you would go home at a reasonable hour," I said. "You're getting too old to be running around all night. You ought to know better."

"Age has nothing to do with wisdom," said Simple. "I know a man fifty-two years old who never does go home except to take a bath and change his underwear. And sometimes before he can do that, his wife runs him out of the house. A woman can really be a thorn in a man's side when she does not understand him. My wife did not understand me, that is why I am out here in the streets tonight."

"Joyce understands you quite well," I said, "yet I see you are not keeping her company this evening."

"I was with her last night," said Simple. "And I am somewhatly doubtful of her understanding. You know the first thing she asked me? She said, 'Where was you the night before?'

"I said, 'I was out, baby, in an after-hours place, and I did not get home till late.'

"She said, 'That is no excuse for you to come around to my house and set up and snooze. I do not pay rent here to receive sleepers. Suppose my landlady was to walk in and catch you sleeping in her parlor.'

"I said, 'So what? When a man is tired, he has to sleep. Besides, I got a headache.'

"She said, 'A licker-ache, that's what! I can smell wood alcohol from your end of the couch to mine. Get out of here and go on home. You ain't no company to me in your condition.'

"Joyce were mad! That is why I am not keeping her company this evening. And that is what I am telling you about a woman not understanding a man. The very time you need to be understood most is the time they let you down. Hang-overed as I was, Joyce should have said, 'Baby, lemme put a cold towel on your head.' Instead of that, she said, 'Get out of here and go home! You ain't no company for me.' Now, if Joyce had come to see me feeling bad, I would have tried to comforther."

"You would not be going with Joyce if she were the kind of girl who gets drunk and has hang-overs," I said.

"True," answered Simple.

"Then why do you expect her to understand you when you come up in that condition?"

"*Because I am a man*," said Simple, "and a woman is suppose to understand. There is nothing worse than a hang-over. So if *ever* there is a time to understand, that time is it. I am disappointed in Joyce."

"Joyce is probably disappointed in you," I said, "spending your money collecting hang-overs in joints like Mojo Mike's after hours."

"After hours is when I needs most to be understood," said Simple, "especially *after* after hours."

19

A Veteran Falls

"It's a sad and sorry thing to see how some of these fellows come back from the war all wounded and crippled up, ain't it?" said Simple.⁹ "Last Saturday night I was climbing that 145th Street hill from Eighth Avenue when it was half raining, half sleeting, and cold. I was just thinking about turning into a bar to have me a drink, when I saw a long tall one-legged soldier coming down the hill on crutches, just swinging it, man, like he was in a hurry on one leg.

"He *was* in a hurry because two dopey dames was behind him trying to keep up with him, and it looked like he was disgusted with both of them. Then something kind of sad happened, man. Right in front of the bar under all them neon lights, one of his crutches skidded on the wet sidewalk and that veteran slipped and fell down. His one good leg went out from under him and he went flat on the pavement.

"But this were the other part—both of them women rushed to pick him up. You could see how that soldier was embarrassed, trying to ignore them homely dames, and here he had done fell down. The tall woman bent over and took him by the arm to pull him up from the sidewalk.

"But the little woman hollered, 'Don't you pick him up, Cassie! I'll pick him up, myself. He's mine! He was trying to jump salty with me tonight—but he's mine right on.'

" 'I will *so* pick him up,' yelled the tall woman. 'He's an old flame and I mean from way back! I will pick him up!'

" 'Charlie's more to me than he is to you,' said the little woman, tugging on his other arm. 'I'll pick him up myself.'

"Both of them was pulling and hauling at that one-legged soldier, and the boy was cussing like mad. When he got to his feet, he shook 'em both loose. I handed him his crutches my own self while them women was yapping at each other. The back of his uniform was all muddy and wet and his pants leg folded back over his stump was wet, too. I reckon he must have been on leave from a hospital because you could tell that leg hurt him. He tried to make out like it wasn't nothing happened. 'What's all this fuss these damn women are making? I just fell down, that's all!'

" 'Any man can fall,' I said. But I could see he was trembling and he couldn't help it. He put his hands over the stump of that leg.

"The little woman was standing at the curb yelling, 'Cab! Cab! Cab!' and taking time out to turn around to see what the other woman was doing. 'Cassie, you leave that man be, I tell you! . . . Cab! Cab! Cab!'

"But you know on a rainy night how hard it is to get a cab. Meantime, the other woman had run one hand down his shirt front and was trying to give him a kiss. But he pushed her away. So she went to the curb and started yelling cab, too. Then in all that cold old drizzly rain them women started yapping at each other all over again. Man, a woman is something!

" 'I'll get a cab,' the tall one yells.

" 'I'll get it and pay for it, too,' hollered the little one. 'I know Charlie snuck off from me to go see you today. But I'm the one he comes to first—like this afternoon—first—soon as he gets in town.'

" 'That's what you think,' says the tall woman. 'Wheeeeeooo! Cab!'

" 'I'm the one he gets a dollar from when he needs it most,' yaps the little chick. 'Long as I'm working, Charlie'll eat! I'll get this cab and pay for it. Do you hear me, Cassie?'

"Some old agitating Negro standing in the doorway of the bar yells, 'One of you women better hurry up and get that taxi or won't neither one of you-all have no man. He'll be gone.'

"The soldier-boy did start to walk, but that leg—he must of hurt them nerve ends when he fell. I imagine it was like a aching tooth and he couldn't keep from grabbing it. Leaning on them crutches trying to keep his hands from going to that sawed-off leg, but he couldn't keep from grabbing it. He just stood still. I didn't know what to say to him, so I thought I would take my handkerchief and wipe some of the wet off the back of his coat.

"But he said, 'Get away, man!'

"It was old Dad Martin what owns that little hamburger stand that did the best thing. Dad come out and said, 'Son, anybody could fall down on this wet night. Is you hurt?'

" 'Naw, Dad, I just slipped, that's all.'

" 'I mean, did it hurt your feelings?' Dad said.

" 'No,' said the soldier.

" 'Then everything's all right,' the old man said.

"Just then Cassie hollered, 'Baby, here's the cab! Come on!'

"The little woman beat Cassie to him, though. 'Here's our taxi, honey! Come on, Charlie, we got a cab.'

" 'You better set between them two women else they liable to tear each other's eyes out,' yells that agitating old Negro in the bar door.

" 'Everything's under control,' said the soldier, 'don't worry.'

"He pulled his own self up in that cab. But the women jumped in after him and there he was between them when the taxi pulled off in the rain— and they was still fussing over who he belonged to. It was funny—still and yet it wasn't funny either.

"You can laugh at a man when he falls if he's got two legs, but I couldn't laugh at him. Couldn't nobody laugh at that soldier like they would laugh at you and me if we fell down trying to ignore a couple of women. That's why it was kinder hard for that boy to take. I aimed to order a beer when I got in the bar but my mouth said, 'A double whiskey!' It damn sure did, after that boy fell down."

20

High Bed

"I told you you should take care of yourself," I said to Simple as I sat down beside his bed. "Running around half high in all this cold weather. If you had taken care of yourself, and not gotten all run down, you would not be here now in this hospital with pneumonia."

"If I had taken care of myself," said Simple, "I would not have these pretty nurses taking care of me."

"Everything has its compensations, I admit. But look at the big hospital bill you will have when you get out."

"Just let me draw two or three weeks' pay or hit one number, and I will settle it," said Simple. "But what worries me is when am I going to get out?"

"You should have worried about that before you got in," I said. "And you will never get out if you do not observe the rules and stop telling folks to bring you beer and pigs' feet and things you are not supposed to have."

"You didn't bring me that Three Feathers I told you to bring," said Simple. "And the nurse would not let me finish that little old sausage Zarita brought in her pocketbook yesterday. She said it would be a bad example for the rest of the patients in this ward. So I have not broken any rules. But if you gimme a cigarette, I sure will smoke it."

"I will not give you a cigarette," I said.

"O.K.," said Simple. "You will want me to do something for you someday."

"You have everything you need right here in this hospital," I said. "You know if you really needed something you are supposed to have, I would bring it."

"They feed me pretty good in here," said Simple. "Only one thing I do not like—they won't let you take your own bath."

"And what is wrong about that?"

"Well, the morning nurse, she comes in before day A.M. and grabs you by the head. When she gets through scrubbing your ears they feel just like they have been shucked. Ain't nobody washed my ears so hard since I got out from under my mother."

"Sleepy-headed as you are, I guess she is just trying to wake you up."

"And, man," said Simple, "when she washes your stomach, it tickles. I told her I was ticklish and not to touch me nowhere near my ribs, nor my navel."

"I do not see why a big husky fellow like you should be ticklish."

"I do not mind when she rubs my back, though. That alcohol sure smells fine."

"Reminds you of something to drink, I presume?"

"It do feel sort of cool and good like the last drop of a gin rickey. But I don't want to think of gin rickey now, pal."

"I shouldn't think you would," I said. "That is why you are here—becoming intoxicated and forgetting your overcoat."

"That is not true," said Simple. "I got mad. Joyce made me so mad I walked out of the house at one A.M. without my coat and the wind was frantic that night. Zero! But being drunk had nothing to do with it. A woman aggravates a man, drunk or sober. But Joyce is sorry now that she ever mentioned Zarita. She come here yesterday and told me so. She is sorry she done caused me to get pneumonia. She knows Zarita ain't nothing to me even if she did accidentally see me talking to her through the vestibule. But I do not want to discuss how come I am in this hospital. I *am* here. I *am* sick. And I cannot get out of this bed. Why do you reckon they make these hospital beds so high?"

"To keep people from getting out easily," I said.

"Well, they are so high that if a man ever *fell* out, he would break his neck. I am even afraid to turn over in this bed. I naturally sleeps restless, but this bed is so high I am scared to sleep restless, so I lay here stiff as a board and don't close my eyes. I mean I am really stiff when morning comes! This would be a right nice bed if it was not so narrow and so hard and so high."

"Everything must be wrong with that bed," I said, "to hear you tell it."

"I don't see why they don't make hospital beds more comfortable. In a place where people have to *stay* in bed, they ought to have a feather mattress like Aunt Lucy used to have."

"If hospital beds were that comfortable," I said, "folks might never want to go home."

"I would, because I don't like even a pretty nurse to be washing my ears. That is one reason I was glad when I growed up, so I could wash my own ears, and comb my own head."

"Has any nurse here tried to comb your hair?" I inquired.

"These nurses are not crazy," said Simple. "My head is tender! Man, nobody here better not try to pull a comb through my hair but me. If they do, I will get up out of this bed—no matter how high it is—and carry my bohunkus on home."

"Calm down," I said. "You'll run your temperature up. Nobody is going to comb your hair, man."

"You can certainly think of some unpleasant subjects," said Simple. "Even if I was dying, I would comb my own head—and better not nobody else touch it! But say, boy, if you want to do me a favor, when you come back bring me a stocking-cap to make my hair lay down. That is one thing these white folks do not have in this hospital. I wonder if it is against the rules to wear a nylon stocking-cap in this here high bed? If it ain't, you tell Joyce to send me one."

"Very well."

"Also a small drink, because you know it's a long time between drinks in a hospital. And sometimes I don't have nothing to do but lay here and think. The other day I got to thinking about the Age of the Air when rocket planes get to be common."

"What did you think about it?"

"About how women will have a hard time keeping up with their husbands then," said Simple.

"How's that?"

"Mens will have girl friends all over the world, not just around the corner where a wife can find out—and sue for divorce. Why, when rocket planes get to be as cheap as Fords, I'm liable to go calling in Cairo any week end."

"Joyce would be right behind you," I said.

"I expect so. Not even in a rocket plane could I keep Joyce from knowing my whereabouts. But you know what I am talking about is true, and in the future it is going to be even better. In 1975, when a man can get in a rocket plane and shoot through the stratosphere a thousand miles a minute—when he can get to London sooner than I can get from Harlem to Times Square—you know, and I know, a guy will meet some woman he likes halfway across the earth in Australia and any night after dinner he will shoot over there to see her while he tells his wife he's going out to play pool. He can be back by bedtime."

"Your imagination is certainly far-fetched," I said.

"No place will be far-fetched when them rocket planes gets perfected," said Simple. "If I can afford it, I sure will own one myself. Then, in my rocket I will rock! You won't see me hanging around no Harlem bars no more. Saturday nights I will rock on down to Rio and drink coconut milk and gin with them Brazilian chicks whilst dancing a samba. Sunday morning I will zoom on over to Africa and knock out some palm wine before I come back to Seventh Avenue around noon to eat some of Joyce's chicken and dumplings.

"Joyce will say, 'Jess, where you been this morning with your hair blowed back so slick?'

"I will say, 'Nowheres, baby, but just out for a little ride in the clouds to clean the cobwebs out of my brain. I drunk a little too much in Hong Kong last night. And don't you know, after them Chinese bars closed the sky was so crowded, it took me nearly ten minutes to fly back to Harlem to get an aspirin. So this morning, baby, I didn't fly nowheres but straight up in them nice cool clouds for a breath of fresh air, then right back home to you.' "

"What are you going to say if Joyce smells that African palm wine on your breath?" I asked.

"How do you know anybody can smell palm wine?" said Simple. "Maybe by that time somebody will have invented something to take the scent out of *all* lickers anyhow. Besides, I won't be drinking enough to get drunk, I'd be very careful with my rocket plane so as not to run into some planet, neither no star. I will keep a clear head in the air."

"That is more than you keep on earth, except when you're in the hospital."

"There you go low-rating me," sighed Simple. "But listen, daddy-o, such another scrambling of races as there is going to be when they gets that rocket plane perfected! Why, when a man can shoot from Athens, Georgia, to Athens, Greece, in less than an hour, you know there is going to be intermarriage. I am liable to marry a Greek myself."

"Are there any colored Greeks?"

"I would not be prejudiced toward color," said Simple, rising on his pillow, "and if I did not like the licker they drink in Greece, I would fly to Nagasaki and drink saki. Or I might come back to Harlem and have a beer with you."

"If you're doing all that flying around, what makes you think I would remain here in Harlem? I might be out in my rocket, too."

"Great stuff, daddy-o! We might bump into each other over London—who knows? Because I sure would be rocking through the sky. Why, man, I would rock so far away from this color line in the U.S.A., till it wouldn't be funny. I might even build me a garage on Mars and a mansion on Venus. On summer nights I would scoot down the Milky

Way just to cool myself off. I would not have no old-time jet-propelled plane either. My plane would run on atom power. This earth I would not bother with no more. No, buddy-o! The sky would be my roadway and the stars my stopping place. Man, if I had a rocket plane, I would rock off into space and be solid gone. Gone. Real gone! I mean *gone*!"

"I think you are gone now," I said. "Out of your head."

"Not quite," said Simple.

21

Final Fear

The next time I visited Simple, I found him convalescent, slightly ashy and a bit thinner, sitting up in bed, but low in spirits. He was gazing sadly at the inscription on a comic book, "*Lovingly yours, Joyce.*"

"She has just been here," he said, "and I feel like I am going to have a relapse."

"If that's the way visitors affect you, then I will depart."

"Not all visitors," said Simple, "just Joyce. I love that girl."

"Then why does a visit from her get you down?"

"A woman brought me into this world," said Simple, "and I do believe women will take me out. They is the fault of my being in this hospital with pneumonia because my doctor told me the mind is worse than my body and from the looks of my chest, I must of been worrying."

"So you too have one of those fashionable psychosomatic illnesses," I said.

"No, it's Zarita and Isabel," said Simple, "plus Joyce. That wife of mine called me up New Year's Eve just when I was starting out to have some fun—long-distance, *collect*, from Baltimore—just to tell me that since another year was starting, she was tired of being tied to me and not being *with* me. She told me again either to come back to her or else get her a divorce. I said which would she rather have after all these years, me or the divorce.

"She said, 'Divorce!'

"I said, 'How much do a divorce cost nowadays?'

"She said, 'Three Hundred Dollars.'

"That is what I am feeling bad about, buddy-o. If I had not paid Five Dollars to marry that woman in the past, I would not have to pay Three Hundred now to get loose."

"Maybe it would be cheaper to go back to her."

"My nerves is wrecked," said Simple. "That woman is incontemptible. She has caused me mental anguish, also a headache. I will not go back. Besides, Joyce has been too good to me for me to cut out now. You see them flowers she brought to this hospital, also these two comic books and four packs of chewing gum. But Joyce is also a headache."

"You are just weak from your recent illness," I said.

"You mean Joyce is weak for me," corrected Simple. "Sitting right here on this bed today, she told me she is not built of bricks. Joyce says she's got a heart, also a soul, and is respectable. Joyce swears she is getting tired of me coming to her house so regular and everybody asking when is we gonna marry. She says I've been setting in her parlor too late for her respectability.

"I said, 'One o'clock ain't late.'

"She said, 'No, but two and three o'clock is, and you sure can't stay till four.'

"I said, 'Baby, it ain't what you do, it's how you do it.' But she disagreed.

"She said 'No, it ain't what you do—it's what folks *think* you do. When folks see you coming out of my place at two-three-four o'clock in the morning, you know what they think—even if it ain't so. I have been knowing you too long not to be married to you. It were not just day before yesterday that we met,' Joyce says."

"Then a divorce would be good for both of you," I interjected. "You could get all those day-before-yesterdays straightened out."

"Days is like stair-steps," said Simple. "If you stumbled on the first day yesterday, you liable to be still falling tomorrow. I have stumbled."

"Anyhow," I said, "it is better to fall up than to fall down. You can get things straightened out when you get well."

"No matter what a man does, sick or well, something is always liable to happen," said Simple, "especially if you are colored."

"Race has nothing to do with it," I said. "In this uncertain world, something unpleasant can happen to anybody, colored or white, regardless of race."

"Um-hum," said Simple. "You can be robbed and mugged in the night—even choked."

"That's right," I said, "or you can get poisoned from drinking King Kong after hours."

"Sure can," said Simple. "Or you *can* go crazy from worriation."

"Or lose your job."

"Else your money on the horses."

"Or on numbers."

"Or policy."

"Or on Chinese lottery, if you live on the Coast."

"Or poker or blackjack or pokino or tonk. And you ain't mentioned Georgia skin," said Simple.

"I can't play skin," I said.

"It's a rugged card game," said Simple. "If I had never learnt it, I might be rich today. But skin's a mere skimption compared to some of the things that can happen to a man. For instant, if you was a porter, your train could wreck. If you was in the Merchant Marines, your boat could sink. Or if you're a aviator, you're liable to run into the Empire State Building or Abyssinia Baptist Church and bust up your plane. It is awful, man, what can happen to you in this life!"

"You talk as though you've had a hard time," I said. "Have any of those things ever happened to you?"

"What're you talking about?" cried Simple, sitting bolt upright in bed. "Not only am I half dead right now from pneumonia, but everything else *has* happened to me! I have been cut, shot, stabbed, run over, hit by a car, and tromped by a horse. I have also been robbed, fooled, deceived, two-timed, double-crossed, dealt seconds, and mighty near blackmailed—but I am still here!"

"You're a tough man," I said.

"I have been fired, laid off, and last week given an indefinite vacation, also Jim Crowed, segregated, barred out, insulted, eliminated, called black, yellow, and red, locked in, locked out, locked up, also left holding the bag. I have been caught in the rain, caught in raids, caught short with my rent, and caught with another man's wife. In my time I have been caught—but I am still here!"

"You have suffered," I said.

"Suffered!" cried Simple. "My mama should have named me Job instead of Jess Semple. I have been underfed, underpaid, undernourished, and everything but *undertaken*. I been bit by dogs, cats, mice, rats, poll parrots, fleas, chiggers, bedbugs, granddaddies, mosquitoes, and a gold-toothed woman."

"Great day in the morning!"

"That ain't all," said Simple. "In this life I been abused, confused, misused, accused, false-arrested, tried, sentenced, paroled, blackjacked, beat, third-degreed, and near about lynched!"

"Anyhow, your health has been good—up to now," I said.

"Good health nothing," objected Simple, waving his hands, kicking off the cover, and swinging his feet out of bed. "I done had everything from flat feet to a flat head. Why, man, I was born with the measles! Since then I had smallpox, chickenpox, whooping cough, croup, appendicitis, athlete's foot, tonsillitis, arthritis, backache, mumps, and a strain—but I am still here. Daddy-o, I'm still here!"

"Having survived all that, what are you afraid of, now that you are almost over pneumonia?"

"I'm afraid," said Simple, "I will die before my time."

22

There Ought to Be a Law

"I have been up North a long time, but it looks like I just cannot learn to like white folks."

"I don't care to hear you say that," I said, "because there are a lot of good white people in this world."

"Not enough of them," said Simple, waving his evening paper. "If there was, they would make this American country good. But just look at what this paper is full of."

"You cannot dislike *all* white people for what the bad ones do," I said. "And I'm certain you don't dislike them all because once you told me yourself that you wouldn't wish any harm to befall Mrs. Roosevelt."

"Mrs. Roosevelt is different," said Simple.

"There now! You see, you are talking just as some white people talk about the Negroes they *happen* to like. They are always 'different.' That is a provincial way to think. You need to get around more."

"You mean among white folks?" asked Simple. "How can I make friends with white folks when they got Jim Crow all over the place?"

"Then you need to open your mind."

"I have near about *lost* my mind worrying with them," said Simple. "In fact, they have hurt my soul."

"You certainly feel bad tonight," I said. "Maybe you need a drink."

"Nothing in a bottle will help my soul," said Simple, "but I will take a drink."

"Maybe it will help your mind," I said. "Beer?"

"Yes."

"Glass or bottle?"

"A bottle because it contains two glasses," said Simple, spreading his paper out on the bar. "Look here at these headlines, man, where Congress is busy passing laws. While they're making all these laws, it looks like to me they ought to make one setting up a few Game Preserves for Negroes."

"What ever gave you that fantastic idea?" I asked.

"A movie short I saw the other night," said Simple, "about how the government is protecting wild life, preserving fish and game, and setting aside big tracts of land where nobody can fish, shoot, hunt, nor harm a single living creature with furs, fins, or feathers. But it did not show a thing about Negroes."

"I thought you said the picture was about 'wild life.' Negroes are not wild."

"No," said Simple, "but we need protection. This film showed how they put aside a thousand acres out West where the buffaloes roam and nobody can shoot a single one of them. If they do, they get in jail. It also showed some big National Park with government airplanes dropping food down to the deers when they got snowed under and had nothing to eat. The government protects and takes care of buffaloes and deers—which is more than the government does for me or my kinfolks down South. Last month they lynched a man in Georgia and just today I see where the Klan has whipped a Negro within a inch of his life in Alabama. And right up North here in New York a actor is suing a apartment house that won't even let a Negro go up on the elevator to see his producer. That is what I mean by Game Preserves for Negroes—Congress ought to set aside some place where we can go and nobody can jump on us and beat us, neither lynch us nor Jim Crow us every day. Colored folks rate as much protection as a buffalo, or a deer."

"You have a point there," I said.

"This here movie showed great big beautiful lakes with signs up all around:

NO FISHING—STATE GAME PRESERVE

But it did not show a single place with a sign up:

NO LYNCHING

It also showed flocks of wild ducks settling down in a nice green meadow behind a government sign that said:

NO HUNTING

It were nice and peaceful for them fish and ducks. There ought to be some place where it is nice and peaceful for me, too, even if I am not a fish or a duck.

"They showed one scene with two great big old longhorn elks locking horns on a Game Preserve somewhere out in Wyoming, fighting like mad. Nobody bothered them elks or tried to stop them from fighting. But just let me get in a little old fist fight here in this bar, they will lock me up and the Desk Sergeant will say, 'What are you colored boys doing, disturbing the peace?' Then they will give me thirty days and fine me twice as much as they would a white man for doing the same thing. There ought to be some place where I can fight in peace and not get fined them high fines."

"You disgust me," I said. "I thought you were talking about a place where you could be quiet and compose your mind. Instead, you are talking about fighting."

"I would like a place where I could do both," said Simple. "If the government can set aside some spot for a elk *to be a elk* without being bothered, or a fish *to be a fish* without getting hooked, or a buffalo *to be a buffalo* without being shot down, there ought to be some place in this American country where a Negro can be a Negro without being Jim Crowed. There ought to be a law. The next time I see my congressman, I am going to tell him to introduce a bill for Game Preserves for Negroes."

"The Southerners would filibuster it to death," I said.

"If we are such a problem to them Southerners," said Simple, "I should think they would want some place to preserve us out of their sight. But then, of course, you have to take into consideration that if the Negroes was taken out of the South, who would they lynch? What would they do for sport? A Game Preserve is for to keep people from bothering anything that is living.

"When that movie finished, it were sunset in Virginia and it showed a little deer and its mama laying down to sleep. Didn't nobody say, 'Get up, deer, you can't sleep here,' like they would to me if I was to go to the White Sulphur Springs Hotel."

" 'The foxes have holes, and the birds of the air have nests; but the Son of man hath not where to lay his head.' "

"That is why I want a Game Preserve for Negroes," said Simple.

23

Income Tax

On March 14th, just the day before his taxes came due, Simple was sitting in a booth across from the bar, figuring, and each time he figured he put his pencil in his mouth.

"Joyce's Fifty-Nine-Dollar birthday wrist watch on time, plus Two Dollars and Seventy-Five Cents cab fare to the Bronx for that wedding reception to which we was late, minus Twenty-Nine Dollars and Eleven Cents old-age dependency insurance, plus miscellaneous Five Hundred and Seventy-Nine Dollars and Twenty-Two Cents, minus One Dollar and Fifteen Cents work-clothes deduction—man! I ain't *never* gonna get it straight."

"What's all this high finance," I said, "concerning birthday watches and nondeductible cab fare?"

"Income tax," said Simple. "I deducts all."

"Pshaw! Just think of the movie stars and Wall Street people who really have to worry about income tax," I said.

"I don't care nothing about them folks," answered Simple. "All I know is that tomorrow the man is *demanding*—not asking—for money that I not only don't have—but ain't even seen."

"The Bureau of Internal Revenue seldom makes mistakes, Jess. If it does, they've got people to check and recheck, and if they miscalculate even as little as two cents, you'll eventually get it back."

"I just like to check for myself," said Simple. "So I been figuring on this thing for three days and it still don't come out right. Instead of them owing me, looks like I owe them something which I don't know where I'm going to get."

"Why didn't you just take your figures to a public accountant and let him figure it out for you?"

"Man, I took 'em to one of them noteriety republicans once and he charged me so much I got discouraged."

"Maybe next year things will be different, old man. According to the papers, Congress is considering a bill to reduce taxes."

"By the time Congress convenes, I'll be without means," said Simple.

"Besides, I don't get enough for my taxes. I wants to vote down South. It's hell to pay taxes when I can't even vote down home."

" 'Taxation without representation is tyranny,' so the books say."

"Sure is!" said Simple. "I don't see why Negroes down South should pay taxes a-tall. You know Buddy Jones' brother, what was wounded in the 92nd in Italy, don't you? Well, he was telling me about how bad them rednecks treated him when he was in the army in Mississippi. He said he don't never want to see no parts of the South again. He were born and raised in Yonkers and not used to such stuff. Now his nerves is shattered. He can't even stand a Southern accent no more."

"Jim Crow shock," I said. "I guess it can be as bad as shell shock."

"It can be worse," said Simple. "Jim Crow happens to men every day down South, whereas a man's not in a battle every day. Buddy's brother has been out of the army three years and he's still sore about Mississippi."

"What happened to him down there?"

"I will tell it to you like it was told to me," said Simple. "You know Buddy's brother is a taxicab driver, don't you? Well, the other day he was telling me he was driving his cab downtown on Broadway last week when a white man hailed him, got in, and then said in one of them slow Dixie drawls, 'Bouy, tek me ovah to Fefty-ninth Street and Fefth Avahnue.'

"Buddy's brother told him, 'I ain't gonna take you nowhere. Get outta my cab—and quick!'

"The white man didn't know what was the matter so he says, 'Why?'

"Buddy's brother said, 'Because I don't like Southerners, that's why! You treated me so mean when I was in the army down South that I don't never want to see none of you-all no more. And I *sure* don't like to hear you talk. It goes all through me. I spent eighteen months in hell in Mississippi.'

"The white man got red in the face, also mad, and called a cop to make Buddy's brother drive him where he wanted to go. The cop was one of New York's finest, a great big Irishman. The copper listened to the man, then he listened to Buddy's brother. Setting right there in his taxi at 48th and Broadway, Buddy's brother told that cop all about Mississippi, how he was Jim Crowed on the train on the way down going to drill for Uncle Sam, how he was Jim Crowed in camp, also how whenever he had a furlough, him and his colored buddies had to wait and *wait* and WAIT at the camp gate for a bus to get to town because they filled the busses up with white soldiers and the colored soldiers just had to stand behind and wait. Sometimes on payday if there were a big crowd of white soldiers, the colored G.I.'s would never get to town at all.

" 'Officer, I'm telling you,' Buddy's brother said, 'that Mississippi is something! Down South they don't have no nice polices like you. Down South all them white cops want to do is beat a Negro's head, cuss you, and call you names. They do not protect Americans if they are black. They lynched a man five miles down the road from our camp one night and left him hanging there for three days as a warning, so they said, to us Northern Negroes to know how to act in the South, particularly if from New York.'

"Meanwhile the Southern white man who was trying to get the cop to make Buddy's brother drive him over to Fifth Avenue was getting redder and redder. He said, 'You New York Negras need to learn how to act.'

" 'Shut up!' says the cop. 'This man is talking.'

"Buddy's brother talked on. 'Officer,' he says, 'it were so bad in that army camp that I will tell you a story of something that happened to me. They had us colored troops quartered way down at one end of the camp, six miles back from the gate, up against the levee. One day they sent me to do some yard work up in the white part of the camp. My bladder was always weak, so I had to go to the latrine no sooner than I got there. Everything is separated in Mississippi, even latrines, with signs up WHITE and COLORED. But there wasn't any COLORED latrine anywhere around, so I started to go in one marked WHITE.

" 'A cracker M.P. yelled at me, "*Halt!*"

" 'When I didn't halt—because I couldn't—he drew his gun on me and cocked it. He threatened to shoot me if I went in that WHITE latrine.

" 'Well, he made me so mad, I walked all the way back to my barracks and got a gun myself. I came back and I walked up to that Southern M.P. I said, "*Neither you nor me will never see no Germans nor no Japs if you try to stop me from going in this latrine this morning.*"

" 'That white M.P. didn't try to stop me. He just turned pale, and I went in. But by that time, officer, I was so mad I decided to set down and stay awhile. So I did. With my gun on my lap, I just sat—and every time a Southerner came in, I cocked the trigger. Ain't nobody said a word. They just looked at me and walked out. I stayed there as long as I wanted to—black as I am—in that WHITE latrine. Down in Mississippi a colored soldier has to have a gun even to go to the toilet! So, officer, that is why I do not want to ride this man—because he is one of them that wouldn't even let me go in their latrines down South, do you understand?'

" 'Understand?' says the cop, 'Of course, I understand. Be jeezus! It's like that exactly that the damned English did the Irish. Faith, you do not have to haul him. . . . Stranger, get yerself another cab. Scram, now! Quick—before I run you in.'

"That white man hauled tail! And Buddy's brother drove off saluting that cop—and blowing his horn for New York City. But me, if I'd of been there," said Simple, "I would of asked that officer just one thing about Ireland. I would have said, 'Well, before you-all got free—kicked around as you was—did you still have to pay taxes to the British?' "

"I can answer that for you," I said. "Of course, the Irish had to pay taxes. All colonial peoples have to pay taxes to their rulers."

"How do you know?" asked Simple. "You ain't Irish."

"No," I said, "but I read books."

"You don't learn everything in books," said Simple.

"It wouldn't hurt you to read one once in a while," I said.

"Not to change the subject, but I need a beer to help me figure up this income tax," said Simple. "Bartender, a couple of beers on my friend here—who reads books."

"I do not like your tone of voice," I said. "I will not pay for beer to entertain a man who has nothing but contempt for the written word."

"Buddy-o, daddy-o, pal, I do not want to argue with you this evening because I haven't got time. You are colored just like me, so set down and help me figure up my taxes for these white folks. What did you say that book says about taxation?"

"Without representation, it's tyranny."

"If you don't know how to add, subtract, multiply, erase, deduct, steal, stash, save, conceal, and long-divide, it is worse than that," said Simple. "Taxes is *hell*! Buddy-o, here's our beer."

"It seems to me you should understand mathematics," I said. "You've been to school."

"I didn't learn much," said Simple, "which is why I have to run my feet off all day long and work hard. What your head don't *under*stand, your feet have to stand."

"Well, you certainly have opinions about everything under the sun," I said. "You ought to have a newspaper since you have so much to say."

"I can talk," said Simple, "but I can't write."

"Then you ought to be an orator."

"Uh-um, I'm scared of the public. My place is at the bar."

"Of Justice?"

"Justice don't run no bar."

24

No Alternative

"Man, you don't know how I have suffered these last few weeks," Simple groaned into an empty glass. "Joyce's birthday, the Urban League ball we had to go to, income tax, hospital bill, and so forth—"

"What's 'and so forth'?" I asked.

"My landlady," said Simple. "That woman has no respect for her roomers a-tall. In fact, she cares less for her roomers than she does for her dog."

"What kind of dog has she got?"

"A little old houndish kind of dog," said Simple. "But is she crazy about that hound! She will put a roomer out—dead out in the street—when he does not pay his rent, but she does not put out that dog, not even when it chews up her favorite Teddy bear which her second husband give her for her birthday. That dog is her heart. She would feed that dog before she would feed me. When I went down in the kitchen last week to give her my room rent, I saw her hand Trixie a whole chicken leg—and she did not offer me a bite."

"Were you hungry?" I asked.

"I could have used a drumstick," said Simple. "It would have meant more to me than it did to that little fice."

"I gather you do not like dogs."

"I love dogs," said Simple. "When my landlady was laid up with arthritis and scared to get her feet wet, I even took that little old she-hound of hers out two or three times to the park to do its duty—although I would not be seen with no dog like that if it belonged to me. All I got was, 'Thank you, you certainly nice, Mr. Semple.' She used my real last name, all formal and everything. 'You certainly nice, yes, indeed.' But did I get a extra towel when I asked for it? I did not. All I got was, 'Laundries is high and towels is scarce.' Yet I seen her dry that dog on a nice big white bath towel, the likes of which she never give a roomer yet. I don't think that is right, to care less about roomers than you do about a dog, do you?"

"Ties between a dog and its master are often greater than human ties."

"Ties, nothing," said Simple. "That lazy little old mutt don't bring her in a thing, not even a bone. I bring in Ten Dollars rent each and every week—even if it is a little late."

"You got behind though, didn't you, when you weren't working?"

"I *tried* to get behind," said Simple, "but she did not let me get far. I told her they was changing from a ball-bearing plant to a screw factory and it might even take three months. But she said it better not take *three weeks*—do, and she would get eviction orders and evict me. So I had to go to the post office and draw out my little money and lay it on the line. That very evening she says, 'Oh, this poor dog ain't been out of the house in five days, bad as my knees ache.' So me, like a chump, I take it out to the park."

"Why doesn't her husband take care of it?" I asked.

"He runs on the road," said Simple. "When he gets through taking care of white folks, he does not feel like taking care of dogs. Harlem is no place for dogs—people do not have time to look after them."

"True," I said, "but Harlemites love dogs, and there are a great many here."

"Almost as many as there are roomers," agreed Simple. "But it is not good for the dogs, because people work all day and leave the dog by itself. A dog gets lonesome just like a human. He wants to associate with other dogs, but when they take him out, the poor dog is on a leash and cannot run around. They won't even let him rub noses with another dog, or pick out his own tree. Now, that is not good for a dog. For instant, take Trixie, my landlady's hound. Spring is coming. I asked her one day last week had Trixie ever been married.

"My landlady says, 'You mean mated?'

"I says, 'Yes, I was just trying to be polite.'

"She says, 'No, indeed! Trixie is a virgin.'

"Now, ain't that awful! That poor dog never had a chance in life, which worried me. So I said, 'Next time I take Trixie to the park, I will see that she meets some gentleman dogs.'

"But, man, don't you know that woman hollered like she had been shot. She says, 'No, indeed, you won't! I do not want Trixie all crossed up with no low-breeded curs.'

"I says, 'You must be prejudiced, madam. Is Trixie got a pedigree?'

"My landlady says, 'She is pure Spotted Dutch Brindle.'

"Before I thought, I said, 'Pure mutt.'

"My landlady jumped salty, I mean salty! She reined in Trixie and yelled, 'You will apologize to this dog, Mr. Semple, else leave my house.'"

"Did you apologize to that dog?"

"I had no alternity. Hard as rooms is to find these days, I do not know which is worse, to be a roomer or a dog."

25

Question Period

"I know one thing," said Simple, "I am sick and tired of radio commentators who don't talk sense."

"Now what's the matter?"

"Aw, Joyce took me to one of them Town Hall lectures the other night and I ain't been the same since. I wouldn't a been caught dead ten blocks near nothing like that if it hadn't been for Joyce. Trust a woman like she is to drag me out in the cold to hear a commentator *in person* when I could've stayed home and heard one on the radio—if I'd a wanted to hear one—just as well."

"A commentator?" I asked.

"A commentator," said Simple. "He's been all over the world and saw the war, atomic bombs exploding, also the conversation of the Nazis to democracy, and stuff like that. He had a whole lot of facts and figures to prove it, too. His subject was 'The World Situation.'"

"Was he penetrating?"

"Joyce made me pay a Dollar Six Bits a head to penetrate other folks' troubles."

"What's wrong with that?" I asked. "I think it was a good idea for Joyce to take you. You need an awareness of world affairs."

"I'm aware, all right," said Simple. "Aware that it costs half of my weekly beer money to hear about problems in foreign countries when I got a Million Dollars' worth of my own! I'm aware that folks are mistreated and starvin' right here at home. They whip my head and poke my eyes out with a billy-club down South. The Ku Klux Klan is trying to scare colored folks out of voting—but I don't hear them lecture commentators talking about that!"

"They overlook a number of pertinent topics," I said, "which simply indicates that the equilibrium of current sociological equations is somewhat irregular."

"Somewhat?" yelled Simple. "Man, for a Dollar Seventy-Five Cents a ticket, that commentator should at least have mentioned lynching that Negro the other day and nobody doing nothing about it."

"I suppose they had a question period after the lecture?"

"They sure did," said Simple. "Joyce wanted to ask a question, but she was ashamed to get up and ask it herself. She kept nudging me in the ribs and telling me to read it off for her since she had it all written down beforehand. I told her if she wanted to know so bad, why didn't she get up and read it herself. But she said she was shy. I said, 'Ain't this a killer. You won't ask him nothing—but it's O.K. for *me* to get up and make a fool out of myself.' "

"Well, did you get up and ask her question?"

"I did not," said Simple. "I figured if I was going to be stared at, I might as well use my *own* brains and ask a question for myself."

"What was your question?"

"I raised my hand and said, 'Mr. Commentator, how come you fellows always know so much about them foreign countries which you can analyze so easy, but when somebody asks you what's going on here as I have before now thought about mailing several questions in to you on the radio and got no answer, don't you have no realization of how bad my colored condition is?' "

"What did he say?"

"He hemmed and hawed and said what was happening in other countries stirred the consciousness of the world more than what went on here at home and that Negroes had to take a long view. So I told him a whipped head was a *whipped* head—no matter whose shoulders it was on, in Europe or here. And if it was on *my* shoulders, that made it twice as bad—I didn't care how long the view was. I also told him that if Negroes' being mistreated *right under his nose* didn't stir his consciousness, then he must be unconscious."

"What happened then?" I asked.

"That near about broke up the forum," said Simple. "Joyce started pulling on my sleeve and talking about 'Now! Now! Set down. You're not the speaker!' "

"If your question caused so much disturbance," I said, "I am curious to know what question Joyce wanted to ask. Is her slip of paper still in your pocket?"

"Yes, right here," said Simple. "Look. With pork chops as high as they are in Harlem, Joyce was going to ask the man, 'If the United Nations took over Trieste, would they also internationalize the suburbs or would the outskirts of town still belong to Yugoslavia, and if so, how far?' That is what Joyce was going to ask!"

26

Lingerie

"Where are you going?" I asked as I bumped into Simple on 125th Street near the Baby Grand.

"I have been where I am going," said Simple.

"At Joyce's?"

"Natch. But she were in a very impatient mood tonight," said Simple as we walked up Eighth Avenue. "Her and another girl were there sewing like mad, so Joyce did not care much about having a gentleman caller. She were busy."

"Joyce sees you practically every night, so no wonder," I said. "You are hardly in the category of a caller. What were they making?"

"Lin-ger-ies," said Simple. "Some friend girl of Joyce's is getting married Sunday, so they are making her some step-ins and step-outs, also some slips, for a present. The other girl were making what she called a bood-war gown—but it looked like a nightgown to me. Joyce says there is nothing so fine as a real handmade lin-ger-ies. And everything were pink. I asked them how come ladies' lin-ger-ies is always pink.

"Joyce said, 'What do you mean, *always?*'

"I said, 'Just about all I ever saw is pink.'

"Joyce says, 'You has no business seeing so much. Besides, that is no fit subject for a man, especially in front of company.'

"She never did answer my question. Maybe you can tell me, daddy-o, why is women's underneath-wears practically *always* pink? For instant, why ain't teddies sometimes light green?"

"I have seen them black," I said.

"I don't mean when they need washing," said Simple. "Nine times out of ten, a girl's lin-ger-ies is pink. I want to know why."

"Let me think a minute and come to some logical conclusion," I stalled. "There must be a reason. I never thought of it before."

"I have never seen purple ones," said Simple. "They is pink—always pink!"

"Maybe the word *lingerie* means *pink* in French," I said.

"Then it must mean *pink* in English, too," said Simple, "because every time a dame says lin-ger-ies, it's something pink—from brassieres to girdles to garters to pants."

"I think I have the reason," I said. "Listen, lingerie was probably invented by Caucasians, so they dyed it pink to blend with the rosy tint of a white woman's complexion."

"That could be so," said Simple. "It sure could! White folks make everything else to suit themselves. But since Negroes ain't pink, why don't Joyce make her friend girl some chocolate-colored sepia-tan lin-ger-ies, because that girl is a nice chocolate-brown. Also *real gone*! I mean a pretty Ethiopian Abyssinimon brown!"

"Are you acquainted with her?"

"I have met her," said Simple, "and in my mind's eyes, I can see that chick right now slipping her chocolate hips into a pair of chocolate step-ins, then sliding her sepia shoulders into a chocolate slip."

"You have a vivid imagination," I said.

"Vivian's not her name. It's *Jean*. And when she gets ready to retire, to dream, relax, lay down, Jean could ease her fine brown frame into a chocolate gown. Man, chocolate is better than pink, any day."

"You are a race man for true," I said. "For you, even lingerie should be *colored*, with a capital *C*."

"It should be," said Simple. "I am going to tell Joyce to make that girl some tan-skin things for her present."

"You're fixing to anger Joyce," I said, "taking an intimate interest in some girl you hardly know."

"She *is* kinder jealous-hearted," said Simple. "But next time I go back to pay Joyce a call—which will be around dinner time tomorrow, since I don't board with Joyce, just accepts her hospitality—I am going to tell her that I have found out why lin-ger-ies is pink."

"Thanks to me," I said.

"Yes, thanks to you," said Simple. "Now I will thank you for a beer. I lent Joyce my last Two Dollars to buy some lace on that girl's gown— which were a mistake because now that spring is coming and she's helping her friend girl to get her honeymoon clothes together, Joyce has done started thinking about a June wedding herself."

"Does Joyce want you to commit bigamy?"

"She knows I can't commit nothing without a divorce," said Simple.

27

Spring Time

"I wish that spring would come more often now that it is here," said Simple.

"How could it come more often?"

"It could if God had made it that-a-way," said Simple. "I also wish it would last longer."

"It looks as if you would prefer spring all the year around."

"Just most of the year," said Simple. "As it is now, summer comes too soon and winter lasts too long. I do not like real hot weather, neither cold. I like spring."

"Spring is too changeable for me—sometimes hot, sometimes cold."

"I am not talking about that kind of spring," said Simple. "I mean June-time spring when it is just nice and mellow—like a cool drink."

"Of what?"

"Anything," said Simple. "Anything that is strong as the sun and cool as the moon. But I am not talking about drinking now. I am talking about spring. Oh, it is wonderful! It is the time when flowers come out of their buds, birds come out of their nests, bees come out of their hives, Negroes come out of their furnished rooms, and butterflies out of their cocoons."

"Also snakes come out of their holes."

"They is little young snakes," said Simple, "else big old sleepy snakes that ain't woke up good yet till the sun strikes them. That is why I do not like summer, because the sun is so hot it makes even a cold snake mad. Spring is my season. Summer was made to give you a taste of what hell is like. Fall was made for the clothing-store people to coin money because every human has to buy a overcoat, muffler, heavy socks, and gloves. Winter was made for landladies to charge high rents and keep cold radiators and make a fortune off of poor tenants. But spring! Throw your overcoat on the pawnshop counter, tell the landlady to kiss your foot, open your windows, let the fresh air in. Me, myself, I love spring!

"Why, if I was down home now, daddy-o, I would get out my fishing pole and take me a good old Virginia ham sandwich and go set on the banks of the river all day and just dream and fish and fish and dream. I might have me a big old quart bottle of beer tied on a string down in the water to keep cool, and I would just fish and dream and dream and fish."

"You would not have any job?" I asked.

"I would respect work just like I respected my mother and not hit her a lick. I would be far away from all this six A.M. alarm-clock business, crowded subways, gulping down my coffee to get to the man's job in time, and working all day shut up inside where you can't even smell the spring—and me still smelling ether and worried about my winter hospital bill. If I was down home, buddy-o, I would pull off my shoes and let my toes air and just set on the riverbank and dream and fish and fish and dream, and I would not worry about no job."

"Why didn't you stay down home when you were there?"

"You know why I didn't stay," said Simple. "I did not like them white folks and they did not like me. Maybe if it wasn't for white folks, I would've stayed down South where spring comes earlier than it do up here. White folks is the cause of a lot of inconveniences in my life."

"They've even driven you away from an early spring."

"It do not come as early in Harlem as it does down South," said Simple, "but it comes. And there ain't no white folks living can keep spring from coming. It comes to Harlem the same as it does downtown, too. Nobody can keep spring out of Harlem. I stuck my head out the window this morning and spring kissed me bang in the face. Sunshine patted me all over the head. Some little old birds was flying and playing on the garbage cans down in the alley, and one of them flew up to the Third Floor Rear and looked at me and cheeped, 'Good morning!'

"I said, 'Bird, howdy-do!'

"Just then I heard my next-door roomer come out of the bathroom so I had to pull my head in from that window and rush to get to the toilet to wash my face before somebody else got there because I did not want to be late to work this morning since today is payday. New York is just rush, rush, rush! But, oh, brother, if I were down home."

"I know—you would just fish and dream and dream and fish."

"And dream and fish and fish and dream!" said Simple. "If spring was to last forever, as sure as my name is Jess, I would just fish and dream."

Part Three

Hard Times

28

Last Whipping

When I went by his house one Sunday morning to pick up my Kodak that he had borrowed, Simple was standing in the middle of the floor in his shirttail imitating a minister winding up his Sunday morning sermon, gestures and all.

He intoned, " 'Well, I looked and I saw a great beast! And that great beast had its jaws open ready to clamp down on my mortal soul. But I knowed if it was to clamp, ah, my soul would escape and go to glory. Amen! So I was not afraid. My body was afraid, a-a-ah, but my soul was not afraid. My soul said whatsoever you may do to my behind, a-a-ah, beast, you *cannot* harm my soul. Amen! No, Christians! That beast *cannot* tear your immortal soul. That devil in the form of a crocodile, the form of a alligator with a leather hide that slippeth and slideth through the bayous swamp—that alligator *cannot* tear your soul!' "

"You really give a good imitation of a preacher," I said. "But come on and get dressed and let's go, since you say you left my Kodak at Joyce's. I didn't stop by here to hear you preach."

"I am saying that to say this," said Simple, "because that is the place in the sermon where my old Aunt Lucy jumped up shouting and leapt clean across the pulpit rail and started to preaching herself, right along with the minister.

"She hollered, 'No-ooo-oo-o! Hallelujah, no! It cannot tear your soul. Sometimes the devil comes in human form,' yelled Aunt Lucy, 'sometimes it be's born right into your own family. Sometimes the devil be's your own flesh and kin—and he try your soul—but your soul he cannot tear! Sometimes you be's forced to tear his hide *before* he tears your soul. Amen!'

"Now, Aunt Lucy were talking about *me* that morning when she said 'devil.' That is what I started to tell you."

"Talking about you, why?" I asked.

"Because I had been up to some devilment, and she had done said she was gonna whip me come Monday. Aunt Lucy were so Christian she did not believe in whipping nobody on a Sunday."

"What had you done?"

"Oh, I had just taken one of her best laying hens and give it to a girl who didn't even belong to our church; to roast for her Sunday school picnic, because this old girl said she was aiming to picnic *me*—except that she didn't have nothing good to eat to put in her basket. I was trying to jive this old gal, you know—I was young—so I just took one of Aunt Lucy's hens and give her."

"Why didn't you pick out a pullet that wasn't laying?"

"That hen was the biggest, fattest chicken in the pen—and I wanted that girl to have plenty to pull out of her basket at that picnic so folks would make a great big admiration over her and me."

"How did your Aunt Lucy find out about the hen?"

"Man, you know womenfolks can't keep no secret! That girl told another girl, the other girl told her cousin, the cousin told her mama, her mama told Aunt Lucy—and Aunt Lucy woke me up Sunday morning with a switch in her hand."

"Weren't you too old to be whipped by then?"

"Of course, I was too old to whip—sixteen going on seventeen, big as a ox. But Aunt Lucy did not figure I was grown yet. And she took her duty hard—because she always said the last thing my mother told her when she died was to raise me right."

"What did you do when you saw the switch?"

"Oh, I got all mannish, man. I said, 'Aunt Lucy, you ain't gonna whip me no more. I's a man—and you ain't gonna whip me.'

"Aunt Lucy said, 'Yes, I is, too, Jess. I will whip you until you gets grown enough to know how to act like a man—not just *look* like one. You know you had no business snatching my hen right off her nest and giving it to that low-life hussy what had no better sense than to take it, knowing you ain't got nowhere to get no hen except out of *my* henhouse. Were this not Sunday, I would whale you in a inch of your life before you could get out of that bed.' "

"Aunt Lucy was angry," I commented.

"She was," said Simple. "And big as I was, I was scared. But I was meaning not to let her whip me, even if I had to snatch that sapling out of her hand."

"So what happened on Monday morning?"

"Aunt Lucy waited until I got up, dressed, and washed my face. Then she called me. 'Jess!' I knowed it were whipping time. Just when I was aiming to snatch that switch out of her hand, I seed that Aunt Lucy was crying when she told me to come there. I said, 'Aunt Lucy, what you crying for?'

"She said, 'I am crying 'cause here you is a man, and don't know how to act right yet, and I done did my best to raise you so you would grow up good. I done wore out so many switches on your back, still you tries my soul. But it ain't *my* soul I'm thinking of, son, it's yourn. Jess, I wants you to carry yourself right and 'sociate with peoples what's decent and be a good boy. You understand me? I's getting too old to be using my strength like this. Here!' she hollered, 'bend over and lemme whip you one more time!' "

"Did she whip you?"

"She whipped me—because I bent," said Simple. "When I seen her crying, I would have let her kill me before I raised my hand. When she got through, I said, 'Aunt Lucy, you ain't gonna have to whip me no more. I ain't gonna give you no cause. I do not mind to be beat. But I do not *never* want to see you cry no more—so I am going to do my best to do right from now on and not try your soul. And I am sorry about that hen.'

"And you know, man, from that day to this, I have tried to behave myself. Aunt Lucy is gone to glory this morning, but if she is looking down, she knows that is true. That was my last whipping. But it wasn't the whipping that taught me what I needed to know. It was because she cried—and cried. When peoples care for you and cry for you, they can straighten out your soul. Ain't that right, boy?"

"Yes," I said, "that's right."

29

Nickel for the Phone

"When I were knee-high to a duck I went to the circus and I saw there Jo-Jo the Dog-Faced Boy, or else it were Zip the Pinheaded Man. I never did know the difference because I were too little. I went with my grandpa and grandma before they died and I were sent back to my mama. Neither one of them old folks could read. They also disremembered what the side-show barker said afterwards, so when I got big I never did know if it were Jo-Jo the Dog-Faced Boy I saw or Zip the Pinheaded Man. Anyway, whichever one it were, *he were awful*."

"What makes you think of that now?" I asked.

"Last night Joyce told me I looked like Zip. I am trying to figure out if it *was* Zip that I saw, because if I look like what I saw in that circus, I sure look *bad*."

"You do not have a pinhead," I told him. "But, come to think of it, you could be said to have a dog-face."

"I know I am not good-looking," said Simple, "but I did not think I looked like a dog."

"The last time I saw her, Joyce told me she thought you were a fine-looking man," I said. "Why has she changed her mind?"

"Because I promised to pass by her house night before last night and I did not go."

"Why didn't you?"

"That's my business, but Joyce wants to make it hers. Womens is curious."

"Naturally."

"So when I did not tell her where I went Thursday night, she jumped salty. She said she did not care where I was nohow. So I says, 'Why do you keep on asking me, if you don't care?'

"She says, 'I *did* care, but you have drove all the care out of me, the way you do.' Then she started to cry. Now, when a woman starts to cry, I do not know what to do.

"So I says, 'Let's go down to the corner and have a rum-cola.'

"She says, 'I do not want to go nowhere with you and you looking like Zip!' That is when I started to wondering who Zip were."

"I have always wondered, too," I said, "never having seen that famous freak."

"Another thing I have wondered is, who is Cootie Brown? Last Saturday night somebody said to me, 'Man, you're drunk as Cootie Brown.' "

"Which meant high as a Georgia pine."

"I know what it meant, but I do not know who Cootie Brown was. Do you?"

"I guess he was just somebody who got pretty drunk all the time."

"And Zip were somebody who looked pretty bad all the time."

"That's about it. But did you effect a reconciliation with Joyce?"

"Only partly," said Simple. "A woman does not like to make up right away. They like to frown and pout so you will pet and beg 'em. But I do not beg nobody."

"What's your method, friend?"

"I leave—till they calm down, daddy-o. Just leave the house and let 'em cool off, put a little distance between troubles and me. Facts, I intend to put several days between myself and Joyce."

"You are not going by there and eat on Sunday as usual?"

"I can eat in Father's for Fifteen Cents—so why should I worry with Joyce?"

"Father Divine's is all very well. But his biscuits are nothing like Joyce's, that time she invited us to dinner last Easter."

"I do not care for biscuits when they are all mixed up with Who-Struck-John. Joyce must think a man don't have no place else to go except to her house. There's plenty womens in this world. And tonight I am dressed up so I know I don't look like Zip. Lend me a nickel, boy."

"For what?"

"To phone, what you think? I want to see how Joyce talks this evening. If she answers with one of them sweet *Hello's*, then changes her voice to a gravel bass when she finds out it's me, I will know she's still got her habits on."

"I thought you said just now you weren't going around there tonight."

"I'm *not* going, no matter how sweet she talks. But what is a nickel? I would just juke-box it away on a record by Duke, so I might as well waste it on Joyce."

"You will want that nickel when times get hard."

"That's right," said Simple. "If this depression-recession gets any worse, *both* of us might want some of her biscuits, huh?"

"You have more foresight than I thought," I said. "Here's a nickel. Go call her up."

30

Equality and Dogs

"Even a black dog gets along better than me," mused Simple. "I have discovered that much since I been up North with these *liberal* white folks. You take this here social equality that some of them is always bringing up. I don't understand it. White folks socialize with dogs—yet they don't want to socialize with me."

"True," I said.

"White dogs, black dogs, any kind of dogs," Simple went on. "They don't care what color a dog is in New York. Why, when I first got here I used to drive for a woman out on Long Island who were so rich she had six dogs. One of 'em, a big black dog, slept in bed with her—right in bed with his rusty back up next to her white feet. But if a Negro set down six tables away from her in a restaurant, she almost had a fit. I do not understand it."

"You see plenty of dogs walking with white ladies on Park Avenue," I said.

"But no Negroes."

"That's right."

"They walk dogs and *work* Negroes," explained Simple. "While them rich white ladies is out walking with their dogs, Negroes are working back in their kitchens. Since the days of defense workers are long gone, that's where we are again. Them rich white folks gave their big old yard dogs they didn't like much to the army during the war, you remember? The army trained 'em to fight just like a man. But the army mostly trained Negroes to work—Quartermasters, Engineers, Port Battalions, Seabees. . . ."

"Yes."

"Um-hum-m-m! But they trained dogs to fight. Why, I saw a picture of a dog getting a medal hung on his chest for fighting so good he tore down a German machine-gun nest. It were in a Southern white paper where I never did see a picture of a Negro soldier getting a medal on his chest. Every time them Southern papers had pictures of Negroes in uniforms during the war, they was always unloading some landing barge or digging on some road. A dog got a better break in the army than a Negro."

"You sound kind of bitter," I said, "about your army."

"How do you figger it's *my* army?" asked Simple as he set his beer glass down.

"You pay taxes for it," I said.

"I do," said Simple, "but it pays me no mind. It Jim Crows me, but it don't Jim Crow dogs. White dogs and black dogs all served together in the army, didn't they? And they didn't have no separate companies for black dogs."

"You've got something there," I said.

"Come another war, I had rather be a dog in the army any time than colored—especially down South. Why, I saw in the newsreels once where they trained army dogs to leap at a man and tear him down—to leap at a *white* man, at that. But if I even as much as raise a hand at a cracker when he pushes me off the sidewalk, my head is beat and I am put in jail. But a dog in the army, they taught him not to let nobody push him off no sidewalk in Mississippi nor nowhere else. Here I am a human, and I get less of a break in the U.S. than a dog! I do not understand."

"Neither do I," I said.

"How come you ain't arguing with me tonight?" asked Simple. "You mighty near always disagree."

"How can I disagree about dogs?" I said.

"I remember in the first depression times before the war, when they had the WPA and the PWA and all those things that it was so hard to get on, and that you got so little from after you did get on 'em. I remember seeing folks come into meat markets and buy great big pieces of good red meat for their dogs, while plenty colored folks, and white, too, didn't have meat for themselves and their children. I said to myself then that it must be good to be a dog. I said, eating *fine* red meat and not having to worry about getting on WPA. Black dogs and white dogs all eating good red meat and no color line between 'em. I tell you, dogs rate better in America than colored folks."

"Anyhow, I love dogs," I said, "and I'm glad they get a break in our paradoxical society."

"I love dogs, too," said Simple, "but I love colored folks better."

"Still you want to take the meat out of a dog's mouth."

"I do not," said Simple. "I just want some meat in my own mouth, that's all! I want the same chance a dog has. Furthermore, I do not care to argue about it. Doggone if I'm going to argue about dogs!"

31

Seeing Double

"I wonder why it is we have two of one thing, and only one of others."

"For instance?"

"We have two lungs," said Simple, "but only one heart. Two eyes, but only one mouth. Two——"

"Feet, but only one body," I said.

"I was not going to say *feet*," said Simple. "But since you have taken the words out of my mouth, go ahead."

"Human beings have two shoulders but only one neck."

"And two ears but only one head," said Simple.

"What on earth would you want with two heads?"

"I could sleep with one and stay awake with the other," explained Simple. "Just like I got two nostrils, I would also like to have two mouths, then I could eat with one mouth while I am talking with the other. Joyce always starts an argument while we are eating, anyhow. That Joyce can talk and eat all at once."

"Suppose Joyce had two mouths, too," I said. "She could double-talk you."

"I would not keep company with a woman that had two mouths," said Simple. "But I would like to have two myself."

"If you had two mouths, you would have to have two noses also," I said, "and it would not make much sense to have two noses, would it?"

"No," said Simple, "I reckon it wouldn't. Neither would I like to have two chins to have to shave. A chin is no use for a thing. But there is one thing I sure would like to have two of. Since I have——"

"Since you have two eyes, I know you would like to have two faces—one in front and one behind—so you could look at all those pretty women on the street both going and coming."

"That would be idealistic," said Simple, "but that is *not* what I was going to say. You always cut me off. So you go ahead and talk."

"I know you wish you had two stomachs," I said, "so you could eat more of Joyce's good cooking."

"No, I do *not* wish I had two stomachs," said Simple. "I can put away enough food in one belly to mighty near wreck my pocketbook—with prices as high as a cat's back in a dogfight. So I do not need two stomachs. Neither do I need two navels on the stomach I got. What use are they? But there is one thing I sure wish I had two of."

"Two gullets?" I asked.

"Two gullets is *not* what I wish I had at all," said Simple. "Let me talk! *I wish I had two brains.*"

"Two brains! Why?"

"So I could think with one, and let the other one rest, man, that's why. I am tired of trying to figure out how to get ahead in this world. If I had two brains, I could think with one brain while the other brain was asleep. I could plan with one while the other brain was drunk. I could think about the Dodgers with one, and my future with the other. As it is now, there is too much in this world for one brain to take care of alone. I have thought so much with my one brain that it is about wore out. In fact, I need a rest right now. So let's drink up and talk about something pleasant. Two beers are on me tonight. Draw up to the bar."

"I was just at the bar," I said, "and Tony has nothing but bottles tonight, no draft."

"Then, daddy-o, they're on *you*," said Simple. "I only got two dimes— and one of them is a Roosevelt dime I do not wish to spend. Had I been thinking, I would have remembered that Roosevelt dime. When I get my other brain, it will keep track of all such details."

32

Right Simple

"Once when I was a chauffeur and yard-man, also relief butler, for that rich old country white lady down in Virginia, she kept me working twenty-five hours a day. She could find something for me to do *all* the time."

"Well, at least, it kept you out of mischief," I commented.

"I still had time to get in trouble," said Simple. "She had a pretty upstairs maid named Polly Joe who were married—but she had been married long enough to get used to her husband. At that time, I were a young boy, sharp, also good-looking—which you might not think to see me now, although there is still something about me womens fall for. Anyhow, I played her cool. I did not let Polly Joe know why I had to come upstairs so often when I should have been polishing the silver or the car. I come near polishing the backs right off of that old white lady's silver comb and brush set just so I could get to set and talk on them upper floors to Polly Joe. And it looked like the more I looked at that girl, the more I wanted to taste some of her lipstick.

"Now, somebody went and told Polly's husband. You know, it is a shame some nice womens is married to such mean husbands. Her husband did not like me a-tall. I were younger than him. He was a deacon in the Zion Baptist Church and did not gallivant. I did. So one evening I says to Polly Joe, 'Honey, baby-girl, dear, I could take you down the road a piece and show you what a juke-joint looks like.'

"Polly Joe says, 'Somebody would be sure to tell my husband if I went out with you.'

"I says, 'You could swear it was a lie, that you was right here on your job that night sleeping in.'

"She says, 'Ain't you afraid of married womens?'

"I said, 'Are you afraid of a married man?'

"She said, 'No, I am just scared of my husband.'

"I said, 'Pay him no mind! He will be home in bed while you and me will be down the road at Sy's listening to that mellow treble and drinking mountain dew. It is not good to work for white folks all day long and half the night and not have no pleasure a-tall. You know that.'

"Polly Joe says, 'I sure do know! I believe I will go out with you—just once. But don't let nobody know it. If my husband——!'

" 'Baby, let's leave your husband out of this,' I said.

"Everything would have been all right had not the cook got wind of it when Polly Joe went to borrow her gold earrings. It happened that of *all* the nights to telephone, that was one night when Polly Joe's husband called up from in town. He says, 'Where is Polly Joe?'

"Old fat cook says, 'She's gone to Sy's.'

" 'Sy who's?' said the husband.

" 'Sy's juke,' said the cook.

" 'My wife has got no business in that joint,' says the husband, 'and me a pillar of Zion Baptist Church!'

" 'She's in good company,' says the cook.

" 'What company?' says the husband.

" 'Jess Semple's,' says the cook.

"Well, sir! That Negro mighty near tore that phone from the wall. He had heard from the womens what a man I am, so he got in his Ford and headed for Sy's Roadhouse. The cook said the language she heard on the phone was not from a Christian. She wondered how could a deacon know such words."

"Get on with the story," I said. "What happened to you that night?"

"I am ashamed to say," said Simple. "When the deacon walked in Sy's place I was dancing, holding Polly Joe closer than a hanger holds a suit. The music were so good I could not afford to move my feet for fear I might miss a beat. I did not know her husband was there until I felt something strike me where I didn't set down again for a week. It were his foot. I also felt something grab me by the collar. It were his hand. Then I felt somebody flying through the door. That were me. Something put a dent in the concrete highway. It were my head.

"Man, I *ran*! I *solid* ran! I did not touch the road, I ran in the air. When I looked back, I did not see Polly Joe neither her husband because I were two miles off. I run so fast I strained a linament in my ankle. Polly Joe's husband made her quit that job. The next maid our old mistress-lady hired were fifty-one years old. And it were a month before my head got back to normal and that knot resided. As many girls as I knowed when I were young, I didn't have to take no married woman out. Sometimes, you know, I think I am right simple."

33

Ways and Means

"You see this, don't you?" said Simple, showing me his N.A.A.C.P. card. "I have just joined the National Organization for the Association of Colored Folks and it is fine."

"You mean the National Association for the Advancement of Colored People," I said.

"Um-hum!" said Simple, "but they tell me it has white people in it, too."

"That's right, it does."

"I did not see none at the meeting where me and Joyce went this evening," said Simple.

"No?"

"No! There should have been some present because that *fine* colored speaker was getting white folks told—except that there was no white folks there to be told."

"They just do not come to Negro neighborhoods to meetings," I said, "although they may belong."

"Then we ought to hold some meetings downtown so that they can learn what this Negro problem is all about," said Simple. "It does not make sense to be always talking to ourselves. We know we got troubles. But every last Italian, Jew, and Greek what owns a business all up and down Seventh Avenue and Eighth Avenue and Lenox in Harlem ought to have been there. Do you reckon they belong to anything colored?"

"I don't expect they do," I said.

"Well, next time I go to a A.A.C.P. meeting . . ."

"N-A-A-C-P meeting," I said.

" . . . N.A.A.C.P. meeting, I am going to move that everybody get a coin can," said Simple, "and go from store to store and bar to bar and hash-house to hash-house and take up collection for the N.A.A.C.P., from all these white folks making money in colored neighborhoods. If they don't give, I will figure they do not care nothing about my race. White folks are always taking up collections from *me* for the Red Cross or the Community Chest or the Cancer Drive or the March of Dimes or something or other. They are always shaking their cans in *my* face. Why shouldn't I shake my can in *their* face?"

"It would be better," I said, "if you got them all to be *members* of the N.A.A.C.P., not just to give a contribution."

"Every last white businessman in Harlem ought to belong to the N.A.A.C.P., but do you reckon they would ever come to meetings? They practically all live in the suburbans."

"They come to Harlem on business," I said, "so why shouldn't they come to the meetings?"

"That is why they go to the suburbans, to get away from the Negroes they have been selling clothes and groceries and victuals and beer all day. They do not want to be bothered with me when they close up their shops."

"Do you blame them?" I said.

"I do," said Simple. "Long as the cash register is ringing, they can be bothered with me, so why can't they come to an N.A.A.C.P. meeting?"

"Have I ever heard of you going out to the Italian or Jewish or Irish neighborhoods to any of their meetings to help them with their problems?" I asked.

"I do not have any stores in the Italian or Jewish neighborhoods," said Simple. "Neither do I own nary pool hall in an Irish neighborhood, nor nary Greek restaurant, nor nary white apartment house from which I get rent. I do not own no beer halls where Jews and Italians come to spend their money. If I did, I would join the Jewish N.A.A.C.P., and the Italian one, too! I would also join the Greek N.A.A.C.P., if I owned a hash-house where nothing but Greeks spent money all day long like I spend money in their Greasy Spoons."

"You put social co-operation on such a mercenary basis," I said.

"They would want me to have mercy on them if they was in my fix," said Simple.

"I did not say anything about mercy. I said *mercenary*—I mean a buying-and-selling basis."

"They could buy and sell me," said Simple.

"What I mean is, you should not have to have a business in a Jewish neighborhood to be interested in Jewish problems, or own a spaghetti stand to be interested in Italians, or a bar to care about the Irish. In a democracy, everybody's problems are related, and it's up to all of us to help solve them."

"If I did not have a business reason to be interested in *their* business," said Simple, "then what business would I have being interested in *their* business?"

"Just a human reason," I said. "It's all human business."

"Maybe that is why they don't join the N.A.A.C.P.," said Simple. "Because they do not think a Negro is human."

"If I were you, I would not speak so drastically unless I had some facts to go on. Have you ever asked any of the white businessmen where you trade to join the N.A.A.C.P.—the man who runs your laundry, or manages the movies where you go, or the Greek who owns the restaurant? Have you asked any of them to join?"

"No, I have not. Neither have I asked my colored landlady's white landlord."

"Well, ask them and see what they say."

"I sure will," said Simple, "then if they do not join, I will know they don't care nothing about me."

"You make it very simple," I said.

"It is simple, because everybody knew what stores to pick out the night of the riot."

"I was in Chicago that summer of '43 so I missed the riot."

"I was in it," said Simple.

"You don't say! Tell me about it. Where you that night?"

"All up and down," said Simple.

"Grabbing hams out of broken windows?"

"No," said Simple, "I did not want no ham. I wanted Justice."

"What do you mean, Justice?"

"You know what I mean," Simple answered. "That cop had no business shooting a colored soldier!"[10]

"You had no business breaking up stores, either," I said. "That is no way to get Justice."

"That is the way the Allies got it—breaking up Germany, breaking up Hiroshima, and everything in sight. But these white folks are more scared of Negroes in the U.S.A. than they ever was of Hitler, otherwise why would they make Jackie Robinson stop playing baseball to come to Washington and testify how loyal we is? I remember that night after the riots they turned on all the street lights in Harlem, although it was during the war and New York had a dim-out. Wasn't no dim-out in Harlem— lights just blazing in the middle of the war. The air-raid drill was called off, likewise the blackout. Suppose them German planes had come with *all* our lights on full."

"You're so dark the cops couldn't see *you* in a dim-out so they had to turn on the lights."

"Make no remarks about my color, pal! You are the same complexion. And I'll bet if you'd been in New York when the riot started, you would have been out there in the streets with me."

"I would have emerged to see the excitement, yes, but not to break windows looking for Justice."

"Well, *I* was looking for Justice," said Simple. "I was tired."

"Tired of what?"

"Of hearing the radio talking about the Four Freedoms all day long during the war and me living in Harlem where nary one of them Freedoms worked—nor the ceiling prices neither."

"So?"

"So I threw a couple of bricks through a couple of windows when the riots started, and I felt better."

"Did you pick your windows or did you just throw?"

"Man, there wasn't no time to pick windows because the si-reens was blowing and the P.D.'s coming. But I aimed my foot at one grocery and my bricks at two big windows in a shoe store that cost them white folks plenty money to put back in."

"And that made you feel better?"

"Yes."

"Why?"

"Well, I figured, let them white men spend some of the profits they make out of Harlem putting those windows back. Let 'em spend some of that money they made out of these high rents in Harlem all these years to put them windows back. Also let 'em use some of that money to put them windows back that they owe my grandmother and my great-grandmother and her mother before that for working all them years in slavery for nothing. Let 'em take *that* back pay due my race and put them windows back!"

"You have things all mixed up, old man," I said, "which is one reason why I am glad you have joined the N.A.A.C.P., so that the next time a crisis comes up, you will have a more legitimate outlet for your energies. There are more effective ways and means of achieving justice than through violence. The N.A.A.C.P. believes in propaganda, education, political action, and legal redress. Besides, the men who owned that shoe store you threw those bricks in probably were way over in Europe when you were born. Certainly they had nothing to do with slavery, let alone your grandma's back pay."

"But they don't have nothing to do now with *Grandma's grandson* either—except to take my money over the counter, then go on downtown to Stuyvesant Town where I can't live, or out to them pretty suburbans, and leave me in Harlem holding the bag. I ain't no fool. When the riot broke out, I went looking for Justice."

"With a brick."

"No! Two bricks," said Simple.

34

The Law

"I definitely do not like the Law," said Simple, using the word with a capital letter to mean *police* and *courts* combined.

"Why?" I asked.

"Because the Law beats my head. Also because the Law will give a white man One Year and give me Ten."

"But if it wasn't for the Law," I said, "you would not have any protection."

"Protection?" yelled Simple. "The Law always protects a white man. But if *I* holler for the Law, the Law says, 'What do you want, Negro?' Only most white polices do not say 'Negro.'"

"Oh, I see. You are talking about the police, not the Law in general."

"Yes, I am talking about the polices."

"You have a bad opinion of the Law," I said.

"The Law has a bad opinion of me," said Simple. "The Law thinks *all* Negroes are in the criminal class. The Law'll stop me on the streets and shake me down—me, a workingman—as quick as they will any old weedheaded hustler or two-bit rounder. I do not like polices."

"You must be talking about the way-down-home-in-Dixie Law," I said, "not up North."

"I am talking about the Law *all over* America," said Simple, "North or South. In so far as I am concerned, a police is no good. It was the Law that started the Harlem riots by shooting that soldier-boy. Take a cracker down South or an o'fay up North—as soon as he puts on a badge he wants to try out his billy-club on some Negro's head. I tell you police are no good! If they was, they wouldn't be polices."

"Listen," I said, "you are generalizing too much. Not all cops are bad. There are some decent policemen—particularly in New York. You yourself told me about that good Irish cop downtown who made an insistent Southerner get out of a Negro's cab."

"I admit since the riots the cops ain't so bad in Harlem, and downtown there are some right nice ones. But outside of New York, you can count the good polices on the fingers of one glove," said Simple. "They are in the minorality."

"You mean *minority*. But what about the colored cops?" I asked. "Not all cops are white."

"Man!" said Simple, "colored cops are *colored*, so they can't bully *nobody* but me—which makes it worse. You know colored cops ain't gonna hit no white man. So when the black Law does get a chance to hit somebody once, they have to hit me *twice*. Colored cops is worse than white. A black Law is terrible!"

"I do not agree with you," I said. "I think there ought to be more colored cops."

"You can add, can't you?" asked Simple.

"Yes."

"Then use your rithematics. A black Law cannot lock up a white man in most cities, and he better not try. So when a colored cop does some arresting he has to lock up *two* or *three* of *me* to fill his quota—otherwise he never would get promoted."

"Well, anyhow, if it wasn't for the police, who would keep you from being robbed and mugged?"

"I have been robbed and mugged both," said Simple, "and there was not a cop nowhere to be found. I could not even find a P.D. car."

"Did you report being robbed?"

"I did the first time, but not no more. Them polices down at the precinct station looked at me like *I* were the robber. They asked me for all kinds of identifications from my driving license to my draft card. That was during the war. I told them, 'How can I show you my draft card when it was in my pocketbook and my pocketbook is just stole?' They wanted to lock me up for having no draft card."

"That does not sound plausible," I said.

"It may not sound possible—but it was," said Simple. "I told the Desk Sergeant that them mugs taken Eighty Dollars off of me at the point of a gun. The Desk Sergeant asked me *where did I get Eighty Dollars!* I showed him my hands. I said, 'See these here calluses? I work for my money,' I said. 'I do not graft, neither do I steal.'

"The Desk Sergeant hollered, 'Don't get smart, boy, or I'll throw *you* in the jug!' That is why I would not go back to no police station to report *nothing* no more."

"Maybe you'll be better treated next time."

"Not as long as I am black," said Simple.

"You look at everything, I regret to say, in terms of black and white."

"So does the Law," said Simple.

35

Confused

"When a Jew changes his name, he stops being Jewish, but I would have to change my color to stop being colored."

"True," I said. "Nature has got us fixed so we can't do a thing."

"Nature has got me in the go-long," said Simple. "No matter what I do, I am still black. I cannot pass for another nation, even if I change my name to Ahboo Ben Anklebar and wear a goatee."

"But being a race man," I said, "I know you are proud of being black."

"Proud as I can be," said Simple. "But sometimes it is mighty inconvenient. I remember once I was driving down South. I got the stomach-ache, but every service-station toilet on the road was marked WHITE. Every time I went near one, they hollered at me like a dog. Lord, I never will forget that! They tell me there are some hotels marked RESTRICTED into which a Jew cannot go. But I have never seen a toilet marked FOR CHRISTIANS ONLY."

"Neither have I," I said. "Besides, it is not so easy to tell with the eye who is a Jew and who is not."

"But me," said Simple, "I am marked for life. I am a Son of Ham from down in 'Bam—and there ain't none other like I am. Solid black from front to back! And one thing sure—it won't fade, jack! The name I take makes no difference either. I have known Negroes named O'Malley, but they wasn't Irish. Anyhow, sometimes if you get your name *too* white, it makes the white folks mad. My second cousin on my stepuncle's side down in Virginia named her first child Franklin D. Roosevelt Brown. But the white folks she worked for told her, 'Mattie Mae, you better take that white name off that black child. That's a Yankee name, anyhow. In fact, a damn-yankee name.'"

"If you were going to pass for white, what name would you take?" I asked.

"Patrick McGuire," said Simple.

"But why pick out an Irish name?"

"I don't know," said Simple, "I just like Irish names. If I was going to pass for white, I might as well pass good. With an Irish name, I could be Mayor of New York."

"A fine Mayor you would make."

"A fine Mayor is right," said Simple proudly. "I would immediately issue a decree right away."

"To what effect?"

"To the effect that any colored man who wants to rent an apartment downtown can rent one and no landlord can tell him, 'We do not lease to colored.'"

"Always bringing in race," I said, "even after you get to be Mayor."

"I would decree a landlord has to rent a house to anybody," said Simple. "I would not allow him to discriminate against colored."

"Remember, now, this is all in case you would be white," I reminded him. "However, if you were white, sir, listen—would you want your daughter to marry a Negro?"

"If my daughter didn't have no better sense," said Simple.

"There you go showing prejudice yourself," I said.

"You got me confused, man! What I meant was . . ."

"Intermarriage is always brought up to confuse the issue," I said, "so don't bother to explain."

"Well, don't confuse *me*!" objected Simple. "In the first place, I am not white. In the second place, I don't have no daughter. And in the third place, if I did have, she wouldn't be white since I'm just passing for Irish myself. So don't confuse the issue. We was having a nice simple argument and you had to go confuse the issue. Buy me a beer."

"You drink too much," I said.

"Please don't confuse *another* issue," said Simple.

36

Something to Lean On

"A bar is something to lean on," said Simple.

"You lean on bars very often," I remarked.

"I do," said Simple.

"Why?"

"Because everything else I lean on falls down," said Simple, "including my peoples, my wife, my boss, and me."

"How do you mean?"

"My peoples brought me into the world," said Simple, "but they didn't have no money to put me through school. When I were knee-high to a duck I had to go to work."

"That happens to a lot of kids," I said.

"Most particularly colored," said Simple. "And my wife, I couldn't depend on her. When the depression come and I was out of a job, Isabel were no prop to me. I could not lean on her."

"So you started to leaning on bars," I said.

"No," said Simple. "I were leaning on bars before I married. I started to leaning on bars soon as I got out of short pants."

"Perhaps if you belonged to the church you would have something stronger on which to lean."

"You mean lean on the Lord? Daddy-o, too many folks are leaning on Him now. I believe the Lord helps them that helps themselves—and I am a man who tries to help himself. That is the way white folks got way up where they are in the world—while colored's been leaning on the Lord."

"And you have been leaning on bars."

"What do you think I do all day long?" Simple objected. "From eight in the morning to five at night, I do not lean on no bar. I work! Ask my boss-man out at the plant. He knows I work. He claims he likes me, too. But that raise he promised me way last winter, have I got it yet? Also that advancement? No! I have not! I see them white boys get advancements while I stay where I am. Black—so I know I ain't due to go but so far. I bet you if I was white I would be somewhere in this world."

"There you go with that old color argument as an excuse again," I said.

"I bet you I would not be poor. All the opportunities a white man's got, there ain't no sense in his being poor. He can get any kind of job, anywhere. He can be President. Can I?"

"Do you have the qualifications?"

"Answer my question," said Simple, "and don't ask me another one. Can I be President? Truman can, but can I? Is he any smarter than me?"

"I am not acquainted with Mr. Truman, so I do not know."

"Does he *look* any smarter?" asked Simple.

"I must admit he does not," I said.

"Then why can't I be President, too? Because I am colored, that's why."

"So you spend your evenings leaning on bars because you cannot be President," I said. "What kind of reasoning is that?"

"Reason enough," said Simple. "If anybody else in America can be President, I want to be President. The Constitution guarantees us equal rights, but have I got 'em? No. It's fell down on me."

"You figure the Constitution has fallen down on you?"

"I do," said Simple. "Just like it fell down on that poor Negro lynched last month. Did anybody out of that mob go to jail? Not a living soul! But just kidnap some little small white baby and take it across the street, and you will do twenty years. The F.B.I. will spread its dragnet and drag in forty suspections before morning. And, if you are colored, don't be caught selling a half pint of bootleg licker, or writing a few numbers. They will put you in every jail there is! But Southerners can beat you, bum you, lynch you, and hang you to a tree—and every one of them will go scotfree. Gimme another beer. Tony! I can lean on this bar, but I ain't got another thing in the U.S.A. on which to lean."

Part Four

Any Time

"So I ordered her some Teacher's. But that girl was thirsty! She drunk me up—at Sixty-Five Cents a shot! I said, 'Bea-Baby, let's get some air.'

"She said, 'Air? I growed up in air! I got plenty of air when I were a child. Sixteen miles south of Selma there weren't nothing but air.'

" 'Selma is far enough South, but *sixteen miles south of there* is too much! How long you been up North, girl?'

" 'Two years,' she said, 'and if I live to be a hundred, I will be up here seventy-five more.'

" 'You mean you are not going back to Selma?'

" 'Period,' she said.

" 'In other words, you are going to stay in Chicago?'

" 'Oh, but I am,' she said.

" 'Well, we are not going to stay in this bar seventy-five years,' I whispered. 'Come on, Bea-Baby, let's walk.'

" 'Walk where?' she hollered, insulted.

" 'Follow me and you will see,' I said.

" 'I will not follow you, unless you tell me where we are going.'

" 'I will not tell you where we are going, unless you follow,' I said.

"But when we got out of that darker-than-a-movie bar, under the street lights on Indiana Avenue, I got a good look at her and she got a good look at me. We *both* said 'Good-by!' In that dim dark old dusky cocktail lounge, I thought she was mellow. But she were not! I thought she was a chippy, but she were at least forty-five.

"And the first thing she said when she saw my face was, 'I thought you was a *young* man—but you ain't. You old as my Uncle Herman.'

"I said, 'I done had so many unpleasant surprises in my life, baby, until my age is writ in my face. *You* is one more unpleasantness.'

"I thought she said 'Farewell,' but it could of been 'Go to hell.'

"Anyhow, she cured me of them dark Chicago bars. *Never make friends in the dark,* is what I learned in Chicago."

"I am glad you learned something," I said.

"Thank you," said Simple. "Now, come on let's have a beer to welcome me back to Harlem. Not to change the subject, but lend me a quarter. I'm broke."

"I'm broke, too."

"Then you can't have a beer, daddy-o," regretted Simple. "What is worse, neither can I."

38

For the Sake of Argument

When I came out of the house about midnight to get a bite to eat, there was Simple in one corner of Paddy's Bar arguing loudly with an aggregation of beer-drinkers as to who is the darker, Paul Robeson or Jackie Robinson. I sat down on the lunch-counter side of the bar and ordered a plate of shortribs. After a while Simple spotted me and took possession of the next stool, although he had no apparent intention of eating.

"You know Robeson is not as light as Robinson," he announced.

"To me it makes not the slightest difference what their gradations of complexion are," I said. "Furthermore, I do not comprehend how you can stand around for hours in bars and on corners just arguing about nothing. You will argue with folks about which railroad has the fastest trains, or if Bojangles could tap more taps per second than Fred Astaire. And none of it is of any importance."

"I do not see how you can sit around looking so smart all the time and saying practically nothing," countered Simple. "You are company for nobody but yourself."

"I do not like to argue," I said.

"I do! I will argue about whether or not two and two makes four just for the sake of argument."

"It has been proven so long ago that two and two make four that I do not see the sense in discussing it. If you were arguing about what to do with the Germans or how to reform the South, then I could go along with you. But I do not like to argue about things on which there is really no argument."

"I do—because my argument is that it is good for a man to argue, just argue," said Simple, walking to the door of the bar and gazing out. Suddenly he turned around. "But I could not argue if you did not argue back at me. It takes two to make an argument. A man cannot argue by his self."

"The trouble with you is that you always wish to *win* the argument," I said. "For me, just an exchange of views is sufficient. But you, you always want to win."

"Naturally, I want to win. Otherwise, why should I be arguing?"

"You are so often wrong, Jess, also loud. You cannot win an argument when you are wrong. There are two sides to every question."

"There are sometimes more than two sides," said Simple, "except to the race question. For white folks that don't have but one side."

"There you go bringing up the race question," I said. "How is it two Negroes can never get together without discussing the race question?"

"Because it is not even a question," said Simple. "It is a hammer over our heads and at any time it may fall. The only way I can explain what white folks does to us is that they just don't give a damn. Why, I once knowed a white man down South who were so mean he wouldn't give a sick baby a doctor's address."

"Where and when was that?" I asked.

"When I were a boy," said Simple. "I was hired out one summer on his plantation. He used to ride all around over the plantation watching everybody work. He rid on a little old girl-horse named Betsy, and Betsy were as mean as he were. In fact, he had taught Betsy how to bite Negroes in the back. 'Boy, hist that there tree out of that ditch!'

"If you did not hist fast enough to suit him—'I can't, Capt'n Boss!'— he would holler, 'Boy, you better, else I'll bull-whip your hide wide open!'

"Then if you still didn't hist, he would tell that little old horse, 'Get him, Betsy!' Betsy would gallop up and nip you right between the shoulder blades."

"You are lying now, I do believe," I said.

"You have never lived down South," said Simple, "so you do not know."

"I admit I am not really familiar with the South," I said, "but sometimes I think conditions are exaggerated. Certainly in recent years they are getting better."

"They've still got Jim Crow cars," said Simple. "And the last time I was down home on a trip, I went to pay a visit on the old white man my uncle used to work for. I had kinder forgot how it is down there, so I just walked up on the porch where he was setting and says, 'Howdy, Mr. Doolittle.'

"He says, 'Boy, take off your hat when you address a white man.' And that is how he greeted me. He says, 'You must have been up North so long you done forgot yourself.'

"You know that kinder hurt my feelings because he used to know me when I was a boy. But I am a man now. That is the trouble with the

South. They do not want to treat a Negro like a man. It's always *boy*, no matter if you are ninety-nine years old. I know some few things is getting better, but even them is slow as molasses. Here, lemme show you a little poem I writ about that very thing last week."

Simple pulled a piece of tablet paper out of his pocket and proceeded to read. "Listen fluently:

> *Old Jim Crow's*
> *Just panting and a-coughing,*
> *But he won't take wings*
> *And fly.*
>
> *Old Jim Crow*
> *Is laying in his coffin,*
> *But he don't want*
> *To die.*
>
> *I have writ*
> *His obituary,*
> *Still and yet*
> *He tarry.*"

"Not bad, old man, except that 'He tarry' is not grammatical," I said. "If you want to be literary, you ought to know grammar."

"Joyce knows grammar," said Simple. "She will fix it up for me. I just have not showed her this one yet."

"A writer should never depend on anyone else to fix things for him. You ought to fix up your own things," I said.

"There are some things in life you cannot fix all by yourself," said Simple. "For me, poetries is one. And the race problem is another. Now you take for instant, we got two colored congressmen down in Washington. But they can't even stop a filibuster. Every time them Civil Rights Bills come up, them old white Southerners filibuster them to hell and gone. Why don't them colored congressmen start a filibuster, too?"

"Probably because they cannot talk as long or as loud as the Southerners," I said. "It takes Southerners to keep a filibuster going, and there are a great many of them in the House. Neither Adam Powell nor Dawson represents the South."

"They are colored and they represent me," said Simple. "If I was down yonder in Congress representing the colored race, I would start a filibuster all my own. In fact, I would filibuster to keep them filibusters from starting a filibuster."

"If you had no help," I said, "you would just have to keep on talking day and night, week after week, because once you sat down somebody else would get the floor. So how would you hold out?"

"How would I hold out?" yelled Simple. "With the fate of my Race at stake, you ask me how would *I* hold out! Why, for my people I would talk until my tongue hung out of my mouth. I would talk until I could not talk no more! Then, I would use sign language. When I got through with that, I would get down on my knees and pray in silence. And nobody better not strike no gavel while I am communing with my Maker. While I am on my knees, I would get some sleep. When I riz up, it would be the next day, so I would start all over again. I would be the greatest one-man filibuster of all time, daddy-o! But I am running dry now. Treat me to a beer."

"I will not," I said.

"O.K., then," said Simple, "you are setting there eating and drinking and here I am empty-handed. You are a hell of a buddy."

"I will lend you a dime to buy your own beer," I said, "but a treat should be an invitation, not a request."

"Just so I get the beer," said Simple. "Now, I will continue. As I were saying, there ain't but one side to this race question—the white folks' side. White folks are setting on top of the world, and I wouldn't mind setting up there myself. Just look around you. Who owns this bar? White folks. Who owns mighty near every shop and store all up and down this street? White folks. But what do I own? I'm asking you."

"As far as I know, you do not own a thing. But why don't you get a bar or a store?"

"Why don't you?"

"Let's consider the broader picture," I said.

"I asked you a question," said Simple. "Why don't you get a bar or a store?"

"I asked you first," I countered.

"I do not get a bar or a store for the same reason that you don't," said Simple. "I have nothing to get me one with. On Saturday I draws my wages. I pay my rent, I get out my laundry, I take Joyce to a show, I pay you back your Two Dollars, I drink a little beer. What have I got left to buy a store with?"

"Do you think Tony the Italian that owns this Paddy's Bar—with its Irish name—also two stores, and a bookie joint, had anything when he came to America twenty years ago in the steerage?"

"Columbus come before him and smoothed the way," said Simple.

"Besides, if you are white, you can get credit. If you are white, you can meet somebody with money. If you are white, you can come up here to Harlem and charge double prices. If I owned a store and charged what they charge, folks would say, 'That Negro is no good.' I tell you, white folks get away with murder. They murder my soul every day and my pocketbook every night. They got me going and coming. They say, 'You can't have a good job. You're black.' Then they say, 'Pay double. You can't eat downtown. We got this grease-ball joint for you in Harlem where it's a dime more for a beef stew. Pay it or else!' A man can't else. That's the way they get ahead when they come to America. Columbus didn't start out with Jim Crow around his neck. Neither did the guy who owns this bar. Any foreigner can come here, white, and Jim Crow me, black, from the day he sets foot off the boat. Also overcharge. He *starts* on top of my head so no wonder he gets on top of the world. Maybe I ought to go to Europe and come back a foreigner."

"While you are over there, in order to change your complexion, you'd have to be born again."

"As colored as I am," said Simple, "I'd have to be born two or three times."

39

Simple Pins On Medals

"Now, the way I understand it," said Simple one Monday evening when the bar was nearly empty and the juke box silent, "it's been written down a long time ago that all men are borned equal and everybody is entitled to life and liberty while pursuing happiness. It's in the Constitution, also Declaration of Independence, so I do not see why it has to be resolved all over again."

"Who is resolving it all over?" I asked.

"Some white church convention—I read in the papers where they have resolved all that over and the Golden Rule, too, also that Negroes should be treated right. It looks like to me white folks better stop resolving and get to *doing*. They have resolved enough. *Resolving ain't solving.*"

"What do you propose that they do?"

"The white race has got a double duty to us," said Simple. "They ought to start treating us right. They also ought to make up for how bad they have treated us in the past."

"You can't blame anybody for history," I said.

"No," said Simple, "but you can blame folks if they don't do something about history! History was yesterday, times gone. Yes. But now that colored folks are willing to let bygones be bygones, this ain't no time to be Jim Crowing nobody. This is a new day."

"Maybe that is why they are resolving to do better," I said.

"I keep telling you, it has come time to stop *resolving*!" said Simple. "They have been *resolving* for two hundred years. I do not see how come they need to *resolve* any more. I say, they need to *solve*."

"How?"

"By treating us like humans," said Simple, "that's how!"

"They don't treat each other like human beings," I said, "so how do you expect them to treat you that way?"

"White folks do not Jim Crow each other," said Simple, "neither do they have a segregated army—except for me."

"No, maybe not," I said, "but they blasted each other down with V-bombs during the war."

"To be shot down is bad for the body," said Simple, "but to be Jim

Crowed is worse for the spirit. Besides, speaking of war, in the next war I want to see Negroes pinning medals on white men."

"Medals? What have medals to do with anything?"

"A lot," said Simple, "because every time I saw a picture in the colored papers of colored soldiers receiving medals in the last war, a white officer was always doing the pinning. I have not yet seen a picture in *no* papers of a *colored* officer pinning a medal on a white soldier. Do you reckon I will ever see such a picture?"

"I don't know anything about the army's system of pinning on medals," I said.

"I'll bet there isn't a white soldier living who ever got a medal from a colored officer," said Simple.

"Maybe not, but I don't get your point. If a soldier is brave enough to get a medal, what does it matter who pins it on?"

"It may not matter to the soldiers," said Simple, "but it matters to *me*. I have never yet seen no *colored* general pinning a medal on a *white* private. That is what I want to see."

"Colored generals did not command white soldiers in the last war," I said, "which is no doubt why they didn't pin medals on them."

"I want to see colored generals commanding white soldiers, then," said Simple.

"You may want to see it, but how can you see it when it just does not take place?"

"In the next war it must and should take place," said Simple, "because if these white folks are gonna have another war, they better give us some generals. I know if I was in the army, I would like to command white troops. In fact, I would like to be in charge of a regiment from Mississippi."

"Are you sober?" I asked.

"I haven't had but one drink today."

"Then why on earth would you want to be in charge of a white regiment from Mississippi?"

"They had white officers from Mississippi in charge of Negroes—so why shouldn't I be in charge of whites? Huh? I would really make 'em toe the line! I know some of them Southerners had rather die than to *left face* for a colored man, buddy-o. But they would *left face* for me."

"What would you do if they wouldn't *left face*?"

"Court-martial them," said Simple. "After they had set in the stockade for six months, I would bring them Mississippi white boys out, and I would say once more, '*Left face!*' I bet they would *left face* then! Else I'd court-martial them again."

"You have a very good imagination," I said, "also a sadistic one."

"I can see myself now in World War III," said Simple, "leading my Mississippi troops into action. I would do like all the other generals do, and stand way back on a hill somewheres and look through my spyglasses and say, 'Charge on! Mens, charge on!' Then I would watch them Dixiecrat boys go—like true sons of the old South, mowing down the enemy.

"When my young white lieutenants from Vicksburg jeeped back to Headquarters to deliver their reports in person to me, they would say, 'General Captain, sir, we have taken two more enemy positions.'

"I would say, 'Mens, return to your companies—and tell 'em to *charge on!*'

"Next day, when I caught up to 'em, I would pin medals on their chests for bravery. Then I would have my picture taken in front of all my fine white troops—*me*—the first black American general to pin medals on white soldiers from Mississippi. It would be in every paper in the world—the great news event of World War III."

"It would certainly be news," I said.

"Doggone if it wouldn't," said Simple. "It would really be news! You see what I mean by *solving*—not just resolving. I will've done solved."

40

A Ball of String

"This makes me mad." My friend frowned as he came back to his stool from the telephone booth at the rear of the bar. "I do not like Zarita nor no other dame calling me up at a bar, having the bartender strewing my right and full name all over the place, 'Hey, there, Jesse B. Semple! One of your womens wants you on the phone. But she's way down at the end of the alphabet—Z, for Zarita.' That bartender ain't got no business letting everybody know my business and I don't care to have my name known to everybody, neither."

"He is not very discreet," I said, "but then, Harlemites have very little training in public service, since they don't get a chance to acquire background in business elsewhere."

"Bartenders are most in generally all right," said Simple, "but some of these waitresses get me down—unless they are damn good-looking. Also some Harlem clerks don't know how to wait on people. The other day I went in a Dime store on 125th Street. Young girl clerk was standing back behind the counter chewing gum and looking like a baby bull moose. I asked for a Ten-Cent ball of string.

" 'I don't have none,' she snaps.

"I said, 'Do you mean to tell me you don't have a Ten-Cent ball of string in all this great big old Dime store?'

" 'It costs *Twelve* Cents,' she said.

" 'Why didn't you tell me that in the first place?' I asked her. 'All I want is what *used* to be a Ten-Cent ball of string. I do not care if it costs Twelve Cents now or not. I need the string.'

"Whereupon she grabs a ball of twine, throws it in a bag, and throws it at me. Now I do not very seldom get mad, daddy-o, but I got mad this time. That girl were colored like me and ought to treat *me* with some politeness. So I says, 'Young lady, look here! If you stop chewing gum long enough to let your ears stay in one place and hear what I have to say, I will tell you something. Do you remember when they did not let any colored clerks work in these white stores here in Harlem? Huh? Do you? Well, I was one of the mens that picketed in the snow in my bare shoes with no overshoes to get you-all these jobs. Now I will picket *to get you out again,* if you do not give me some kind of decent service!'

" 'I give you what you wanted,' she snaps. 'That is the trouble with colored folks, they always expect more out of us than they do out of white clerks. You've got your string.'

" 'Yes, I've got my string,' I said, 'but I would not have had it had I listened to you in the first place, telling me, Naw, you didn't have any, when what you should have said was, Yes, we have it, but the price is gone up to Twelve Cents—even if this is a Dime store. I cannot figure out why colored clerks say "No" so much.'

" 'You should ask for what you want,' said the girl, lowering her head at me and chewing like a young cow.

" 'I did ask for what I want—string,' I said. 'But I am no clerk, so how do I know to ask for *Twelve-Cent* string when it used to be Ten? Don't pull no teck on me, young lady, and me as black as you.'

" 'You talk like you've never been mistreated by no white clerks in a store,' she says.

" 'That is just why I picketed to get colored clerks in this store,' I says, 'so I wouldn't be snipped up and ignored. Now here you come telling me, Naw, you don't have no string, when you do. Then getting technical about Two Cents' difference in the price. I got a good mind to report you to the manager.'

" 'That's what I say about Negroes—always running to the white man,' said the young woman. 'What do you want, madam?' she says to a large lady who has been waiting all this time.

" 'A box of sealing wax,' said the woman.

" 'That is not at this counter,' snaps the girl, so the woman wandered on off looking all around to see if she could see any sealing wax laying loose somewhere.

"I said, 'Why didn't you tell that woman where the sealing wax is?'

"She says, 'Because I don't know, that's why! I'm not supposed to know where everything in this store is.'

" 'If you knew a little more, you might get a little further,' I said. *'No! I don't know! No! I don't have! No! No, ma'am! No!* Sometimes I think all you clerks know is *No!* Is that so?'

" 'No,' she snaps, 'it's not so! No!'

"Then I says, 'Tell me then where the shoe-polish counter is.'

"She says, 'I think it's in the rear.'

" 'You think?' I says. 'Then you do not know? How long have you been working here?'

" 'Four years and none of your business,' she says.

" 'Then I should think you would know where *something* is in this store,' I said.

" 'Stop heckling me!' she said.

" 'I heckled to get you in here,' I said.

"About that time a young slick-headed dude come up and says, 'Say, baby, how you doing? What time you gonna be ready to cut out of this joint and run by Slim's and Mary's with me, huh?'

"She says, 'Daddy, you know I told you I'm not going around to Mary's any more after she talked about me like a dog.'

"I said, 'Young lady, do you realize you still got a customer?'

"She says, 'Where?'

"I said, 'Don't you consider me a customer?'

"She says, 'No—because you got your string.'

"I said, 'I got my string—but I don't have satisfaction.'

"She says, 'We don't sell that at this counter.'

"Whereupon that young cat what didn't even work there hollers, 'Are you trying to insult my girl friend?'

"Buddy-o, what I said to him will not bear repeating! Me and that cat would have tangled right in that Twelve-Cent Dime store if not an old lady had come up and said, 'Now, sons, sons, you-all are acting just like Negroes.' That made me ashamed, so I cut out."

"Were you acting like a Negro?" I asked.

"I was acting like myself," said Simple.

41

Blue Evening

When I walked into the bar and saw him on the corner stool alone, I could tell something was wrong.

"Another hang-over?"

"Nothing that simple. This is something I thought never would happen to me."

"What?" I asked.

"That a woman could put *me* down. In the past, I have always left womens. No woman never left me. Now Joyce has quit."

"I don't believe it," I said. "You've been going together for two or three years, and getting along fine. What happened? That little matter of the divorce from your wife, the fur coat, or what?"

"Zarita," said Simple.

"Zarita! She's nothing to you."

"I know it," said Simple. "She never was nothing to me but a now-and-then. But Zarita has ruint my life. You don't know how it feels, buddy, when somebody has gone that you never had before. I never had a woman like Joyce. I *loved* that girl. Nobody never cared for me like Joyce did."

"Have a drink," I said, "on me."

"This is one time I do not want a drink. I feel too bad."

"Then it *is* serious," I said.

"It's what the blues is made out of," said Simple. " 'Love, oh, love, oh, careless love!' Buddy, I were careless."

"What happened, old man?"

"Zarita," said Simple. "I told that woman never to come around to my room without letting me know in advance. Joyce is too much of a lady to be always running up to my place, which is why I love her. Only time Joyce might ring my bell is when she can't get me on the phone due to my landlady is evil and sometimes will not even deliver a message. Then maybe Joyce might ring my bell, but she never comes upstairs, less it is to hang me some new spring curtains she made herself or change my dresser scarf. What's come up now is Zarita's fault, plus my landlady's.

Them two womens is against me. That word *Town & Country* uses for female dogs just about fits them."

"I understand. They are not genteel characters. But what exactly took place?"

"It hurts me to think of it, let alone to talk about it. But I will tell you. Zarita not only came around to my room the other night, but she brought her whole birthday party *unannounced, uninvited,* and *unwanted*. I didn't even know it were her birthday. I had just come in from work, et a little supper at the Barbecue Shack, and was preparing to take a nap to maybe go out later and drop by to see were Joyce in the mood, when my doorbell rung like mad nine times—which is the ring for my Third Floor Rear. It were about nine P.M. I go running downstairs in my shirttail, and sixty-eleven Negroes, male and female, come pouring in the door led by Zarita herself, whooping and hollering and high, yelling they come to help me celebrate her birthday, waving three or four bottles of licker and gin.

"Zarita says, 'Honey, I forgot to tell you I'm twenty-some-odd years old today. Whoopeee-eee-e! We started celebrating this morning and we still going strong. Come on up, folks! Let's play his combination. This man has got some *fine* records!'

"I didn't have a chance to say nothing. They just poured up the steps with me trailing behind, and my landlady looking cross-eyed out of her door, and Zarita talking so loud you could hear her in Buffalo. Next thing I knowed, Louis Jordan was turned up full-blast and somebody had even put a loud needle in the victrola. Them Negroes took possession. Well, you know I always tries to be a gentleman, even to Zarita, so I did not ask them out. I just poured myself a half glass of gin—which I do not ordinarily partake. Then I hollered, 'Happy birthday,' too.

"Well, the rest of the roomers heard the function and started coming in my room. Boyd next door brought his girl friend over, and before you knowed it, the ball was on. The joint jumped! To tell the truth, I even enjoyed myself.

"By and by, Zarita said, 'Honey, send out and get some more to drink.'

" 'Send who?' I said. 'We ain't got no messenger boy.'

"She said, 'Just gimme the money, then, and I will send that old down-home shmoo who has been trying to make love to me since four o'clock this afternoon. That man ain't nothing to me but a errand boy.'

"So we sent the old dope after a gallon of beer and pretzels. Soon as he left out the door Zarita grabbed me close as paper on the wall and started to dance. She danced so frantic, I could not keep up with her, so I turned her loose and let her go for herself. She had a great big old pocketbook on her arm and it were just a-swinging. Everybody else stopped dancing to watch Zarita, who always did want to be a show girl. She were really kicking up her heels then and throwing her hips from North to South. All of a sudden she flung up her arms and hollered, 'Yippeee-ee-ee-e!' whilst her pocketbook went flying through the air. When it hit the ceiling it busted wide open. Man, everything she had in it strewed out all over my floor as it come down.

" 'Lord have mercy!' Zarita said. 'Stop the music! Don't nobody move a inch. You might step on some of my personal belongings.'

"Just about then the downstairs doorbell rung nine times—my ring. I said, 'Somebody go down and let that guy in with the beer, while we pick up Zarita's stuff.'

"Zarita said, 'You help me, baby. The rest of you-all just stay where you are. I ain't acquainted with some of you folks and I don't want to lose nothing valuable.'

"Well, you know how many things a woman carries in her pocketbook. Zarita had lost them all, flung from one wall to the other of my room—compact busted open, powder spilt, mirror, key ring with seven keys, lipstick, handkerchief, deck of cards, black lace gloves, bottle opener, cigarette case, chewing gum, bromo-quinine box, small change, fountain pen, sun glasses, big old silver Bow-Dollar for luck, address books, fingernail file, three blue poker chips, matches, flask, also a shoehorn. Her perfume bottle broke against the radiator so my room smelt like womens, licker, mens, and a Night in Paris.

"Zarita was down on her hands and knees scrambling around for things, so I got down on my hands and knees, too.

" 'Baby,' she says to me, 'I believes my lipstick has rolled under your bed.'

"We both crawled under the bed to see. While we was under there, Zarita kissed me. She crawled out with the shoehorn and I crawled out with her lipstick—some of it on the side of my mouth. Just as I got up, there stood Joyce in my door with a package in her hand.

"Have you ever seen a man as dark as me turn red? I turned red, daddy-o! I opened my mouth to say 'Howdy-do?' but not a sound come out. Joyce had on her gold earrings and I could see they were shaking. But she did not raise her voice. She were too hurt.

"Zarita said, 'Why, Joyce, tip on in and enjoin my birthday. We don't mind. Just excuse my stuff flying all over the room. Me and Mr. Semple is having a ball.'

"Joyce looked at the black lace gloves, playing cards strewed all over the place, cigarette case, compact, poker chips, address book, powder, Bow-Dollar, and nail file on the floor with all them strange Negroes setting on the bed, in the window sill, on the dresser, everywhere but on the ceiling, and lipstick on my cheek. She did not say a word. She just turned her head away and looked like tears was aching to come to her eyes.

"I says, 'Joyce, baby, listen,' I says, 'I want a word with you.'

"She said, 'I come around here to bring you your yellow rayon-silk shirt I ironed special for you for Sunday. Since your landlady said you was at home, she told me to bring it on upstairs myself. Here it is. I did not know you had company.'

"Just then that old down-home Negro come up with the beer yelling, 'Gangway! The stuff is here. Make room!' and he almost run over Joyce.

"Joyce says, 'Excuse me for being in your guests' way.'

"She turned to go. In facts, she went. I followed her down the steps but she did not turn her head. That loud-mouthed Zarita put the needle on Louis Jordan's bodacious 'Let the Good Times Roll,' and the ball were on again. When I got to the bottom of the steps, my landlady was standing like a marble statue.

"Landlady says, 'No decent woman approves of this.' Which is when Joyce started crying.

"Boy! My heart was broke because I hates to be misunderstood. I said, 'Joyce, I did not invite them parties here.'

"Joyce says, 'You don't need to explain to me, Jess Semple,' getting all formal and everything. She says, 'Now I have seen that woman with my own eyes in *your* bedroom with her stuff spread out every which-a-where just like she was home. And people I know from their looks could not be *your* friends because I never met any of them before—so they must be hers. Maybe Zarita lives with you. No wonder you giving a birthday party to which I am not invited. Good night, I am gone out of your life from now on. Enjoy yourself. Good night!'

"If she had fussed and raised her voice, I would not have felt so bad. But the sweet way she said, 'Enjoy yourself,' all ladylike and sad and quiet, as if she was left out of things, cut me to my soul. Joyce ought to know I would not leave her out of nothing.

"I would of followed her in the street, but she said, 'Don't you come behind me!'

"The way she said it, I knowed she meant it. So I did not go. When I turned back, there was my landlady. All I said to that old battle-ax was, 'Go to hell!' I were so mad at that woman for sending Joyce upstairs.

"She started yelling as I went on up the steps, but I didn't hear a word she said. I knowed she was telling me to find another room. But I did not care. All I wanted was to lay eyes on Zarita, stop them damn records from playing, and get them low-down dirty no-gooders out of my room. Which I did before you could say 'Jackie Robinson.' But after they left, I could not sleep. It were a blue evening.

"Some of Zarita's stuff was still on the floor next day when I went to work, so I gathered it up and brought it down here to the bartender and left it for her. I do not want to see Zarita no more again. The smell of that Night in Paris water is still in my room. I'll smell it till the day I die. But I don't care if I die right now. I don't know what to say to Joyce. A man should not fool around a bad woman *no kind of way* when he's got a good woman to love. They say, 'You never miss the water till the well runs dry.' Boy, you don't know how I miss Joyce these last few days."

"Haven't you tried to see her?" I asked.

"Tried?" said Simple. "I phoned her seventeen times. She will not answer the phone. I rung her bell. Nobody will let me in. I sent her six telegrams, but she do not reply. If I could write my thoughts, I would write her a letter, but I am no good at putting words on paper much. The way I feel now, nobody could put my feelings down nohow. I got the blues for true. I can't be satisfied. This morning I had the blues so bad, I wished that I had died. These is my bitter days. What shall I do?"

"I don't know."

"You never know anything important," said Simple. "All you know is to argue about race problems. Tonight I would not care if all the race problems in the world was to descend right on New York. I would not care if Rankin himself would be elected Mayor and the Ku Klux Klan took over the City Council. I would not care if Mississippi moved to Times Square. But nobody better not harm Joyce, I'm telling you, even if she has walked out of my life. That woman *is* my life, so nobody better not touch a hair of her head. Buddy-o, wait for me here whilst I walks by her house to see if there's a light in her window. I just want to know if she got home from work safe tonight."

"She's been getting home safely by herself all these years," I said, "Why are you so worried tonight?"

"Please don't start no whys and wherefores."

"I sympathize with you—still, there are always ameliorating circumstances."

"I don't know what that word means," said Simple, "but all that rates with me now is what to say to that girl—if I ever get a chance to say anything. If she does not come to the door when I ring this time, if I see a light I am going to holler."

"Since she lives on the third floor, you can hardly play Romeo and climb up," I said. "Still, I don't believe Joyce would relish having her name called aloud in the street."

"If she don't let me through the door, I will have to call her," said Simple. "I can explain by saying that I have lost my mind, that she has driv me crazy. And I will stand in front of her house all night if she don't answer."

"The law would probably remove you," I said.

"They would have to use force to do it," said Simple. "I wouldn't care if the polices broke my head, anyhow. Joyce done broke my heart."

"You've got it bad," I said.

"Worse than bad," moaned Simple. "Here, take this quarter and buy yourself a beer whilst you wait till I come back."

"I have some affairs of my own to attend to," I protested, "so I can't wait all night."

"I thought you was my ace-boy," he said as he turned away. "But everybody lets you down when trouble comes. If you can't wait, then don't. To hell with you! Don't!"

I started to say I would wait. But Simple was gone.

42

When a Man Sees Red

"I may not be a red," he said as he banged on the bar, "but sometimes I see red."

"What do you mean?"

"The way some of these people a man has to work for talks to a man, I see red. The other day my boss come saying to me that I was laying down on the job—when all I was doing was just thinking about Joyce. I said, 'What do you mean, laying down on the job? Can't you see me standing up?'

"The boss said, 'You ain't doing as much work as you used to do.'

"I said, 'A Dollar don't do as much buying for me as *it* used to do, so I don't do as much for a Dollar. Pay me some more money, and I will do more work.' "

"What did he say then?"

"He said, 'You talk like a red.'

"I said, 'What do you mean, red?'

"He said, 'You know what I mean—*red, communist.* After *all* this country has done for you Negroes, I didn't think you'd turn out to be a red.'

"I said, 'In my opinion, a man can be any color except yellow. I'd be yellow if I did not stand up for my rights.'

"The boss said, 'You have no right to draw wages and not work.'

"I said, 'I have *done* work, I *do* work, and I *will* work—but also a man is due to eat for his work, to have some clothes, and a roof over his head. For what little you are paying me, I can't hardly keep body and soul together. Don't you reckon I have a soul?' I said.

"Boss said, 'I have nothing to do with your soul. All I am concerned about is your work. You are talking like a communist, and I will not have no reds in my plant.'

"I said, 'It wasn't so long ago you would not have no Negroes in your plant. Now you won't have no reds. You must be color-struck!'

"That got him. That made him mad. He said, 'I have six Negroes working for me now.'

"I said, 'Yes, out of six hundred men. You wouldn't have them if you could've got anybody else during the war. And what kind of work do you give us? The dirty work! The cheapest wages! Maintenance department—which is just another way for saying *clean up*. You know you don't care nothing about us Negroes. You getting ready to fire me right now. Well, if you fire me, I will be a red for sure, because I see red this morning. I will *see the union, if you fire me*,' I said.

" 'Just go on and do your work,' he said, and walked off. But I was hot, pal! I'm telling you! But he did not look back. He didn't want to have no trouble out of that union."

"Now I know he will think you are a red," I said.

"Is it red to want to earn decent wages? Is it red to want to keep your job? And not to want to take no stuff off a boss?"

"Don't yell at me," I said. "I'm not your boss. I didn't say a thing."

"No, but you implied," said Simple. "Just because you are not working for white folks, you implied."

"There you go bringing up the race issue again," I said. "I think you are too race-conscious."

"I am black," said Simple, "also I will be red if things get worse. But one thing sure, I will not be yellow. I will stand up for my rights till kingdom come."

"You'd better be careful or they will have you up before the Un-American Committee."

"I wish that old Southern chairman would send for me," said Simple. "I'd tell him more than he wants to know."

"For instance?" I said.

"For instant," said Simple, "I would say, 'Your Honery, I wish to inform you that I was born in America, I live in America, and long as I have been black, I been an American. Also I was a Democrat—but I didn't know Roosevelt was going to die.' Then I would ask them, 'How come you don't have any Negroes on your Un-American Committee?'

"And old Chairman Georgia would say, 'Because that is un-American.'

"Then I would say, 'It must also be un-American to run a train, because I do not see any colored engineers running trains. All I see Negroes doing on the railroads is sweeping out coaches and making beds. Is that American?'

"Old Chairman Georgia would say, 'Yes! Sweeping is American.'

"Then I would say, 'Well, I want to be un-American so I can run a train.'

"Old Chairman would say, 'You must be one of them Red Russians.'

" 'No, I ain't neither,' I would say. 'I was born down South, too, like you. But I do not like riding a Jim Crow car when I go home to Dixie. Also, I do not like being a Pullman porter *all the time*. Sometimes I want to *run* a train.'

" 'I know you are a Red Russian!' yells that old Chairman. 'You want to tear this country down!'

" 'Your Honery,' I says, 'I admit I would like to tear *half* of it down—the Southern half from Virginia to Mobile—just to build it over new. And when I built it over, I would put *you* in the Jim Crow car instead of me.'

" 'Hold that Negra in contempt of court!' yells Chairman Georgia.

" 'I thought you just said I was a Red Russian. Now here you go calling me a Negro. Which is I?'

" 'You're both,' says the Chairman.

" 'Why? Because I want to drive a train?'

" 'Yes,' yells the Chairman, 'because you want to drive a train! This is a white man's country. These is white men's trains! You cannot drive one. And down where I come from, neither can you ride in a WHITE coach.'

" 'You don't have any coaches for Red Russians,' I said.

" 'No,' yells the Chairman, 'but we will have them as soon as I can pass a law.'

" 'Then where would I ride?' I asked. 'In the COLORED coach or in the RED coach?'

" 'You will not ride nowhere,' yells the Chairman, 'because you will be in jail.'

" 'Then I will break your jail up,' I said, 'because I am entitled to liberty whilst pursuing happiness.'

" 'Contempt of court!' bangs the Chairman."

Just then the bartender flashed the lights off and on three times, indicating that it was time to close the bar, so I interrupted my friend's imaginary session of the Un-American Committee.

"Listen," I said, "you're intoxicated, and when you are intoxicated, you talk right simple. Things are not that simple."

"Neither am I," said Simple.

43

Race Relations

"Don't let's talk about it," he said when I asked him about Joyce. "Don't let's even mention her name. I can't stand it. I have tried every way I know to make up with that woman. But she must have a heart like a rock cast in the sea. I have also tried every way I know to forget her. But no dice. I cannot wear her off my mind. I've even taken up reading. This week I bought all the colored papers from the *Black Dispatch* to the *Afro-American,* trying to get a race-mad on, reading about lynchings, head-whippings, barrings-out, sharecroppers, cheatings, discriminations, and such. No dice. I have drunk five bottles of beer tonight and I'm still sober. Nothing has no effect. So let's just not talk about Joyce.

"There is a question, anyhow, I want to ask you because I wish to change the subject," said Simple.

"Them colored papers are full of stuff about Race Relations Committees functioning all over the country, and how they are working to get rid of the poll tax and to keep what few Negroes still have jobs from losing them, and such. But in so far as I can tell, none of them committees is taking up the real problem of race relations because I always thought *relations* meant being related. Don't it? And to be related you have to have relations, don't you? But I don't hear nobody speaking about us being kinfolks. All they are talking about in the papers is poll taxes and jobs."

"By relations, I take it that you mean intermarriage? If that is what you mean, nobody wants to talk about that. That is a touchy subject. It is also beside the point. Equal rights and fair employment have nothing to do with intermarriage."

"Getting married," said Simple, "is also a equal right."

"You do not want to marry a white woman, do you?" I asked.

"I do not," said Simple, "but I figure some white woman might want to marry me."

"You'd better not let Joyce hear you talking like that," I said. "You know colored women do not like the idea of intermarriage at all."

"I know they don't," said Simple. "Neither do white men. But if the races are ever going to relate, they must also mate, then you will have race relations."

"Race relations do not necessarily have to be on so racy a basis," I said. "At any rate, speaking about them in such a manner only infuriates the South. It makes Southerners fighting mad."

"I do not see why it should infuriate the South," said Simple, "because the South has always done more relating than anybody else. There are more light-skinned Negroes in the South whose pappy was a white man than there is in all the rest of this whole American country."

"True," I said, "many colored people are related to white people down South. But *some* relationships are private matters, whereas things like equal job opportunities, an unsegregated army, the poll tax, and no more Jim Crow cars affect everybody, in bed or out. These are the things Race Relations Committees are trying to deal with all over the country. It would only complicate the issues if they brought up intermarriage."

"Issues are complicated already," said Simple. "Why, I even got white blood in me myself, dark as I am. And in some colored families I know personally down South, you can hardly tell high yellows from white."

"My dear fellow," I said, "the basic social issues which I am talking about are not to be dealt with on a family basis, but on a mass basis. All Negroes, with white blood in them or not, in fact, everybody of whatever parentage, ought to have the right to vote, to live a decent life, and to have fair employment."

"Also to relate," said Simple.

"I keep telling you, race relations do not have anything to do with that kind of relating!"

"If they don't," said Simple, "they are not relations."

"Absurd," I said. "I simply will not argue with you any more. You're just as bad as those Southerners who are always bringing up intermarriage as a reason for *not* doing anything. What you say is entirely beside the point."

"The point must have moved then," said Simple.

"We are not talking about the same thing at all," I said patiently. "I am talking about fair employment, and you are talking about . . ."

"Race relations," said Simple.

44

Possum, Race, and Face

"Since you just came in, how come you've got to go so soon? If you was a good buddy, you'd wait until I have one more beer," said Simple about two A.M. Saturday night in the crowded bar. "I have to get up kinder early in the morning myself, at least by noon. I am going to have Sunday dinner with Joyce! We have made up, man! And she is cooking especially for me. I wish I could invite you, but I can't, 'cause Joyce just invited me *alone*."

"I'm happy to hear you're reunited," I said. "In truth, I am delighted. How did you two effect your reconciliation?"

"We just couldn't stand not to see each other no longer."

"Who gave in first?" I asked. "You or Joyce?"

"We both gave in at once, man. You know how those things is. I forgived her—and she forgived me. Now she is cooking again—and I have got my appetite back."

"What are you going to eat tomorrow?"

"Chicken, since it is Sunday," said Simple, "but I wish it were possum."

"Possum! Now I know you are intoxicated. Where on earth can you get a possum in New York?"

"As many Negroes as there are in Harlem, there ought to be at least one possum around in the fall of the year. Listen, man, tonight if I had a lantern and a hound dog and a gun, and if there was a persimmon tree on Sugar Hill and that possum was up that tree, I'll bet you I would get myself a possum this very night. I bet on that!"

"So you used to hunt possum down home?"

"He could be up a nut tree, too, or whatever kind of tree he was up, me and my hound would find him out and bring him down," declared Simple.

"Do you suppose Joyce knows how to cook a possum?" I asked.

"She might not admit it," said Simple, "but I'll bet you if I brought her one, she would not give it up for silver nor gold. Between her and an oven, that possum would come out good. But I don't reckon nobody in America could cook a possum like my Uncle Tige. The way Uncle

Tige cooked a possum, man, you would not want nothing better on this earth, *never*!"

"I never heard tell of your Uncle Tige before. Who was he?"

"I lived with him and Aunt Minnie for a time when I were ten, eleven, twelve."

"You sure lived with a lot of different relatives."

"I was passed around," explained Simple. "When I were a child, I was passed around. But not even with Grandma Arcie did I eat so good. Not *no* place did I eat so good as with Uncle Tige. Him and Aunt Minnie both liked to eat. They both could cook. And sometimes they would see who could outcook the other. Chitterlings—man, don't talk! Hog jowl, hog maw, pig tails, pig feets! They tasted like the Waldorf-Astoria *ought* to taste—but I know it don't. Corn dumplings, turnip greens, young onions! Catfish, buffalo fish, also perch! Cabbage with cayenne pepper! Tripe! Chime bones and kraut! On Sunday two hens stuffed with sage dressing! Also apple dumpling! Umm-m-huh!

"When they sent me back to my Aunt Lucy, I was so big and fat the schoolteacher looked at me and said, 'Boy, how come you're only in the fourth grade? Big as you is, you ought to be in the low ninth.'

"I had done et so much cracklin' bread I was oozing out grease and so many hominy grits with gravy till my hair was oily and laid down just like a Indian's. I did not have to use no Murray's Pomade then. But that was long ago. And I have not et like that since I come to New York. I would give all the ducks, chickens, and turkeys in the world for a possum.

"A possum for Sunday dinner, man, would be perfect, cooked like my Uncle Tige used to cook him. First singe him in hot ashes, then clean him, then bake him—and that possum all stuffed with apples and fruits and pineapples with great big old red yams laid around his sides, plenty of piccalilli and chowchow and watermelon-rind pickles setting in little cut-glass dishes all around the table. And a great big old jug of hard cider to drink along with that possum. Aw, man, Sunday would be perfect then! But since we will not have a possum, I will have a good dinner tomorrow right on. Joyce is making hot biscuits. And if there is anything I like in this world, it is biscuits."

"Me, too," I said.

"I also like beer," said Simple.

"Then why don't you set us up?"

"Because I haven't got a dime left. I stashed my money home this week since I intend to take Joyce out to a show or something every night now that we made up. But if I ever get hold of a possum in Harlem, you will get some of it. You are my friend."

"Give us a beer, Tony," I said. But the bartender didn't hear me with the juke box going.

"Sometimes I set and remember when I were nothing but a child," Simple continued. "In this noisy old bar I set sometimes and remember when I were a child, and I would not want to be a child again. But some things about it was good—like possum. There was other things I don't like to remember. Some of them things keep coming back to me sometimes when I set in this bar and look in the bottom of my beer glass and there ain't no more beer."

"Another round, Tony!"

"When I were a growing boy and lived with my Aunt Lucy, I used to hear the old folks saying, 'Take all this world and gimme Jesus!' Aunt Lucy were a great Christian, so she used to go to church all the time, facts, she were a pillar of the church. It was her determination to go to Beulah Land, and I do believe she went. In this life she had very little to look forward to—except some more hard work. So no wonder she said, 'Take all this world—but gimme Jesus!' Well, the white folks have taken this world."

"What makes you think that?"

"The earth don't belong to me," said Simple. "Not even no parts of it. This bar does not belong to me. It belongs to Italians. The house I live in does not belong to me. It belongs to Jews. The place I work at belongs to an Irishman. He can fire me any time he gets ready. The insurance I'm in belongs to white folks. And I reckon the cemetery I'll be buried in belongs to them, too. The only thing I own is the clothes on my back—and I bought them from a white store."

"You could at least belong to a colored insurance," I said.

"My mama put me in the Metropolitan when I were knee-high to a duck, and I never did get around to changing my policy," said Simple. "But you are getting me off my point—which is that this *world* belongs to white folks."

"Have you been all over the world?"

"No," said Simple, "but I reads. I listens to world news on the radio every day. I am no dumbbell. I hear all about the Dutch in Java, the Americans in Japan, and the English in Africa, where I hear they have Jim Crow cars. Don't tell me o'fays don't own the world."

"That doesn't necessarily mean they are going to keep it forever," I said, competing with the music on the juke box and the noise at the bar. "The colonial system is bound to come to an end."

"When?" asked Simple.

"Before long. The British Empire is on its last legs. The Dutch haven't got much left."

"But the crackers still have Mississippi, Georgia, Alabama, and Washington, D.C.," said Simple.

"I admit that, but when we start voting in greater numbers down South, and using the ballot as we ought to up North, they won't be as strong as they might have been."

"I hope I live to see that day," said Simple. "Anyhow, the next time I go to church, I am going to pray for the Lord to give back some of this world to colored folks."

"I am glad you intend to go to church. But what you ought to pray is *not* to have the world split up between colored and white nations, but instead, to have the spirit of co-operation enter into *everybody's* soul so that we all could build a decent world together."

"If I was to really pray what is in my mind," said Simple, "the Lord would shut up His ears and not listen to me at all. If I was to pray what is in my mind, I would pray for the Lord to wipe white folks off the face of the earth. Let 'em go! Let 'em go! *And let me rule awhile!*"

"I'll bet you would do a fine job of ruling," I said sarcastically.

"I would do better than they have done. First place, with white folks wiped out, I would stop charging such high rents—so my landlady could charge *me* less. Second place, I would stop hoarding up all the good jobs for white folks—so I could get ahead myself. Third place, I would make the South behave. Fourth place, I would let Asia and Africa go free, and I would build them all schools and air-cooled movies and barbecue pits— and give everybody enough to eat, including possum. Then I would say, 'If you-all colored folks in Africa and Asia and elsewhere, including Harlem, don't behave yourselves, I will drop an atom bomb on you and wipe you out, too—just like the Lord wiped out the white folks!' I would make everybody behave themselves."

"In other words, you would repeat the same old mistake of force and violence that the white nations have been guilty of," I said.

"Except that I would *force* people to be *good,* and get educated, and run themselves, and enjoy Lena Horne and Bing Crosby, and eat aplenty. I would make people do *right.* I would not let them do wrong."

"You would do more than God is doing," I said.

"Man, I would be *a hell,*" cried Simple, "a natural hell!"

"I think you must be drunk," I said. "Stop yelling so loud, or that white bartender will think you're a disgrace to the race."

"Oh," sighed Simple, "there are certainly a lot of disadvantages in being colored. The way that juke box is blaring, a body has to yell. Yet you can't even holler out loud without somebody saying, 'Shsss-ss-s! Don't be so rowdy in front of white folks.' You can't even get drunk and walk staggle-legged down the street without somebody accusing you of disgracing the race. I think Negroes should have as much right to get drunk and misbehave in front of anybody as the next person has, without somebody always throwing it up in our faces about disgracing the race."

Simple paused for a long drink of beer, gulped, took a deep breath, and went on.

"If a colored man even gambles a little penny ante and the place gets raided, there is a big headline in the papers:

HARLEM VICE DEN RAIDED

"But at them downtown clubs they gambles hundreds of dollars every night, never do get raided, and nobody calls them a vice den. But just let a colored man roll one roll—and he is a disgrace to the race. Or take murder and manslaughter, for instant. A white man can kill his wife, cut her up, put her in a trunk, ship her to California, and never get her body out of the baggage room, yet nobody talks about he is a disgrace to the white race. But just let a Negro carve somebody once lightly with a small knife and the papers say:

BIG BLACK BUCK RUNS AMUCK

"Then everybody in Harlem says, 'What a shame for a Negro to act that way,' and 'How is the Race ever gonna get anywhere?' Why, hundreds of white folks kills hundreds of other white folks every day, and nobody says, 'What a shame for a white man to act like that.'"

"Well, being a minority race," I said, "we have to save face. We have to act better than white people act, so they won't brand us as being worse."

"Being worse?" cried Simple, topping Louis Jordan's loudest riff on the juke box. "How could colored folks be worse? Hitler was white and he killed up more folks in *three years* than all the Negroes put together have kilt since B.C. Just look at all them colored mens Southerners have lynched and burnt! How could we be any worse? But me—if I even have one *small* penknife in my pocket that I never use, and I get caught and locked up, they fingerprint me, take my picture and put it in the papers with a big headline:

HARLEMITE BRANDISHES WEAPON

and make out like I am a black disgrace to the U.S.A. I do not think that is right, and if I was ruling the world it would not be. I think I should have as much right as the next one to be a disgrace—if I want to be—without anybody talking about my race."

"*Nobody* has a right to be a disgrace," I said. "That is where you are wrong. I do not appreciate your argument."

"I don't mean people *ought* to kill and murder," said Simple. "But let's get back to what I started with, getting drunk. I see plenty of white men get on the busses drunk, and nobody says that a white man is a disgrace to his race. But just let a colored man get on the bus drunk! Everybody says, 'Tuc-tuc-tuc!' The white folks say, 'That's just like a Negro.' And the colored folks say, 'It's a shame. A disgrace to our group.' Yet the poor man hasn't done a thing but get drunk."

"Nobody, white or colored, has any business getting on a bus or streetcar drunk," I said. "If you are drunk, you should take a taxi home. Drunks are nuisances, staggering around and talking out of turn—like you when you are high. I do not agree with you this evening."

"If you agreed, there would be no point in having an argument," said Simple, pushing back his glass.

"There is not very much point to *your* argument," I said.

"Except," said Simple solemnly, "that I think colored folks should have the same right to get drunk as white folks."

"That is a very ordinary desire," I said. "You ought to want to have the right to be President, or something like that."

"Very few men can become President," said Simple. "And only one at a time. But almost anybody can get drunk. Even I can get drunk."

"Then you ought to take a taxi home, and not get on the bus smelling like a distillery," I said, "staggering and disgracing the race."

"I keep trying to tell you, if I was white, wouldn't nobody say I was disgracing no race!"

"You definitely are not white," I said.

"You got something there," said Simple. "Lend me taxi fare and I will ride home."

45

A Letter from Baltimore

As I walked into Paddy's, there stood Simple grinning from ear to ear. He greeted me like a long-lost brother, pulling me toward the bar as he announced, "This evening the beers are on me and I have the where-with-all to pay for two rounds and a half, so pick up and drink down."

"What, may I ask, is the occasion for this sudden conviviality? Tonight is not Saturday."

"No," said Simple, "but it is a new day right on, a new week, and a new year. They say a man's life changes every seven years. I am in the change. Here, read this letter that I found laying on the radiator in the hall this evening when I come in that I know my landlady tried to peer through the envelope. It's from my wife, Isabel."

"I have no desire to pry into your personal correspondence," I said.

"Read it, man, read it," urged Simple. "Desire or not, read it. I want to hear it in words *out loud* what Mrs. Semple says—because I cannot believe my eyes. Unfold it, go ahead."

"She writes a nice clear hand," I said, "big round letters. You can tell this woman is a positive character. I see she's still in Baltimore, too. Well, here goes:

Dear Mr. Semple:

Jess, at last I have found a man who loves me enough to pay for my divorce, which is more than you was ever willing to do and you are my husband. Now, listen, this man is a mail clerk that owns two houses, one of which he has got rented and the other one he needs somebody to take care of it. His first wife being dead so he wants me for his second. He knows I have been married once before and am still married in name only to you as you have not been willing to pay for the legal paper which grants freedom from our entanglement. This man is willing to pay for it, but he says I will have to file the claim. He says he will get a lawyer to furnish me grounds I have to swear on and that you also have to swear on unless you want to contest. *I do not want no contest,* you hear me? All I want is my divorce, since I have found a nice man, willing to marry me and pay for it, too. I am writing to find out if you will please not make no contest out of this because he has never done nothing to you, only do you a favor by bearing the expenses of the grounds that rightly belong to a husband. Let me hear from you this evening as he has already passed the point where he could wait.

Once sincerely yours but not now,

Isabel

"I suppose you would have no intention of cross-filing," I said.

"I would not cross that wife of mine no kind of way," said Simple, "with a file nor otherwise. My last contest with that woman was such that the police had to protect me. So that man can have her. He can have her! I do not even want a copy of the diploma."

"A divorce paper does not look like a diploma," I said.

"I knew a woman once who framed her divorce and hung it on the wall," said Simple. "But if my wife serves *me* with one, I will throw it out."

"That would render it invalid," I said, "also null and void. You will have to sign all the papers and mail them back to Baltimore so the proceedings can go through."

"Just so they get out of my sight," said Simple. "Joyce would not want no other woman's divorce papers hanging around. If she did, Joyce could have bought them papers herself by now. I gave her the opportunity."

"I am always puzzled as to why you have been so unwilling to pay for your own divorce," I said.

"I told Isabel when we busted up that she had shared my bed, she had shared my board, my licker, and my Murray's, but that I did not intend to share another thing with her from that day to this, not even a divorce. That is why I would not pay for it. Let that other man pay for it and they can share it together."

"But it will free you to marry Joyce," I said.

"Joyce will be free to marry me, you mean."

"Joyce is not being divorced from anyone. You are the one who is being divorced."

"Which means I will no longer be free, then," said Simple. "I will be married again before the gold seal is hardly out from under the stamper."

"That will be good for you. Perhaps you will settle down, stay home, stop running around nights."

"I will," said Simple, "because I will have a home to stay at. I will not have to live in bars to keep from looking at my landlady in the face."

"Maybe married you can save a little money, and get somewhere in the world."

"Them would be my best intentions," said Simple. "Facts is, I always did have ambitions. When I were a little boy in Virginia, my grandma told me to hitch my wagon to a star."

"Did you try?"

"I did," said Simple, "but it must have been a dog-star."

"Well, now things will be different. Joyce is a good girl. You love her and she loves you, so this time you should make a go of it. And I will dance at your wedding."

"You will be my best man," said Simple.

"Well, of course, I'd be delighted—but—but maybe you'd like a relative or some other more intimate friend for your best man. After all, Joyce doesn't know me very well."

"*I* know you," said Simple, "which is enough. As many beers as you have bought me right here at this bar, and as often as you lent me a buck when I was trying to make the week, you deserve to be my best man. So no arguments! Now that my luck is turned, daddy-o, you'll be there at the finish."

"Thanks, old man," I said. "Certainly you seem to be coming out ahead at last—a *free* divorce from a wife you don't like, no contest, no expenses, and, all but for the formalities, a new wife you love."

"I *am* coming out ahead for once," said Simple, "which just goes to prove what's in that little old toast I learned from my Uncle Tige. Listen fluently:

> *When you look at this life you'll find*
> *It ain't nothing but a race.*
> *If you can't be the winning horse,*
> *Son, at least try to place.*

"I believe I have placed—so let's drink to it."

"You have won," I said.

"Providing that Negro in Baltimore keeps his promise to my wife. If he don't, as sure as my name is Simple, I will go down there and beat his head."

"Do you mean to say you'd lay hands on your first wife's second husband?"

"Listen! I married Isabel for better or for worse. She couldn't do no better than to get a free divorce," said Simple. "That man made my wife a promise. *He better not betray her.* If he does, he'll have me to contend with because I dare him to stand in *my* way. I'll fix him! just like that toast says:

> *If they box you on the curve, boy,*
> *Jockey your way to the rail,*
> *And when you get on the inside track—*
> *Sail! . . . Sail! . . . Sail!*
> *In a race, daddy-o,*
> *One thing you will find—*
> *There ain't* NO *way to be out in front*
> *Without showing your tail*
> *To the horse behind."*

"One regrets," I said, "that, after all, life is a conflict."
"I leave them regrets to you," said Simple.

Simple
Takes a Wife

(1953)

To Helen E. Brown

The author and publishers of *Simple Takes a Wife* are grateful to the *Chicago Defender* and to *Phylon* for permission to reprint some of the material in this book.

Contents

Part Two: Manna from Heaven

Part Three: Sassafras in Spring

Part One

Honey in the Evening

1

Seven Rings

Early blue evening. The street lights had just come on, large watery moonstones up and down the curbs. April. The days were stretching leisurely. This particular evening had become too old to eat dinner and too young to do much of anything else. It was unseasonably warm. Tasting spring, Harlem relaxed. Windows, stoops, and streets full of people not doing anything much. In spite of his landlady's request *not* to sit on the steps in front of her house, Simple was sitting there. Harlem has few porches. In his youth in Virginia, Simple had been accustomed to sitting on porches. His youth was some thirty-odd years gone, but the habit remained. The lights looked pretty in the smoke-blue evening of sudden spring. But did Simple see the lights? Who knows? He didn't see me as I came down the street. His legs were stretched out over three steps and he leaned back staring at nothing.

"Good evening," I said, "if you're not too tired to open your mouth."

"Tired, nothing. Man, I'm natural born disgusted," said Simple. "My divorce didn't come through."

"What?"

"That fool man that promised to marry my wife and pay for our divorce, too, did not pay her lawyer to clinch the proceedings," said Simple, "and until he does, the judge will not hand down no decree. Divorces and money is all mixed up in Baltimore. In fact, I believe divorces costs more there than they do here in New York. The last time I asked about a divorce in Harlem, the man told me Three Hundred Dollars. My wife writ me that her present boy friend is paying Four Hundred for hers—and she ain't got it yet—which is hindering *me*, because I am due to marry Joyce. If it had not been that I showed Joyce Isabel's last letter, I do believe Joyce would have thought I am standing her up. But you know as nice as Joyce is to me, I would almost marry that girl *without* a divorce."

"Joyce would hardly want to marry a man who is already married," I said.

"No, but she wants me so bad that if I was to press her, she might even lend me the money to pay for the rest of my wife's divorce. Joyce swore she would never *outright* pay for no other woman's divorce, but a loan is a different thing."

"Why don't you accept the loan?"

"Because I do not want the shadow of nothing having to do with Isabel hanging over me and Joyce. I swore and be damned I wouldn't pay for no divorce for Isabel. Neither will I let Joyce pay for it. If that man in Baltimore who wants to marry Isabel can't even pay for a little old decree for her, he ain't much good. And he is bugging me!"

"I thought you told me the man is a widower who owns two houses and is a very solid citizen."

"That's the jive Isabel wrote. But Isabel might just be trying to shame me by comparison, because I never owned nothing. All I do know is, I wish the man would hurry up and pay that lawyer so me and Joyce can complete our arrangements. Isabel had no business getting my expectations up like this.

" 'I have got all my trousseau clothes,' Isabel wrote me, 'and everything but the decree'—which is where I reckon the man's money went. Isabel done made him buy her a whole lot of clothes. Then she writ on, 'If you was any kind of a husband, Jess Semple, you would help me to get this decree. You ought to want a divorce as much as I do. The least you could do is to assist my husband-to-be pay for your wife-that-was to get rid of you.' "

"What did you answer to that?"

"Nothing," said Simple. "The only answer would be money—and money I do not have. They say silence is golden—which is all the gold she can get out of me. Are you walking toward the corner?"

"Yes."

"I will keep you company as far as the bar. Maybe a little further. Maybe I will take a walk, too."

He rose, sighed, stretched, and, as we filed through the crowded block, for no good reason whatsoever started singing:

> *Two things, Miss Martin,*
> *I cannot stand,*
> *A bow-legged woman*
> *And a cock-eyed man.*

"Kindly lower your voice," I requested.

> *Two things, Miss Martin,*

I adore,
One is some loving—
And the other is
Some more!

"Cease your rowdyism," I said. "People will conclude you're drunk."

Two things, Miss Martin,
That bug a man . . .

Cars sped by. The city hummed like a mechanical beehive. Beneath the street lights among the crowded stoops, the broken end of the song got lost in the early blue. With his mouth open Simple stopped indecisively at the corner to look slowly up and down the street.

"Which way are you going?" I asked.

"Come with me," said Simple, "and I will show you where I am going—to Joyce's."

"There is no point in my going with you to see Joyce. She's not *my* girl."

"You can keep the ball rolling," said Simple. "With me, Joyce is kind of silent these days. But if you are there, she will act like we got company—then *I* can talk, too. Otherwise, she will just *um-hum* when I say something and let it go at that. There is nothing worse than a woman that will not talk. You get so used to women rattling away, that when they keep quiet you are scared they will explode. Are you coming with me or not?"

"If I am going to be in an explosion, I'll go. I'd like to see Joyce give you a good dressing down. Here you are, a man in your prime—and can't pay for one divorce. Why, some men at your age are already paying three alimonies."

"White men," said Simple. "The most alimonies I ever knowed a Negro to pay was *one*—and he didn't keep that up to date. What I like about Joyce is she would never alimony me. Joyce works and makes her own money and does not want anything out of me but love."

We stopped in front of the neat brownstone house around the corner from Seventh Avenue where Joyce roomed. He rang seven times.

"Joyce knows my ring," said Simple.

Nobody came to the door. He rang again, counting out loud from one to seven.

"Maybe Joyce is in the bathroom."

No answer.

"I wonder should I ring for her big old fat landlady?"

"You have walked way over here," I said, "so you might as well find out if she's home or not."

Simple rang one long ring and two short, the landlady's private signal. Presently the floor boards creaked. The inner door opened. An enormous figure filled the vestibule. Then the outer glass door cracked just a crack.

The landlady said, "I knowed it was you all the time. Joyce is not here. She went to a movie."

"You don't know which one?"

"Joyce does not tell me her business. There's a draft in this door, Mr. Semple. Excuse me."

The door closed.

"Um-huh! You see," said Simple. "Joyce has done made that woman mad at me, too. Done told her something. Her landlady is most in generally more pleasanter than mine, but you see how she acts tonight. When a woman is mad at a man, she always wants every other woman to be mad at him, too. Well, daddy-o, let's go have a beer. We done took our walk."

So we went and had a beer. Simple drank in silence, but not for long. As he ordered a second round, he said dolefully, "These are dark days for me, man. Joyce is as touchous as a mother hen done lost her chicks. She knows she has not lost me—she just has to wait a little longer. But she acts like I have put her down. That girl is bent, bound and determined to marry me. She has asked me seven times already.

" 'I'm tired of not seeing hair nor hide of neither ring, license, orange blossoms or veil,' Joyce told me last week. 'I try to keep my head up and my back straight—but how straight can a girl's back be without breaking? You know I don't believe in no common-law stuff. But in the framework of marriage, that's different. Jess Semple, my patience is about done wore out with you.'

"I said, 'Joyce, don't render me liable to commit bigamy.'

"Whereupon, she stuck her hands on her hips and yelled, 'Bigamy? Every time I mention marriage to you, *bigamy* is the first thing that jumps into your mind. I'm warning you, Jess Semple, for the last time, if you don't hurry up and think of something more respectable to commit besides bigamy, you're going to see mighty little of me. I have never known any one Negro so long without having some kind of action out of him.'

"I said, 'Baby, you talk like you have been married before.'

"Joyce said, 'No, I have not been married before. But I have been proposed to. You have not even yet, in going on several years, formally proposed to me, let alone writing my father for my hand.'

"I said, 'I did not know I had to write your father for your hand. This is the first time you mentioned that, honey. I thought this here living-together business, when it does come off, would be just between us.'

"She says, 'I do not like that *living-together* phrase, Jess Semple. We will be legally married as soon as you get legally divorced—and there will be no *living together* to it. Also, you will write my father.'

" 'Joyce, you know I cannot write good,' I said.

" 'Then I can dictate for you, and tell you what to say.'

"I said, 'I know what to say. But I still do not understand how a girl as big and old as you are has to have somebody ask her father if she can get married.'

" 'Marriage involves changing *my* name to *your* name, that is why,' says Joyce. 'Since I bear my father's name—although he is only my step-father—you have to ask him can you change it. Then I will cease to be *Miss* Lane and become *Mrs.* Semple—as soon as that woman in Baltimore lets loose of your name. Do you reckon she will ever do so?'

" 'The wheels of justice grind slow. But, Joyce, you know I mean well. I would have taken your hand long ago, had it not been for bigamy.'

" 'I thought your first wife's name was Isabel, not *Bigamy*.'

" 'Don't be funny,' I says. 'You know what I mean. I do not want to get in jail and leave you in disgrace. I love you, woman! I want all to be well with us, also between us. I will even write your old man tomorrow, if you say so.'

" 'My *father*,' says Joyce, 'not my *old man*. I never did like crude-talking people. I bet no child of mine better not call you *old man*, nor me *old lady*. Any child of mine will be brought up after me, not after you.'

" 'That's good,' I said. 'One thing, Joyce, for which I admires you is your culture. Was your old man cultured? I mean, *your father*?'

" 'He is a bricklayer,' said Joyce, 'but my mother was a Daughter of the Eastern Star, also a graduate of Fessenden Academy. She always worked around fine white folks. She never did work for no poor white trash. In fact, she wouldn't. Poor folks have nothing to give nobody—least of all culture. I come by mine honestly.'

" 'Well, you will have to tell me what to ask your father because I am not used to writing no man for a woman's hand.'

" 'When the time comes, I will put you straight,' said Joyce. 'But do not let it be too long. After all, I am only human and June don't come but once a year.'

" 'Meaning what?'

" 'Meaning I might meet some other man before next year,' said Joyce.

"That is what hurt me about our conversation, daddy-o. Pulling all them technicalities on me, then talking about *she might meet some other man*. Joyce better not meet no other man. She better not! Do, and I will marry her right now this June, in spite of my first wife, bigamy, or her old man—I mean, her father. Don't Joyce know I am not to be trifled with? I am Jesse B. Semple."

2

What Can a Man Say?

Sweep, rain, over the Harlem roof tops. Sweep into the windows of folks at work, not at home to close the windows. Wet the beds inside bedrooms almost as narrow as the bed against the window. Sweep, rain! Have fun with the brownstone fronts of rooming houses full of people boxed in *this* room, *that* room, seven rings, two rings, five, nine.

"Who are they ringing for? It ain't me, is it? Did you count how many rings?"

Turn into a spring equinox, rain, and blow curtains from Blumstein's until they flop limp-wet. Dampen drapes. Soak shades until they won't pull up or down. Make folks mad who come home from work and find everything all wet.

" 'It was so hot this morning any fool might have knowed it was going to rain. What did you leave the windows open for? It ain't summer yet. You just don't think,' says my big old landlady to me.

"Yet and still, it ain't my fault," said Simple, "she's got arthritis-rheumatis so bad she can't get up the steps to shut the windows when it starts raining. Now she comes blaming me for letting *my* things get all wet! I come home from work tonight and find a puddle of water in the middle of the floor. Mattress soaked where I pushed the bed up against the window on account of the heat. The Bible my grandma gave me with my birth date writ in it looking like somebody run it through the laundrymat. Ink all blurred. Nobody'll ever know when I was borned.

"Old landlady says, 'Ain't you got a birth certificate?'

"I says, 'No'm.'

"She says, 'Why, even my dog has got one on his pedigree.'

"I says, 'I am not a dog, so I has no pedigree. And everything I own has got wet upstairs today, madam.'

" 'I *tells* you roomers to pull down your windows when you leave the house. I cannot be running up and down steps looking after you-all. That is not my responsibility. You due to protect my house. Who's gonna pay for my rug when it moulds and mildews that this rain done wet up in your room? Who's gonna buy me a new mattress for your Third Floor Rear when that one wets out? Mr. Semple, *I could charge you* with destroying my property. Don't come down here telling me about your things got all wet today. If you had a wife to stay home and shut the windows, instead of running around with them gals from the corner bar—that Zarita, for instance, passing here yesterday with her head looking like a hurrah's nest, switching worse than a dog. Trixie has got more respect for herself than that bar-butterfly with that red streak in the front of her hair.'

"'Madam, you are talking about my friends. I will thank you to hush. As much as I have walked your dog for you, is that the thanks I get?'

"'My dog is at least a lady. Ain't you, Trixie?'

"'That dog makes me sick. I cannot stand such talk. I am going upstairs and hang my bed clothes up to dry.'

"'Bring your dirty sheets down here and I'll give you some fresh ones—*this once*. Your week's almost up anyhow.'

"'Three flights up—three flights down—three flights back up again! Thank you. Don't do me no favors. Do, and you'll want me to be walking that lady hound of yours around again. Madam, I am not a dog walker. And I reckon my sheets will dry out by the time I get ready to go to bed.'

"'Which is three, four A.M. Every night the Lord sends I hear you coming in staggle-legged.'

"'Don't you never sleep?'

"'With roomers in the house, how can I? No telling what you-all might do. I'm responsible.'

"'Well, I wish you'd be responsible for folk's things getting all wet when a thunderstorm comes up and a man is at work. That is more important than hearing who comes in when.'

"'I know what my responsibilities is. You don't need to tell me. And if you just must keep on chewing the rag, complaining and arguing, you move.'

"'I have been here seven years, madam, but you liable to find me gone *soon*. Then who will walk your dog for you? Don't none of your other roomers do it. Neither your husband. Madam, you will miss me when I move. Won't she, Trixie?'

"'Don't try to get on the good side of me through Trixie.'

"'Madam, have you got a good side?'

"'Mr. Semple, I am hurted by that last remark. I tries to treat everybody nice. I do! And I am hurted. As often as I let you slip a week, sometimes two, on your rent. Nice as I been to you compared to most landladies, I tell you, I am hurted. You can just move, if you want to. Move.'

" 'Madam, I do not wish to move. And I did not mean what I said. You got three or four good sides. I expect more. If it wasn't so damp right now I would walk Trixie for you.'

" 'Trixie! Trixie! Trixie! Do you think that nobody else lives downstairs here in this Dutch basement but Trixie? Ain't you got no regard for me?'

" 'Madam, does you want me to walk *you?*'

" 'I likes to go out once in a while myself. And you ain't never so much as invited me to Paddy's for a beer in all these years you been living in my house.'

" 'But you got a husband, madam.'

" 'It were my understanding that you also had a wife when you moved in here. But that does not, and has not, stopped you from running with every woman that wears a skirt—and some in pedal-pushers.'

" 'But, madam, you always said you did not drink.'

" 'What I say and what I do are two different things.'

" 'Do you want me to bring you back a can of beer when I go out?'

" 'Oh, no! Don't worry about *me,* Mr. Semple. Just bring Trixie some dog food—since you are so concerned about her. And excuse me, I am going to fix my husband's dinner. I don't need a thing. Excuse me.'

" 'You are excused,' I said, to which she did not answer. Wrong again! What can a man say to a woman that is not wrong, be they landladies, wives, or Joyce?"

3

Empty Room

One night Paddy's bar for once was strangely quiet. I soon learned why. Watermelon Joe was going around taking up a collection to bury a fellow who had just died that day, a boy everybody around that corner knew. The bartender said the fellow had been in Paddy's drinking just a few nights before, now he was gone. The juke box was not playing as continuously that evening because most of the men had given their last spare change to help put their late bar-buddy away. Everybody was a little sad.

"Zarita has just been in here, cried, and gone," Simple said. "I expect she knew that boy better than she makes out—Zarita being a woman. We all knew him pretty well. Just to think, here today, gone tonight! I can't quite get it. You know, pal, I have not been around people dying very much."

"Neither have I," I said.

"But once in Baltimore, in the first house where I roomed, a man died quick like that. It was before me and Isabel got married so I was living alone, being just a young man. I did not know this fellow who died very well, but he roomed next to me on the same floor, three rings. Sometimes I would hear him stumbling around in his room, humming and singing to himself:

> *I got the Dallas blues*
> *And the Fort Worth*
> *Heart's disease . . .*

Once in a while we shared a quart of beer together and talked about the weather. But I never went nowhere with the man and he never went nowhere with me, and I only ran into him once on the street, so I did not know him very well. But when he died I missed him. Just like sometimes when somebody dies in the papers that you did not know, President Roosevelt, or a movie star. You never did know them to speak to them a-tall, but you miss them right on.

"Well, when this same-floor roomer of mine died, I were asleep. The next morning, they told me he was dead. It was hard to believe because

I had just seen the guy the night before in the hallway going to the bathroom to soak his corns.

"He told me, 'My feet's been giving me hell today.'

"I said, 'Not you, but me. I do believe black feet hurt worse than white.'

"We laughed. He said, 'Dark men, dark feet, dark days.'

"That were the last thing that man said to me. Next morning he were gone.

"Where do people go when they are gone? And why? One day, here, the next day, gone. They could not find no address for that man's people for nobody to claim the funeral. Maybe none of his kinfolks had the money to pay for it. And he did not have no insurance. Anyhow, he went unclaimed. The city came and took him away, Baltimore City, which is a prejudiced town, so I do not know what they do with colored folks who have died, maybe give them to the medical students, because even when you are alive they do not treat you very well. Anyhow, the city taken that man. I did not see him come down the hall no more that day, nor never.

"I have not seen nobody die in their presence, so I do not know how that roomer went except that he went in the night when he were alone by hisself. I would not want to go like that. I would want somebody with me. I want some woman to hold my hand, some slim tall sweet old gal like Joyce to say, 'Baby, don't go! I do not *know* what I can do without you.'

"I would want somebody to miss me—even *before* I am gone. I want somebody to cry real loud, scream and let the neighbors know I am no longer here. I want my passing to be a main event, 'Dear Jesus, Jesse B. is gone! The one I love is gone! Why did you take him this evening, Lord?'

"In fact, if there are more than one woman crying over me, I will be glad. If there are three or four, or seven, I would not care. Let the world, the rest of the womens in it, and everybody know that I have been here and gone, been in this world, and passed through, and left a mighty mourning. I want some woman to yell, 'Why? Why did you take him, Lord?'

"When I go, I would not like to die like that fellow in Baltimore with nobody to claim his body, nobody to lay out Five Hundred Dollars for a funeral, nobody to come and cry. Only a lonesome few roomers knowed when he were taken down the steps with his room door left open—and it were empty in there. Empty, empty, and quiet.

"No, I would not want to be carried out that way, feet first. I would really like to walk down the steps, out to my own funeral—if I had to go at all. Anyhow, after I'm gone, I would like there to be such another weeping and wailing as you never heard. Not quiet like it were that day in Baltimore.

"Not having been around people very much who are dying, I did not know until then how it felt to see somebody walking down the hall tonight, then not see them in the morning because they are gone. *Gone* with a big letter, *gone* with a capital *G*. I mean *solid and really* not-here-no-more—gone. Silent, with nobody to scream. Nobody like Zarita around to make a big noise, nor Joyce to cry sweet and polite. Nobody to yell, 'He's gone.' His name I can't recall. But maybe why I remember that man in Baltimore so well is because there was no human to cry, 'Gone! He's gone!'

"The landlord said to his wife the next day, 'Put that sign—ROOM FOR RENT—back in the window. But don't let nobody have that room unless they pay a full week in advance.'

"That's all anybody said after that roomer were gone. But one night somebody come and rung his bell, three rings. He were not there."

4

Better than a Pillow

"After that man's dying I got to thinking about myself—suppose I was to die upstairs all alone *by myself* in a lonesome room! Man, I hustled up quick on a stick-close gal before the year was out. I had had three or four on-again-off-agains and plenty of fly-by-nights since I'd arrived in Baltimore City. But before I got married, this was the first woman I ever stayed with regular, the one I'm gonna tell you about. I lived with her so long she started to calling herself Mrs. Semple."

"You never told me about her," I said.

"I know I didn't. There are some things I have not told God—He has to find out for Himself. I am somewhatly ashamed, even now."

"I am not God, so I won't pass judgment," I said.

"Well, I will tell you. She was the first woman I ever went with steady. Also she was the first woman for which I ever kept a job. Yet and still, I did not love that woman, I don't believe. There was always other womens I had my eyes on, younger and sharper, like Marvalene, or that fly baby-faced chick named Cherie. And I did not have to give that woman I lived with my money. She did not ask for it—so I spent it on other womens. But I always went back to her. That woman was home to me.

"Now, that's funny, ain't it? I did not give her my money, yet for her sake I kept a job, respectable. Up to that time I had quit and rested any time I wanted to. She settled me down, in fact, almost got me housebroke. She were a good influence in my life. I wasn't but nineteen, twenty, something like that. We lived together going on two years. She didn't leave me. I left her. But I bet right now if I was to write that woman and ask her for something, she would send it to me.

"Do you want me to tell you what that woman was like? Boy, I don't know. She was like some kind of ocean, I guess, some kind of great big old sea, like the water at Coney Island on a real hot day, cool and warm all at once—and company like a big crowd of people—also like some woman you love to be alone with, if you dig my meaning. Yet and still, I wasn't *in love* with that woman. Explain me that, daddy-o."

"That's deep psychology," I said. "It'd probably take Freud to explain why you think of water when you think of that woman. I didn't get *that* far in college, so I can't explain it. You haven't told me anything about her, anyhow, except generalities. Who was she? Where did you meet her? Was she a rich widow, or what?"

"She were not rich," said Simple, "but she were settled. She worked out in service for wealthy folks and she got up early and come home late, and she did not have but two Thursday afternoons and every other Sunday off. Before she met me, she slept on the job. But after she met me, and we got acquainted, we taken a furnished room together. She was considerable older than I were."

"Now I begin to get a clearer picture of the liaison," I said.

"I didn't lay it on," said Simple. "It just kinder growed on both of us. I met her in a beer garden one Sunday night on the way to church and she asked me to go with her. It were a friendly Baptist Church, so the next Sunday I met her in the bar again—and we went to church again. She asked me did I want to escort her home, so I rid way out in the suburbans on the streetcar with her to the white folks' mansion where she stayed. She kissed me goodnight. Then I rid way back downtown to my cubbyhole. She asked me did I want to come out some night to dinner, or else some Thursday afternoon when she was off. She said she would cook me a pot of greens. Well, you know I will ride a long, long ways for greens. So I went out, et, and kissed her goodnight. She was kind of settled for a young boy like I was then, but she had nice ways, no glamour ways, just nice ways. But I did not try to spend the night."

"What was her name?"

"Mabel," said Simple, "just plain old Mabel. One evening she told me, 'Honey, I might adopt you if I could get the consent of your parents.'

"I said, 'Baby, my parents don't even know where I am at. They ain't hardly kept track of me since they borned me.'

"Mabel said, 'You are a good-looking black boy, Jesse. I just like to set and look at you.'

"Sometimes she looked at me so hard I would turn my eyes away. Anyhow, we kept getting acquainted better and better. Mabel had some friends in town so she took me around there to meet them, church people older than I were, nice married respectable folks who got high on just *one* quart of beer, all of them, including Grandma. It were at their house that it happened on a Sunday evening.

"They had a nice fire going in the base-burner and it were warm as toast and we had et a nice big Sunday dinner kind of late in the afternoon that Grandma had cooked. Long about dusk-dark it started snowing outside and kept on coming down. It were November. Mabel told her friends she did not have her overshoes with her so she did not see how she could go with them tramping through the snow to evening services with nothing on but open-work sandals.

"So Wilbur said, 'Why don't you and Jess stay here and keep the fire burning while we run around to the church? Hattie Belle is on the Usher Board so she has to go. And Grandma would die if she didn't get there to put in her Dollar Money, not having attended this morning.'

"So Wilbur and his wife put their two kids to bed, and they and her mother bundled up and went on through the snow to the church. Mabel and me was left setting in the parlor with the radio on when they departed. There wasn't but two lights in the room, and Mabel turned one of them out, which left just the red one—and the fire glowing through the cracks of the stove, friendly. We set on the davenport. By the time them folks got back from Zion Baptist Church we was the same as married in the sight of God.

"Wilbur's family was respectable folks, and, his wife being an usher in the church, Mabel did not want them to think nothing like that what had happened *had* happened whilst they was away. So, long before they got back, all the lights in the parlor was turned on again—including lights that hadn't even been burning when they left. We was listening to Walter Winchell.

"Wilbur's wife had brought some ice cream so we all sat around the kitchen table and talked a while. Then I spent Two Dollars and Fifteen Cents to take Mabel out to where she worked in a taxi and get myself back to the car line, whence I rid in to town.

"The next night I had a date with that young chick, Cherie, but I did not go, being broke. I called up old Mabel instead and we talked a long time. I put three nickels in the phone before we got through. That coming Tuesday, I went out to see her, but I did not stay overnight. She would not let me.

"Mabel said, 'I am working for respectable people with children in the house, and I have never kept no Negro here with me overnight—not even a child.'

"She were digging me on account of my young age. I reckon she was about thirty-five. The next coming Thursday, when she were off, was the first time she had visited my little old beat-up furnished room.

"She said, 'I am going to make some curtains for you.'

"She did. She also made me a pair of pajamas with a monogram *J-S* on them and give them to me for Christmas, the first pajamas I ever had. They helped to keep me warm for that were a hard winter in Baltimore.

Most of the time it blowed and snowed and blowed. And I caught cold from going out to see Mabel so much. She gave me some hot lemonade with a shot of whiskey in it.

"Mabel says, 'Jess, I believe I ought to move in town so's I can look after you. I do not *have* to sleep on my job. I was just saving rent, being's as how I did not have nobody. Sometimes I get so lonesome I hold my own hand for company. Now that I have got someone, I do not like to be way out yonder in the suburbans amongst nothing but white folks on these cold nights. Let's me and you get ourselves a room next week.'

"That is how we shacked up. The day she moved, I moved. It was a good thing we was *together* in that big old furnished room, too, because it was so cold that winter we both would have friz if we had not kept each other warm. In fact, it was so cold we moved again. We found a house that at least had heat, if not much of anything else. There we settled down.

"I found out how much better it is to lay your head on somebody's arm than on a pillow. But womens are sensitive. They get shame-faced. Mabel would not go around to see Wilbur and his wife much no more, neither did she attend their church.

"She said, 'What will they think, especially Grandma, about me, a woman going on thirty-five years old living with a young man like you? That is why I don't want to go around to their house.'

"I said, 'I would not care what they think.'

"She said, 'You are a man. Wilbur is, too. But his wife is a woman. Maybe if I had not had such a hard road to go, and my first two husbands had not been so no-good, I wouldn't do this. It ain't respectable. But I work hard for a living, and I got a right to have somebody. You don't think I'm a bad woman, do you? Even if I am a fool, Jesse, honey, I love you.'

"Very often she would say she must be a fool at her age, liking a young boy like me. Then I would kiss her, and she would say, 'I love you.'

"I would lie like in a moving picture, 'I love you, too.'

" 'Two husbands,' she would say, 'and neither one of them as sweet as you, nowhere near. One dead, and left no insurance. The other one quit, and took my radio and my electric clock.'

"I natural born felt sorry for that woman and I liked her, so I would say, 'Don't worry about it, Mabel. Don't talk about the past, baby.'

"And she would say, 'You're *my* baby to me. But I had a rocky road, Jess, a rocky road.'

"Afterwhile we would go to sleep and sleep till the alarm rung. Cold old dawning of another day."

"Mabel sounds like a pretty good old girl to me," I said. "You haven't mentioned any fights, quarrels, arguments, or anything like that, such as you went through later with your wife."

"We had none," said Simple, "until the last one—and that was terrible. Mabel and I did not fuss and fight, never. Maybe it was because she were not my wife, also she were older and wiser than Isabel. Mabel had a good heart and she talked soft. She just looked, and cried, when her feelings were hurt—not like that woman I married, who *hollered*."

"But didn't your wife have a good heart, too?"

"Isabel talked so fast and so loud I never found out about her heart. But Mabel was soft-spoken, like I just told you. If I even growled at her, she would hang her head. If I barked, she would cry. But if I barked at my wife, she would bark right back at me, also bite if she got close enough. Isabel were a hell on wheels. I have heard tell, from men who have had lots of womens, that a wife is always worse than your girl friend, and I believe that to be true. I never did argue with no woman as much as I did with the one I married."

"Mabel never suggested marriage?"

"Her second husband didn't leave her no divorce when he departed," said Simple, "and he were not dead. Anyhow, Mabel knowed she was too old for me, thirty-five, and me nineteen-like. She always said, 'Jess, honey, the time will come when I will be no good to you. Maybe that's why I just like to lay here now and look at you.

"I'd say, 'You will always be good to me—and *for* me, too.'

"She would say, 'June-time is a good month, sugar, but it goes away and stays all winter. When it comes back in the spring, it don't always come back the same. And for some folks, June don't come back a-tall.'

"I would say, 'I'm no June-bug. Kiss me, baby.'

"Then Mabel would laugh and say, 'I'm no baby.'

"I would say, 'You're my baby to me.'

"Then she would laugh some more. And sometimes, when she was laughing, I thought she was crying. Afterwhile I would go to sleep with my head on her arm, which was better than a pillow. Maybe she was still looking at me. But before you knowed it, that old alarm clock would be ringing, and it seemed like the middle of the night. But it wasn't. It was morning."

5

Explain That to Me

"I love to be woke up easy," continued Simple. "Maybe that is what I liked about Mabel. On them cold mornings after the alarm went off, if I turned over and snoozed a little while more, she would let me sleep until she got dressed, then wake me up gentle-like before she went to work, since she had to be on her job early. But I had time to make myself some coffee before I went out. Her white folks was crazy about Mabel because she never missed being at work in time to cook breakfast for their children and get them off to school. Then she got breakfast for the old man to get him down to the office. Then she made toast and coffee for the Madam about ten. By that time she had been at work a long time. And she worked hard.

"But I was ashamed of Mabel. Just as she didn't like to take me around to Wilbur's house any more, or to none of her church friends after we started to living together, because I was a young boy, so I didn't take her around to none of my friends or to the bar where they hung out, because she was a settled woman. She didn't know the jive and couldn't lindy-hop the first step. She were neat and clean, but not young and sharp. She were sweet but didn't have what the boys call *class*. You know what I mean, no glamour. You see them around Harlem by the thousands—nice respectable womens that don't have but one boy friend at a time—which may be the reason they're so nice. They don't have class. They look like women who keep house fine and cook good—but a cat can't show them off at the Shalimar, neither the Theresa Bar. At Sugar Ray's they would be out of place.

"As nice as Mabel was to me, I ought to've been ashamed to be ashamed of her. But a young man do not have much sense. So when I fell for that little teen-age, Cherie, I started not being home nights when Mabel would get home from work. I started coming in any old time, twelve, one, two o'clock in the morning, then eating what Mabel had brought me.

"All she would say was, 'Baby, you won't get enough sleep to go to work in the morning.'

"I would say, 'Don't worry about me,' as I et from the thank-you pan.

"She would say, 'I does worry about you. I can't help it.'

"But she never did ask me where I had been—until one night I stayed out *all* night. Then she said, 'Jess, where did you stay?'

"When I said, 'None of your damn business,' Mabel cried.

"I thought I was supposed to be a man and ignore her. But I guess that were the beginning of the end. She did not get much sleep that winter whilst I was running around with Cherie, taking her to dances over in Washington, and staying out till all hours. Mabel got thin and dark circles came under her eyes. Sometimes she would leave a note in the empty bed if she left for work before I got home in the morning:

> *Baby, please wait for me this*
> *evening before you go out.*

I usually got home from work about six o'clock. Mabel didn't get home until maybe nine or ten P.M. after the white folks had been served their dinner. She wanted me to wait for her. But it was always the *very* day that she would leave a note that I would not wait. I reckon I wanted to show Mabel who was the man in the house, also that I were not a child she could tell when to come and go. But it was not until I stayed out three days straight one week-end which were her Sunday off, that she turned her back on me in the bed. I slept on my own arm that night. I did not hear her crying, but the next morning her pillow were wet.

"That were the week-end I spent in Washington with Cherie at the Whitelaw Hotel, and we had a high old time. But who should I run into on 'U' Street in Washington on Saturday afternoon but Wilbur and his wife, Hattie Belle, who had come over to see the cherry blossoms which bloom in the spring! They went back to Baltimore Saturday night. And it were that Sunday morning, of all Sundays, that Mabel went to church. Being home by herself in that big old furnished room without me, she decided to go and worship.

"At church the first thing Wilbur's wife said was, 'Mabel, we seen Jess in Washington yesterday with a pretty high-yellow, dressed back, hanging onto his arm.'

"When I returned from Washington about two o'clock Sunday night—or rather Monday morning—Mabel did not say a word, although her eyes were open when I turned on the light. She just looked at me while I took off my clothes. When I got in bed, she turned her back.

"I was tired, so I slept good, anyhow, not worried about a thing— too beat to worry. Had I been older, I might've been afraid Mabel would have killed me in my sleep. But when you are young, you don't have sense enough to be afraid of women nor beasts. I slept. The next morning when I just barely heard that old alarm go off, I didn't wake up enough to realize it was almost time to go to work. Mabel left me in bed and departed. When I did wake up, I saw where her pillow was wet. And that night she did not leave a note for me to wait.

"If I was quitting, I should have quit her then. But not knowing my own mind, I made it hard for Mabel, keeping late hours, igging her, and playing Cherie. Then, one day while Mabel was at work, I packed my clothes and left. But I did not do her like her second husband did—I did not take our clock nor her radio, just myself.

"I thought I was going to move right in with Cherie. But Cherie said, 'No, baby, I ain't situated right to have you living with me.' In fact, she acted real surprised. 'Honey, you are more serious than I took you to be. Besides, I thought I told you, I got a nice old married man who pays my rent. He wouldn't like me rooming with you.'

"Chump that I was, I kept on seeing her, though, taking her out, and giving her half my pay check each and every week. Cherie had class—and I paid to gaze upon it. The way the boys I worked with made admiration over her when we passed tickled me no end. She was a beautiful thing to have hanging around on your arm. Daddy-o, she *was* fine, and only eighteen. I was fascinated by that woman. I knowed she was nothing but a playgirl, like Zarita is now, but I didn't care. She was the first sure-enough glamour chick I ever had contact with and I felt like a solid ton.

"I put down Marvalene, who was an older kid about my own age of twenty or so that I kind of liked and used to meet sometimes in the candy store in the early evening. I put down all my other interests for Cherie. In fact, Cherie took so much of my dough that I had nothing left to spend on anybody else anyhow—except that I did manage to buy myself a fall suit on credit so I could look hep when I took Cherie out.

"I had on this new suit, draped down, reet-pleated and pegged, the night Mabel no doubt must have saw me as I escorted Cherie down the avenue to the Morocco Bar. When I looked up from the booth we was snuggled in, Mabel were standing there looking me dead in the eyes.

"What did I say? Nothing. I were struck dumb. I was not scared. But it was like a wave had washed over me. I was confused.

"Cherie was not very comfortable herself. 'Do you know this woman, Jess?' Cherie asked me. 'What's she standing here looking at us for?'

"Mabel did not raise her hand nor her voice. She just stood and looked at Cherie, one of them long silent looks.

"All of a sudden Cherie screamed. People thought there was a fight in the bar. But there wasn't no fight. Mabel did not do a thing but stand like a statue just outside that booth and look at us.

"Cherie screamed again. She jumped up and scrambled out of the booth and ran past Mabel out of the bar. She ran out the side door, screaming all the time, although Mabel didn't do a thing but just look at her that long quiet look.

"When Cherie had gone, Mabel said, 'Jess, come home with me and talk.'

"Thinking I was due to be a man in front of all them big-time bar-friends of mine, I said, 'Woman, if you want to talk to *me,* talk here.'

"She said, 'I do not want to talk to you in this place.'

"I said, 'I'm through with you, anyhow.'

"She said, 'I am through with you, too. But I hate to get through like this.'

"I said, 'Like what?'

"She said, 'Like this.'

"I didn't answer. That was the longest minute I ever spent. She didn't say nothing, and I didn't say nothing. Then all of a sudden her eyes screamed. Not a sound came out of her mouth, but her eyes screamed.

"Mabel drew back and picked up a bottle on the bar and threw it at me. I ducked. Then she picked up Cherie's glass from the table and broke it into a thousand pieces on the wall behind me. Then she snatched another glass and it flew over my head. Then everything Mabel could lay her hands on made a bull's-eye out of each place from where I had just dodged. She not yet had said a word, nor cried the first cry—until the bartender grabbed her and put her out. Then Mabel cried.

"I was backed up in that booth, as pale as possible, wet and glass-splintered, but not hurt. Mabel could've cut me to death with all that glassware if her aim had been good. But she didn't even hit me—I was a dodging soul. My suit had to go to the cleaners, but not me.

" 'Why don't you slap her head off?' the barflies asked. 'Man, run and catch her and knock her block off before she gets to the corner.'

" 'Aw, let that woman go,' I kept saying to those guys at the bar. 'She don't mean nothing to me. That old has-been don't mean a thing. She's just my used-to-be. She don't mean nothing.'

"I went to the GENTS' ROOM and bent down to wash my face. It seemed like the floor was slipping out from under me in there, like sand does at Coney Island, when a big old wave goes sucking itself backwards into the ocean, pulling out from under your feet, water and sand from under your feet. I was sick when I bent over that washbowl to run the water. Explain that to me, daddy-o. I was sick as hell."

6

Baltimore Womens

"Maybe if Mabel had only hit me just once when she aimed at me, I could've felt *mad*—instead of just sick, sad, and bad. The reason I don't tell nobody about it hardly is because I hate to look back on it. The way I treated that woman, I can't hardly believe it myself. But I did. Like when you look at somebody who has done something awful wrong, you say, 'I can't believe you did it!' But he did do it. But neither one wants to believe it, least of all the one who did it. That's how I hate to believe I ever treated Mabel the way I did. But I did. I did do it. Which is why I reckon I got sick.

"The next time I saw Cherie, Mabel had scared her so bad she started to run from *me*. That made me so mad I thought I might run after her and bop her one, but I didn't. I lost my admiration for that girl, so I put her down. Cherie never got another dime of mine, nor drunk another drink. That July-August I did not have no women to drop in on and visit, which is not good for a fellow. After he gets through working hard all day every man ought to have a little honey in the evening. But that summer, my honey had done turned to fly paper. I was stuck in bad luck.

"Then I met Isabel, coffee-brown, fine-hipped, young and dizzy, with gold hoop earrings in her ears, sharp as a tack, jack! She were just my age. But I did not realize she were *twice* as old as me in the head. To look at that girl, I ought to have knowed she could outsmart me at every turn.

"Isabel worked nights just coining tips in a hot-dog stand. She knew all the big-time jokers in town. But I told her she hadn't met anybody until she met me! And don't you know, she fell for that jive. She could hardly make change for the customers when I was setting on one of her stools. At that time I wore my hair conked—shining like patent-leather. I looked like Kid Chocolate.

"After Cherie took off like a sprint-dasher, I had to taste some kind of lipstick once in a while. So every time I thought about a woman I bought a hot dog. And every time I bought a hot dog, I asked Isabel what time she got off from work so I could walk her home. At first she wouldn't give me any satisfaction.

"Finally she said, 'Ask me some Monday.'

"On Monday evening I was right there. I said, 'This is our night. What time do you check out, leave here, put it down?'

"She said, 'Twelve P.M.'

"I said, 'I'll be waiting right on this stool.'

"Isabel said, 'No, wait on the corner. I don't want nobody to see who I leave the job with.'

"It seems like she portioned each fellow a different night, she had so many. Mine was Monday for a time. But later on I got to know all her boy friends, including Walter, just by eating hot dogs and setting on her stools. When some fellow wouldn't show up at midnight to take Isabel home, there I would be. From then on his night was mine. Man, I were a lover in those days—with a capital L. Lover Man Semple, that was me.

"It were really Isabel's idea that we get married. So we did. And we might have made out right well in the beginning, had we had anything solid to build on—since we started with love. But I had not saved a penny in my whole life and neither had she. When I bought the license and paid for the wedding party—which were a supper with invited friends, since didn't neither one of us have any relatives in Baltimore at that time—I were cold in hand. So we spent our honeymoon in a hotel on Druid Hill and *took up residence*—as they say in the society columns—in a furnished room. Isabel had a lot of clothes. The closet were not big enough to hold her clothes and mine, too, so I hung my one suit on a hanger behind the door.

"Isabel dressed down, and was built, man, built! I loved to tell her, 'Baby, latch on my arm and let's walk down the street this evening.'

"So I made her quit her night job so she could be home when I come and we could go out sporting together. She started to work daytimes in a FISH RESTAURANT and every night she brought home the best old fish sandwiches for her daddy.

"Isabel were right sweet—until she asked me for that *first* fur coat, and I could not produce. The depression were coming on, but I did not realize it. All I knowed was when I got out of work at the foundry, the next job I got as a porter in a dress shop paid less, and the job after that didn't hardly pay nothing at all. When that place closed down, I was broke, busted, and disgusted—with a wife on my hands who could make more money than me and eat where she worked, too. Some of her customers tipped her a dollar. Yet she would take *my* money to buy herself some jewelry. Isabel wore more bracelets on one arm than Sheba had on two.

"We was living when we first got married in a one-room kitchenette in a house full of chinches and Negroes. Negroes I love, but not bedbugs. One nice thing about Harlem is that it does not have as many bedbugs as Baltimore. Harlem has rats, roaches, wine-o's, reefer-heads, and no-good womens, but Harlem does not have bedbugs—except in very dirty places.

"The further South you go, the more bedbugs you see. A friend boy of mine in Richmond took a girl to a hotel one night which he did not investigate. There were so many bedbugs in the room he could not sleep. So he got up and said to the chinches, 'See here, you-all, I rented this room.'

"A great big old bedbug looked up at him and said, 'You just rented this room for one night, buddy. We live here *all* the time.'

"Well, anyhow, to get back to Baltimore, me and Isabel did not wish to be disturbed by bedbugs, so as soon as we moved into that kitchenette, we started battling. First I went out and bought some spray—but the bedbugs stayed. Then we got some coal-oil and oiled the springs. Them bedbugs thought it was Coca-Cola and lapped it up. One night when I come home from work, I took the whole can of kerosene and poured it all over the bedsprings and set fire to it to smoke them out. A woman down the hall got scared and nearly jumped out the window. But it did not scare them bugs. The next night they was back stronger than ever.

"We put shoe-polish tops full of water under the bed-legs, but they swum. Some climbed up on the ceiling and parachuted down. Every morning I was bit everywhere except under the soles of my feet since I slept with socks on.

"The next Sunday after the kerosene burning, I told my old lady to take the bed down, scrub it, and put it in the back yard to air. Also the covers.

"Everything aired all day from our mattress to the kewpie doll that Isabel set on the pillows when I were not home. No good. That night new chinches come out of the walls fresh and strong and hungry. I got so mad, I heated six kettles of hot water and scalded a battalion. Then I set up in the chair the rest of the night. Isabel said nothing could drive her out of her bed, so she stayed put. But when she woke up she were evil.

"She said, 'I could have married Walter and not lived in no rundown place like this with you and all these chinches.'

"I said, 'Go marry Walter then—but you will pay for your own divorce, if you ever get one. Just because Walter's got a car, you think his house don't have bedbugs?'

"She said, 'At least I could go out riding at night and get some fresh air.'

" 'You can go out walking and get some now.'

"And don't you know, Isabel left me that morning without cooking my breakfast! All because of them bedbugs. I started to burn the mattress up but I did not have the cash to buy another one. Besides, the whole house needed burning up. So I just went on out to work. But one of them bedbugs had the nerve to go to work with me! Along about half-past ten A.M. he came crawling out of my coat and said, 'Good-morning!'

"I said, 'If you say another word to me, I will bust you wide open!'

"That is what I started to do when that chinch hit the floor and run like mad. Amongst all them white folks I would be embarrassed to chase him, so I let that bedbug go. But when I got home, I took it out on his relatives.

"As soon as one of them housing projects opened up, me and Isabel moved in, fumigated all our clothes, bought new furniture on credit and, thank God, never did see another bedbug the rest of our married life. It were not bedbugs that brought our happiness to an end. It were Isabel herself. Both womens and bedbugs can *really* bug a man. I don't know which I hate to remember worse, Baltimore womens or Baltimore bugs."

7

Less than a Damn

"At any rate, it were not another woman that caused Isabel and me to break up," Simple continued. "It were Isabel. She was two women in one—one good, one bad. And the depression added to that. The less I brought in, the more she got depressed, mad and bad. She would rag and nag. I would cuss and fuss. She'd raise her voice and I'd raise mine, until finally it came to the point where I almost had to raise my hand. She dared me—and raised a flat-iron. So no blows passed. But my patience broke down completely."

"That is your side of the story," I said. "But no doubt she had some reason to condemn you."

"I'll be con-damned if she did," said Simple. "I tried to treat that woman right. It was not me brought on the depression. How did I know when I got married that in a couple of years I wouldn't be making enough to keep a bird alive, let alone myself. But birds scramble for themselves. That my wife objected to.

"She said, 'You the man of the house. I did not marry you to work my fingers to the bone. I was doing right well when I met you, not begging anybody for my meals. Now, if I get something decent to eat I have to not only cook it, but *pay for it*, too. A wife ought to be able to set down at home, dress up when she goes out, and not worry about a thing. I worried more since I married you than I ever did in all these twenty-some-odd years I have lived before. Besides, my mama thinks I am a fool.'

" 'I did not marry your mama,' I said, 'so I give less than a small damn about her opinion. She's come up here to Baltimore from the Eastern Shore as soon as we got married, expecting to settle her big fat frame down on us. Just because this apartment is too small for even a dog, plus a couple, she gets sore and starts talking about why don't we get a big house and live like folks. We lucky to have this, Isabel, young as we is and just starting out in life. It will take us another two years to pay for these three rooms of furniture—so what would we put in a big house?'

" 'I knowed I should have married Walter all the time,' says Isabel.

"Walter were her Thursday night Negro when she was working at the hot-dog stand, her main dancing man. Walter bell-hopped and also wrote numbers, and sold as much of his *own* licker to the hotel guests as he toted from the bar. Walter were a slick hustler, with a Buick car and no morals. I told Isabel if she so much as said *Wal,* let alone *ter,* again, I would slap her down. Then it was when she raised the iron—after which she started sleeping on the davenport in the parlor."

"Did she ever take up with Walter again?"

"Not that I knows of. Walter had fifteen chicks and did not need Isabel."

"So you could not name Walter as a co-respondent if you were to cross-file your current divorce case?"

"Money were the correspondent," said Simple. "Walter did not enter into the picture, except on Isabel's tongue. Anyway, it were shortly after that that I left town—which is maybe why I drank so much when I first come to Harlem, trying to wear that woman off my mind. I had found out by then that she did not really care a thing about me, only what I had in my pocket."

"I think perhaps you exaggerate," I said. "She probably loved you, but naturally she wanted to be fed, too."

"Fed and furred both, you mean," said Simple. "She were always throwing it up to me that we had been married two years and I had not yet bought her that fur coat I promised."

"Did you make such a promise?"

"You know a man will promise anything when he is trying to make a point, and all I had to go on when I was courting Isabel was my mouth. I guess I have a way of talking real positive, because women seem to believe everything I say—even Joyce. Womens are simple when it comes to a man."

"And men are simple when it comes to women."

"You got something there, daddy-o. Joyce has been planning all winter to marry me in June and I was too simple to tell her I hadn't heard hair nor hide of my divorce since Isabel first wrote that it was started. Finally I got worried and wrote Isabel and Isabel writ back that the second and third payments was still missing. It were a sorry day last month when I broke that news to Joyce, which is why she ain't herself this spring. I wish it were not against the law to commit bigamy because Joyce had her mind set on a honeymoon this June. I reckon, just to remind me of it, last week she went and got a whole lot of vacation folders. She also purchased herself a pocket *Travelguide* for our race, which is a very good book as to where Negroes can stop in different towns.

"I said, 'Joyce, them books is all very pretty, but you know we ain't ready to travel yet.'

"Joyce says, 'I reckon you will be ready perhaps maybe sometime before I die. So I can dream, can't I?'

"Which made me feel bad. And she didn't hardly say nothing to me the rest of the evening. But when her big old fat landlady came down the hall, Joyce asked her which place she thought was the best for honeymooning, the Grand Canyon or Niagara Falls.

"Old landlady said, 'It's all as to whether you prefer a dry climate or a wet one.'

"I said, 'It makes me no difference.' But Joyce did not even answer me."

"Were you ever at the Grand Canyon?" I asked Simple.

"I were," he replied.

"And were you ever at Niagara Falls?"

"I also were," he answered. "In fact, I was at Niagara Falls, and I were at the Grand Canyon."

"I do not wish to criticize your grammar nor change the subject but, listen, my friend, why do you sometimes say, 'I *were*,' and at other times, 'I *was*'?"

"Because sometimes I *were*, and sometimes I *was*," said Simple. "I *was* at Niagara Falls and I *were* at the Grand Canyon—since that were in the far distant past when I were a coach-boy on the Santa Fe in my teens running out of Chicago. I was more recently at Niagara Falls."

"I see," I said. "*Was* is more immediate. *Were* is way back yonder."

"Somewhatly right. But not being colleged like you, I do not always speak like I come from the North."

"Regional differences have nothing to do with it," I said. "Plenty of Southerners speak correct English. I am not trying to make a Harvard man out of you—I am only concerned about your verbs. It is *not* correct to say, 'I were.'"

"Not even when *I were*?" asked Simple.

"You never were 'I were,'" I said. "There is no 'I were.' In the past tense there is only 'I was.' The verb *to be* is declined, 'I am, I was, I have been.'"

"Did you say, 'I have *bean*?'" asked Simple.

"I am not from Boston, so I did not say, 'I have *bean*.' A bean is a vegetable, not a verb. I said, 'I have been,' with a slight intonation."

"O.K.," said Simple, "I have bee-ee-een dry for the last half hour. Buy me a beer."

"Why should I buy you a beer?"

"Because I take for granted you are my friend."

"You take a great deal for granted when it comes to beers."

"What you do not take, you do not get," said Simple. "If you can afford it, I will take a bottle. If not, I will take a glass."

"You will accept a glass," I said. "Bartender, fill them up. Now to get back to grammar. I often wonder why so many colored people say, 'I taken,' instead of, 'I took'?"

"Because they are taken, I reckon," said Simple. "Lord knows I have been taken in more ways than one—for a ride, for my week's salary, my good name, and everything else but undertaken. Someday I will be undertaken, too, and it will cost me Five Hundred Dollars. Funerals is high."

"Funerals *are* high," I said.

"Neither *is* or *are* reduces expenses," said Simple. "Funerals and formals is both high, so what difference do it make?"

"What difference *does* it make," I said. "Your verbs are frequently wrong, old man. I wish you would speak correct English."

"I am American, not English," said Simple, "so if I want to say, 'I were,' I will say, 'I were.' Likewise, 'It do.' Also, 'She ain't.' Now, don't tell me *ain't* ain't in the dictionary."

"It is in the dictionary, but only as a colloquialism. It's not Oxford or Boston or Washington English."

"I am glad it ain't Washington English since I do not like that Jim Crow town. I do not know where Oxford is. And Boston, I have never *bean*. So about them, I give less than a damn. I ain't bothered."

"Didn't I just tell you 'ain't' isn't correct?"

"What if it aren't?" he said.

8

Picture for Her Dresser

It was a warm evening not yet dark when I stopped by Simple's. His landlady had the front door open airing the house, so I did not need to ring. I walked upstairs and knocked on his door. He was sitting on the bed, cutting his toenails, listening to a radio show, and frowning.

"Do you hear that?" he asked. "It's not about me, neither about you. All these plays, dramas, skits, sketches, and soap operas all day long and practically nothing about Negroes. You would think no Negroes lived in America except Amos and Andy. White folks have all kinds of plays on the radio about themselves, also on TV. But what have we got about us? Just now and then a song to sing. Am I right?"

"Just about right," I said.

"Come on, let's go take a walk." He put on his shoes first, his pants, then his shirt. "Is it cool enough for a coat?"

"You'd better wear one," I said. "It's not summer yet, and evening's coming on. You probably won't get back until midnight."

"Joyce is gone to a club meeting, so I won't be going to see her," he said. "She's expecting her sister-members to elect her a delegate to the regional which meets in Boston sometime soon. If they don't, she'll be a disappointed soul. She used to skip meetings, but that regional is why she goes regular now. Let's me and you stroll up Seventh Avenue to 145th, then curve toward Sugar Hill where the barmaids are beautiful and barflies are belles. I have not been on Sugar Hill in a coon's age.

It was dusk-dark when we reached the pavement. Taxis and pleasure cars sped by. The Avenue was alive with promenaders. On the way up the street we passed a photographer's shop with a big sign glowing in the window:

HARLEM DE-LUXE PHOTOGRAPHY STUDIO
IF YOU ARE NOT GOOD-LOOKING
WE WILL MAKE YOU SO
ENTER

"The last time I come by here," said Simple, "before my lady friend started acting like an iceberg, Joyce told me, 'Jess, why don't you go in and get your picture posed? I always did want a nice photograph of you to set on my dresser.'

"I said, 'Joyce, I don't want to take no picture.' But you know how womens is! So I went in.

"They got another big sign up on the wall inside that says:

RETOUCHING DONE

" 'I don't want them to *touch* me, let alone *retouch*,' I told Joyce.

"Joyce said, 'Be sweet, please, I do not wish no evil-looking Negro on my dresser.' So I submitted.

"Another sign states:

COLORED TO ORDER—EXPERT TINTING

"I asked, 'Joyce, what color do you want me to be?'

"Joyce said, 'A little lighter than natural. I will request the man how much he charges to make you chocolate.'

"About that time a long tall bushy-headed joker in a smock came dancing out of a booth and said, 'Next.'

"That were me next. There was a kind of sick green light blazing inside the booth. That light not only hurt my eyes, but turned my stomach before I even set down.

"The man said, 'Pay in advance.'

"My week's beer money went to turn me into chocolate to set on Joyce's dresser—providing I did not melt before I got out of there, it were so hot.

"The man said, 'Naturally, you want a retouching job?'

"I said, 'You know I *don't* want to look like I am.'

" 'That will be One Dollar extra,' he stated. 'Would you also wish to be tinted?'

" 'Gimme the works,' I said.

" 'We will add Three,' he additioned. 'And if you want more than one print, that will be Two Dollars each, after the negative.'

" 'One is enough,' I said. 'I would not want myself setting around on my *own* dresser. Just one print for the lady, that's all.'

" 'How about your mother?' asked the man. 'Or your sister down home?'

" 'Skip down home,' I said.

" 'Very well,' said the man. 'Now, look pleasant, please! You have observed the sign yonder which is the rule of the company:

IF YOU MOVE,
YOU LOSE.
IF YOU SHAKE—
NO RE-TAKE!

So kindly hold your position.'

" 'As much of my money as you've got,' I said, 'I will not bat a eye.'

" 'Tilt your head to one side and watch the birdie. Don't look like you have just et nails. . . . Smile! . . . Smile! Smile! . . . Brightly, now! That's right!'

" 'I cannot grin all night,' I said. 'Neither can I set like a piece of iron much longer. If you don't take me as I am, *damn*!'

" 'No profanity in here, please,' says the man. 'Just hold it while I focus.'

"I held.

"He focussed.

"I sweated.

"He focussed.

"I said, 'Can't you see me?'

"He said, 'Shussh-ss-s! Now, a great big smile! . . . Hold it!'

"*F-L-A-S-H!*

"I were blind for the next ten minutes. Seven Dollars and a Half's worth of me to set on Joyce's dresser! When I go to get that picture out next week it better be good—also have a frame! As touchous as Joyce is these days, I want her to like that picture."

By that time we had reached the Woodside. The corner of 141st and Seventh was jumping. King Cole was coming cool off the juke box inside the bar.

"Daddy-o, let's turn in here and get a beer," said Simple. "I never was much on climbing hills and if I go any further, I'll have too far to walk back. Besides, I got to wake myself up in the morning. My Big Ben won't alarm, my wrist watch is broke, and my landlady is evil. She says I don't pay her to climb three flights of steps to wake me up—so I have got nobody to wake me in the morning. That is one reason why I wish I was married, so I would not have to worry about getting to work on time. Also I would have somebody to cook my breakfast. I am tired of coffee, crullers, coffee and crullers, which is all I can afford. Besides, I hate an alarm clock . . . Two beers, bartender! . . . I like to be woke up gentle, some woman's hand shaking saying, 'Jess, honey, ain't you gonna make your shift?'

"And if I was to say, 'No,' she would say, 'Then all right, baby. You been working too hard lately anyhow. Sleep on. We will all get up about noon and go to the show.'

"That is the kind of woman I would like to have. Most womens is different. Most womens say, 'You better get up from there, Jess Semple, and go to work.' But even that would be better than a *brr-rrr-rr-r!* alarm clock every morning in your ears. I rather be woke up by a human than a clock."

"So you would make your wife get up before you, *just to wake you up,* would you?"

"Which is a woman's duty," said Simple. "He that earns the bread should be woke up, petted, fed, and got off to work in time. Then his wife can always go back to bed and get her beauty sleep—providing she is not working herself."

"No doubt a woman of yours would have to work."

"Only until we got a toe-holt," said Simple, "then Joyce could stay home and take care of the children."

"I haven't heard you speak of children before," I said. "You'll be too far along in age to start raising a family if you don't soon get married."

"You don't have to marry to have a family," said Simple.

"You wouldn't care to father children out of wedlock, surely?"

"A man slips up sometimes. But I don't need to worry about that. Joyce is a respectable woman—which is why I respects her. But she says as soon as we are wedlocked she wants a son that looks like me—which will be just as soon as that Negro in Baltimore pays for Isabel's divorce. So far that igaroot has only made one payment."

"I thought that man loved your wife so much he was willing to pay for the *whole* divorce. What happened?"

"I reckon inflation got him," said Simple. "Some things makes me sad to speak of. It takes three payments to get a decree. He made the down payment. Isabel writ that if I would make one, she would make one, then everybody could marry again. But I cannot meet a payment now with food up, rent up, phones up, cigarettes up, Lifebuoy up—everything up but my salary. Isabel wrote that divorces are liable to go up if I don't hurry up and pay up. I got a worried mind. Let's order one more beer—then I won't sleep restless. Have you got some change for this round?"

"I paid the last time."

"Except that *that* were not the last time. This round will be the last time. Just like a divorce in three installments, the last time is not the *last* time—if you still have to pay another time. Kindly order two beers."

"What do you take me for, a chump?"

"No, pal—a friend."

9

Cocktail Sip

Along about nine o'clock Sunday evening, Simple emerged grinning from the dusky backroom of Paddy's Bar to spy me at the front. I was surprised to see him so early and so hilarious. He was half high.

"Mulberries, sweet, my Lord," he cried, "also the lips of a woman!"

"You sound like an Elizabethan," I said. "What's up?"

"Lizzie who?" asked Simple.

"Poets of long ago I studied in school."

"It must have been long ago, because you have been out of school a long time."

"I still remember some of their poems, though. For instance:

> *Drink to me only with thine eyes,*
> *And I will pledge with mine,*
> *Or leave a kiss but in the cup,*
> *And I'll not ask for wine.*"

Meanwhile, Simple was beckoning the bartender, and the juke box was blaring.

I said, "Are you listening?"

"I'm listening fluently," he protested. "But I would like some beer. Besides, these kisses I'm talking about were not in no cup."

"You're probably in your cups," I said.

"I am not," said Simple. "I am half sober. See this lipstick on my handkerchief? I just got through wiping my mouth."

"Whom, may I ask, were you kissing?"

"Zarita—in the phone booth."

"Are you running with that light-o'-love again?"

"Only occasionally," said Simple. "This evening is one of the occasions."

"If Joyce catches you, you will run *from* Zarita, not with her."

"I hope Joyce don't catch me," said Simple. "Sometimes a man likes a woman with experience."

"Then you ought to like Zarita a lot."

"I do and I don't. Zarita is strictly a after-hours gal—great when the hour is late, the wine is fine, and mellow whiskey has made you frisky."

I quoted over the juke-box blare:

> *"The thirst that from the soul doth rise*
> *Doth ask a drink divine . . ."*

"Zarita will drink anything," said Simple. "She is like me in that respect, from beer to champagne. But this Sunday, we been to a Five O'clock Cocktail Sip where they empty all the different left-over bottles on the bar into the shaker, shake it up, put in a cherry—and call it a Special. We had several Specials.

"I did not know I was going to meet Zarita there, but I did. She were unescorted, so we sipped together. Then we danced together. Then we sat together. Then I went by her house. Then she came by my house. After which, we both came here to cool. I still had to kiss her one more time in the phone booth before she shoved off. She spends every Sunday night with her foster-mama, so she has to go now. In fact, I think she already went out the side door because she does not like Buster to see her in here with me. Old funny-looking Buster standing over there thinks he likes her."

"It's a good thing you are not jealous," I said.

"I have an open mind about Zarita. I am only jealous of Joyce. I may not see Zarita again for a month. But somehow or other, her kisses make me think of mulberries—that sloe gin they colored them cocktails, I reckon."

"It's a wonder you are not rocking and reeling."

"Rocky, but not really. I feel like hey! hey! hey! Come on, have a beer!"

"On you?"

"On me," said Simple. "My generosity has come down on me! I am glad I run into you while I still have some change left. I spent Three Dollars and a Half at the Cocktail Sip, threw a Dollar to the shake dancer when the floor show come on, tipped the waiter Fifty Cents, checked out my hat—then borrowed Five Dollars from Zarita that she said Buster give her—so it all come out even. Zarita is a good old girl. She will give you the shirt off her back, also take yours off your back. But in due time, we more than gets it back, both of us. So nobody's worried. What did you say about that kiss in the cup?"

> *"Leave but a kiss within the cup*
> *And I'll not look for wine . . ."*

"I sure won't," said Simple. "Won't and don't! But lately there ain't been nary kiss in *my cup*."

"You mean where you ring seven bells?"

"That's right," said Simple. "Joyce is still acting like she just met me—like I was a total stranger with no divorce—which maybe is why I fell into Zarita's arms today, which were wide open. You don't need a decree to relax with Zarita. You know, I usually spends Sundays with Joyce. But she said she were going to Jersey to see her godchild this afternoon. I wonder if she went? I did not ring seven to find out. Sometimes if her landlady catches me when Joyce ain't home, she just wants to talk and talk and talk, and I did not feel like talking to that woman today. So when I passed by the Heat Wave and saw that sign up—COCKTAIL SIP—I went in."

"And what did you find but sin—in the form of Zarita. 'When the cat's away, the mouse will play.'"

"Did Lizzie Beasley say that, too?"

"That's not Elizabethan, that's doggerel," I stated, "simple but true."

"Do you think I'm simple? If I wasn't drunk, I would feel bad. But I do not feel bad. I feel like if Joyce had rather go see some godchild than to see me, okay. Let the good times roll! They have rolled this evening! Look, am I wrong?"

"I am neither Judge Rivers nor Judge Delany, so I will not pass judgment on you," I said.

"I had rather go up before them than to go up before a lady judge. If my case ever got in front of any lady judge, I bet she would make me pay for Isabel's divorce. Lady judges is tight, tight, tight. But let us not mention judges this evening, partner. As long as I know what I am doing, I will never appear before one."

"You had better stop mixing your drinks then. You've been drinking cocktails, now you are drinking beer—so after a while you will not be clear as to what you are doing. Have you had your dinner yet?"

"You know I don't like restaurant cooking. And Joyce—let's not talk about her—no invite there this Sunday. I believe I will go home to bed right now, up to my Third Floor Rear. I told Zarita I might wait till she comes back, but I changed my mind. Them Specials is wearing off. Tell her I have went. If she's got any more kisses for me, tell her to leave 'em in a cup."

10

Apple Strudel

"I do believe if I was a woman I would be a nervous wretch," said Simple. "They are always worrying about dusting something, cleaning up something, or washing something, especially in the spring. Now, you take Joyce, every time I go by her place, either she, or her landlady one, is bulldozing the house—sweeping or mopping or dusting or washing out curtains, or ironing slip-covers. I swear there is many a thing to keep clean in a house. But a man do not worry about it as much as a woman."

"That's true," I said. "Still, a man has to worry about a few things, mostly personal. They take up enough time."

"Right," said Simple. "If you got any clothes at all, you have to keep them pressed. And laundry! I don't know which is worse, to have too little shirts or too many. If you only got three, you rotate them. If you got a dozen, it costs you more than you make to get them washed. And shoes, one pair ain't so bad to keep shined. You can do it yourself. But if you got three or four pair, skippy! Shining them is a nuisance. And paying good money to have them shined is more so, especially when the shine boy's hand is out for a tip each and every time."

"Well, anything one owns demands care," I said. "Did you ever read Thoreau's *Walden* when you were in school?"

"I never got that far."

"Thoreau says that his few belongings took up so much of his time when he was living in the woods trying to write and think, that he started to simplify life by eliminating things. He said to himself, 'More than one chair just means another one to dust,' so he threw out his chairs. 'Shelves are things on which one accumulates more *things*,' so he threw them out. Then he said, 'I can sleep on the floor,' so he discarded his bed. After a while his house was bare. But he didn't have to worry about a thing."

"He really cleaned house," said Simple. "But there ain't a Negro living would throw out his bed. A Negro might throw out his rug if it was summertime. He might throw out his chairs if they broke down. But bed, uh-uh, no, never would a Negro throw out his bed. It is too useful—even if it do have to be made up every morning and the sheets changed every week. Beds and Negroes go together."

"You certainly are race-conscious," I said. "Negroes, Negroes, Negroes! Everything in terms of race. Can't you think just once without thinking in terms of color?"

"I *am* colored," said Simple. "That man you was talking about were white. He could afford to throw out things. White folks have got plenty of things. Almost all we got is problems, especially the race problem. Everybody's talking about it. The white folks down where I work is always discussing this race problem. I tell them that white folks can measure their race problem by how far they have come. But Negroes measure ours by how far we have got to go.

"Them white folks are always telling me, 'Isn't it wonderful the progress that's been made amongst your people. Look at Dr. Bunche!'

"All I say is, 'Look at me.'

"That jars them because I don't look nothing like Dr. Bunche.

"Then they say, 'Well, take Marian Anderson.'

"I say, 'Take Zarita,' which shakes them, because when I get through describing all the furnished-room gals in Harlem that never heard of Marian Anderson they change the subject.

"Sometimes they say, for example, 'Years ago, Mr. Semple, Negroes could not stay at the Waldorf-Astoria.'

"I say, 'Mr. Semple can't stay there right now—because Mr. Semple ain't able.'

"They say, 'But in your case it's money, not race.'

"I say, 'Yes, but if I were not of the colored race, smart as I am, I would have money.'

"That shakes them again so they switch around to something else. 'Look at Dawson and Powell, those fine men you colored folks have in Congress.'

" 'Yes,' I say, 'just two in Washington all by their lonesome. As many Negroes as there are in the U.S.A. there might to be *two dozen* colored Congressmen. But half the Negroes in the South is scared to vote.'

" 'The Supreme Court says Negroes have the right to vote.'

" 'Can a Negro take time off from work to go running to the Supreme Court every time the Klan keeps him from voting? We can't enforce no laws by ourselves.'

" 'You are most pessimistic about things,' says the white folks.

" 'You would be, too, if you was black,' I say.

"They mean well, them white folks I work with, but they just don't know. One white fellow last week says, 'Here. I was telling my wife about you and she baked some apple strudel and sent you one for a present for you and your girl.'

"I said, 'Thank you,' because I knew he meant well. He would also like to do well. Still and yet, he is one of the very ones who will argue with me most about how the Negro problem is improving, beat me down that things is getting *so* much better, how we got so many white friends in America. Just because he gives me an apple strudel, does he think I can give everybody in Harlem a slice?

"I wish I could. To tell the truth, I really wish we could."

11

Belles and Bells

It was Palm Sunday. On the way home from church, I saw Simple, hat at the back of his head, in a tieless white shirt, decorating the railing of his stoop.

> *Hey, now, moo-cow,*
> *Gimme a little milk . . .*

he chanted as I approached.

"Disturbing the Sabbath, as usual."

"Well, I milked the milk," he said, "but just when I got ready to pick the bucket up, the cow kicked it over."

"That seems to be a parable," I observed, pausing at the foot of the steps, "but I do not understand your meaning."

"The meaning is that sometimes I act like a cow myself. It takes me a week to make my money, but only one night to spend it. Last night were that *one* night—Saturday, daddy-o, and I have kicked my own milk over. In fact, I have milked myself."

"Your allegories are somewhat mixed," I said, "but I think I understand what you mean."

"Joyce is cool, anyhow, and mad because I do not have a cent. So instead of inviting me to dinner today she starts talking about food is too high for money to buy—unless me, she, or somebody makes more money."

"Surely you do not call on a belle just to eat?"

"No, but I generally manages to ring her bell around dinner-time. You see, Joyce gets to bed early, so I go calling early."

"You don't have to go *that* early, do you?"

"Well, for one thing, her landlady objects to my ringing her bell late. Seven rings is a lot for ten or eleven o'clock at night. So I go at six-thirty or seven. Then I only have to ring once—which is seven times. If I go later and nobody hears me, I have to ring twice—which is fourteen times.

And if I ring three times—which is three times seven—twenty-one times is too much for the landlady's nerves.

"Old landlady told me the other night, 'Looks like common sense would tell you Joyce ain't here. Are you gonna ring ninety-nine times?' "

"Colored rooming houses certainly have a lot of different bell signals," I commented.

"You told that right!" said Simple. "I lived in a house once that had up to twenty-one rings, it were so full of roomers. Mine was twelve. I often used to miscount when somebody would ring. One time I let in another boy's best girl friend by mistake—she were ringing eleven. He had his second best girl friend in the room. The wrassle was a hassle then! I think each roomer should have a bell in his own room, instead of them different numbers of rings on the house bell. But landladies is too cheap to give everybody their own bell. As high as rents is, we ought to have such, though."

"Suppose you were a landlord," I said. "Would you give everybody a bell of his own? Think how much that would cost."

"I would not count the cost," said Simple. "If I was a landlord, as I intends to be when I get married, money would mean nothing to me. I would be making so much that I would not care about a few little old bells. I would give everybody a bell—then dare them to ring it after *I* went to bed. I would not want to hear bells ringing all over my house all night long."

"What do you mean, all night? You don't go to bed before morning."

"I mean *if* I went to bed," said Simple. "Furthermore, I would not have no balling and brawling in my house—unless I were invited also to ball. Anybody that had a party would have to invite me, the landlord. I would not permit no Sneaky Pete to be served there, neither King Kong. All licker would have to be good licker—pure whiskey, beer, gin, wine, or rum."

"You certainly would impose your preferences on the tenants," I said. "In fact, you sound almost as bad as you say your present landlady is. I do not believe you would be a good landlord."

"I would so," said Simple. "I would keep the hot water hot—because I like hot water. I would also keep the steam on when it is cold—since I like to be warm. I would not put no little old ten-watt bulb in the bathroom—because I would not want to cut myself while shaving. And my main rule would be posted on a sign:

WHEN THERE IS A PARTY—INVITE ME—ELSE MOVE

"You would not only take your roomers' rent, but you also would drink up their refreshments. For shame!"

"For shame, nothing," said Simple, "for fun."

12

Bop

Somebody upstairs in Simple's house had the combination turned up loud with an old Dizzy Gillespie record spinning like mad filling the Sabbath with Bop as I passed.

"Set down here on the stoop with me and listen to the music," said Simple.

"I've heard your landlady doesn't like tenants sitting on her stoop," I said.

"Pay it no mind," said Simple. "Ool-ya-koo," he sang. "Hey Ba-Ba-Re-Bop! Be-Bop! Mop!"

"All that nonsense singing reminds me of Cab Calloway back in the old *scat* days," I said, "around 1930 when he was chanting, 'Hi-de-*hie*-de-ho! Hee-de-*hee*-de-hee!'"

"Not at all," said Simple, "absolutely not at all."

"Re-Bop certainly sounds like scat to me," I insisted.

"No," said Simple, "Daddy-o, you are wrong. Besides, it was not *Re*-Bop. It is *Be*-Bop."

"What's the difference," I asked, "between *Re* and *Be*?"

"A lot," said Simple. "Re-Bop was an imitation like most of the white boys play. Be-Bop is the real thing like the colored boys play."

"You bring race into everything," I said, "even music."

"It is in everything," said Simple.

"Anyway, Be-Bop is passé, gone, finished."

"It may be gone, but its riffs remain behind," said Simple. "Be-Bop music was certainly colored folks' music—which is why white folks found it so hard to imitate. But there are some few white boys that latched onto it right well. And no wonder, because they sat and listened to Dizzy, Thelonius, Tad Dameron, Charlie Parker, also Mary Lou, all night long every time they got a chance, and bought their records by the dozens to copy their riffs. The ones that sing tried to make up new Be-Bop words, but them white folks don't know what they are singing about, even yet."

"It all sounds like pure nonsense syllables to me."

"Nonsense, nothing!" cried Simple. "Bop makes plenty of sense."

"What kind of sense?"

"You must not know where Bop comes from," said Simple, astonished at my ignorance.

"I do not know," I said. "Where?"

"From the police," said Simple.

"What do you mean, from the police?"

"From the police beating Negroes' heads," said Simple. "Every time a cop hits a Negro with his billy club, that old club says, 'BOP! BOP! . . . BE-BOP . . . MOP! . . . BOP!'

"That Negro hollers, 'Ooool-ya-koo! Ou-o-o!'

"Old Cop just keeps on, 'MOP! MOP! . . . BE-BOP! . . . MOP!' That's where Be-Bop came from, beaten right out of some Negro's head into them horns and saxophones and piano keys that plays it. Do you call that nonsense?"

"If it's true, I do not," I said.

"That's why so many white folks don't dig Bop," said Simple. "White folks do not get their heads beat *just for being white*. But me—a cop is liable to grab me almost any time and beat my head—*just* for being colored.

"In some parts of this American country as soon as the polices see me, they say, 'Boy, what are you doing in this neighborhood?'

"I say, 'Coming from work, sir.'

"They say, 'Where do you work?'

"Then I have to go into my whole pedigree because I am a black man in a white neighborhood. And if my answers do not satisfy them, BOP! MOP! . . . BE-BOP! . . . MOP! If they do not hit me, they have already hurt my soul. *A dark man shall see dark days.* Bop comes out of them dark days. That's why real Bop is mad, wild, frantic, crazy—and not to be dug unless you've seen dark days, too. Folks who ain't suffered much cannot play Bop, neither appreciate it. They think Bop is nonsense—like you. They think it's just *crazy* crazy. They do not know Bop is also MAD CRAZY, SAD CRAZY, FRANTIC WILD CRAZY—beat out of somebody's head! That's what Bop is. Them young colored kids who started it, they know what Bop is."

"Your explanation depresses me," I said.

"Your nonsense depresses me," said Simple.

13

A Hat Is a Woman

"A hat is a woman—and a woman is a hat," said Simple when I ran into him late one evening toward the end of the week in Paddy's. It was evident he and Joyce had made up. Simple, it seemed, had just come from her house and was grinning from ear to ear.

"Old man, it's O.K. When I phoned her tonight, she gave in and told me to come over. 'It's Lent,' Joyce said on the phone, 'and I do not want to harbor nothing in my heart against nobody when I go to church Easter, not even you. Besides, I got something to show you, Jess.' Naturally, I was curious, so I rung seven."

"What did she have to show you?"

"A couple of freakish hats. Womens is so crazy about hats they ought to be born with one on. Joyce has just got *two* hats for Easter. She couldn't make up her mind which hat she liked best, so she got two. Now she can't make up her mind which one to wear Easter Sunday. So she just puts one hat on—and looks at herself. Then she puts the other one on—and looks at herself. It's a wonder she ain't wore her mirror out looking in it."

"Which one of the two do you like?"

"Neither one," said Simple. "But I do not count when it comes to hats. I dare not express my opinion."

"What are the hats like?"

"One's little and small with a dagger-feather in it. The other one's big and round, the top all flowers. Both of them are supposed to set down over one ear—which makes Joyce look like she is drunk. I wished I had a drink because I were cold stone sober when she put on that first hat, and I were mighty near asleep when she got through trying on the second.

"Joyce says, 'Baby, ain't you got no interest in my new millinery? You would not want me walking in the Easter parade looking like Mother Goose, would you?'

" 'I dead sure would not,' I replied. 'On the other hand, I don't want you to look like Lady Jackass, either.'

" 'You talk right simple,' Joyce said. 'If you do not like the hats this season when they range all the way from one style to another, you are just hard to please. If we go to that tea at the Theresa Hotel, I want to look my best.'

" 'If we go to *any* tea,' I says, 'I want to be high before we get there. Let's start early so I can stop in Sugar Ray's and have a beer.'

" 'Beer is all you think about,' said Joyce. 'It looks like I am not company enough for you, Jess Semple. Every time I go out with you, you want to wrap your hand around a cold bottle. On Easter Sunday, we are going to church. From church you are going to take me for a bus ride down Fifth Avenue to see the Easter Parade. From there we are returning uptown to the tea.'

" 'All of that without stopping for a beer?'

" 'Well, we could stop in Sugar Ray's for a minute. I like those lighted-up pictures he's got on his wall. But I am not going to spend the day in there, you hear me, Jess?'

" 'I hear you,' I says. 'Being outdoors so much, I think you better wear that little hat that latches onto your left earring, because if the wind is blowing, I do not want to have to run after that big hat.'

" 'I'm so glad you like my cute little hat,' says Joyce.

" 'I'd like anything you put on your head, baby,' I says. 'Now, *please* take 'em both off and come over here and set by me.'

"But do you know what that woman said?"

"No," I answered.

"Joyce said, 'I am keeping Lent, honey. Besides, I got to dye some Easter eggs for my godchild's cousin's niece. Come on in the kitchen and help me.'

"That is why I am in this bar so early, because the *last* thing I had on my mind tonight was dyeing Easter eggs. A woman will let you down every time just when you need her most. Worried as I am about what to write my wife about our divorce—since Isabel has made that second payment and is waiting for me to make the third—it looks like Joyce should try to take my mind off my troubles instead of dyeing Easter eggs. Anyhow, I addressed Isabel an envelope today so she will hear from me after Easter.

"I bought a Three Cent stamp—which didn't look like any Three Cent stamp I ever saw before. Once you could tell a Three Cent stamp when you saw it, but now you can't any more. It used to always be the same size, purple and small, and have a man's head on it. But now sometimes it is long and blue and got a statue on it. Then again it might even have a buffalo or a pony on it. Or it runs length-ways and has a picture of a woman and a Red Cross. You can't tell what a Three Cent stamp will be any more, the government has done got so fancy. Why do you reckon they put out so many different kinds of Three Cent stamps lately? I do not like them."

"They are not put out for *you* to like," I said. "There are plenty of people who go wild about any kind of a new stamp. They are philatelists."

"What?"

"Stamp collectors. They love new stamps, and buy whole sheets of them just to save, or exchange with other philatelists around the world."

"Huh!" said Simple. "Why don't they make all these different kinds of stamps just for them collectors then, and stick to the good old regular purple Three Cent stamp I have always knowed—for me? But if they just *have* to make all them different kinds of stamps every week, then why don't they print some with Negroes on them? I ain't seen a Negro on a Three Cent stamp yet, and I have seen many another varmint thereon."

"If I am not mistaken, I saw Dr. Carver once on a stamp."

"Not I," said Simple. "And even if he were, that is just *one* Negro. As many different stamps as the government makes, let's put some *more* Negroes on them, not just one."

"Who, for example?"

"Joe Louis on one end and Jackie Robinson on the other, also Satchel Paige, or Ralph Bunche, Mother Bethune, and maybe Joyce. Or one of them fINE Brandford models—or me."

"Why *you*?"

"To show the government is not prejudiced," said Simple.

14

Formals and Funerals

Suddenly spring had turned off cold again. The day after Easter it was drizzling rain. Easter Monday night I was standing under the Theresa Hotel's protecting canopy watching the cars cutting and curving around each corner at 125th and Seventh. Simple was walking against the wind with his head down, his coat collar up, and his hat dripping.

"Where are you going this cold night with the rain raining and the elements blowing?" I asked.

"Hi, there!" he said. "I am ankling to the flower shop to buy a corsarge. Come on with me."

"In this rain! Are you simple?"

"Somewhatly," he said, "but I got to do it."

"So you and Joyce are going out sporting this evening, I divine."

"You know it's not me and no other woman," said Simple. "I *certainly* would not spend Ten Dollars for a corsarge for nobody else, even if she is paying half of it herself."

"You mean to say Joyce has to go halfers on her own corsage," I asked, "when *you* are taking her out?"

"She is liable to have to go *more* than half before this evening is done," said Simple. "We are going to a formal, the Beaux Noirs Annual Easter Monday Dance. Do you know what a formal is? It is a function where you have to wear a tux with a shirt that buttons only with studs and a tie that is a bow. Joyce has got herself an evening gown that is cut so low it looks like she is trying to show how little she can wear and not catch pneumonia. If you are anybody in society at all at a formal you have to have a box to retire to between dances. Me and Joyce is sharing our box with another couple, which makes us only have to pay half, which is Twelve Dollars, the box costing Twenty-Four to seat eight. When you go to a formal it is necessary to invite guests to set in your box, so we have invited two couples. Since Joyce and me and the other couple are the hosts, we have to furnish the licker. I got one bottle of White Mule and one bottle of White Horse. The Horse is for Joyce—since she says a lady drinks nothing but Scotch at a public formal.

"I'm telling you, a formal is something! Right there, daddy-o, I have done spent Twenty-Three Dollars and Eighty-Two Cents, not counting renting the tux which also required a Ten Dollar deposit in case I snag it or do not bring it back. Raining and blowing like it is tonight, I got to take Joyce in a cab, which is another Dollar and a Half. Fifty Cents for the checkroom girl, tips for the waiter that brings the set-ups, another tip for extra ice. Then after the dance, womens always have to eat even if it is mighty nigh breakfast time, so you have to take them for four A.M. barbecue at Ribs-In-The-Ruff, so they can gaze at Sidney. Man, a formal costs almost as much as a funeral! Since Joyce just *has* to go to a formal, what reason is it she shouldn't pay half? It were not my idea in the first place."

"One doesn't take a woman out on her own money," I said.

"I do," said Simple, "when she insists on going some place I can't afford. Why can't they have a formal without all this rigmarole? I had rather die than put on a stud-buttoned shirt. And I do not understand why it takes a formal for Joyce to wear a dress cut so low everybody can see almost as much of her as I could if I was married to her."

"Maybe that is why folks like formals," I said, "because women reveal their hidden charms."

"Such charms should be reserved for husbands."

"You're as old-fashioned as a Sultan. In Turkey in the old days Sultans made their wives put on veils when they went out, and wrap up from top to toe."

"Here," said Simple, "women take off practically everything when they go out. Joyce is liable to catch her death of cold unless I buy her a *great big* corsarge to cover up her chest. How many dozen orchids do you reckon you get for Ten Dollars?"

"About one," I said. "Not one dozen, but *one orchid.*"

"I am going to get her carnations," said Simple.

"If you do, Joyce will never speak to you again. An orchid is *the* flower for a formal."

"Are orchids made of gold?"

"Of course not."

"Neither am I," said Simple.

15

Science Says It's a Lie

When I met him again, "It were wonderful," he said. "Soft lights, pretty womens, and a jam-up band. I really enjoyed my fool self. So did Joyce. And she looked like a dreamboat, jack! Brownskin, all in white, floating like a cloud. Like a sail in the sunset, like the Queen of Sheba, like Josephine Baker! She were righteous! From the minute we hit the floor, folks started making admiration over Joyce. And everything was going fine at the formal until Jimboy—who's gotten kind of famous lately as a jazz piano-player—brought his wife up to our box to introduce her to the ladies."

"What happened then?"

"The ladies friz up," said Simple.

"Why?"

"Jimboy's wife is white."

"That's right," I said, "he did marry a white girl, didn't he? I haven't run into him since he got married."

"Dorothea is not only white, *she is pretty*," said Simple. "There is nothing a colored woman hates more than to see a colored man married to a *pretty* white woman. If she's some old beat-up strumpet, they don't care much. But Jimboy's wife is a nice girl. So when he come up to our box with Dorothea, the womens just friz up, Joyce included."

"That was not very polite," I said.

"Of course it were not," said Simple, draining his beer. "It were right embarrassing. Besides, I wanted to ask Jimboy's wife for a dance, but I did not dare after I saw that *no-you-don't* look in Joyce's eyes.

"I just said, 'Excuse me, folks, I have got to go to the MEN'S ROOM.'

"When I come back Jimboy and his wife was gone, and Joyce and her women friends was talking like mad about them.

" 'That little old white Southern hussy,' they says—because Jimboy's wife is from Arkansas. 'The idea of her coming up here to Harlem and marrying a Negro! Why didn't she marry one of her own?'

" 'Why didn't he marry one of *his* own?' another one says. Man, they carried on just like Bilbo."

"It's too bad we have prejudices, too," I said.

"Too bad," nodded Simple. "But Jimboy's son is going to be a smart child. He is about six months old now, and he started to teaching his mama before he was born."

"What do you mean, started teaching his mama before he was born?"

"Ain't you heard that story about how Jimboy's son was born? Where have you been lately? That child refused to be born in Arkansas."

"Quit kidding," I said.

"I am not kidding," declared Simple. "What I am telling you is true. That baby knows a colored man married to a white woman is against the law in Dixie. Last fall Jimboy's wife wanted to be with her mother and the rest of her white folks when her first child was born. So she went down to Arkansas. Jimboy could not go because he were working. He knew if he gave up his job, he's liable not to get another one soon.

"So when her time were about come, Dorothea was put on the train by her colored husband and went on home—home being where mama is in Dixie. Me, myself, I would not marry a woman who thought home was where mama is. When a woman marries a man, like the Bible says, she should cleave unto *him*—not run looking for mama when his offspring is due. *My wife would stay with me.*"

"A lot of help you would be in childbirth," I said.

"There's a Medical Center with nurses, not midwives," said Simple. "But Jimboy does not have much influence over his wife, I reckon. Being blonde, I expect he is scared of her. So she left the free North and went back South to birth her child—her family being *liberals*, so she told her husband. She regretted it, likewise Jimboy. While he were waiting for the great event, looking each and every day for a telegram, 'It's a boy,' else 'A girl,' Jimboy grew twenty-two gray hairs, missed three nights at the club, lost his touch on the piano, and had heartburn."

"What happened?"

"A new page in history," said Simple, "which science would say was a lie."

"Don't keep me in suspense," I demanded. "Did his wife have the child or not?"

"Dorothea had the child, but not in Arkansas. When she got there, it were time. But nothing happened. One week went by, two weeks, three, an extra month—almost two."

"Then what?"

"Another month. By that time it were *too* long. Dorothea got worried herself. Jimboy in Harlem got gray-headed. He wired his wife in Arkansas to go to the hospital anyhow. It was way overdue. So she went—which is the story. When that white girl got in the hospital, naturally a white doctor proceeded to examine her. He had a thing with earphones they press on the belly of the mother-to-be to listen for the unborn child's heartbeats. Well, sir, the doctor pressed them earphones on Jimboy's wife—but what that doctor heard was not heartbeats at all. He heard Jimmy's unborn baby singing the blues in a real strong voice just like Sugar Chile Robinson. That brownskin baby was singing real loud:

> *I won't be born down here!*
> *No, sir, I won't be born down here!*
> *If you want to know*
> *What it's all about—*
> *As long as South is South,*
> *I won't come out!*
> *I won't be born down here!"*

"That is really a tall tale," I said.

"Ask Jimboy if it ain't so," said Simple. "Dorothea had to come on back to New York to have her baby. Their child were born in Harlem Hospital where he had no fear."

16

Joyce Objects

"That Joyce is still talking about the nerve of Jimboy introducing his white wife to her friends at the formal," said Simple, calling for another beer. "When I went by the house tonight, Joyce and her old landlady was still low-rating Jimboy. Besides, they had just read in the *Afro-American* where another famous Negro had married a white woman. These colored papers can really upset you, if you are colored. One week it's lynchings. Next week it's race riots. Another time you can't vote in South Carolina. Or you can't eat some place else. Or you can't rent a house here.

"But now it ain't what you *can't* do that's got Joyce upset. It's what you *can* do—leastwise up North—and that is marry white. Joyce is almost as upset as Talmadge or Rankin would be about intermarriage. In fact, she is mad. Joyce says she don't see why a colored woman is not good enough for any of our colored big shots. Why should so many band leaders, race leaders, prize fighters, and musicians marry white, Joyce wants to know. She declares it ain't right. According to her, white women are out to wreck and ruin the Negro race."

"I have always considered marriage a private matter," I said, "so I cannot agree with Joyce."

"That is what I would say, too," said Simple, "if I dared to say anything. But I eat Joyce's food almost every night, so I daresn't open my mouth. Intermarriage is a sore subject with Joyce. And her big old landlady backs her up on it. Both of them says when a colored man is in public life, he *belongs* to the public. He has got no business letting the race down by marrying a white woman. Besides, Joyce says, too many big Negroes with good incomes are up and marrying white—and she never reads about no white woman marrying a *poor* Negro. Since Jimboy makes a good salary playing the piano, according to Joyce, women like his wife are just taking money away from the race."

"Joyce has love and economics slightly mixed up."

"Um-m-m!" said Simple. "But I dare not dispute her, riled as she is about my divorce anyhow.

"Her big old fat landlady egged her on by saying, 'Honey, you is right! Them womens is out to *ruin* the black race, financially and every which a way. You just wait until another Scottsboro Case comes up. Them white womens will say to their colored husbands, *Don't you-all go to the defense of them boys, daddy. How do you know but what them Negroes are guilty? They ain't in your intelligent position to marry white, so probably they did rape that girl.*' "

"That is a very evil thought," I said.

"Colored womens is evil when it comes to intermarriage. Joyce says there ain't no white man ever asked her if he could marry her," said Simple. "All white mens wants to do is *buy* colored womens, according to Joyce. But colored mens will run after a white woman like a dog—and marry her, too, when they get up in the world, which is a disgrace!"

"Joyce sounds just like a Dixiecrat," I said.

"She is from Dixie," said Simple, "and she is a race-woman, for true.

"Joyce says, 'With all the nice-looking, good-looking, educated young colored girls in the race, I don't see why no black man has to go outside of Harlem to find a wife. We got from dark chocolate to vanilla cream right in our own group. We even got colored blondes.' She looked dead at me.

"I said, 'Baby, I ain't thinking about marrying no blonde. I am thinking about marrying you.'

"Joyce says, 'Actions speak louder than words, Jess Semple, so make me know it! Even if you don't marry me, I better not catch you marrying no white woman. Every time I pick up a paper, another Negro has gone and committed the act and it is always some big-shot jigaboo making a whole lot of loot who can afford to put diamond rings on lily-white fingers and alligator shoes on her rose-pink toes. I wish I could get hold of some of these big Negroes for just about two minutes. I would put some sense back into their heads,' Joyce says, frowning at me. Why, you would think I was the guilty party—the way she lit into me.

" 'Listen, Joyce, baby,' I says, 'you know I aims to marry *you*. I ain't fixing to marry no white woman.'

"Joyce says, 'I wouldn't put it past you, Jess Semple. You're a man, ain't you? No telling what a man will do, white or colored. But at least, thank God, Jackie Robinson has not taken unto himself a white wife.'

" 'Jackie is already married for years,' I told her.

" 'So was some of them other Negroes,' yells Joyce, 'but that don't stop them! No! The woman that has stuck by them during all their hard struggles when they warn't nobody, they cast aside. When they get up in the world, they marry white. As soon as them big checks start coming in, they cast us aside.'

" 'I have not cast you aside,' I said.

" 'You ain't nobody, neither,' said Joyce.

"Now, that kinder hurt my feelings coming from Joyce. So I guess I said something I am forced to regret."

"What did you say?"

"I said, 'Joyce, maybe white womens are more sympathetic to a man when he is trying to get somewhere.'

"That is all I said, but it made Joyce mad. I should not have said it at dinner time, because she just kept on gnawing the same old bone.

" 'That black king in Africa who was forced to give up his throne on account of marrying some English typist,' Joyce says. 'It's good enough for him! Any black king that wants to marry a white woman ain't got no business with a throne on which to sit. Let him sit on a park bench.' "

"What did you say to that?" I asked.

"Not a word," said Simple. "When Joyce and that big old fat landlady of hers get together on a subject, there's no use of me trying to put a word in edgewise. I did call Joyce's attention to the fact, however, that the Prince of Wales once gave up his throne for the woman he loved.

"Joyce says, 'Yes, but he were white. In fact, both of them were white. They did not give up nothing *but* a throne to marry each other. But this African king gave up his *blackness* to marry that white woman. If I was a man,' says Joyce, 'I would not give up my race for nobody—least of all a white woman. I do not see how that king can expect his subjects to have any respect for what he has done. I do not respect these Negroes here in New York who are marrying white women each and every week—and they ain't even kings.'

"Her big old fat landlady chimes in, 'You right, honey! You is dead right. If any man of mine left me for a white woman, I would fix his little red wagon, I mean, good!'

"Both of them womens looked at me," said Simple. "I do not know why, because I had not said or done a thing. I was just setting there eating chicken and dumplings and keeping my mouth shut. But the way they looked at me made me feel right uncomfortable, so I repeated for the umpteenth time, 'I ain't fixin' to marry nobody but this girl right here. Joyce, I mean you. So I wish you would not cut your eyes at me that way. I am not a king, but if I was, and if I had a throne, wouldn't nobody sit on it but Queen Joyce.'

"That kind of toned her down. Joyce says, 'Baby, will you have some chocolate pudding with whipped cream, or would you rather have some of that tapioca that you liked so well last night?'

"I started to say, 'tapioca.' Then it occurred to me that tapioca were white, so I said, 'Chocolate pudding.' I did not want to get in bad with Joyce no kind of way. Do you blame me, daddy-o?"

17

The Necessaries

The television was going full flicker in Paddy's but since there were no fights on that night, few were watching. Its racket only interfered with conversation. Everybody shouted at everybody else. But Simple seemed slightly subdued.

"One sure thing, you can't have your beer and drink it, too," he said, gazing at his empty glass. "To think I have come to this—another winter gone and not a penny. Now it's spring—and I am ragged as a jaybird."

"I sympathize with you," I said, "but sympathy is *all* I can do. I am not thirsty myself." I made no effort to order beers, being slightly out of pocket. Simple fell silent and turned away from me to examine the bar. He was trying to judge the financial status of those nearby.

"You see that fellow over there, Watermelon Joe?" he asked. "He still owes me a quarter from last year. If he don't pay me soon, I'll sure as hell take it out in melons this summer. When he starts pushing his cart, I will demand my slice."

"By now he owes you interest on that Twenty-Five Cents," I said.

"He can keep the interest. In fact, anybody who is as ugly as Watermelon Joe, I really should give him a quarter. That man is homely! Do you see his head? Bootsie[1] has nothing on him. Do you dig his feet? His feet are so big they look like animals starting to breathe. His nose is the size of Uncle Wambo's. That is one messed-up man!"

"You should talk, Apollo Belvedere," I said.

"Don't 'dearie' me," objected Simple. "I ain't no woman. I might not be handsome, but one thing sure—out of eight million people in New York, I'm the *only* one who looks like me."

"A unique distinction, but the same could be said for Watermelon Joe!"

"You can beg my apology if you put me in a class with Joe. I may look like Zip, but I do not look like Joe. Anyhow, the womens love me."

"I don't see any women taking care of you," I said.

"I'm independent. I would not let a woman take care of me unless I was married to her. All I want from a woman is love. As I told Joyce the other night:

> *A preacher's heart is food.*
> *A woman's heart is kindness.*
> *A young man's heart is money—*
> *But my heart is love."*

"Joyce said, 'That is so beautiful! Jess, say it again.'

"So I repeated myself. Facts, if I had another beer, I could repeat some more toasts. I got a new one for you."

"As entertaining as I find your toasts," I said, "I cannot afford to let *all* my money flow over the bar tonight."

"Do you mean to say a beer would take your last dime?"

"Almost," I said, relenting. "But here goes. My final quarter."

"Two beers for two steers! Bartender, I don't mean water. Now I will say you a toast:

> *If you want a good reason for drinking,*
> *A great one just entered my head—*
> *If a man don't drink when he's living,*
> *How can he drink when he's dead?*

That's one I learned in Dallas, from a Negro who were so well-off he not only changed clothes every day, he changed diamonds. It were prohibition times, too, when they were selling around-the-corner hooch."

"What is around-the-corner hooch?" I asked.

"Take one drink, walk around the corner—and die! That's how bad it were. But I survived. I have survived a great many things. Now, if I can just get Watermelon Joe to return my quarter! I believe I will approach him. I see him down at the end of the bar sporting 'em up. Protect my stool until I come back. If Watermelon gives me a quarter, the next beer is on me."

"I accept with pleasure," I said.

"Don't be too pleased," said Simple, "because if what you expect don't happen, then what don't happen is what to expect. Is that clear? I will now request my quarter."

A couple of comedians were getting yocks from the television audience, but none from the barflies. Nobody paid the TV screen the least mind. Shortly Simple returned to his stool grinning. He had gotten the quarter and promptly proceeded to spend it. Two beers and a nickel in the juke box. Broke again! So he started talking.

"I went window-shopping tonight with no money," said Simple. "All up and down 125th Street—Howard's, Crawford's, Wolfe's, Hollywood

Al's. I thought to myself, broke as I was, look at all those clothes a Harlem Negro is expected to wear! Last night at the Victoria Joyce and me saw a picture about Africa and the only thing the man had on there was a lion-cloth. All the ladies wore was a sarongish little wrap-around which didn't pay no attention to the upper-round. Think how much money they save! Also how much time they save getting up in the morning—just slipping on one piece. And they don't have to remember what sizes they wear, because everything is the same size. I never remember what size my hat is, how long my shirtsleeves is supposed to be, or if I wear a eight or a twelve shoe. And right now I am ragged from tip to toe. I really ought to be half-way sharp to take Joyce out. But do you know how much money it would take to dress me up this spring? Do you know how many pieces of clothes I have to buy to look brand new? I figured it out last night and it is *some* figure."

"How many, and how much?" I asked.

"Starting at the bottom," said Simple, "which is basic, No. 1, shoes. The kind I want costs $18.50. Next, sox, three pairs, $1.00 each, which is $3.00. After that, garters, $1.50. Next, to cover my modesty, drawers, $1.50. Undershirt, $1.00. Now getting to what the public sees—the *main* thing, suit, $58.00—$60.00 at a pinch. A sweater if the suit ain't warm enough, $6.85. Shirt, white, $4.95. Tie, $2.00. Overcoat, not less than $60.00 if it's warm. Skypiece, $8.00. Pocket handkerchief, 60¢. One to blow my nose, 25¢. Muffler to keep from catching cold, $2.00. Gloves, $2.50. Belt, $2.50. Suspenders, $1.50. Oh, yes, a tie-clasp. And pajamas when I take everything else off, for night wear, to keep from being bare, $3.00. These are the twenty-two necessaries a man must have to be dressed up in the U.S.A. Not counting the pennies, they comes to One Hundred and Seventy-Eight Dollars."

"When do you start shopping?" I asked.

"Man, it would take me one hundred and seventy-eight years to get *all* them items at once. Each and every time I buy a suit, my shoes is wore out. Before I can get new shoes, the suit is old. I get a muffler in the fall. Before I can purchase a topcoat, I lose the muffler. I buy a pair of shorts. Before I've got a undershirt to go with them, the shorts have split. I am telling you, man, Africans have sense! They just grab one rag, put it on, and are dressed. Daddy-o, I would not care if I were an African."

"You *are* an African, just born out of place and out of time."

"Out of money, too," said Simple, "and yet I need all them necessaries."

18

Second-Hand Clothes

"Speaking of clothes, do you know where Karl, who owns the Second-Hand Store next door, gets his clothes from?"

"No. I am not interested in second-hand clothes," I said. "Where does he get them?"

"From the Morgue," said Simple.

"Do you mean to tell me Karl's Second-Hand Store is stocked with clothes from the Morgue?"

"They ain't from nowhere else," said Simple.

"How did you find out?"

"Because I bought a suit there once and wore it a week before I knowed it had belonged to a dead man."

"Who told you it came from a corpse?"

"Another second-hand man. He said, 'Don't buy nothing from Karl's. His clothes ain't even second-handed. They are *last-handed*. Nobody ought to wear them any more because they come off of men what was murdered, gassed, stabbed, run over, poisoned, drunk under the table, drowned, or taken for a ride. I would not wear no clothes from Karl's. He gets them from the Morgue.'

" 'Where do you get all these old suits you sell?' I asked him.

" 'Mine I buy from people walking around living, people who need a little bit of change, get caught short, want a bottle of sherry wine, so sell me a coat, a suit, maybe overcoat in summer time when they forget how winter feels. When it turns cold folks come running to buy warm clothes. That's how my clothes change hands, living to living. But Karl, he takes from the dead.'

" 'I believe you just telling me that to knock Karl's business,' I said. 'If I thought this old work suit I bought was off a dead man's back, I would take it back, and get my money right now, and tell Karl you told me these clothes was off a dead man's back.'

" 'What really difference does it make?' he said. 'The wool that suit is made from is off a *dead* sheep's back! The buttons is from a *dead* whale's bone. The thread is from *dead* cocoons. The dye is from *dead* flowers. The padding in the shoulders is from *dead* horses' tails. Everything in a suit is dead. What difference does it make? Why take it back? But I'm just telling you every one of Karl's suits is from a *dead* man.'

" 'Aw-ooo-oo-o!' I hollered. 'Don't tell me no more! I'll be running buck naked in the streets wearing no suit at all. I am not dead.'

" 'That is why Karl can mark his suits two-three-four dollars cheaper than I can,' the other dealer said, 'because they come from the dead.'

" 'Good-bye,' I said. I walked out. I do not believe I will ever buy another second-hand suit to work in unless I know who wore it before me, because I didn't know they might come from Morgues where they take the unknown dead! Did you?"

"No," I said. "But if it is true, I'm certain the Board of Health requires that second-hand garments be cleaned and fumigated before they are resold, so it makes no difference anyway, except in the mind."

"My mind is upset," said Simple.

"Don't worry," I said, "the dead man's ghost will hardly come back. If he did, he couldn't fit into that suit with you in it at the same time."

"He better not try!" said Simple. "Anyhow, you know I don't believe in ghosts. But every time I pass Karl's place lately, it looks like I see dead men hanging up on his racks instead of suits. Why do you reckon that is?"

"You have an impressionable mind."

"Anyhow, one night when I had that Morgue suit on, I put my hand in my coat pocket—and I thought I felt *another* hand in there—a soft, cold hand. I mighty near fainted."

"You were probably drunk."

"I were sober as a judge. And nobody was standing near me."

"Then it must have been your imagination. What color was the other hand in your pocket, black or white?"

"That was one time color did not matter," said Simple.

19

Fancy Free

"Before spring is over, if I can't get no spring clothes, at least I would like to have me a real good mess of greens."

Simple stood at the bar and uttered this statement as though it were of great importance. Then he shook his head with a gesture of despair.

"But there is no place in New York to pick greens. Maybe that is why womens do not cook them much in big cities. Not even a dandelion do I see growing in Morningside Park. If there was, it wouldn't stay there long because some Negro would pull it and eat it."

"Greens *are* good," I said.

"Don't talk!" cried Simple. "All boiled down with a side of pork, delicious! Greens make my mouth water. I have eaten so many in my life until I could write a book on greenology—and I still would like to eat that many more. What I wouldn't give right now for a good old iron pot full! Mustard greens, collard greens, turnip greens, dandelions, dock. Beet-tops, lamb's tongue, pepper grass, sheepcress, also poke. Good old mixed greens! Spinach or chard, refined greens! Any kind of fresh greens. I wonder why somebody don't open a restaurant for nothing but greens? I should think that would go right good up North."

"I hear you always talking about going into business," I said. "Why don't you open one?"

"Where would I get the greens?" asked Simple. "They don't grow around here. Wild mustard has never been known to be found sprouting on Lenox Avenue. And was I to see poke in New York, I would swear it were a miracle. Besides, even if they did grow here, who would pick 'em? That is woman's work, but I would not trust it to Joyce. She might not know greens from poison weeds, nor pepper grass from bridal mist. Joyce were not raised on dandelions like me. I don't expect she would be caught with a basket picking greens. Joyce is cultural."

"She likes greens, though, doesn't she?"

"Eats them like a horse," said Simple, "when somebody else serves them. The same by chitterlings. Joyce tried to tell me once she did not eat pig ruffles, would not cook them, couldn't bear to clean them, and *loathed* the smell. But when my cousin in the Bronx invited us to a chitterling supper, I could hardly get near the pot for Joyce. I do not believe people should try to pass."

"What do you mean, *pass*?"

"Pass for non-chitterling eaters if they are chitterling eaters," said Simple. "What I like, I like, and I do not care who knows it. I also like watermelon."

"Why not?" I asked.

"Some colored folks are ashamed to like watermelon. I told you about that woman who bought one in the store once and made the clerk wrap it up before she would carry it home. She didn't want nobody to see her with a watermelon. Me, I would carry a watermelon unwrapped any day any where. I would eat one before the Queen of England."

"A pretty picture you would make, eating a slice of watermelon before the queen."

"I would give the queen a slice—and I bet she would thank me for it, especially if it was one of them light green round striped melons with a deep red heart and coal-black seeds. Man, juicy! Oh, my soul! Sweet, yes! And good to a fare-thee-well! I wish I had a pot of greens right now, a pitcher of buttermilk, and a watermelon."

"You would have a stomach ache."

"It would be worth it! But let's talk no more about such things. I would settle for a cold bottle of beer on you here."

"I see no reason why I should buy you a bottle of beer."

"I am broke and I have dreamed you up a beautiful dream," said Simple. "You know you like them things, too. If I had not dreamed them up, you might not of thought of watermelon or greens tonight—greens, greens, greens!"

"Thinking of greens is not the same as eating them," I said.

"No," said Simple, "but at least we can share the thought. It was my thought. Don't you intend to share the beer? O.K. Draw two, bartender! Pay the man—and let us wash down those greens we have thought up. Pass the corn bread. I thank you, daddy-o! Now, hand me the vinegar, also the baby onions."

"You are certainly indulging in a flight of fancy! In fact, your imagination is running riot. Beer is not free."

"No, but fancy is, and if I had my way," said Simple, seizing his beer, "I would be a bird in a meadow full of greens right now!"

"Why a bird? Why not a horse, or a sheep?"

"A bird can fly high, see with a bird's eye, and dig all that is going on down on earth, especially what people are doing in the springtime."

"Birds are not customarily interested in the doings of human beings," I said, "except to the point of keeping out of their way."

"I would keep out of people's way," said Simple, "but also I would observe everything they do."

"Suppose they captured you and put you in a cage?"

"No, I would not be a pretty bird, the kind anybody would want in a cage. I would be just a plain old ugly bird that caws and nobody would want. That way I would be free. I would sail over towns and cities and look down and see what is going on. I would ride on tops of cars in Italian weddings, on top of hearses in Catholic funerals, I would light on the back of fish-tail Cadillacs in Harlem, and when I wanted to travel without straining myself, I would ride the baggage rack of a Greyhound bus to California.

"Before I left I would build me a nest on top of the Empire State so that when I came home I could rest on top of the world. I would dig worms in Radio City's gardens and set underneath a White House bush when I visited Washington. I would wash my feet in every fountain from here to yonder, and eat greens in every meadow. Down South I would ignore FOR WHITE and FOR COLORED signs—I would drink water anywhere I wished. I would not be tied to no race, no place, nor fixed location.

"I would be the travelingest bird you ever met—because everywhere that Jackie went, I would go. Every time Robinson batted a ball over the fence, I would be setting on that fence. I would watch Joe Black daily, and caw like mad for Campanella. I would outfly the Dodgers from New York to St. Louis, and from Boston to Chicago. Everywhere they went, there would be old me. Ah, but I would fly! On summer evenings I would dip my wings in the sea at Southampton and in winter live on baby oranges in Florida—if I did not go further to the West Indies and get away from Jim Crow. In fact, come to think of it, I believe I would just fly *over* the South, stopping only long enough to spread my tail feathers and show my contempt.

"If I was a bird, daddy-o, I would sometimes fly so high I would not see this world at all. I would soar! Just soar way up into the blue where heaven is, and the smell of earth does not go, neither the noise of juke boxes nor radios, television or record shops. Up there, I would not hear anything but winds blowing. I would not see anything but space. I would not remember no little old taw-marble called the world rolling around somewhere with you on it and Joyce and my boss and my landlady and her hound-dog of a Trixie. There would not be no paydays up there, neither rent-days nor birthdays nor Sunday. There would not be nothing but blue sky—and wind—and space. So much space!

"But when I got real lonesome looking at space, I would head back towards earth. I would pierce old space with my beak and cleave the wind with my wings. Yes, I would! I would split the sky wide open to get back to earth. And when I come in sight of Lenox Avenue, man, I would caw once real loud. Everybody would look up and think it was a horn honking on the Chariot of God. But it wouldn't be nobody but me—coming back to Harlem.

"I would swoop down on Seventh Avenue at six P.M. in the evening like a bat out of hell, do two loop-the-loops over the Theresa, and land on 125th Street by the Chock-Full-O'-Nuts. Then I would change myself back into a human, take the bus to my corner, put my key in my old landlady's vestibule, go up to my Third Floor Rear, wash my face, change my clothes, lay my hair down, and go see Joyce, and tell her I am tired of eating raw greens—to cook me up some ham and collards. I could not stand to be no bird anyhow if Joyce were not with me. Also, I would miss my friends. I would see how lonesome it were all day long up there in the heavenly blue and I would come back to this earth and home. Two beers, bartender!"

20

That Powerful Drop

Leaning on the lamp post in front of the barber shop, Simple was holding up a copy of the *Chicago Defender* and reading about how a man who looks white had just been declared officially colored by an Alabama court.

"It's powerful," he said.

"What?"

"That one drop of Negro blood—because just *one* drop of black blood makes a man colored. *One* drop—you are a Negro! Now, why is that? Why is Negro blood so much more powerful than any other kind of blood in the world? If a man has Irish blood in him, people will say, 'He's *part* Irish.' If he has a little Jewish blood, they'll say, 'He's *half* Jewish.' But if he has just a small bit of colored blood in him, BAM!—'*He's a Negro!*' Not, 'He's *part* Negro.' No, be it ever so little, if that blood is black, '*He's a Negro!*' Now, that is what I do not understand—why our *one* drop is so powerful. Take paint—white will not make black *white*. But black will make white *black*. One drop of black in white paint—and the white ain't white no more! Black is powerful. You can have ninety-nine drops of white blood in your veins down South—but if that other *one* drop is black, shame on you! Even if you look white, you're black. That drop is really powerful. Explain it to me. You're colleged."

"It has no basis in science," I said, "so there's no logical explanation."

"Anyhow," said Simple, "if we lived back in fairy tale days and a good fairy was to come walking up to me and offer me three wishes, the very first thing I would wish would be:

THAT ALL WHITE FOLKS WAS BLACK

then nobody would have to bother about white blood and black blood any more. And my second would be:

THAT ALL POOR FOLKS WAS RICH

which would include my relatives—so I wouldn't have to worry about them any more. After that I'd wish:

250

THAT ALL SICK FOLKS WAS WELL

then nobody would suffer."

"Do you think things are that simple?" I asked. "If everybody in the world were the same color, nobody was poor, and everybody was well, do you really think there would be no more problems?"

"All *mine* would be solved," said Simple.

"There would still be the problems of the heart."

"Joyce is *my* heart and I can take care of her," said Simple. "But if I just had one more wish, my fourth and final wish would be:

THAT I HAD MY DIVORCE

—from Isabel, so I could marry Joyce."

"Your divorce is on the way, isn't it?"

"Somebody still has to make that final payment, I told you."

"Since you are making so free with your wishes," I said, "why don't you wish for a little foresight, so you wouldn't start so late doing what you should have done long ago. You have been courting Joyce five or six years. For the last two or three years you have been intending to marry her. And you still haven't saved enough money to pay for even one installment on a three-way divorce. Why is that?"

"You know why that is," said Simple. "I don't make enough money. Since the war plants closed down, who in Harlem has made any money— except politicians, number writers, and dope pushers? Have you? And you are colleged. People with an education should always have money. So if I had another wish, I would wish:

THAT YOU ALWAYS BE STANDING PAT

because you have been on the up and up with me. You are one of my few buddies who will always buy me a beer when I am broke. Naturally I include you in my wishes. In fact, I wish I had a Piel's right now."

"Do you realize this is the middle of the week, also that you've had four beers already, and that excess in anything is sin? Since you are changing the world by wishes tonight, why don't you wish that you were free from sin?"

"Sin ain't free," said Simple. "That costs money, too."

21

Never No More

_____

"If sin was free, this world would be ruint. Mens pay for sin just like everything else. You know, since I have been in Harlem, if I had back all the money I have spent on Zarita, I could buy me a house. I have swore off from that woman more times than once. But the thing about Zarita is she's so handy. All you have to do is turn around on your bar stool, and there she is. Even when a man is not idle, the devil sends his wenches after you. Last night I did something I regrets now."

"Well, what did you do it for?"

"Because I am a rumble-seat lover from way back. And when that boy come by the bar with his Methuselah of a car and asked me did I want to take a ride, I said, 'Yes.'"

"I haven't been in a rumble seat for so long, I thought they didn't make them any more."

"You are too old to get in a rumble seat," said Simple, "but not me. Me and Zarita was in one at this very time last night. I did not go riding alone."

"I thought, now that you are planning to get married, you would no longer associate with Zarita."

"A man cannot go riding in a rumble seat alone, I tell you. And Zarita were right there handy, so I just said, 'Come on.' That was all it took. Next thing I knew, me and Zarita, and Coleman and his girl, was heading across the George Washington Bridge to Jersey, and hair were blowing in my face."

"Stop lying," I said.

"I did not say _my_ hair," said Simple. "It were Zarita's. She done bought herself one of them Josephine Baker horse tails. It is a good thing she had it, too, because even if it is spring, it were cold, so she finally wrapped it around her neck for a scarf. You know a lot of air blows in a rumble seat, and even if Zarita were in my arms, she were cold. I were cold myself, which is why I am sniffling today. And I reckon Zarita ended up with pneumonia because I do not see her here in the bar tonight. But I hope I never lay eyes on her again. Don't you know, she got in a roadhouse juke joint over there in Jersey and cut up like a clown.

"We hadn't even got there before Coleman's old roadster run out of gas, so I had to put in a dollar to buy some, which left me with nothing but small change. All I could offer Zarita on arrival were a beer. Well, some other cat what did not know how much Zarita can drink, and what had never laid eyes on her before, offered her a drink. Zarita ordered Scotch, thinking she should show him she were from New York. He must have been a numbers banker because she could not drink him out of money, and he could not drink her down. Meanwhile all I got is small beers, and all Coleman got is his girl in his arms, because we were both broke. Meanwhile them Jersey mosquitoes is having a meal on my ankles whilst Zarita is having a ball.

"About 3 A.M. I says, 'Zarita, babes, let's cut on back to Harlem.'

"Zarita says, 'Just because I come over here with you, Jesse B., is no sign I'm going back with you. You are just my play-cousin. After all, buses do run. I can get back to Harlem. Even maybe my friend here has a car.'

" 'I will drive you home,' says the old Scotch-buying Negro, which made my Indian blood rise.

"I says, 'Zarita, you come on here with me!'

"I grabs her. Knowing good Scotch when she drinks it, she pulls away. Whereupon, I grabs her again. And don't you know, that other Negro ups his dukes to me. I let Zarita go to paste him one. But before my left landed, his right had hit my chin—and I were flat on my back. He cold-cocked me for fair.

"When I come to, I were dumped in Coleman's rumble seat by myself and he was crossing the bridge to New York. It were the motor sputtering that woke me up and brung me to, because just about then that car broke down for good and would not run another inch, neither a foot, right there in the middle of the George Washington Bridge with the wind just a-blowing through my hair.

"By the time we got towed off that bridge by the police, it were 7 A.M. and time for me to be starting to work. I did not get there. I were chilled to the bone and had to go home and drink a hot toddy. Also my jaw hurt. So I not only lost my money last night, but I lost my time today, also my pay. And I have lost a friend, because I will not speak to Zarita again—except to tell her what I think of her, which I cannot say here. I swore to put Zarita down a long time ago, as you know. But I backslid.

It is not bad to backslide, but to be knocked on your back, daddy-o, that is too much, especially over a chick that don't mean a thing. Also I never intends to get in Coleman's old broken-down car no more. From here on in I stick to this bar stool."

"You had a real joyride last night," I said.

"Except that it were no joy."

22

Simply Heavenly

"Once, when I were a child, I were kicked by a small mule. Neither the mule nor I had any sense. I were trying to make the mule go one way, but the mule was trying to make me go another. I were for hitching the mule onto a plow. The mule were for nibbling grass. So, after that kicking, I learned right then and there to respect animals and peoples when they are not of the same mind as you are."

"What prompts you to make these remarks?" I asked.

"Joyce," said Simple.

"Why?"

"Because last night it were her determination to see Tyrone Power's picture at the Rex along with Tarzan, and it were my determination to see Ava Gardner at the Lincoln."

"I know you ended by seeing Tyrone Power."

"We did," said Simple. "Joyce can be stubborn as a small mule— although she has not kicked me yet. But sometimes she rubs me the wrong way. I said, 'Baby, they ain't neither one of them double features nothing but movies. Me, I had much rather set up in a bar and have a cold beer.'

" 'You never think of nothing but beer, Jess Semple,' Joyce says. 'You know I am a respectable girl and do not like to be seen setting up in no bar like Zarita. I pay my church dues regular, attend services every first Sunday, and would sing in the choir if I had not lost my voice in the flu. Neither beer, whiskey, gin, nor bars appeals to me.'

"I said, 'Joyce, that is one reason I like you because you are a good woman. But I don't believe a little beer ever hurt anyone.'

" 'You do not stop with a little,' says Joyce. 'You go the whole hog. When you was courting me, and I was weak for you and followed you around, I have seen you set up and drink as many as six bottles—after which you expected me to see you home, instead of *you* seeing me home like a gentleman should a lady. Alcohol gives you loose thoughts, which is no way for a man not divorced to behave. A good girl always has expectations, otherwise she is loose, too. Have you ever known me to be loose, Jess Semple?'

" 'I have not,' I says. 'You always have been a lady. In fact, at times you have been too much of a lady. But just as bar booths was made for kissing, you know me—I do not believe in going to a movie *just* to look at pictures. And in the dark, baby, I cannot always see you.'

" 'If you are referring to my complexion,' says Joyce, 'go get yourself one of them bleached blondes and see if I care. Just because I asked you to go to a show with me tonight, you must be trying to make an issue or something. I am going upstairs and dress.'

"And she went upstairs, leaving me sitting in the landlady's front room. Joyce knows I did not intend to mean to hurt her, but, after all, she hurted me."

"How?" I asked.

"By trying to make me out ignorant and a lickertarian. A woman thinks she knows everything, and Joyce is a woman. Sometimes she tries to be two women at once and outtalk herself. Me and her landlady began having a nice pleasant conversation—for a change—whilst I were waiting downstairs for Joyce to dress. But when she come down, she took it up. And she crossed me again."

"What was the subject of the conversation?" I asked.

"Marriage," said Simple. "Old landlady said she thought nobody had a right to get married less they owned their own house, could afford to set a woman down and not let her work, just let her keep house and get her husband's dinner. Too many colored womens, she said, had to work, keep house, *and get dinner, too*. Now I agreed that that were not the best thing but, I said, if every colored man waited until he owned a house to get married, most men would not get married at all. Also if women waited for a man who made enough loot each and every week to say, 'Here, baby, take this money and set down—this will cover all expenses and leave you some spending change, too,' most colored womens could never get married. Black men ain't white men making One Hundred Dollars per week.

"Old landlady admitted I had a point. We was having a real pleasant time chewing the rag when Joyce come down the steps and heard the last words I said and from there on in, murder!

"Joyce said, 'Jess Semple, Simple ought to be your name, instead of your nickname. If you don't make money, you ought to. I don't call a man ambitious who can't take care of a wife without her going out and slaving every day. Besides, don't say 'most colored women' because I know plenty of women married to men who can take care of them—but good, too.'

" 'Baby,' I says, 'don't take it so serious. Me and your landlady were just discussing. I did not mean no harm. Don't you feel good?'

" 'I felt all right until just a few minutes ago,' says Joyce, 'but I hate to hear anybody talk ignorant. Also I believe in looking on the positive side. If you don't *have,* make an effort to get. You do not make an effort.'

" 'What do you call that which I make each and every day from eight A.M. till the five o'clock bell rings?' I asked. 'Furthermore, how come you gets so personal, Joyce? Me and your house lady were talking theoretical—till here you come getting personal. Womens have to bring every conversation down to their own level—which is them.'

" 'Women want a decent home. We don't want to ride that crowded subway to work and back every day before we can enjoy home,' says Joyce. 'When working women get home at night we're too tired to take pleasure in it—and then have to clean up and cook for some great big old—'

" 'Don't say it,' I said. 'Don't call me no kind of name, not even a decent one! Joyce, do not call me a great big old nothing. I am not your husband—yet. And if I am going to have to earn One Thousand Dollars a week to be your husband, skippy! Shame on you! It will never be.'

"Now that is what hurt her feelings. She thought I meant we would never get married. What I really meant was I would never make a Thousand Dollars a week. Hardly even a Hundred. But Joyce took it the wrong way like I was saying she were not worth a Thousand Dollars. Her feelings was bruised. But she had bruised mine, too. I felt hurted and she felt hurted. I got mad and she got mad.

"Her landlady just waddled on back to the kitchen and started singing 'Precious Lord, Take My Hand.' After a while, Joyce and me went down the street, but Joyce were still salty.

"She said, 'You don't need to spend nothing on me tonight. I got my own money.'

"I *was* kinder embarrassed in the pocket, so I said, 'Since you got money, lend me Five. I will spend it on *you,* but I'll give it back.'

"Just to prove she still loved me, I reckon, Joyce came through with the loan. She knowed I did not intend to mean to hurt her, also that I would buy her a house and a car, too, if I could.

" 'Let's go see Tyrone,' I says, as if she hadn't suggested it herself. I give in to Joyce on the picture—just as I give in down South to that little old small mule after I got kicked. A woman can always find words to get a man's goat, have her way, hurt his feelings, and make him do what she wants him to do.

"When we got to the movies, I said, 'Joyce, lay back in my arms and rest yourself and have a piece of gum.'

"But Joyce refused to lay back, so in no time I were asleep—the picture not being a Western nor Ava Gardner. When I woke up, instead of Joyce laying in my arms, I were laying in *hers*—which is just as good. And which proved there wasn't nobody really mad after all.

"I said, 'Joyce, is you feeling all O.K.?'

"She looked right into my eyes and whispered, 'Simply heavenly!'

"So I went back to sleep again."

Part Two

Manna from Heaven

23

Midsummer Madness

Pavement hot as a frying pan on Ma Frazier's griddle. Heat devils dancing in the air. Men in windows with no undershirts on—which is one thing ladies can't get by with if they lean out windows. Sunset. Stoops running over with people, curbs running over with kids. August in Harlem too hot to be August in hell. Beer is going up a nickel a glass, I hear, but I do not care. I would still be forced to say gimme a cool one.

"That bar's sign is lying—AIR COOLED—which is why I'd just as well stay out here on the sidewalk. Girl, where did you get them baby-doll clothes? Wheee-ee-oooo!" The woman did not stop, but you could tell by the way she walked that she heard him. Simple whistled. "Hey, lawdy, Miss Claudy! Or might your name be Cleopatra?" No response. "Partner, she ig-ed me."

"She really ignored you," I said.

"Well, anyhow, every dog has its day—but the trouble is there are more dogs than there are days, more people than there are houses, more roomers than there are rooms, and more babies than there are cribs."

"You're speaking philosophically this evening."

"I'm making up proverbs. For instance: 'A man with no legs don't need shoes.' "

"Like most proverbs, that states the obvious."

"It came right out of my own head—even if I did hear it before," insisted Simple. "Also I got another one for you based on experience: 'Don't get a woman that *you* love. Get a woman that loves YOU!' "

"Meaning, I take it, that if a woman loves *you*, she will take care of you, and you won't have to take care of her."

"Something like that," said Simple, "because if you love a woman you are subject to lay down your all before her, empty your heart and your pockets, and then have nothing left. I bet if I had been born with a silver spoon in my mouth, some woman would of had my spoon before I got to the breakfast table. I always was weak for women. In fact, womens is the cause of my being broke tonight. After I buy Joyce her summer ice cream and Zarita her summer beer, I cannot hardly buy myself a drink by the middle of the week. At dinner time all I can do is walk in a restaurant and say, 'Gimme an order of water—in a clean glass.' "

"I will repeat a proverb for *you*," I said. " 'It's a mighty poor chicken that can't scratch up his own food.' "

"I am a poor rooster," said Simple. "Womens have cleaned me to the bone. I may give out, but I'll never give up, though. Neither womens nor white folks are going to get Jesse B. down."

"Can't you ever keep race out of the conversation?" I said.

"I am race conscious," said Simple. "And I ain't ashamed of my race. I ain't like that woman that bought a watermelon and had it *wrapped* before she carried it out of the store. I am what I am. And what I say is: 'If you're corn bread, don't try to be an angel-food cake!' That's a mistake. . . . Look at that chick! Look at that de-light under the light! So round, so firm, so fully packed! But don't you be looking, too, partner. You might strain your neckbone."

"You had better take your own advice," I said, "or you might get your head cut off. A woman with a shape like that is bound to have a boy friend."

"One more boy friend would do her no harm," said Simple, "so it might as well be me. But you don't see me moving out of my tracks, do you? I have learned one thing just by observation: Midsummer madness brings winter sadness, so curb your badness. If you can't be good, be careful. In this hot weather with womens going around not only with bare back, but some of them with mighty near everything else bare, a man has got to watch his self. Look at them right here on the Avenue—play suits, sun suits, swim suits, practically no suits. I swear, if I didn't care for Joyce, I'd be turning my head every which-a-way, and looking every which-a-where. As it is, I done eye-balled a plenty. This is the hottest summer I ever seen—but the womens look cool. That is why a man has to be careful."

"Cool, too, you mean—controlled!"

"Also careful," said Simple. "I remember last summer seeing them boys around my stoop, also the mens on the corner jiving with them girls in the windows, and the young mens in the candy store buying ice cream for jail bait and beating bongos under be-bop windows. And along about the middle of the winter, or maybe it was spring, I heard a baby crying in the room underneath me, and another one gurgling in the third floor front. And this summer on the sidewalk I see *more* new baby carriages, and rattles being raised, and milk bottles being sucked. It is beautiful the way nature keeps right on producing Negroes. But the

Welfare has done garnished some of these men's wages. And the lady from the Domestic Relations Court has been upstairs in the front room investigating twice as to where Carlyle has gone. When he do come home he will meet up with a summons."

"I take it Carlyle is a young man who does not yet realize the responsibilities of parenthood."

"Carlyle is old enough to know a baby has to eat. And I do not give him credit for cutting out and leaving that girl with that child—except that they had a fight, and Carlyle left her a note which was writ: 'Him who fights and runs away, lives to fight some other day.' The girl said Carlyle learned that in high school when he ought to have been learning how to get a good job that pays more than thirty-two dollars a week. When their baby were born, it was the coldest day in March. And my big old fat landlady, what always said she did not want no children in the house, were mad when the Visiting Health Nurse came downstairs and told her to send some heat up.

"She said, 'You just go back upstairs and tell that Carlyle to send me some money down. He is two weeks behind now on his rent. I told him not to be setting on my stoop with that girl last summer. Instead of making hay while the sun were shining, he were using his time otherwise. Just go back upstairs and tell him what I said.'

" 'All of which is no concern of mine,' says the Health Nurse. 'I am concerned with the welfare of mother and child. Your house is cold, except down here where you and your dog is at.'

" 'Just leave Trixie out of this,' says the landlady. 'Trixie is an old dog and has rheumatism. I love this dog better than I love myself, and I intends to keep her warm.'

" 'If you do not send some steam upstairs, I will advise your tenants to report you to the Board of Health,' says the Health Nurse.

"She were a real spunky little nurse. I love that nurse—because about every ten days she came by to see how them new babies was making out. And every time she came, that old landlady would steam up. So us roomers was warm some part of last winter, anyhow."

"Thanks especially to Carlyle and his midsummer madness," I said. "But where do you suppose the boy went when he left his wife?"

"To his mama's in the Bronx," said Simple. "He is just a young fellow what is not housebroke yet. I seen him last night on the corner of Lenox and 125th and he said he was coming back soon as he could find himself a good job. Fight or not fight, he says he loves that girl and is crazy about his baby, and all he wants is to find himself a Fifty or Sixty Dollar a week job so he can meet his responsibilities. I said, 'Boy, how much did you say you want to make a week?' And he repeated himself, Fifty to Sixty.

"So I said, 'You must want your baby to be in high school before you returns.'

"Carlyle said, 'I'm a man now, so I want to get paid like a man.'

" 'You mean a white man,' I said.

" 'I mean a *grown* man,' says Carlyle.

"By that time the Bronx bus come along and he got on it, so I did not get a chance to tell that boy that I knowed what he meant, but I did not know how it could come true. . . . Man, look at that chick going yonder, stacked up like the Queen Mary! . . . Wheee-ee-ooo! Baby, if you must walk away, walk straight—and don't shake your tail-gate."

"Watch yourself! Have you no respect for women?"

"I have nothing but respect for a figure like that," said Simple. "Miss, your mama must of been sweet sixteen when she borned you. Sixteen divided by two, you come out a figure 8! Can I have a date? Hey, Lawdy, Miss Claudy! You must be deaf—you done left! I'm standing here by myself.

"Come on, boy, let's go on in the bar and put that door between me and temptation. If the air cooler is working, the treat's on me. Let's investigate. Anyhow, I always did say if you can't be good, be careful. If you can't be nice, take advice. If you don't think once, you can't think twice."

24

Morals Is Her Middle Name

"It takes a whole lot of *not* having what you want, to get what you want most," said Simple, cooling off at the bar.

"Meaning?" I asked.

"Meaning you have got to do without a lot of things you want in order to get the main thing you want."

"What do you want?"

"Joyce," said Simple, "to be my wife—*soon.*"

"And what is it that you will have to do without?"

"My beer and my sport," said Simple. "I am on an allotment, in other words, a budget. I have made up my mind to make that final payment on my first wife's divorce myself, so I can be free to marry my final wife. So now I do not buy but one glass of beer per day—which is my allotment. After hours I no longer sport around a-tall, neither gamble—which is my budget. I have opened a savings account and I put Ten to Fifteen Dollars in it each and every week. I soon will have that One Hundred and Thirty-Three Dollars which is the third payment on my divorce. Since my wife's husband-to-be made the first payment, and Isabel made the second, I have now made up my mind to make the third."

"I think it is no more than right," I said.

"It is *not* right," said Simple. "Isabel run me out of the house. If she wants a divorce, she should pay for it herself. But now that she has found a chump who will marry her, and pay a third of it, too, I figure it will speed things up if I meet that other third—since I want to marry Joyce before I get old as Methuselah."

"All this time you've been standing Joyce off waiting for your divorce; you should consider yourself lucky. She certainly has more patience than most women."

"Joyce is a saint," said Simple. "She knows my heart is in the right place even if my pocketbook is empty. That girl knows I love her. But life ain't all that long, that a girl so good should be stood up indefinite. Joyce says if I don't marry her this year, skippy! She says she is tired of paying room rent by herself. Also if she stays *Miss* much longer, she will have missed the boat. Joyce says she is going to get on board some kind of boat this year even if it is a tug.

"I told her, 'Baby, don't put me in a class with no tug. I am a big-time excursion boat, myself. I hauls the finest only, that is why I am waiting now to take you on my deck.'

" 'When will your decks be clear?' asks Joyce.

" 'When I have saved One Hundred,' I said, 'which will be when I have done without *One Thousand* glasses of beer.' "

"You have counted carefully," I said.

"Which is why, daddy-o, I have give up drinking, also any other kind of sport which takes money. I even skipped seeing the Dodgers play this season, and only looked at Jackie on television, in order to prove to that woman that I will do a whole lot of not having what I want, to get what I want—which is her. Joyce is sweet, I mean! In my heart she is a queen! My desire, my fire, my honey—the only woman who ever made me save my money!"

"I am glad to see your mind made up," I said.

"A man has to make his mind up," said Simple, "to get a woman to make his bed down. You know, Joyce is not like a lot of these women around New York. She don't have no truck for trash that don't act right. Just this evening she was reading and it were a colored paper, and she asked me why it is that every time she looks in it they got on the society page the picture of some colored pimp or racketeer or low lady stuck up there as representative of society. That I do not understand myself."

"I understand it," I said. "The racketeer people and night-life folks are about the only ones in these days of high prices who have got the money to entertain lavishly."

"Well, money or not," said Simple, "Joyce says she do not see why they is got to be set up as examples for kids to imitate. She tried to make a issue out of it with me, even, when I told her that Sweet Beak Charlie was after all a nice guy, even if he did have an apartment on Sugar Hill, a house in Long Island, two Cadillacs, a wife, and six other womens, and made his money out of numbers. Naturally, him and his wife is bound to go in society."

"They are way up there," I said.

"They are," said Simple, "but Joyce won't admit it, even if they do give cocktail parties all winter and garden parties all summer.

"Joyce yells, 'They ain't no society to me, them and nobody else like them! I know how too many of them got their money, and they did not get it right. They got it out of crooked dice, good-time houses, reefers, bootlegging, and not paying off when somebody hits for more than a quarter—like I did once—and haven't got my money till this day. I do not see how such people rate to be society, their pictures always stuck up on the Society Page of our papers.'"

"Joyce is a pretty strict moralist," I said.

"Morals is her middle name," said Simple. "But she says them other folks do not have neither morals or manners.

"I says, 'Well, at least, they have got money.'

" 'Money is not everything,' says Joyce.

" 'No,' I says, 'but it will do till everything comes along.'

"That makes Joyce mad all over again. 'Do?' she hollers. 'Do for what? Money cannot give back a prostitute her virginity! Neither can money give a P.I. back his good name, nor turn a dope pusher into a Christian. Any woman with money can buy a mink coat, but that does not make her a lady. Any hussy in society can hire a cater to cater a party and roast her a ham and grind it up and ruin it for appetizers when everybody has got an appetite already and would rather have ham sandwiches without calling them hore-do-beers on crackers. I would not care if I served chitterlings,' says Joyce, 'I would rather have my good name, even if I never get it in the papers.'

"Man, Joyce really raved—and she looked at me like as if I was in society. And I ain't never even been in jail—let alone society—but once."

"What were you in jail for?" I asked.

"Not for doing nothing wrong," said Simple. "I just happened to be present when they raided a house."

"What kind of a house?"

"A gambling house."

"Then you were contributing to crime," I said, "by supporting the place."

"I sure did support it," said Simple, "because they got all I had. But I did not run it. It belonged to Sweet Beak who's always got his wife's picture in the society columns nowadays for giving parties."

"Racketeers are not in the papers just for the parties they give," I said. "They often donate a lot of money to charity, or marry one actress after another, or open night clubs, or do something sensational. If good people want to be news, they have to do sensational things, too. Just being good is not enough—at least, not for the newspapers."

"It's not enough for making money either," said Simple.

25

Party in the Bronx

Over all the noises at the bar plus Dinah Washington on the juke box, Simple proceeded to inform me that, speaking of parties, his Cousin Myrtle in the Bronx had fallen out with her best girl friend.

I said, "I do not know your Cousin Myrtle, so I am not interested, fellow."

"I will tell you how it was, anyhow," said Simple. "It were her anniversary."

"What anniversary?"

"Her fifth. She and Alonzo's been married seven years. But they were not together for two, so they just count five."

"Well, it does seem wise *not* to celebrate the years they were separated," I said.

"Anyhow, Myrtle and Alonzo gave a party," Simple went on. "They thought, since it was their fifth anniversary, it would be nice to invite just five couples. Also their apartment is small and licker is high. So they invited me and Joyce, and four more. But nearly everybody brought somebody extra. Annabelle brought five people besides her boy friend—three womens and two men. That made Myrtle mad."

"You should never bring uninvited guests to a party," I said.

"Not when the apartment is small," agreed Simple. "Two of the womens Annabelle brought were so big and fat they took up practically the whole studio couch when they set down. The couch sunk so low in the middle that the biggest woman was practically setting on the floor. It were bad for Myrtle's furniture."

"What did Myrtle say?"

"Myrtle was cold toward them. But she did pass them a drink—which they gulped down like it was their own party. Myrtle said in front she did not want nobody to get drunk, to just have a nice polite social time. So I was thinking of going home early—providing I could get Joyce out of there. But after about seven drinks, one of them uninvited men guests started the ball rolling and passed it to Alonzo who cut a great big hog by saying, 'Yeah, man.' "

"Yeah, man, to what?"

"To, 'Let's play some blackjack,' which burned Myrtle up, 'cause she had some of her pastor's best amen-corner friends there. But Alonzo had already got half high and forgot. So before Myrtle could get back from the kitchen cracking ice, the cards was out and I had put my money down.'"

"It's a wonder Myrtle did not get mad at you, too," I said.

"I did not start the game," said Simple. "It were them extra mens Annabelle brought. Well, sir, every time they dealt, up come a winning 18–19–20, else 11 for them, or blackjack for the dealer, and a low 16–17, else bust for everybody else around the table—even for Alonzo whose cards they was. Alonzo got kinder impolite.

"Annabelle says, 'I hope you do not think my friends is cheating?'

"Alonzo hollers, 'I don't know what I think.'

"One of the uninviteds says, 'You can think anything you want to, but you better not raise your voice no higher at me!'

"Alonzo hollers, 'I *will* raise my voice in my own house. This is my party, my deck, my licker—also *my money* I am losing, so I will raise my voice.'

"It was then that Myrtle asked Annabelle to take her friends out.

"Myrtle says, 'This is my fifth wedding anniversary in seven years so I only invited five couples—and these folks are not a part of them, for whom no collation is prepared. Furthermore, I do not allow no blackjacking in my house. Alonzo knows that. If he do not care to abide by his Christian upbringing, Alonzo can go, too.'

" 'Myrtle, I pays the rent for this apartment,' said Alonzo.

" 'You paid *one* month's rent,' said Myrtle, 'but I bought the furniture. Every stick in here is mine—and you know it. There will be no more cards dealt on this table. I abominates gambling.'

"Myrtle hauled off and knocked the dropleaf table down. Cards, dimes, and dollar bills went every which-a-way. Alonzo and Myrtle raised their voices at each other—also at Annabelle. In fact, at all but me and the big fat lady who never moved from the middle of that studio couch. We just poured ourselves another drink.

"Finally Joyce got Myrtle out in the bedroom whilst Annabelle took her folks and left—and they carried *all* my money with them. Now Myrtle does not speak to Annabelle who were once her best friend.

"I said, 'I hated to see them folks leave with my dough. If this had not been a nice polite social party, Myrtle, they wouldn't have got out of here, either—except over my dead body.'

"Myrtle says, 'That's what I appreciates about you, Jess— you know how to behave yourself at a function.'

"To which Joyce agreed. 'Honey, I never want you indulging in no low arguments.'

"I said, 'Don't worry, Joyce, I never will.'

"But I did not tell her that I know all them card-sharpers by sight, also where they hang out down by the Braddock, and I intends to cut them a brand-new one. I am the baddest Negro God's got. I am just too well raised to show my badness at functions."

26

Last Thing at Night

"When you see a little old lady with a head like a pet bird, she can really talk," said Simple as we walked up the street.

"I never did notice a pet bird's head," I remarked.

"Well, you must have noticed my next-door neighbor's, name of Miss Amy," continued Simple. "She's the one who sets on the stoop next to my landlady's in the cool of the evening all summer long and talks to every human that passes. That Miss Amy will talk to *anybody* who comes by, know them or not. I usually try to approach my place from the opposite end of the street when I arrives home from work, so she don't get a hold of me. Sometimes I have not et and I do not want to be held up. Else I have a date coming up and I am in a hurry. But, regardless, that old lady will halt you."

"What does Miss Amy talk about?" I asked.

"Any and everything," said Simple, "to any and everybody, from blackeyed peas to Eisenhower, from Adam Powell to Adam and Eve. This evening that old lady shook me. Just as I was starting up my stoop, with heads out windows all up and down the street—and her voice is shrill, too, you know—she asks me, 'Has you ever been married to a white woman?'

" 'Who, me?' I says.

" 'I am talking to nobody but you,' says she, 'neither to your shadow nor your soul-case. I addressed you.'

" 'Why do you ask *me* such a question, Miss Amy?'

" 'Because I wants to know how it feels to be black married to some-body white who less than a hundred years ago just got through selling your grandpa, and who lynched your papa no time ago—and even Jim Crowed you last week. If you was married to a white woman, dark as you is, what would you think when you was with her?'

" 'I would not be thinking about what took place a hundred years ago, you can be sure of that. My mind would be on the NOW, not the then.'

" 'Um-hum!' said Miss Amy. 'I just wanted to know. It is hard to kill the man in any human, no matter what color the woman may be. A man is just like a dog—doggish! But if I were a black man, I would not be enticed by no white woman. No indeedy! I would think about my mother.'

" 'Miss Amy,' I said, 'you would not do no such thing—think about your mother—were such a time to come. Setting out here on this stoop in the sunshine, it is all right to think now what you would think. But there are other times when thoughts do not much matter. And you do NOT think about your mother at such times.'

" 'A rascalian like you does not,' says Miss Amy. 'But I have thought about my mother at all times. As long as she lived, I thought about her.'

" 'Miss Amy, I think you forgets. There must have been times in your life—which I would declare to be long—when you must have put your mother out of your mind. Meaning no disrespect, mind you. But there are times when folks just do not think about mama, I swear there is. Have you ever been married?'

" 'Two or three times, at least,' said Miss Amy. 'But as long as she lived, my mother always came first.'

" 'First thing in the morning, you mean, maybe,' I said.

" 'My mother were always uppermost in my mind,' said the old lady, 'first thing in the morning *and* the last thing at night—except for my prayers.'

"To this all I could say was, 'Aw, Miss Amy.' "

27

They Come and They Go

"Do you know what happened to me last night when I got home?" said Simple.

"How could I—when I haven't seen you since?"

"F.D. was setting in my room."

"Who in the world is F.D.?"

"Franklin D. Roosevelt Brown."

"I haven't the least idea whom you are talking about," I said.

"I am talking about the fact I never did think I would be being a father to a son who is not my son, but it looks like that is what is about to happen to me."

"A son?"

"Same as," said Simple. "I've been adopted."

"It's beyond my comprehension."

"Mine, too," said Simple. "But his name ought to make you remember what I told you once about my Cousin Mattie Mae's baby being born down in Virginia a long time ago when she were working for them rich white folks, and she named that baby Franklin D. Roosevelt Brown. Them rich old Southerners got mad when they heard it, and told Mattie Mae she better take that white name off that black child. Mattie Mae told them she'd quit first, which she did.

"Well, when I got home high last night at one-two A.M.—having fell off my budget—and come creeping up the steps not to disturb my old landlady, I saw a light under the crack of my door. I thought maybe Zarita had got in my room by mistake, since sometimes she do inveigle my landlady. But when I opened the door, I hollered out loud, also damn near turned pale. I had not expected to see no Negro setting on my bed. I thought he were a robber. Every hair on my head turned to wire. But it were not no robber. It were a boy.

"When he riz up grinning, instead of fighting, I yelled, 'If I knowed who you was I'd grab my pistol out of that drawer and shoot you before you could speak your name, but I do not want to kill nobody I don't know. Who *in the hell* is you?'

" 'F.D.'

" 'F.D. who?' I said, still shaking.

" 'Don't you remember me? I'm your Cousin Mattie Mac's boy, Franklin D. Roosevelt Brown. You saw me when I was five years old.'

" 'You sure ain't five now,' I said, 'and you done scared the hell out me, setting on *my* chair in *my* room at this time of night, and I ain't seen you since you was a baby. You big as I am. How old are you?'

" 'Seventeen, going on eighteen,' he said.

" 'What are you doing out so late?'

" 'I'm not just out, Cousin Jess. I'm gone.'

" 'Gone! From where?'

" 'Home. I left.'

" 'Left what home? I ain't heard tell of you, nor Mattie Mae neither, in ten years. Where do you live, Brooklyn?'

" 'Virginia,' he said.

" 'Your mother sent you here?'

" 'My mama does not know I am gone,' he said. 'I ran away.'

" 'Well, how come you run *here*?'

" 'Because you're my favorite cousin. I got your address from Uncle George William. I've heard tell of you all my life, Cousin Jess. Folks at home're always talking about you. And I never will forget that hard big-league ball you bought me when I was five years old, and you came home on that visit. I broke my mama's lamp with it and got whipped within an inch of my life. But I never did blame you for it—like the rest of them did. I sure am glad to see you now, Cousin Jess. Howdy!'

" 'Set down,' I said. He set. 'On what did you come here—hitch-hike?'

" 'No, sir. Train. I didn't dream of getting to New York, Cousin Jess, wasn't even thinking of it. But I've been wanting to come, ever since my step-father raw-hided me. Then when Mama Mattie just keeps on telling me I'm just like my father, no-good, I was thinking of running away to Norfolk and joining the navy, till somebody told me I wasn't old enough without my parents' consent. Then I thought I'd run as far as Baltimore maybe before frost sets in. But all this was just kind of vague in my mind. Then, last night, I was hanging around the station watching the trains come in and the girls eating ice-cream cones when a colored man got off the streamliner from the North and he said to me, *Here, boy, here is a ticket for you. The rest of this here round-trip, I do not want it. Use it, sell it, tear it up, or give it away. I don't care.*

" 'I looked at it and saw that it was a ticket to New York—a great long yellow ticket. I said, *Aren't you going back up North?*

" 'The man said, *I been up North. They comes and they goes. You go.*

" 'He cut out and left me standing there on the train platform with the ticket in my hand. So when the night train came along in a few minutes heading North, I got on. Here I am.'

" 'Here you is, all right,' I said.

" 'I always did want to come North, Cousin Jess, so I come to you—'

" 'Don't get *me* confused with the North! I ain't the North.'

" 'And I always wanted to see New York and—'

" 'My room ain't New York. Out yonder is New York.'

" 'You are all the Harlem I knew to come to, so—'

" 'Excuse me from being Harlem, because I ain't. Where are you going to sleep? Also eat?' I said. 'How are you going to live?'

"Then that kid took his eyes off me for the first time. He looked down. In fact he looked like he were going to cry.

" 'O.K.,' he said, 'I guess I can't sleep here. And I'm not hungry. So so long, Cousin Jess.'

"He got up and reached for his hat which were on my dresser. In my mind I was going to say, 'Go on back home.'

"Instead I heard my mouth say, 'Hey, you, F.D.! Hang your clothes on the back of that chair. You can sleep over there next to the wall—I got to jump out early when the alarm goes off. I'm telling you, though, I'm a man that snores when I'm in my licker, so if you can sleep through—'

" 'If you don't mind a fellow that kicks in his sleep, Cousin Jess—'

" 'Did you bring your toothbrush?'

" 'No, sir, just the clothes on my back.'

" 'Well, you can get a toothbrush tomorrow.'

"So that's the way it were. My big old landlady let F.D. in to wait for me when I wasn't home. Now, what am I gonna do?"

"You say he's going on eighteen. He's practically a man, isn't he? So he'll know his way around soon."

"I don't know my way around yet," said Simple.

28

A Million—and One

"When I first come to Harlem, I remember, some of them folks that was here then are gone now. It's true, all right, as that man told F.D., 'They come and they go.' New York is too much for them. Some can't make the riffle, just can't stand the place. Some go to Sea View, some to Lawnside Cemetery, some to Riker's Island, and some go back home. Some get off trains back down South where they come from—and stay. They *been* North, like that man said.

"If I had not told so many lies myself in my time, I would believe F.D. was lying. But I know that sometimes a lie is the truth. And some things that really happen are more like lies than some things that don't. F.D. couldn't make up nothing like his story about that ticket that would be *that* true. So I know it was true. That boy wanted to come to New York so bad he wished himself up on a ticket. Then he had sense enough to believe the ticket was real. It were real. And here he is!

"Do you think I will tell F.D. to go home? I would not!" said Simple. "I remember when I first come to Harlem, nobody had better not tell me to return back home. I do not know if I looked like that kid or not. But I can see F.D. now setting there last night on that chair with one million dreams in his eyes and a million more in his heart. Could I tell him to go home?"

"What kind of kid is F.D.?"

"About the darkest *young* boy I ever seen. And he has the whitest teeth which, when he smiles, lights up the room. He also looks like he has always just taken a bath, he is so clean. Fact is, I would say F.D. is a handsome black boy, but my judgment might be wrong. I want you and Joyce to meet him. He's a husky young cat, done picked so much tobacco he's built like a boxer. Also plays basketball, says his high-school team were the county champeens last spring. He's graduated and got a diploma, too. I know he's smart because the first thing he asked me for this morning when that alarm clock went off, was, 'Cousin Jess, you got any books I can read while you're at work?'

"You know, I couldn't find nothing but a comic book. But I borrowed a dollar from my landlady and told him, 'Go out and look at Harlem today—till I find my books. There ain't but about a million Negroes in Harlem. You will make One Million and *One*. Get acquainted with your brothers.'

"You mean you turned him loose on the town unaccompanied, just like that, and he's never been here before?"

"Could I stay off from work just to go sightseeing with F.D.?"

"I suppose not, but—"

"And do I know anybody else rich enough to be off from work in the day time? I do not. That young boy did not want to be cooped up in that hot room in the warm summer time with nobody there. And it was a good thing I turned him loose this morning, too, because do you know what he did?"

"No."

"F.D. found himself a job the *first* day he was here. I'm telling you the Semple family is smart even on the Brown side."

"How did he accomplish that miraculous feat?"

"He asked a boy running for the subway if he knew where a job was. The boy said, 'I'm running to my job now. If you can keep up with me, there might me another one down where I am.'

"So F.D. run, too. He like to lost that boy in the subway rush, but he pushed and scrooged along with him, and ended up in the garment center. When that boy run in and grabbed a hand-truck loaded with ladies' garments, F.D. grabbed a hand-truck, too. So the man thought he was working there all the time and give him a invoice to deliver. When he come back, he give him another one. And they put F.D. down on the payroll as hired. That boy just went to work on his nerve."

"It runs in the family," I said. "That's the way you drink, on your nerve—and your friends."

"Come Saturday, I can borrow from F.D.," said Simple.

"Where is he now while you're supporting the bar?"

"I sent him to the movies. He is too young to invite in a bar. But if it was left up to me, I would rather have him in this nice noisy café which ain't no more immoral than them jitterbug candy stores where they sell reefers and write numbers for kids. More junkies hang around a candy store than in a bar, also dope pushers, which I hope F.D. do not meet. What am I going to do with that boy when he starts getting around? Harlem is a blip. He cannot just go to movies every night."

"What you are going to do about sending him back home or, at least, getting in touch with his parents, is the problem it seems to me you should be considering."

"I should?" asked Simple. "I took for granted F.D. were here to stay. I ain't none of his close relations that I have to correspond with his ma. And from what he told me tonight whilst we was eating in the Do-Right Lunch, in my opinion, he just as well not be with Mattie Mae. She's married again and got seven children by another man, not F.D.'s father. They got more mouths than they can feed now. Which is maybe why that boy is so smart. He's been working since he were eight-nine years old. So if he has to look out for his self anyhow, it might as well be in New York where the color line will not choke him to death. I ain't even thought about F.D. going back home."

"Don't you suppose his mother will worry about where he is?"

"I will tell F.D. to drop Mattie Mae a card tonight when I get in. I do not intend to stay out until A.M. and set a bad example for that boy. And he better be home when I get there."

"Do you intend to start bossing the boy around immediately?"

"I intend to start keeping him straight," said Simple. "I know some of the ropes in New York, and if I find him pulling on the wrong ones, I will pull him back."

"Do you intend to keep him with you in that small room of yours?" I asked. "That will cramp your style slightly for entertaining, will it not?"

"Zarita better not light around that room while F.D. is there," said Simple. "I will ask Joyce to take him to church to meet some nice young girls what attends Christian Endeavor or B.Y.P.U. Since I am F.D.'s favorite cousin, he is going to meet some of Harlem's *favorite* people, you know, society, *up there*—the kind I do not know very well myself, but which Joyce knows. I will not let a fine boy like F.D. down. I might even try to meet a few undrinking folks myself—just to have somebody to introduce F.D. to. He ain't got around to the point of asking me yet where I go when I go out. But if he gets curious I'm liable to end up at Abyssinia's prayer meeting some night."

"For you," I said, "I think that would be carrying things a little far. That boy will like you just as well when he finds out your true character. With young people, just be yourself, and you'll get along. Kids don't like four-flushers, nor false fronts, you can be sure of that. Take my advice and just be yourself with F.D."

"There's something else you can give me tonight besides advice, daddy-o. Maybe you'll lend—"

"My good man, please don't start that again. Always borrowing—"

"You thought I was going to say money, didn't you? Uh-uh! Fooled you for once. I was going to say, lend me some extra books you got around your place for that boy to look at."

"Happy to, of course. When?"

"Right now, tonight," said Simple. "I don't want that boy to wake up nary another morning and I ain't got a single book in the house. He will think I am ignorant. Give me some books now."

"Suppose I am not going home now?"

"I very seldom ask of you a favor outside a bar."

"You have *never* asked me for one like this before. Come on, let's go get the books. The Lord must have sent that boy up North to bring a little culture into your life. Joyce has been trying all these years without success. Thank God for Franklin D. Roosevelt Brown!"

"Mattie Mae had a point when she gave that boy that powerful name," said Simple. "It has done took effect on me. I might even read one of them books you are going to lend me. I got to have something to talk about with my cousin. He's educated. Virginia schools for colored ain't as bad as they used to be, so he has learned a lot more than I. Of course, I can talk with you because when you drink beer you come down to my level. But F.D. is too young to drink, so I got to come *up* to his. Am I right?"

"I think you are very right."

"Then pick me out a book I can read *now* this evening," said Simple.

"They say *Knowledge cannot be assimilated overnight*," I reminded him.

"I don't care what they say," said Simple. "It can be laying there ready to assimilate in the morning."

29

Two Loving Arms

"I am glad F.D. got a job in that Jewish dress factory," said Simple, "because he will learn something. It is good to work around some other kinds of people than Gentiles. I thought all white folks was white folks until I come North to Maryland. I did not know some were Jews. In Virginia I do not recall that it made any difference. The better-class folks is more gentlemen down there than to use bad names about somebody's race. But in Baltimore at the shipyards where I worked, folks flung words around right freely about Jews and Negroes, too. But I would fling the dozens right back at them—and back up the dozens with my fists. You see this scar over my left eye? Well, the white man what give it to me got a worse scar over his right lip. I was the baddest Negro God's got when I were young.

"Anyhow, when I first got to Baltimore, before I worked in either the foundry or the shipyards, I worked in a Jewish dress store where colored people could not try on a dress. You know, most downtown stores in Baltimore is like that. A colored woman has to buy hats, dresses, and shoes by sight, without trying them on, if she buys them at all, less'n she shops in the colored neighborhood. Baltimore is worse than way down South in some things.

"Anyway, Mr. Harris what owned this store was a right nice man and he told me it were not his fault Baltimore had them kinds of customs because in the Old Country where he come from there was no prejudices against colored folks, just against Jews. He said some places was RESTRICTED to Jews in the Old Country when he was a kid. That was the first time I knowed this. We used to talk about race problems quite a heap, because Mr. Harris were what he called a 'liberal,' which meant he voted for Roosevelt three times.

"I used to love to hear them Jewish people talk in their own language to each other and with their hands, too. I got so I used my hands a lot myself, throwing them up in the air, which is maybe why Isabel thought sometimes I was going to hit her. I never hit no woman—although I have sometimes been forced to protect myself and push them *off of me*. The only woman I sometimes wish I had hit now is Cherie—that girl that run when Mabel looked her in the eyes in the beer booth. Cherie were really no-good—like Zarita. Except that Zarita will drink you up for fun, whereas Cherie drunk you up only for money. But I did not know that then. I used to talk big around the store about little slick Cherie and how glamorous she was. I never did mention Mabel at work, only Cherie. I used to tell the nice old head Jewish lady clerk about how swell she looked.

"That old lady must of knowed I was young and foolish because she would say to me, 'Swell—*smell*! Swell is what swell does, not how swell she looks!'

" 'But this girl is beautiful!' I'd say.

" 'Beautiful, *snootiful*,' this old Jewish lady clerk said— which was just about right. Cherie was snooty. As long as a man was putting down cash, she was O.K. But don't pay, and she snubbed you in public. When the contest come, she run off and left me to face Mabel in that booth by myself. She rooked me, then shook me. If I had not met Isabel, I would have been alone again.

"Working in that dress shop, I used to hear the Jewish people talking all the time about Palestine, like the Irish talk about Ireland. I wondered how come Negroes don't talk much about Africa. But we don't. And practically nobody wants to go back there. I guess because it is so different and so dark and so far away. We been here in America longer than lots of other folks have, yet we can't even buy a pair of shoes in them downtown shops in Baltimore. That is Baltimore. That is one reason why when I got here to Harlem, I stayed."

"I see you stayed," I said. "Yet ever so often you speak of the South with longing. You're like those foreign people you spoke of—who come to America, but still remember home. You're a kind of displaced person yourself."

"I'd be a *displeased* person if I had to live down South again," said Simple. "Harlem has got everything I want from A to Z. Here, like the song says, 'I have found my true love.' Them Baltimore womens was just preliminaries, my A-B-C's."

"You've certainly told me plenty about the A-B-C's of your love life in Baltimore," I said, "but not too much about your X-Y-Z's in Harlem."

"*J* is as far as I go nowadays," said Simple. "I stops with Joyce. I can't spell with letters no further down in the alphabet than A-B-C-D-E-F-G-H-I-J-O-Y-C-E."

"Zarita begins with a Z."

"Hers is one name I will never write on no paper. Yet and still, I likes

Zarita. When you are happy, she is happy. Zarita likes to be happy with people."

"That's why they call women like her *playgirls,*" I said.

"I reckon it is," said Simple. "And she can be a right good plaything. But don't get me wrong, bud, I don't love Zarita. She is always broke. And when I am hang-overed, Zarita is hang-overed. Zarita ain't good for but one thing, to have fun with. Cherie in Baltimore was like that too, and being young, I made the mistake of loving her. Never no more! That is not really love."

"Just what do you call love, I'd like to know?"

"Love is when you are broke and hungry, she says, 'I don't mind being hungry either.' When you are hang-overed, she says, 'I will put a cold towel on your head.' When you are happy, she will say, 'You make me happy, too.' Instead of, 'Why don't you get out of here and earn me some money?' Or, 'How come you didn't come home sober?' Or, 'I can't see nothing to be so happy about when I ain't got a rag to put on my back?' Do you see what I mean by *love?*"

"Long-suffering," I said.

"Exactly," said Simple. "Some women pretends they like to suffer, but when a man is really suffering, they ain't got no sympathy for him. Cherie runs. Isabel raised a flat-iron, even Joyce just turns cool. Don't womens know a man's got feelings, too, as well as they have? When you're broke you need company. When you got a hang-over, you need sympathy. And when you're happy, you need somebody to be happy along with you."

"You want an angel," I said, "not a woman."

"I wouldn't want to be bothered with all them wings an angel's got," said Simple. "Wings might fly up and hit me in the eye. Arms is all I need, just two pairs of arms."

"*One* pair, you mean, don't you?"

"Whatever two arms is called—just so they're loving," said Simple.

30

All in the Family

"F.D. says he don't know which one is the biggest, my landlady or Joyce's. And don't you know both of them evil old landladies is just crazy about that boy!"

"So you took F.D. around to meet Joyce?"

"I did. And Joyce said, 'Jess, when we get married, we're going to adopt F.D.'

"I said, 'In another year F.D. will be big enough to adopt you. He's mighty near grown now.'

" 'We will need a big brother for our babies,' says Joyce. 'And F.D. is a fine boy. He likes culture.'

"Joyce were referring to the fact that he read one of them books you lent us. I ain't read mine yet. But F.D. has done read one and started on mine, too. So when he gets through and tells me what it's all about, I won't have to read mine. He is a very nice young boy, and polite to womens. Southern folks raises their kids better than Northerners, I do believe. F.D. has got manners—even if he is got the nerve to call me *coz* already—short for cousin. One thing, he is about the most pleasantest young fellow I been around, always talking and smiling that big old bright smile of his. I do not mind having him in my room at all. In facts, he is company for me. Also he has offered to pay half the rent."

"Did you accept?"

"What do you mean, did I accept? F.D. has not been here hardly a week yet. He is a young boy just getting started in New York and I am his kinfolks. You know I would not accept no rent from that boy. What good is relatives if they can't do a little something for you once in a while? None of mine never helped me since Aunt Lucy died. But if somebody had of helped me just a little bit when I were in my young manhood, I might of gotten somewhere further by now, not just laboring from hand to mouth. I am going to help this boy, and he is going to get somewhere. F.D. is already helping me."

"How do you mean, helping you?"

"With somebody around to talk to, I don't spend so much dough in bars any more, as early as Joyce goes to bed."

"You don't mean to tell me you keep that young man up all night long talking to you after you get home from your rounds?"

"I get home early now—to see if he has got home. I done commanded F.D. to be in the house by midnight. Just so he won't think I'm spying on him, I comes home about twelve-thirty or one. He's laying on his side of the bed reading a book. I do not want to put the light out while he's reading—also I am not sleepy so early—so I start talking to him. And we talks sometimes till two-three in the morning."

"It must run in the family," I said, "both of you are night-owls. What can you find to talk about with a youngster like F.D.?"

"Life," said Simple.

"That covers a very wide range of subjects," I said.

"F.D. ain't no baby. When you are going on eighteen now, it is just like going on twenty-eight when I were a child. Besides, he were raised by Mattie Mae, and even though she's my cousin, she never was known to be no lily."

"You don't need to tell everything you know about your Cousin Mattie Mae," I said.

"I say that to say this," said Simple, "Mattie were not bashful with nobody. So I know she did not raise F.D. on Sunday school cards alone. He knows the facts of life. You know what he asked me already? I were telling him about the reason I have started putting Five or Ten dollars in the leaves of the Bible every week is because I am preparing to pay for my divorce.

"F.D. says, 'Then you were married legally, and not common law?'

" 'I regrets it, but I were,' I said.

"F.D. said, 'But, coz, I always heard common law is better since it doesn't cost so much to get loose.'

"I did not think it would be good morals to agree with F.D., so I said, 'Boy, where did you hear that?'

" 'From mama,' said F.D.

" 'Mattie Mae said that?' I acted like I was surprised.

" 'Yes, but mama didn't really believe it herself, after she saw the results,' said F.D., 'because after my third brother and sister came, she told my step-father he had *better* marry her—or she would get out an injunction to keep him from rooming at our house. So they got married. Which was all right by me,' says F.D., 'except that he thought his fatherly duty was to tan *my* hide, which I never did like, not being his child. And you know I am too big to whip now. But look at these scars on my legs.'

"F.D. stretched one leg out from under the sheet and raised it up, then he pulled the other one out. Both of them were whelped up.

" 'Mama should not have let him whip me like this, should she? But she is crazy about that Negro.'

" 'I will whip you myself,' I said, 'if you talk to anybody else that way about your mama, F.D. After all she is *my* cousin. 'Course, you can talk to me—since it's all in the family. But let's keep it there.'

" 'Naturally,' says F.D."

31

Kick for Punt

" 'Did you know who my father was, Cousin Jess?' F.D. asked me last night, 'because I never even as much as laid eyes on him.'

" 'I knowed the Negro,' I said. 'I met him once when I were home on a visit before I settled permanent in the North. He were a big black handsome man. Folks called him John Henry because he worked on the railroad and were just passing through with the construction.'

" 'I wonder where the construction gang went on to?' asked F.D.

" 'That, son, I do not know,' I said. I meant *coz*. But not being around that boy since he was five, he seemed more like a son to me than a cousin, even a third or fourth cousin. I always think of cousins as being around my age. Anyhow, I told him I did not know much more about his father than his mother did, except that he were a great one for bawling and brawling, laughing and joke-telling, drinking and not thinking. I wanted to say, 'F.D., I am surprised at you taking to books because all your father could read were the spots on the cards. But he really could play skin, blackjack, and poker. How I know is he beat me out of my fare back to Baltimore, then laughed, and took me out and bought me all I could drink.' But I did not tell that boy that about his father. I said, 'Coz, he were a right nice fellow, always smiling and good-natured just like you, so you come by it naturally. And if he had ever seen you, he would have been crazy about you because you were sure a lively boy-baby. It is too bad that construction gang moved on before you were born. They was working Northwards. I wouldn't be surprised if your daddy warn't somewhere in Harlem by now.'

" 'I wish I could find him,' said F.D. 'But he wouldn't know me and I wouldn't know him, we never having seen each other. But I wish I would find him.'

" 'Wishing that hard, I expect you will find him,' I said, 'just like you wished up a ticket to come to New York.'

" 'I wish I would,' he said, half asleep by that time, and he went on to sleep. So I turned out the light—but not before I jumped into my shirt and pants, and come on out here to the bar to grab myself a couple of more beers. You see I ain't got on nothing now but house shoes, don't you?"

"That boy is liable to wake up and wonder where in the hell you have gone," I said.

"If he do, it won't be the first time he has missed a relative in the middle of the night, I bet. I have been behaving myself right good since I had F.D. under my wing. At least I do come home, even if I might maybe sneak right out again soon as he goes to sleep."

"Why you think you have to deceive that boy about your night-prowl habits, I don't know," I said. "You do nothing vicious or wrong, and I am sure he's not the kind of boy who would look down on a man for imbibing a bit of beer, would he?"

"No, he would not," said Simple. "But I do not want him to think because I am out all night, he should maybe be out, too. So I come in— and come out again when he is unconscious. Just like it took Joyce two or three years to find out I did not go *right* home to bed when I used to leave her house. She knows it now, though."

"And she loves you right on. Just as this boy will still like you when he finds out you don't need more than three or four hours' sleep. He'll probably admire you just for that."

"Next week will be time enough for him to find out, though, won't it? This week lemme set a good example."

"Good examples are not set by deceit," I argued.

"Oh, but sometimes they are," said Simple. "A congressman is a good example until somebody catches him with a deep freeze. A minister is a good example until he gets caught with the deacon's wife. I am a good example as long as F.D. *thinks* I am in my bed asleep. I don't have to always be there in person, do I?"

"Getting your proper rest would do you no harm, however."

"Vacation's coming up. I'll rest then. So don't worry about me."

"Last year you went to Saratoga, didn't you? Where are you going this time?"

"I know where I *ain't* going—and that is to the country. Yes, I know the poem says, 'Only God can make a tree.' But I sure am glad God let Edison make street lights, too, also electric signs. I like electric signs better than I do trees. And neon signs over a bar, man, I love! A bar can shelter me better than any tree. And a tall stool beats short grass any time. Grass is full of chiggers. It is too dark in the country at night, and sunrise comes too early. In the daytime you don't see nothing but animals. Horses, pigs, cows, sheep, birds, chickens. Not a one of them animals ever said one interesting word to me. Animals is no company. I like them in zoos better. Trees I like in parks, birds in somebody else's cages, chickens in frozen-food bins, and sunrise in bed. No, daddy-o, I will not go to the country this summer. I like lights too well."

"You see Tony flashing these lights off and on, don't you? He is about to close the bar. We'd better get out or there won't be any light—except daylight."

"Doggone if it ain't four A.M.," said Simple. "Yonder is dawn breaking. Dawn never was as pretty in the country as it is sneaking over Lenox Avenue. Lemme get on home and see is F.D. done kicked the pillow out from under his own head. That is the kickingest boy! Punt formation! He dreams he's playing football in his sleep—drop-kicks, place-kicks, punts, goals. Dream on, coz, but damn if I want to be the ball! If you kick me this morning, I sure will kick you back."

"You won't get much sleep anyhow, going to bed this late."

"Yes, I will, too," said Simple. "I sleep quick."

32

Night in Harlem

"I come up out of that hot subway tonight at 135th and Lenox, and I saw so many Negroes in the streets I started to turn around and go back down again. I believed I'd lost my boundaries," said Simple. "Since I have seen so many movies these recent years about how bad off I am in this *Home of the Brave,* I swear I believe I *am* worse off than I am.

"There are sure a lot of Negroes living around 135th and Lenox, including me. When I saw all them Negroes tonight, I started to holler out loud. I were shocked. There are so many dark folks in the world, I started to butt my head on the pavement and holler, 'Dark, dark, dark!' Up the street and down the street, nothing but colored. When that boy in *Lost Boundaries* come up out of the subway in the middle of Harlem and saw all of them Negroes, he were shocked, too, because he did not realize how many colored folks there are. I were like him—tonight I had a temporary blackout."

"Harlem is nothing to joke about," I said.

"Can't I make up a movie, too?" asked Simple. "Dig this: it is a tragic situation I finds myself mixed up in surrounded by all colored—and *No Way Out.* I am too dark to pull a *Pinky,* so I come up from the subway and go mad, disturb the peace. The next thing I know I am up before some old white judge. Judge says, 'Boy, why did you disturb the peace?'

"I say, 'Because I have lost my boundaries.'

"Judge says, 'You better find them again, damn quick, else I will give you ninety days.'

"I says, 'Your Honery, Judge, in this home of the brave, I thought a man had a right to lose his boundaries?'

" 'Not and disturb the peace, too,' says Old Judge.

" 'Peace is disturbing me,' I says. 'I expect it would disturb you if a thousand colored folks come crowding into your Court Room. I bet you would go flying out the back door with your robes floating,' I says. '*Intruders in the Dust,*' you would holler, 'Vamoose! Vamoose!'

" 'Respect the dignity of this court,' yelled Old Judge. 'I would do no such thing.'

" 'Well, I would,' I said. 'Because when you lose your boundaries, you lose your mind. Your judgment goes blind. It is hard to be sane if you ain't among your kind. Judge, if you saw all them movies about my race during the last few years, you'd know what I mean. *Pinky* was light, but not right. That boy in *Lost Boundaries* was near white, but things was tight. In *Home of the Brave* all we could do was rave—there were *No Way Out*. Couldn't even jump in *The Well*—because it were hell! So, I ask you, Your Honery, what's it all about?'

" 'Case dismissed!' Judge says."

"Now that you have acted out your fantasy," I said, "I still can't see your point."

"It is too dark to see," said Simple. "But all jokes aside, when I come up out of the subway this evening and saw my people, it were really just the other way around. I were delighted! I would not have gone back downtown for nothing. I fell in on Lenox Avenue like a fish falls back in a pool when it gets off the hook. In Harlem night time is the best time, because folks have the *best* time. Night is the coo-oo-ool time when breezes blow, the sun don't hurt your eyes, you are full of dinner, relax and dream and see your girl, walk and go to the movies, order a beer in a nice cool bar. Daytime, nothing but work. Night time—fine! There is as much difference between day and night as there is between colored and white."

"The social scientists say there is *no* difference between colored and white," I said. "You are advancing very unscientific theory."

"Do I look like Van Johnson?" asked Simple.

"No, but otherwise—"

"It's the *otherwise* that gets it," said Simple. "There is no difference between me and Van Johnson, except *otherwise*. I am black and he is white, I am in Harlem and he is in Beverly Hills, I am broke and he is rich, I am known from here around the corner, and he is known from Hollywood around the world. There is as much difference between Van Johnson and me as there is between day and night. And don't tell me day and night is the same. If you do, I will think you have lost your mind."

"Night is simply the absence of day," I said.

"Night is also the absence of time-clocks, and bosses! 'Do this! Do that!' And running for the bus, run out to lunch, run back to work, run to get uptown before the laundry closes to get a clean shirt out, run, run, run all day, run! Night you walk easy, set on a stoop and talk, stand on a corner, shoot the bull, lean on a bar, ring a bell and say, 'Baby, here I am!' Night time is the right time! And me and night is both the same color. If I had my way it would always be night, calm and cool and dark and easy on the eyes like Marian Anderson or Delores Martin or Joyce who is my favorite woman in this world. And the sky would be always all lit up with stars—like them eyes of Joyce's. And along about eleven P.M. the moon would rise—just like when Joyce smiles—to light up the sky and me. Along about midnight A.M. I would hear music and it would be Sarah Vaughan on the juke box because I would be standing in a bar. And I would lift up a cool glass of beer and say to some pretty little gal setting there on a stool:

> *Here's to the night!*
> *It's a delight!*
> *With you on my right,*
> *May it never be,*
> *Goodnight."*

33

Staggering Figures

"If you had a Million Dollars and no poor relatives, what would you do with your money—buy a saloon?" I asked Simple.

"First I'd marry Joyce," said Simple. "And I would not buy no saloon, since I can come in here and drink. I would buy a house. After I bought the house, I would set Joyce up in business, so she would not always be around the house."

"That's a strange thing to say," I said. "Most men want their wives to stay home and keep house."

"I like to drop ashes on the floor sometimes," said Simple, "so I would want Joyce to be home in the daytime only to cook because, if I had a Million Dollars, I would be home all the time myself. I would not go out to work nowhere—I would just rest and get my strength back after all these years I been working. I could not rest with no woman around the house all day, not even Joyce. A woman is all the time saying, 'Do this' and 'Do that.' And 'Ain't you cut the grass yet?'"

"I would say, 'No, I ain't, baby. Let it go till next week.'"

"Then, if she's like the rest of the women, she would say, 'You don't take no pride in nothing. I have to do everything.' And she would go out and cut it herself, just to spite me.

"That is why, if I had a Million Dollars, first thing I would do if I was married would be to set my wife up in business so she wouldn't worry me. Womens like to be active. They *hate* to see a man set down. So I would give my wife some place else to be active other than around me."

"In other words, you would make your wife work," I said.

"I would rather make her work than to have her make *me* work. Of course, if she was the type that just liked to lounge around and eat chocolates, which I have never known no colored woman to do, that might be different. Colored women are so used to working that they can't stop when they get a chance to set down. And they hate to see a man do nothing. Why do you reckon this is?"

"You've supplied the answer yourself. Activity over a long period of time breeds intolerance to inactivity," I said. "One has to be accustomed to leisure to know how to enjoy it."

"I am not accustomed to it," said Simple, "but I really could enjoy it. Why, man, if I had a Million Dollars, I would not stir a peg nor lift a finger! Of course, I might tap my own beer keg. But I doubt if I would even do that. I would have a house-man to tap it for me. I would also have a butler serve it. And I would have a valet to press my clothes, so all I would have to do would be to get in my car and go downtown to see how my wife was running her business. If I found her with time on her hands, I might say, 'Baby, come on home and cook me some lunch.' "

"You certainly do have old-time ideas about women," I said.

"I cannot put them in force," said Simple. "Lend me a dime for that last beer so I can get home and see if F.D. is in the house. I am not only broke tonight, but beat. Buddy, you are heaven-sent! Any man who will lend me a dime is O.K. by me any time. Money talks! Big money hollers! I couldn't hear my ears if I had a Million Dollars! I don't like noise—so gimme *just* a dime, and we'll have a drink."

"No! I've set you up twice already. I do not intend to break a dollar, not having a million."

"Loan your dollar to me and I will break it. Buddy, I am as free from money now as a Christian is from sin. Gimme the dollar. I will treat you."

"Calm down, calm down! What are you celebrating anyhow?"

"I'm celebrating just because it's Monday. Tuesday I'm always too broke to celebrate. Wednesday I'm too tired. Thursday I'm disgusted. Friday, exhausted. But Saturday, Sunday, and sometimes even Monday—whoopee! So let's have another one. If I go to sleep sober I might dream I'm handling money, and wake up screaming. I don't trust myself. My left hand might short change my right. Let's have one for the road. Go ahead and break your dollar. What difference do it make?"

"With my dollar intact," I said, "I'm only $999,999 away from having a million."

"Such figures staggers me," said Simple.

34

Tickets and Takers

There was an aura of nothing and nowhere about the night. But the night was lying—for there she sat at the bar, pert as a pussycat in process of purring—which, as soon as Simple saw her, made the evening electric.

"What's your name?" he asked.

"Guess," she said.

"Delores?"

"No."

"Mamie?"

"No."

"Betty Jane?"

"No."

"What then?" asked Simple.

"Lay-overs to catch meddlers," she said.

"I ain't heard that one since I was a child," declared Simple. "You must be older than you look. I thought you was a baby."

"A baby in a bar? Haven't you been around?"

"A little," said Simple, "but I have seen nothing like you nowhere I have been. Neither have I seen you in here before. Where've you been hiding?"

"I'm from Philly," she purred.

"Oh! Visiting?"

"I came to stay if I have my way. Buy me a drink."

"I thought we'd get around to that," said Simple, mounting a stool beside her and beckoning to the bartender. "My name is Jesse B."

"Um-hum! Nice to know you. Married?"

"Naturally," said Simple, "about to about to get married again—maybe to you if my A-1 turns me down. You don't look like you've got any solid attachments—out here in the jungle by yourself at this bewitching hour."

"I am waiting for someone," she said, "so don't get too comfortable. I did not come in here just to set and drink alone."

"Waiting for me?"

"Only till my 100 Proof comes along."

"Baby, cannot you tell I am bottled in bond, also aged in wood?"

"You do look aged. But to tell the truth, I love settled men. They make the best providers."

"You like to talk serious," said Simple.

"Also to look ahead," said the girl. "Which is why, if I were to tell you my name, you might want to speak to me the next time we meet. And I might be with Joe. And Joe does not like me speaking to strange men. Thank you for this drink!"

"Is Joe bigger than me, blacker than me, or what—that you think I can't deal with Joe?"

"Joe is a man who does not take no tea for the fever," she stated. "If I wasn't a woman, I would be scared of Joe myself."

"Most womens *would* put their head in a lion's mouth," said Simple. "But as pretty as your head is, wouldn't no lion bite it off. But some man might knock it off."

"Joe aims the other way," said the girl. "When he gets through, there is *him* and *me* standing there. But *you* are on the ground."

"How do you figure *me*? I would like to see Joe or any other bo lay me low! How come you got to get personal with me?"

"You got personal with me," said the girl. "I was not bothering you, because I am reserved—but you come up and asked me my name. Are you the F.B.I.?"

"I am only Mr. Drinks-I-Buy," said Simple. "Good-bye!"

He was clearly frustrated. He went to the far end of the bar, then came up to where I was, but he could not keep his eyes off the girl. Shortly another fellow was buying her drinks and going through the same routine, trying to guess her name. When he left, another one took his place. The girl just sat there drinking all evening with gentlemen who fell for her guessing game. But when the night was done, still nobody knew who she was. Joe never came. Finally she left.

"I always heard Philadelphia womens are reserved," said Simple. "Which is why maybe Joe didn't show. But if I was Joe I would stick so close to that chick nobody would ever get a chance to ask her name. She is fine."

"You are just weak for women," I said.

"I do have a weak heart," said Simple.

"I would say, *head*," I said.

"Just because I can't guess her name?"

"Not just because you can't guess her name. A man may lose his head over a woman, but a woman always comes out ahead."

"Every time," said Simple. "Where paying is involved, every time. But if Joyce was in town, I wouldn't be trying to make no slick chick like that. Bartender, gimme a beer."

"Joyce is not in town?" I asked.

"She's gone up to Boston for the week-end," said Simple, "to some kind of summer conference of colored women's social clubs. I just come from the station buying her ticket. You know, I have bought train tickets in mighty near every railroad depot in this U.S.A., and I have never yet seen a colored man selling tickets in *no* station where I have been. Why do you reckon that is?"

"I don't know," I said.

"I know," declared Simple. "It is because white folks do not want Negroes near money, that's why. When you get on the train and the conductor comes through and asks for your ticket, who is he? A white man. They do not even want Negroes taking up tickets. We buy tickets. We ride trains. Why cannot we sell tickets, also take up tickets? Huh? I'm asking you."

"You have already answered your own question," I said.

"As many colored folks as ride trains," insisted Simple, "we ought to sell *some* tickets *somewhere* in this U.S.A. But have you ever seen one of us, yellow, black, brown or meriney, setting behind a station window selling tickets? I have not. Now why should that be? We are citizens as well as train riders. Down at the Grand Central tonight seeing off Joyce, I saw all them rows of ticket windows selling tickets every which-a-where—and not *one* Negro in nary window selling a ticket nowhere. The only Negroes I saw in that station was Red Caps toting bags. The only Negroes Joyce will see working on that train is porters. I bet my boots the conductor is not black, neither the engineer, neither the fireman. *Carry and clean,* that is all they let Negroes do on trains and in stations, *carry and clean, carry and clean.* If I'm man enough to buy a ticket, I do not see why I'm not man enough to *sell* a ticket."

"Is it your ambition this late in life to be a railroad ticket seller?"

"It is always my ambition to be more than I is," said Simple. "I am of this American nation, bred, born, and reared here. A man can come right from Europe and never speak English as good as me, still he can get a job selling tickets in an American station, or taking up tickets on an American train. How come I can't?"

"Why do you ask such foolish questions?"

"The question may be foolish," said Simple, "but the answer is criminal. The answer is, 'No, you cannot sell a railroad ticket. You are black.'

"I say, 'But I am an American.'

"They answer, 'You are a *black* American.'

"That is criminal. Do you agree?"

"It may be criminal, but nobody is arrested for it."

"There are lots of crimes for which nobody is arrested," said Simple. "Women who drink men up without telling their names ought to be arrested. I wonder who that cute little slick chick was, Miss F.B.I.?"

"No, man, just Miss Drinks-*You*-Buy."

"That," said Simple, "is no lie! Lemme get home and see about F.D."

35

Subway to Jamaica

"F.D. were not there when I got back home last night in spite of the fact that it were 12:30, past P.M., so I came back out. I did not see you, so I went back in—and I come back out again. I broke my money-savings rule not to drink more than one beer on myself so I can pay for that divorce. I bought four, also a drink of whiskey. I was worried about that boy being a new boy in the block and a stranger in town—some of them young hellions might of ganged him.

"I stood on the corner of Lenox Avenue and looked up and down. No F.D. I walked to Seventh Avenue and looked up and down. No F.D. All the movies was closed. Nothing but bars open, so I went in a bar I had never been in before.

"Then I said, 'To hell with F.D.! He's big as me, so I ain't responsible. I do not care where he's at. What right has he got to worry me like this? I ain't his daddy.'

"I returned back to my Third Floor Rear. He still were not there—going on four in the morning. So I took off my clothes and went to bed. I did not sleep.

"F.D. come in later than me by twice. But I give that boy credit he did not try to tiptoe. If he just had come in with his shoes in his hands sneaking up the steps, I would have riz up mad and caught him with, 'Where the damnation you been, arriving back this time of night?'

"But when F.D. come walking in loud like nothing had happened, creaking every step and hitting on his heels, I pretended to be asleep. F.D. set down on the bed to take his shoes off. I grunted and groaned, 'Uh-er-ummm-uh! Man, why don't you turn on the light so you can see?'

" 'Cousin Jess, I've been having a ball,' he said. 'Listen! We've been to the Savoy. It's fine up there! Two bands and a rainbow chandelier that goes around. I'm learning the mambo. I had to take a girl all the way home to Brooklyn.'

"I could not help it but say, 'Late as it is, I thought maybe you had gone to Georgia.'

" 'No, I got on the wrong subway coming back and forgot to change. I went all the way to some place called Jamaica.'

" 'That happens to every Negro what ever comes to New York, at least once,' I said. 'I think they just made that Jamaica line to confuse Negroes, because everybody knows somebody that lives in Brooklyn, and the first time you start back to Harlem you *always* end up in Jamaica. Don't you have to work in the morning, F.D.?'

" 'Yes, Sir.'

" 'Then fall on over in this bed and get your rest.'

" 'She's a sweet little number, coz.'

" 'Um-hummmm, well, tell me about her tomorrow.'

" 'Were you asleep, coz?'

" 'Yes, I were asleep—till you woke me up.'

" 'I got her phone number.'

" 'Um-hum! Well, I suppose you'll be running to Brooklyn every night now.'

" 'Not every night. I couldn't get a date in edgewise till Sunday. That girl is popular. Sunday we're going to Coney Island.'

" 'I want you to bring that girl up here and let me look her over before you-all get too thick. You hear me, F.D.?'

" 'Yes, sir, but I'll bet you're gonna like her, Cousin Jess. Her name is Gloria. She's eighteen and keen. Dresses crazy—had on a big wide leather belt with green shoe strings in the front and a little tiny waist about the size of this bed post. You gonna like her.'

" 'Turn over and go to sleep, boy. And next time, don't get mixed up on no subway to Jamaica. What you due to take is the *A Train* to Harlem. Otherwise, you will arrive at nowhere, square.'

" 'She don't think I'm a square, Cousin Jess.'

"I made out like I were snoring so that boy would stop talking. Next thing I knew, we was both asleep. F.D. must have been sleeping real good because in a few minutes he hauled off and kicked me, which woke me up. In another half-hour the alarm went off. So I didn't get much rest last night. But I'm glad that boy had fun, though. If you do not have a good time in your young years, you might not know how when you get old. And the sooner you find out what train to take to get to where you are going in this world, the better. The Jamaica train does *not* run to Harlem. It goes somewhere else."

36

No Tea for the Fever

"Joyce says she rid back from Boston with Mrs. Sadie Maxwell-Reeves," said Simple. "Now you can hardly touch her with a ten-foot pole, she is so proud."

"You can't much blame her, can you?" I said. "Mrs. Reeves is one of Harlem's leading club ladies."

"*The* leading, according to Joyce, always giving banquets and teas and things. So cultured she wears her glasses on her bosom. I met her once. Well, anyhow, on the train she told Joyce, 'Darling, you are a clever woman, such as our race needs. Your club ought to make you a delegate to the National Convention next spring, not just to a Summer Regional.'

"So now you know there will be no getting along with Joyce come next winter. She will have me tromping through the cold selling more tickets to teas and forums and recitals than enough. The more tickets Joyce sells, the better club worker she is. She could pay her own fare to the National seven times over, were it meeting in California, if all the work it takes to sell them tickets was put into a *paying* job. Somehow or another Joyce has got the idea that a tea uplifts the race."

"You ought to be glad Joyce has some social and civic interests," I said. "You don't want just a stick-in-the-mud for a fiancée, do you?"

"I want somebody who is going to stick by me," said Simple, "which Joyce has been doing right well until lately. But, buddy, as the summer gets hotter, that girl is getting increasing cool. I told her last night, 'Baby, I done saved Fifty-Five Dollars toward paying for our—I mean *my*—divorce. So it won't be long now.'

"Joyce says, 'It's been too long already. You know I wanted to get married *last* June. All my friends are talking about how you been stringing me along. They think you don't take me serious.'

" 'Look here,' I says to her, 'if I don't get the rest of that money together by Labor Day, baby, I am going to borrow it—some maybe from F.D. who is working like a man, and some from my best bar-buddy, who will do me a favor, I know.' Meaning, of course, you."

"Meaning me!" I exclaimed. "You realize, I suppose, that I have obligations too, though I may not be so vocal about mine."

"I didn't know you're taking singing lessons," said Simple. "Are you a baritone—or a nary tone?"

"I can't carry a tune," I said, "so I'm not taking vocal lessons. But I do have other things to do with my money."

"Whatever you've got to do with your money, I know you'll lend me Twenty or Thirty if push comes to shove. I got to get together One Hundred and Thirty-Three Dollars and Thirty-three and One-Third Cents to make up my share of that Four Hundred Dollar divorce. I writ Isabel I would send it soon. I am getting tired of them proceedings dragging on forever. Nothing but money is holding things up. Joyce is getting ready to go on her vacation and I want to have them divorce papers to show her when she gets back."

"Where is Joyce going this year?" I asked.

"She will not tell me," said Simple. "Joyce is acting salty about almost everything this summer. But I expect she will go over to Jersey and spend it with her friends and her god-child. She is crazy about that little varmint. Joyce pretends like she wanted to spend her vacation with me— that is, had we been married. But she knows I don't get off at the same time she does. Her vacation comes in August, and mine is always in September.

"She says, 'Any man with any gumption could arrange it so he's off the same time as his wife,' she says, 'and if you don't, I will, if and when we are ever united. I will go down and see your boss myself.'

"I says, 'Joyce, it is not that I don't want to. It's just, what's the use? You have told me yourself morals is your middle name, and you would not go nowhere for no two weeks with a single man—nor a married one neither that you are not married to yourself. That is why I did not get my vacation changed.'

" 'You always got an explanation for everything,' says Joyce. 'If you are late getting to heaven, you will give Saint Peter some jive excuse. Well, I will go on my vacation alone, as usual. I had expected this vacation this year to be my second honeymoon—had we been married last spring. But I'm going to have a bang-up good trip anyhow. My vacation will not be no dud, with or without you, Jess Semple. My plans is laid.'

" 'Laid where?'

" 'You will find out in due time. I intends to relax and have myself a ball wherever I go. I have been working hard all winter and all summer. Now I am going to relax.'

"The way she said that word *relax,* daddy-o, I do not feel so good about. What do you reckons she means?"

"Probably just lying in a hammock and reading a book," I said. "You don't have to worry about Joyce."

"I may not have to, but I do," said Simple. "And this is one time I do not want her going off nowheres without me. To tell the truth, if I find out where she is going, I'm liable to take a week off from my work and relax with her."

"You might be unwelcome," I said, "since you say she's holding you at arm's length these days."

"My arm is as long as hers. I will reach out and snatch her bald-headed if she fools with me. She must not know who I am. I am Jesse B. Semple. I loves that girl, and I have come to the point where I will not take no tea for the fever. In fact, I will get rough."

"Do you intend to state all that to Joyce?"

"My statement is being considered," said Simple.

37

That Word *Black*

"This evening," said Simple, "I feel like talking about the word *black*."

"Nobody's stopping you, so go ahead. But what you really ought to have is a soap-box out on the corner of 126th and Lenox where the rest of the orators hang out."

"They expresses some good ideas on that corner," said Simple, "but for my ideas I do not need a crowd. Now, as I were saying, the word *black,* white folks have done used that word to mean something bad so often until now when the N.A.A.C.P. asks for civil rights for the black man, they think they must be bad. Looking back into history, I reckon it all started with a *black* cat meaning bad luck. Don't let one cross your path!

"Next, somebody got up a *black-list* on which you get if you don't vote right. Then when lodges come into being, the folks they didn't want in them got *black-balled*. If you kept a skeleton in your closet, you might get *black-mailed*. And everything bad was *black*. When it came down to the unlucky ball on the pool table, the eight-rock, they made it the *black* ball. So no wonder there ain't no equal rights for the *black* man."

"All you say is true about the odium attached to the word *black*," I said. "You've even forgotten a few. For example, during the war if you bought something under the table, illegally, they said you were trading on the *black* market. In Chicago, if you're a gangster, the *Black Hand Society* may take you for a ride. And certainly if you don't behave yourself, your family will say you're a *black* sheep. Then if your mama burns a *black* candle to change the family luck, they call it *black* magic."

"My mama never did believe in voodoo so she did not burn no black candles," said Simple.

"If she had, that would have been a *black* mark against her."

"Stop talking about my mama. What I want to know is, where do white folks get off calling everything bad *black*? If it is a dark night, they say it's *black* its hell. If you are mean and evil, they say you got a *black* heart. I would like to change all that around and say that the people who Jim Crow me have got a *white* heart. People who sell dope to children have got a *white* mark against them. And all the white gamblers who were behind the basketball fix are the *white* sheep of the sports world. God knows there was few, if any, Negroes selling stuff on the black market during the war, so why didn't they call it the *white* market? No, they got to take me and my color and turn it into everything *bad*. According to white folks, black is bad.

"Wait till my day comes! In my language, bad will be *white*. Blackmail will be *white* mail. Black cats will be good luck, and *white* cats will be bad. If a white cat crosses your path, look out! I will take the black ball for the cue ball and let the *white* ball be the unlucky eight-rock. And on my blacklist—which will be a *white* list then—I will put everybody who ever Jim Crowed me from Rankin to Hitler, Talmadge to Malan, South Carolina to South Africa.

"I am black. When I look in the mirror, I see myself, daddy-o, but I am not ashamed. God made me. He also made F.D., dark as he is. He did not make us no badder than the rest of the folks. The earth is black and all kinds of good things comes out of the earth. Everything that grows comes up out of the earth. Trees and flowers and fruit and sweet potatoes and corn and all that keeps mens alive comes right up out of the earth—good old black earth. Coal is black and it warms your house and cooks your food. The night is black, which has a moon, and a million stars, and is beautiful. Sleep is black which gives you rest, so you wake up feeling good. I am black. I feel very good this evening.

"What is wrong with black?"

38

Boys, Birds, and Bees

"Joyce is gone," said Simple.

"Where?"

"That is just it. I do not know where. She must of left right from work yesterday, which were Friday, because when I rung them seven bells last night, her big old fat landlady waddled to the door and hollered, 'Joyce is gone.'

" 'Gone where?' I says.

" 'You ought to know. You closer than her shadow.'

" 'Madam, I am asking you a question.'

" 'You know her vacation has started. She told me to tell you she would be away for a fortnight, whatever that is.'

" 'A fourth-night?'

" 'Them is her words, not mine, so figure it out for yourself.'

"And she waddled on back through them double doors. What is a fourth-night?"

"Two weeks," I said.

"Well, why didn't Joyce say so? That girl is been around that Maxwell-Reeves woman too much. She's talking in tongues. Two weeks! Well, she can stay gone *two years* for all I care. Facts is, Joyce can *stay* gone. She do not need to come back to me."

"Consider well what you are saying, old boy."

"Don't worry about what I am saying. When she returns, I will close my door against her. I'm a good mind to go home right now and get that money out of that sock I been saving and blow it all in, every damn penny."

"Before I let you do that," I said, "I'll treat you to a whole bottle of beer myself. Bartender, set 'em up! And you, I do not want to hear you talking like that just because Joyce is a little piqued."

"I wish I could peek on her wherever she is at now. Relaxing! I would unlax her."

"Let that girl relax alone and get herself together, calm her nerves, think things over, and come back refreshed. You'll be so glad to see her you won't know what to do."

"She better let me know where she's at by Monday morning," said Simple. "if she do not drop me a line at once *now*, she will find herself dropped. Joyce is embarrassing me. F.D. thinks I know all about womens, and here I don't even know where my own woman is at.

"Last night I took F.D. upstairs to see Carlyle who has come back to his wife and baby. I told F.D., 'Carlyle is a young man a year or two older than yourself. He can give you some good advice which has got me stumped to talk over with you. You been running over to Brooklyn a mighty lot these nights lately, spending time with that keen kitty with the leather belt. Carlyle is a married man. He can tell you *how* he got married.'"

" 'Midsummer madness,' " I started quoting.

"That's right," said Simple. "Now, you take F.D. These young peoples nowadays know a plenty and they act like they knows more. But when you come right down to it, sometimes they don't know B from bull-foot—especially when it comes to subtracting the result from the cause. Sometimes it does not even take nine months to have the answer on your hands. Then they are surprised. F.D. is at the age where a boy needs somebody to talk to him."

"Why don't you talk to him? He seems to respect you."

"That's just it. He *do* respect me. And I don't know how to talk about them things without using bad words. That is all right amongst grown men. But F.D. ain't old enough yet to be drafted. Still and yet, he's old enough to do what the Bible says Adam did—and which has been going on ever since. I don't know what to say to a young boy at that age. I gets somewhatly embarrassed."

"So you turn F.D. over to Carlyle for the birds and bees, eh?"

"Carlyle is more near about his same age. But Carlyle's done had experience with which he walks the floor each and every night."

"Do you expect Carlyle's sex vocabulary to be any cleaner than yours?"

"Dirtier," said Simple. "But F.D. do not respect Carlyle."

39

On the Warpath

"Have you met F.D.'s girl yet?"

"I did," said Simple. "My landlady did also. She passed comment on her, 'Cute as a bug in a rug! Your cousin has better taste than you have, Mr. Semple, being seen in public with streak-haired characters like Zarita.'

"I reminded my landlady that I also knows Joyce.

" 'Which helps a little bit,' she said. 'But I give that young boy, F.D., credit. He did not take up with no trash when he come to New York. Gloria is a real sweet kid. Brooklyn girls is raised. They don't just grow, like they do here in New York. If I was to rear a family,' she continues, 'I would move to Brooklyn—which is a quiet suburb—and leave all you loud-mouthed roomers behind here in Harlem to make out the best way you can. Harlem is no place for a child.'

"Not wishing to carry on the conversation, I did not reply. I were not feeling talkative. Do you know what Joyce wrote me?"

"No."

"Just one word scrawled across the middle of the card like she were in a hurry—*Greetings!* No address, no nothing, but the picture of a beach and some white folks in swimming."

"You could tell from the postmark where it was, couldn't you?"

"It were so pale all I could make out was *AT*—and the rest was hardly there. But it must be Atlantic City, which is where I know Joyce has been before and likes."

"The Paradise, the Harlem, there are some fine night clubs there. Bars, music, dancing."

"I better not go down there and find Joyce setting up in no night club."

"What have you got against night clubs?"

"Nothing. It's what I got against guys who take girls to night clubs. I would not take no woman to a cabaret and spend all that loot on her that I did not intend to take further. A man is always thinking ahead of a woman."

"You have a suspicious mind," I said. "But I am sure Joyce would know how to resist any too intimate encroachments, even if she did accept some handsome stranger's bid for a date."

" '*Bang-up good time—I intend to relax,*' were the last words she said. It's that very last word, *relax,* that keeps running through my mind. On a vacation, you have to relax *with* somebody. If I go down to Atlantic City Sunday, I better not catch Joyce relaxing on the Boardwalk with no other joker. I will run him dead in the ocean. And he better know how to walk the water because he darest not come back to shore with me on the warpath."

"I am sure an exhibition of that nature would perturb Joyce," I said, "and do no credit to your own intelligence."

"About myself I do not care," said Simple. "As for Joyce, it would be worth a round-trip ticket to Atlantic City just to put the fear of God into her heart. Joyce do not realize who she is messing with, upsetting me like this. Here I am ready to give her the best years of my life, soon as that decree comes, and she cuts out on me for a fourth-night leaving no address whatsoever. *Greetings!* Don't she know no more words than that to write to me? She could say, *Dear Jess.* She could say, *Having a wonderful time, but something is missing—you!* She could say, *Hope you are well!* How much do it cost to go to Atlantic City?"

"Damned if I know."

"Lend me a dime," said Simple. "I am going to phone the bus station and find out. Don't let me catch no other Negro down there on no beach relaxing with Joyce when I get there, either!"

"Think carefully, old man," I said, "before starting on a wild goose chase."

"Wild goose, nothing!" cried Simple. "He'll be a dead duck."

40

A Hearty Amen

Monday evening Simple greeted me with a grin.

"Did you locate Joyce?" I asked.

"I did not have to locate her. She located me! I have not been nowhere this week-end but to East Orange across the river. Joyce come phoning me Saturday from Jersey that she were lonesome and to come over there and take her to a movie. Man, I hopped a bus so fast it would make your head swim."

"I thought you were angry with her."

"When my old landlady called me to the phone and I heard that sweet voice, 'Hello, Jess,' I forgot to be mad.

" 'Where are you, Joyce?' I said. 'Atlantic City?'

" 'No, darling,' she answers, 'just right over in Jersey with my god-child's two parents. Sugar Pie, say hello to your Uncle Jess.'

"And don't you know she put that child on the phone and held me up for five minutes. I do not think no child is cute on the phone, especially when it can't hear good. Finally the little varmint dropped the receiver and I got Joyce back. Man, Joyce sounded like old times.

" 'I was just in Atlantic City a hot minute,' she said. 'My friends drove me down there for the day to let me catch some cool breezes. I thought about you, Jess. Come on over here and spend the week-end. Willabee and Johnny say you can sleep on the sleeping porch tonight. They got good screens and the mosquitoes are not bad.'

" 'I am poison to mosquitoes, baby. The last one that bit me died himself. I will be there no sooner than it takes the bus to go through the Holland Tunnel.'

"And, man, I really enjoyed myself over there in that small suburban. Joyce's friends make everything so pleasantlike—Budweiser in the ice box, Canadian Club on the sideboard. Righteous, man! Sunday they invited me to church which, to tell the truth, I enjoyed. Setting there with Joyce smelling like a flower, the old folks singing them old-time hymns, I started thinking about my Aunt Lucy and how she used to love Sunday-morning sermons.

"When the minister said, 'Bow your heads and pray,' I prayed I could keep on being good like Aunt Lucy taught me.

"When I raised my head, the sunlight was coming through them pretty colored windows. I put my hand over Joyce's hand. And the choir sung. And the man said, 'May the Lord watch between me and thee while we are absent one from another.'

"I said, 'Joyce, don't you be absent from me too long.'

"Joyce whispered, 'Jess, I'm coming home Tuesday. I'm going to spend half of my fortnight near you.'

"At that point the minister said, 'Amen!'

"I Amen-ed also."

"All of which leads me to the conclusion that you and Joyce are back on an even keel," I said.

"If keel means back in the groove, then there's nothing left to prove. Come seven, manna from heaven! Cool, fool!"

"Dispense with the hep talk. You're not at Birdland. By the way, how's your protégé getting along?"

"My who?"

"Your young cousin."

"More hep than me—F.D. is wearing Harlem for a sport coat. He works, he plays. But he comes home in time to get himself enough sleep to get up and work and play some more. He does not drink. And he has not taken to dope yet, which, according to the papers, all young Negroes do. Neither does he smoke reefers. He says he had rather buy himself some clothes, take his girl to Coney Island, else mambo with his money. Also to Birdland to hear bop. That boy gets around, him and Gloria. But he do not get run down—being's he's an athlete, he's got to keep his wind. He says he got four letters in high school. Now, what does F.D. mean by that?"

"Football, baseball, basketball, and track, I think. They must have a pretty good high school where he comes from."

"Virginia schools is not bad," said Simple. "One thing about his mama, Mattie Mae, was she probably didn't want F.D. in the house much nohow, so she let him stay in school *all day long* every day. She didn't care how much he studied or played, as long as he were away from home, so she could play in her way. F.D. had sense enough to stay in school, and still have himself a little job shining shoes in a hotel, else picking or packing tobacco, making his own money, till he graduated. Which is why he left home, one reason. That big old no-good stepfather of his would whip that boy if he didn't give him half his shine money for board and keep. He also made him be home in bed by ten o'clock, being some kind of religious frantic."

"Fanatic."

"Um-hum! Anyhow, he grabs F.D. and whips him once too often, and F.D. starts thinking about running away. Upshot, I got him on my hands."

"I believe you've handled the situation pretty well, old boy. But you are lucky in that he is such a decent boy, not a juvenile delinquent. Suppose your cousin were one of these tough young jitterbugs you read about, running around in gangs, smoking marijuana, always getting into trouble. What would you have done with him then?"

"Done with him?" said Simple. "Nothing. I'd just call in my landlady and say, 'You let him in here, madam, so *you* get him out.' I bet that boy would have left there flying. My heavy-hipped old landlady can put out bigger mens than I am. I would have no trouble were F.D. inclined to disturbing the peace. Neither would I have to call the law. Just my landlady, that's all."

"But suppose you had to solve the problem of getting him out yourself if he had turned out to be rowdy? How would *you* get him out?"

"Knock him out," said Simple.

"So force would be your only solution for the problems of juvenile delinquency?"

"I would not be trying to solve no problem but my own," said Simple.

41

Colleges and Color

Six plays for a quarter. Play Frankie Laine six times.

> *Sing a song of juke boxes*
> *In ice-cream bars*
> *Garlanded by comic books*
> *And shiny prints of record stars:*
> *Dinah Washington, Johnny Ray,*
> *Billy Eckstine, Mel Tormé,*
> *Lena Horne, Kay Starr,*
> *And other chirpers favored*
> *In an ice-cream bar.*
> DOUBLE-THICK MALTED.
> *Eat it with a spoon.*
> *It's too darn good*
> *To go so soon!*
> *Nickel for the juke box,*
> *The malted, Twenty-Five:*
> *F.D. and Gloria—*
> *Great to be alive!*

" 'Cousin Jess.'

" 'What?'

" 'Gloria says she wants me to go to college.'

" 'She do? When?'

" 'This fall. Gloria's going. So I already wrote and got my applications. Now all I got to do is write home to the high school and get my basketball transcript, and my football record, and my grades.'

" 'Didn't you tell me you played baseball, too, in school?' I didn't want him to forget nothing important," explained Simple.

"Look here," I interrupted, "would F.D. be going to college to *play*— or to study?"

"Both," said Simple. "So if I live and nothing happens—and I get straight—I am going to send him the money for his first pair of football shoes."

"Well, if F.D. goes to college, what you should think about helping him buy is not football shoes, but books. Men go to college to study, not to play football."

"Footballing is all I ever read about them doing," said Simple. "Since I do not know any college boys, I thought they went there to play."

"Of course, the ones who play football get their names in the papers," I said. "But there are thousands of other students who graduate with honors and never even see a football game. What sort of college is F.D. planning to go to, may I ask? A white college? Or a colored college?"

"I hope to a colored college," said Simple.

"Why?" I inquired.

"So he can get a rest from white folks."

"A student doesn't go to college to get a rest from anything. He goes to gain knowledge."

"At a colored school he can dance with the girls, and not be no wallflower."

"A *man* is hardly likely to be a wallflower," I said. "But I see what you mean. At a colored college he can be among his own race and have a well-rounded social life. Still, I insist, you don't go to college to dance. You go to get educated."

"If I was going to college," said Simple, "I might not get educated—but I would come out with a educated wife."

"Football, dancing, marriage, are all side issues. A college is for the propagation of knowledge—not fun or sex."

"I don't see how you are going to keep sex out of a boy's life, nor fun, neither. If F.D. was a son of mine, not just my cousin, I would say, 'F.D., son, go have yourself a good time whilst you are learning, because in due time you will be married like Carlyle and cannot enjoy yourself like you can in school. Also, go to a colored college where you will get to know better your own folks—because when you come out of college, if you don't work with colored folks, you are going to have to work *for* white folks. And the jobs white folks give educated colored mens are few and far between. If you get to be a doctor, you will have to doctor *me*. I am black. How can you doctor me good if you don't know me?' That is what I would say to my son."

"You have a point there," I said, "but I still insist the prime purpose of college is education."

"Do you mean book-learning?" asked Simple.

"Approximately that."

"Then you are approximately wrong," said Simple. "I do not care what you know out of a book, you also have to know a lots out of life. Life is hard for a colored boy in the manhood stage to learn from white folks. If F.D. does learn it around white folks, he is going to learn it the hard way. That might make him mad, or else sad. If he gets mad, he is going to be bad. If he's sad, he is going to just give up and not get nowheres. No, I will tell F.D. tonight not to go to no white school and be snubbed when he asks a girl for a dance, and barred out of all the hotels where his football team stays. That would hurt that boy to his heart. Facts is, I cares more about F.D.'s heart, anyhow, than I do his head."

"I admit there has to be a balance," I said. "And certainly there are good Negro colleges like Lincoln, Howard, or Fisk, where a boy can learn a great deal, and have fun, too. But the way you talk, fun is first and foremost. You imply that there is no fun to be had around white folks."

"I never had none," said Simple.

"You have a color complex."

"A colored complexion," said Simple.

"I said *complex,* not complexion."

"I added the *shun* myself," said Simple. "I'm colored, and being around white folks makes me feel *more* colored—since most of them shun Negroes. F.D. is not white. He's not even light, so F.D. would show up very dark in a white college."

"That would make him outstanding," I said.

"*Standing out—all by himself,* you mean," said Simple, "and that is just where the 'shun' comes in."

"You are confusing the issue," I said.

"I had rather confuse the issue than confuse F.D.," said Simple.

42

Psychologies

"I do not know why it is that vacations tire Negroes out."

"Neither do I," I said.

"But they do," said Simple. "Negroes go on a vacation and come back so tired they can't hardly get to work. In fact, sometimes they have to take an extra week off to recover from their vacation. Vacations rest up white folks, *but they almost kill Negroes*. Somebody ought to find out the reason for this."

"You probably have some theories on it," I said, "or you wouldn't have brought the subject up."

"My theory is that Negroes play too hard. They always play like they're never going to get a chance to play again. If they do not have but one week's vacation, they try to crowd seven weeks of fun, fading, and fast living into *seven days*. If Negroes go to Saratoga they try to have fun at *all* the night clubs, drink at *all* the bars, pass by *all* the springs, fade the dice on *every* table, and jive *every* cute little chick on Congress Street. That is why a Negro comes back from Saratoga—which is supposed to be a healthy place—completely broke down.

"If a Negro goes to Idlewild he tries to play society jam up, sit in on every bridge or canasta game there is, play poker with every doctor and dentist, dance all night, then swim and dive all day, too. It is too much for him. He cannot make his job when he returns.

"If he goes to Atlantic City, the chorus girls in the Paradise and the Harlem will drive him mad, whether he knows them or not, they are so pretty, and know so many places to go, until his tongue hangs out trying to keep up with them. If he goes to Asbury Park, he's liable to suntan himself to death and come back all peeled and blistered and cannot get no rest because there is no part of his body he can lay on. So how can he go to work?

"And don't let a Negro go to Europe! just talking about his trip will keep him tired for months to come. And the memory of Paris for a summer is enough to tire anybody out for the winter. A Negro that goes to Paris should have the whole winter off to rest."

"How do you know?" I said. "You've never been to Paris."

"No, but I have met some of these big-time sports who have, and they was too tired to sport around when they got back. Couldn't do nothing but sleep. It do not seem to make any difference where a Negro goes on his vacation, though, when he comes back he is tireder than when he went. I never saw it fail. Why do you reckon?"

"Some kind of desperation is involved, I believe," I said. "Vacations for Negroes are hard to come by. Sometimes you have never had one before in your life, so when you get it, naturally you run it into the ground. Sometimes you take your only savings to have some real fun on a vacation. Figuring you might not have another one for a long time, you do that one up brown. Negroes are not rich like millionaires who can take a spring vacation in the Carolinas, a summer vacation in Maine, an autumn vacation in Virginia, and a winter vacation in Florida. When you take three or four vacations a year, you get used to them. You don't have to make every minute count. But when you get a vacation only once in a coon's age, you try to enjoy yourself around the clock. Therefore, one has to rest when one returns. Don't you agree?"

"Must be," said Simple. "I know the last time I had a vacation, it took me a month to catch up on my rest when I got back home. I could not just lay down in bed for three or four hours and sleep quick like I usually do. I found myself going to bed with the chickens at eight-nine o'clock, and getting up twelve hours later still sleepy. This year I did not go on a vacation, so I feel twice as good as I did last year. I just stayed right in Harlem this summer and drank beer. If I had gone to Atlantic City or Idlewild or Asbury Park or Saratoga, I would have drunk licker. I would also have courted and sported. I would have tried my luck on all the different kinds of games from galloping dominoes to the wheel-of-fortune. And I would have been broke, busted, disgusted, and sleepy on my return. I am beginning to believe that the best vacation is right at home."

"That is because you have no self-control," I said.

"Ain't there some kind of saying about, 'When in Rome, do as the Romans do?'" asked Simple. "Well, on a vacation, everybody is roaming. Me, too. And it sure do tire you out. So I am glad I did not go anywhere this year. It looks like the closer I come to marrying Joyce, the more I want to be near her, anyhow, so I just changed bars instead of going away."

"I noticed I hadn't seen you for ten days or so."

"I been hanging out at the Glamour Bar which is fine—with beautiful bar maids. A man has to have some kind of change of scenery. But I am glad to get back here to Paddy's tonight."

"Welcome to your second home," I said. "How about a beer?"

"Sure," said Simple. "Hi, Zarita!"

As she headed for the back room, Zarita chirped a pleasant good evening. Like a magnet, she pulled Simple's eyes right on back with her.

"But this is one time I will fool her," he said. "I will not follow in her footsteps. Here is one lamb Zarita has led to slaughter for the last time."

"No comment," I said. "By the way, what happened to F.D.? Did he go to college?"

"He went to Lincoln," said Simple.

"Lincoln is a good college," I said.

"And colored," said Simple.

"But it may not be colored long. Being in the North, it doesn't have to contend with state Jim Crow laws. And all the trends in education nowadays, I'm happy to say, point toward integration."

"Um-hum," said Simple paying more attention to a new record than he was to me. "I wonder if they teach bopology at Lincoln? Listen at Ella on that juke box, boy, singing like a bop bird. Who said bop was dead? Lay it, Miss Fitzgerald!"

"Bop has left its mark on contemporary music all right," I said, "so I wouldn't be surprised if the colleges do soon have a course in it. Its only trouble is, bop was never meant for dancing."

"Joyce could dance to it," said Simple. "That woman can dance to some of the most off-time music you ever heard. Since returning from her vacation, Joyce has started back to dancing school, expressing herself again, posing and dead-panning and stretching one leg up on the mantelpiece like it were an extra hand on the clock. Downtown they dances to nothing but classics, Show-Pan and Straw-Whiskey."

"Chopin and Stravinsky," I corrected.

"That's right. And them records Joyce buys costs Three Ninety-Five apiece. They sure do play long. The reason I like Ella is because she sings short—like I sleep. Miss Fitzgerald is O.K. by me. She expresses myself, also Mr. B. and Ruth Brown. I sometimes likes Rosemary Clooney, too. I like them short hot kind of records that keeps you jumping. I goes to sleep on Joyce's music."

"I don't imagine Joyce appreciates that."

"Joyce don't care. She's too busy figuring out in her mind which position her foot goes on what bar. In my dancing days, if you could shake it, you could make it. When the lindy and the jitterbug come in, all you had to do was fling. The mambo is simple, too. Just make like you're boxing in time to the rhythms. Box with your hips, too, naturally. But the kind of dancing Joyce is doing, which is expressionistical, aw, man! That takes too much study. But I don't care since it keeps her out of mischief."

"As if Joyce were the type to get into mischief."

"Joyce is a woman, ain't she? From Eve on up, womens always have their eye on the apple."

"You're the apple of her eye, and have been for a long time, so what have you got to worry about?"

"Who she met in Atlantic City," said Simple.

"Just one day there? Joyce hardly had time to meet anybody."

"She got two letters from Atlantic City lately which she keeps fanning under my nose. Last night I grabbed one. I got so mad I almost turned black."

"Incriminating?"

"The first one said:

Baby doll, here is your snapshots—

from which two pictures of Joyce in a bathing suit fell out. Also one of him, long, tall, and grinning.

"I said, 'Joyce, who is this Negro?'

"Joyce says, 'Oh, just some old boy, name of Kite, I met with a Kodak. I wouldn't know him if I was to see him again.'

" 'Who gave him *your* address?'

" 'My friends, I reckon. He were playing with our godchild on the sand and we all got acquainted. Everybody is friendly on vacation.'

" 'Who is that other letter from you holding?'

" 'Kite, too.'

" '*Kite, too!* What's in it?'

" 'He just wants to know did I get the snapshots, since I didn't answer him yet. But if you keep on suspicioning me like this, I will answer him, just to make you jealous.'

" 'Woman, turn off that LP and listen to me. Set down. I bet that Negro has got your snapshot in that white bathing suit setting up on his dresser right now. *Kite!* What kind of a named guy is that for you to be knowing? Were I to see him he sure better *fly*. I never thought you'd be knowing no Kite. Joyce, you makes me feel right bad. You hurts me, Joyce, I swear you do.'

"Nobody said nothing for about five minutes. Then tears come in her eyes. Joyce thought I was gonna get all mad and fuss at her. But I fooled her. Instead, I melted her heart. Joyce showed me that other letter which were nothing but:

> *Dear Miss Lane,*
>   *Did you get the pitchers? Reply rite off plese. This is from*
>   *Your boon coon,*
>   KITE

And the last word were spelled wrong, p-l-e-s-e for *please*. Nothing there, just ignorance, talking about 'your boon coon.' But I looked so hurted on purpose until Joyce cried out loud. She thought I was jealous. Womens is simple.

"Of course, I were jealous until I found out that that Negro could not even spell *please*. Joyce, being cultural, I know would not fall for no dumb simp like Kite. She were just teasing me.

"I said, 'Turn back on your Show-Pan record, baby. Maybe it will calm my nerves.'

"Joyce said, 'I need something more than Chopin to calm mine. Daddy, kiss me.'

"So you see how it worked? I know psychologies. Joyce asked me to kiss *her* for once. I did. And that were the end of the argument. But I will never let her go on a vacation alone no more. It is dangerous for a woman to go on a vacation by herself."

43

Must Have a Seal

"Chicken tender as a mother's love, stewed down with dumplings—that is what we had for dinner Sunday."

"At Joyce's?"

"Sure, at Joyce's. That woman can really mess with pots and pans. Cornbread that melted right out of sight. I didn't leave a piece on the plate. Oh, man, I can't describe that dinner!"

"If Joyce cooks like that now, and you are not even married, what kind of meals will you eat when you set up house-keeping and have your own kitchen?"

"It will be better than cooking in some old landlady's kitchen. Every time Joyce's landlady lets Joyce use her kitchen, she invites herself to eat with us. That's what I was about to tell you," said Simple. "She eats like she never had a pot full of nothing herself. Sunday she slayed that succotash, murdered the beets, completely annihilated the candied sweet potatoes, and drunk a small gallon of coffee. When we got down to the dessert, she was too full to eat more than a ladle of jello, but she put whipped cream on that twice. I'm telling you, it were such a fine dinner, I do not blame that landlady much for scarffing. Joyce buys her vegetables and groceries downtown nearby where she works. The foods is better. Everything is two-three-four cents a pound higher in Harlem. And Joyce likes good groceries. When she gets through salting and seasoning, man, it is scrumptious! That girl is a cook."

"Well," I said, "you have given me an ample description of the dinner. But dinner tables are set as much for conversation as they are for eating. What did you good people talk about Sunday?"

"Politics," said Simple. "November is political times, and Joyce's big old fat landlady took over. She said all them years that she had been persuading all her roomers to vote Democratic, ain't no precinct leader ever presented her with a mink coat, not even a rabbit skin, which is why she switched to Eisenhower. She says, 'The Republicans can bring the country back to normal and keep it there.'

"'You must think the Republicans is God,' I said to her. 'Back to normal would mean I could ride the bus for a nickel, get a shine for a dime, and buy a new suit almost any old time. You know can't nobody bring them miracles to pass.'

" 'I knows no such thing,' says Joyce's landlady. 'That is what politics is for, to bring things to pass. Building inspectors, health inspectors, all of them never bother me at all, since I'm in politics. They know I helps get out the vote, so they leave me alone—which is a miracle. And when I change my vote, every last roomer in my house had better vote like me, else out they goes.'

" 'That, madam' I says, 'is against the law. You can't *make* people vote your way.'

" 'Oh, can't I?' she says. 'Now, take you, Mr. Semple, if you was running for Mayor of New York, you'd want me to swing my votes your way, wouldn't you?'

" 'I'd appreciate it,' I said. 'Would you?'

"She leaned across the table and stated in a loud voice, 'No! I would not! Never! No!'

"Which embarrassed Joyce—and made me mad."

"So that is why you enjoyed the food more than you did the conversation," I said.

"That is one reason," said Simple. "The other reason is that if you don't know anything about anything, like Joyce's landlady, you should not open your mouth."

"Your ruling would practically put an end to conversation," I said. "Almost nobody knows much about anything. Do you want to plunge the world into silence?"

"Only landladies," said Simple, "and wives. Isabel is trying to bug me again by mail. Look what I found on the hall table today from Baltimore!"

He proceeded to read her letter:

"Dear Mr. Semple, My Former Husband,

   This is the very last letter you will ever get from me because I have asked you to do something for me and you do not do it, now I will do it myself. I will pay with my own money my own self for the last installment on our divorce. If I don't, the man I love might get out of the mood of marrying me at all, he has waited so long for you to do your husbandly duty. Jesse B. Semple, I do not think much of you, and have never did. You are less than a man. You marry a woman, neglect her, ignore her, then won't divorce her, not even when your part is only one third of the payment. So you go to hell! The next thing you will get from me will be the Decree, and the lawyer will send that. You do not deserve no gold seal on that paper because you have not put a cent into it and unless a gold seal goes with it free, you will not get one. From now on, you kiss my foot!

ISABEL ESTHERLEE JONES

P.S. I have taken back my maiden name until I get freshly married as I do not want no parts of you attached to me any longer.

MISS JONES

"That is an insult," said Simple. "I will not let Isabel get the last word in on me. I will send that lawyer my part of the money tomorrow. Right now I got saved $92.18. Lend me $41.16."

"In the middle of the week? If ever. Are you out of your mind?"

"This is an emergency. But if I can't emerge with it tomorrow, I will on pay day. I'll add my whole pay check to that money I got in my sock and send it off—because when I get that paper, I want to be sure mine has a gold seal on it, too. A paper don't look like nothing without a seal."

44

Shadow of the Blues

"I got it," said Simple when I ran into him on Saturday.

"Got what?"

"One Hundred and Thirty-Three Dollars and Thirty-Three Cents."

"How?"

"By not paying my landlady, not getting my laundry out of Won Hong Low's, letting my hair stay long, getting no pressing done, neither a shoeshine. And if I don't spend this dollar tonight—which I am about to treat us to a beer with now—I will have One Hundred and Thirty-Four. I am going to send it off to Baltimore early Monday morning, which Money Order will change *Divorce Pending* to *Divorce Ending*—signed, gold-sealed, and delivered. When I get it, it will be like manna from heaven. If you see Joyce, don't say nothing. I want to surprise her with them papers. No more talking."

"Not a word will I say. In fact, I will believe it myself only when I see it."

"You will see it," said Simple. "I have sacrificed for that day."

"So have I," I said.

"You have treated me royal," said Simple, "which is why I am happy to break this One Hundred and Thirty-Fourth Dollar to treat *you* tonight. What will you have?"

"A beer."

"Since I'm busting this dollar, I might as well put a quarter in the juke box. What would you like to hear?"

"If they've got any old-time blues on it, play them."

"Will do," said Simple. "But there ain't no Bessie these days. Do you remember Bessie Smith?"

"I certainly do. And Clara?"

"I bet you don't remember Mamie?"

"Yes, I do—all three Smiths, Bessie, Clara, and Mamie."

"Boy, you must be older than me, because I only heard tell of Mamie. I am glad I am not as ageable as you. You's an *old* Negro!"

"Come now! Let's see what else you might remember, before we start comparing ages. Speaking of blues singers, how about Victoria Spivey?"

"You've gone too far back now if you remember Victoria."

"How do you know how far back she was if you can't recall her?"

"I just recall my Uncle Tige had one of her records when I were born which he used to play called 'The Blacksnake Blues.' I almost disremembers it."

"I see. I wonder if you recall when a boy had to be fifteen or sixteen to wear long trousers. Did you ever wear knickers as a child?"

"Knickerbockers," said Simple.

"Then your life span dates back quite a way. Did you ever see Theda Bara in the nickelodeons?"

"My mama told me about Theda."

"Did you ever see *Uncle Tom's Cabin*?"

"Simon Legree, Little Eva, Eliza and the bloodhounds? My grandma told me about all them. But I remember Clara Bow."

"The 'It Girl' of the flapper age."

"She really had *It*. Also I remember Nina Mae McKinney."

"Since your interest in women goes away back, I'm wondering if you remember when girls wore corsets instead of girdles?"

"They didn't wear neither one in them woods where I came from. Besides I didn't start investigating womens until I were eight. Up to then I was playing agates and yo-yo's."

"Oh, so you remember when each youngster had a yo-yo. That's not exactly a recent toy. You were probably in your teens when boys were making crystal-set radios with ear phones."

"If I were making them, I will not admit it," said Simple. "But I do remember when folks didn't have Frigidaires. My mama used to get her ice from an ice-man in town. And Aunt Lucy hung her butter down in the well in the country. In those days a kid would do an errand for a penny—because a penny was worth a nickel. Now it is hard to get one to do an errand for a dime. *Damn* was a bad word then—even without God in front of it. Ladies didn't smoke. And Madam Walker's would lay it down when nothing else would—so slick a fly couldn't get his bearings. When a boy had a birthday, your uncle gave you a dollar watch—an Elgin. Them was the days!"

"Watch out, you're giving yourself away if your memory goes back that far. You're ancient, man, you're ancient!"

"I only heard about them things."

"Anyhow, to get back to the blues. Let me ask you about one more personality we forgot—Ma Rainey."

"Great day in the morning! Ma! That woman could sing some blues! I loved Ma Rainey."

"You are not only as old as I am, you're older! I scarcely remember her myself. Ma Rainey is a legend to me."

"A who?"

"A myth."

"Ma Rainey were too dark to be a mist. But she really could sing the blues. I will not deny Ma Rainey, even to hide my age. Yes, I heard her! I am proud of hearing her! To tell the truth, if I stop and listen, I can still hear her:

> *Wonder where my*

Yee-ooo!

> *Easy rider's gone . . .*

Great day in the morning!

> *Done left me . . .*
> *New gold watch in pawn . . .*

Or else:

> *Troubled in mind, I'm blue—*
> *But I won't be always.*
> *The sun's gonna shine in*
> *My back door someday . . .*

"One thing I got to be thankful for, even if it do make me as old as you, is I heard Ma Rainey."

Part Three

Sassafras in Spring

45

Nothing but Roomers

Autumn in New York. No burning leaves, no woodsmoke in the air. But skyscrapers at dusk burst into a kind of golden glare. There's coolness, then coldness, then maybe snowflakes in the air. Bang on the radiator—if you've got the nerve—and try to get some heat. The law says they got to turn the heat on by October 15th. Simple's old landlady says, "The law? What law? I am the law in here!"

"Well, anyhow, madam, if you don't care nothing about me—my name being Jesse B. Semple—nor about Mr. Ezra Boyd, nor none of the other tenements in your house, remember there's babies upstairs—Carlyle's baby and that little girl-baby down underneath me. It ain't them babies' faults they're nothing but roomers."

"It ain't my fault they're babies. I told *everybody* when they moved in here, 'No children in this house.' And then them gals had to come up pregnant! I had nothing to do with it. Now, with all the gas they are using heating milk, washing diapers, burning the light all night with the colic, I don't make a cent out of this house. The law says to turn on the heat October 15th, so you say. Well, this is still Indian summer."

"I am part Indian, madam, and it do not feel like summer to me."

"You are all run down, that is what is the matter with you, also run out. At your young age, you got no business being cold-natured, Mr. Semple. Now, you take my husband who is a settled man, he is not cold. Neither am I. But I keeps heat on downstairs for Trixie, that is the reason. She is old and her hair is thin."

"Them babies is young and ain't got no hair a-tall yet. How about them?"

"Can I help it if babies are hairless? Who is running my business—you or me? Just because you been living here seven years, don't think you nor any other roomer can take over, Jesse B. Semple. This is still a private house, a home, and I runs this house like a home. You are my guests. But you are not in charge. I intend to send some heat upstairs as soon as them radiators get drained. That is why there is no heat—I do not want to flood this place. So just hold your horses before you come running down here accusing me of being the kind of woman who freezes babies, I don't care whose they are—even if they were bred by accident."

"Madam, there's no telling how many of us was accidents."

"I'll have you know *my* father and *my* mother was married two years before I was born. I was their third child."

"Three children in two years? Two was twins?"

"No twins—one girl—one boy—then me—a year apart, stair-steps."

"Then that first step must have been a misstep."

"What?"

"I mean three babies in two years is going pretty fast, isn't it, unless somebody got a head start somewhere?"

"I will thank you to leave my presence and stop reflecting on my parents—and on me. The facts are, I must have disremembered. They were really married *three* years when I were born—which, I know now, is what I meant to say. Us stair-steps was three years apart."

"Excuse me, madam, for catching you up. I always was good at mathematics."

"You can't seem to figure out how to keep ahead on your rent. You are almost always behind. Explain me that, if you are so good at figures."

"If I was always on time, would you give me a bonus, a discount for cash on the line?"

"Why don't you try getting ahead sometime and see? One thing I will do, if you showed your appreciation for me by paying promptly every week *absolutely on time,* I would hang you some new winter drapes that would make your room more presentable. You seems to take no interest at all in decoration yourself. Nothing up on your walls but them nude calendars, and they are blondes. I'll bet you, you would not have them white naked nudes up on your walls down South. As race-minded as you pretend to me, I wouldn't have them up on my walls here. Don't your licker store nor bar have no colored girls on their calendars?"

"They do, but they all got clothes on."

"Naturally, no colored woman would have her picture taken with each and every point bared to the breeze. We are more modest. Never would I pose in a meadow for nobody without my clothes on."

"I hope not, madam."

"*Meaning* by that—?"

"Meaning you have such a beautiful character you do not have to show your figure. Your soul does it, madam. There is sweetness in your face. F.D. loved you like a mother."

"I thank you. Have you heard from F.D.?"

"That boy's done got on the freshman football team. He sure is a kicker. And he sends you his regards."

"Thanksgiving I'll send that F.D. a fruitcake. You have a smart young cousin, Mr. Semple. I am one who likes to see young people get ahead in this world. Were I young again, I would go to college myself."

"Where did you get your education, madam?"

"The hard way. I was working in a tobacco barn when I was fourteen. I first married when I was sixteen and started buying a house. This man is my third husband. This house is my fourth house. And this house I swear I am gonna keep. Neither husbands nor mortgages is gonna take this house from me. I handles this business myself now. This property is in my own name—and all the papers. Losing husbands and losing houses is what has been my education. Now I say, 'To hell with husbands—I am going to hang onto this house!' I'll tell any woman, a roof over your head is better than a husband in your bed! A good woman can always get a man, but a house costs money.

"Set down, Mr. Semple. If you're interested in my education, I'll tell you. Me and my No. 1 husband—that Calvin were as young as Carlyle when I married him—we mortgaged our house to start a barbecue restaurant in Charlotte in *his* name, with a juke box. Don't you know that Negro put all his profits in the piccolo, playing records, entertaining every chippie that come in, trucking, sanding, dancing our dimes away, lindy-hopping all day long, rainbow lights just flashing in the vendor. The concession what owned that tune-box come every week with twelve new records, and lugged off twelve tons of nickels out of it, mostly what Calvin had put in. That's where our profits went. Husband lost the business, I lost the roof over my head.

"Husband No. 2, I said we'll put the house and the business in *both* our names. We did. Started buying a nice little cottage, too, in Durham with a yard. Opened up a nice little soda-pop, newspaper, shoeshine stand. Instead of selling soda pop, Renfroe started selling moonshine—without fixing the cops up in front. You can't fool no cop when he sees a man set down at a soda fountain sober and get up drunk. Renfroe went to jail. Lawyers, bails, fines, a little present of some folding money for the judge to let him off light. Shoeshine and soda fountain stand padlocked. Me worried out of my mind. Lost the house again. I divorced that Negro.

"This man I got now, I make him work for himself. I owns this house *myself*. I runs it. My home and my investment is all in one so I can stay home and keep an eye on my business, too: ROOMS FOR RENTS. No man is mixed up in my finances no more. From now on a husband might share my bed, but not my bankbook. Oh, no! I have learned my lessons. When a woman wants to get ahead, she cannot tie a millstone to her feet. Most men is millstones."

"I am sorry, madam, you have such a low opinion of mens, but it looks like all your experiences have been disfavorable. You should have met *me* in your young life."

"God forbid! Joyce can have you. But I hope you and Joyce have laid your plans to buy a nice little home when you get married, which she will put in *her* name. Y'all certainly can't live here. Your room ain't big enough for two, neither is it a kitchenette. Besides, I do not want no couples—and no more babies. That is a *single* room."

"Don't worry, madam, me and Joyce do not plan to room with no-body. Facts are, we intends to buy a house and keep roomers ourselves. But only roomers with recommendations, Joyce says."

"It's a good thing you will be *married* to her then, otherwise you couldn't live in that house yourself."

"You wouldn't give me a recommendation, was I to need one?"

"What have you ever gave me except a frown when I remind you your rent is due?"

"I have walked your dog—which is a favor for any man to be seen with."

"I am beginning to understand that you just don't have a nature for dogs, you mentions that so frequent. I will not ask you to walk Trixie again. I hope, however, you will never be crippled up with rheumatism yourself and need somebody to walk a dog for you."

"I will turn my dog loose in the back yard and let him run around in circles."

"Then your dog will be just a plain old cur, I reckon, that can get his exercise by chasing his own tail."

"Which would be good exercise right on. His hind feet would never catch up with his front ones nor his front feet with his hind."

"Just like you never catch up with your rent."

"If you keep harping on that, madam, you will make me hot."

"Good—because you sure ain't gonna get no heat upstairs this evening."

"Goodnight, madam."

"Goodnight."

"*Damn* goodnight!"

"What did you say?"

"*Goodnight!*"

46

Here Comes Old Me

"You know my Aunt Pearl?" asked Simple.

"I do not know her," I said, "but I have heard you speak of her."

"She is my Cousin Myrtle's mother. And she is all upset. She has had a calamity."

"A calamity?" I said. "What do you mean, a calamity?"

"Something has happened to Aunt Pearl that has got her down which she does not know how to get out from under."

"From under what?"

"What has taken place," said Simple. "Aunt Pearl is a good woman. She likes to do things right, but she don't know what to do about this."

"Well, tell me, or don't," I said. "What happened to your Aunt Pearl?"

"She picked up the phone this morning," said Simple, "and out of the clear blue skies, the other party said, 'Baby, here is ole me!'"

"Aunt Pearl said, 'Ole who?'"

"And the man said, 'You know, ole me! Roscoe!'"

"Whereupon, Aunt Pearl like to fainted."

"Why?"

"Because it were her husband speaking, and she had taken him to be dead in the war. She said, 'I ain't heard tell of you in eight years, Roscoe, I thought you was *Missing In Action*!'"

"Roscoe said, 'I were, but I found myself. Wouldn't nobody else find me, so I found myself. I have just got back from Honolulu. I been two years out from the hospital, and made over new. Baby, it's ole me!'"

"Well, she must have been happy," I said.

"She were not," said Simple. "Aunt Pearl has done found herself a man more suitable to her type, and she is not studying Roscoe. Anyhow, she thought he was dead. The War Department had long gone reported Roscoe *Missing In Action,* so Aunt Pearl had put him out of her life."

"What I do not understand," I said, "is how—old as you are—you've got an aunt young enough to have had a husband in the army?"

"Roscoe is somewhat younger than Aunt Pearl," said Simple. "But he never did turn out to be what she expected. Roscoe wouldn't work. If he did, he didn't bring his money home. Fact is, Aunt Pearl went and had him put in the army herself. She told the Draft Board she wasn't dependent on Roscoe, if she was she would starve. So they put him in i-A and sent him to the rumble. When the word came he was *Missing In Action,* Aunt Pearl cried a little and took her blue star down. Now she is going with a nice settled mail clerk, more her own age and ambitions, with a home in Jamaica, and he told her to stop going out to work for Miss White Lady, just stay home and rest. So you can imagine how bad Aunt Pearl felt today when she picked up that phone and heard the other party say, 'Here comes ole me!' In fact, it made her mad!"

"I can see where it would," I said. "If a woman thinks she's got rid of a no-good husband, then he turns up, it must be embarrassing."

"For Aunt Pearl it's worse than that!" said Simple. "It means she'll have to go back to work."

"What is she going to do?" I asked.

"That is what she sent for me for," said Simple, "to get my advice. She also wants my protection, because she is scared of Roscoe. He was phoning from the Army Hospital, and he said soon as they turn him loose, he would be home—maybe tomorrow. Aunt Pearl says she does not want that Negro to set his feet under her table no more."

"What did you advise her to do?"

"I told her to sit tight. I would handle the situation."

"How?" I said.

"I will inform Roscoe that my Aunt Pearl has changed her mind about him."

"After all these years?"

"Yes! Therefore, I will tell him to stay out of her face from now on—else he will get hurt."

"Who's going to hurt him, you or her?"

"Aunt Pearl does not fight," said Simple. "But me, when I get riled, or somebody does something to Joyce or my relatives, daddy-o, I am bad. What business did Roscoe have to go and find his self *Missing In Action*? Nobody wanted that cat to find his self, least of all Aunt Pearl. Roscoe is not good, never was no good, and never will be no good! He done upset my Aunt Pearl so that ever since she picked up that phone, she's near about had nervous breakdowns. That ain't right! If Aunt Pearl wants to marry a man what owns a house, she is *going to marry a man what owns a house,* and I will protect her! I never did like Roscoe nohow, talking about, 'Here comes ole me!' I hope I'll be there when he shows up! Harlem is too small for Roscoe and me both!"

"I hope you know what you are doing," I said. "But be careful! There is a law against assault and battery."

"It will not be assault," said Simple, "neither will it be batteries! Roscoe will just be *Missing In Action* again—providing he can still run!"

47

Strictly for Charity

"Now, you take this here business of women selling tickets," said Simple, "it is enough to give kin folks high blood pressure, heebie-jeebies, and a nervous prostitution. Joyce's club is having a Fall Tea for charity and she has to sell fifty tickets."

"Nervous prostration," I said, correcting him. "And why does she have to sell so many tickets?"

"I do not know," said Simple. "But she wants me to sell half of them—which is twenty-five. I told her, 'I don't know a soul who wants to go to a tea.'

"Joyce said, 'After all these years, you ought to know some decent people, Jess Semple. As much as you hang out in bars, you should have a lot of friends who would do you the favor of buying a ticket.'

"I said, 'Very few of my friends have Fifty Cents to spend on tea.'

" 'If it were a jump-steady party, I bet they would go,' said Joyce. 'Or had it some kind of gambling or numbers connected with it, Fifty Cents would not be a thing for them to put out. Your friends do not appreciate a cultural hour.'

" 'Listen, Joyce,' I said, 'I will buy and *pay* for ten of them tickets myself rather than listen to a lot of who-struck-John. You know I am not a tea-drinking man, neither a good ticket seller, besides I am liable to lose them somewhere and have to pay for them anyhow. So pay day I will just give you Five Dollars as a contribution. Gimme the tickets and hush.'

"But that did not satisfy Joyce. In fact, it hurt her feelings. She said, 'The purpose of selling these tickets is to popularize the club so as to let people know what we are doing for charity, and to get a crowd there. If you was trying to do something to build up a good movement, Jess, *I* would help you and get my friends to help. But no, you take the easiest way out by giving me Five Dollars as a contribution. Well, give me Five Dollars—then sell the tickets anyhow.'

"So rather than hear no more of it, I agreed. Now here I am stuck with twenty-five cardboards to a tea. Man, can I sell you a couple?"

"No," I said.

"That is why I had rather die than try to sell tickets. I hate to be turned down," said Simple. "When I tell Joyce you did not buy a pair, she will be mad at you. I have seen Joyce not speak to her best friend for a week because she would not buy some kind of tickets Joyce were selling. I'm telling you, women and tickets are a pain in the neck. I cannot take these twenty-five tickets back to Joyce, so I will try you one more time.

"*Daddy-o, do you want to go to a nice cultural charitable tea Sunday afternoon on the 25th of next week?* It will not hurt you none. It might even do you good. You can take your girl or your wife. If you do not take either one, you might meet some FINE old chick there who will sweeten your tea. And you will be sure to hear some sonaties out of this world played by Professor Percival which will not be jazz. It will be pure culture. A large lady will sing an area in no language you ever heard. A tall tenor will lock his hands on 'Trees.' Some young girl will get up and say, 'I will now play a piece in two renditions'—meaning you should not applaud until she gets through, even if she do pause. But some folks will applaud in the middle, anyhow, hoping she is done. A small child will recite a poem. All of that for Fifty Cents—and tea, too."

"Will you be there?"

"Not if my Sunday-morning hang-over can prevent me," said Simple. "After I donate Five Dollars and sell tickets, too, I have done my duty by charity, also by Joyce. The last time I tried to balance a teacup on one knee and a plate full of salad on the other, I could not let go of neither one to take my cigarette out of my mouth. A man ought to have three knees when he goes to a tea. I don't have but two, so I am forced to stay home. If you buy just one ticket, daddy-o, I will *give* you nine."

I gave him Fifty Cents.

"Thank you! That's fine. Now order a beer. I need another one myself. My nerves is kinder rattled this week. In fact, I think I am charged, or else everything else is charged. Anyhow, I am sure glad I did not buy Joyce a fur coat this fall."

"What has a fur coat got to do with anything?"

"It has got to do with what I am talking about," said Simple. "Not only would I have to pay for the fur coat—and be shocked at the price tag—but I would also be shocked every time I touched her, since the air is so full of electricity these days. Haven't you noticed it?"

"Yes," I said, "I have. Almost every time I touch a taxicab door lately I get a shock. But I don't have any explanation for it, do you? Unless it is the dryness of the autumn weather."

"I think they must be testing atom bombs somewhere—or else H-Bombs—and the air has just got filled up with so much electricity that now every morning when I comb my hair it crackles. The other day my landlady asked me to take her little old fice-dog for a walk in the park—which is another thing I do strickly for charity. To pick up the dog chain to clamp it on her neck, I grabbed the dog. The dog and me both got such a shock that we parted company permanently.

"My landlady says, 'What are you doing to Trixie?'

"I said, 'Madam, what is Trixie trying to do to me—electrocute me? I do not have any fur on my hide, but every time I touch fur, the sparks fly. I will not take that dog for a walk today.'

"My landlady thereupon took occasion to remind me that I owed her a half week's rent behind, and I must be just using this shock business as an excuse to keep from doing her a small favor—and she so crippled up with lumbago she cannot take her dog out to do its duty in bad weather herself.

"I said, 'Madam, if you do not think your hound give me a shock, *you* touch her and see if she won't give you a shock.'

"She said, 'I have never been shocked by my own dog yet. Come here, Trixie!'

"Trixie came wiggling and waggling up to my big old fat landlady's knee and she reached out her hand to its head. What I was praying to God would happen, did happen. Sparks flew. Trixie yelped. My landlady hollered. I laughed. But what did I do that for?

"My landlady backslid in her religion right then and there and used some words that I had never heard her use before. Then she turned on me. She said, 'You put the devil into that dog, else brought this electricity into this house yourself—some of that bad licker you been drinking is giving off sparks! I'll thank you to leave my room.'

"I said, 'Madam, you do not want this Five Dollars that I owe you?'

"She said, 'Yes, I will take my money.'

"Whereupon I took out the last Five Dollar bill that I had, just out of pride, pulled it through my left hand real good, and handed it to her. That old woman was so greedy for cash that her whole hand closed over that Five Dollar bill. For once I got my money's worth. She got such a shock she almost dropped that half week's rent.

"She shrieked, 'Jess Semple, you must be possessed of the devil! I been hearing tell of everybody getting shocked from touching this and that and the other thing, but up until this evening, I had not experienced such an experience myself. Now you have shocked both me and my dog, and I'll really thank you to remove your over charged self from my presence.'

"I left. But just out of devilment, that night I borrowed another Five Dollars from Joyce to give her in advance. I don't know which shocked my old landlady most that second time, getting paid ahead—or my static electricity. Anyhow, she didn't say, 'Thank you.'

"She just backslid again."

48

Once in a Wife-Time

"I'm still hoping it will get here in time for Christmas," said Simple.

"What?"

"My divorce. But I just got word from that lawyer in Baltimore that he had been held up until he got my money before completing the process. He also writ me concerning on what my wife bases our divorce, now that I have paid. And, don't you know, that woman claims I deserted *her*."

"Well, did you?"

"I did not. She put me out."

"In other words, you left under duress."

"Pressure," said Simple.

"Then why don't you refute her argument? Contest her claim?"

"That is just why we separated, we argued so much. I will not argue with Isabel now over no divorce. She writ that she did not want to contest. Neither do I. I never could win an argument with that woman. Only once in a wife-time did I win, and I did not win then with words."

"How did you win?"

"I just grabbed her and kissed her," said Simple.

"Why didn't you try that method more often?"

"Because as soon as I kissed her she stopped arguing and started loving. Sometimes it is not loving a man wants. He wants to *win*—especially when he knows he is right. She told me one time that I had forgot and left the front door unlatched when I went to work.

"I said, 'I know I did not.'

"She said, 'I know you did.'

"It were on from there on in. The truth was I left her at home that morning. She was late to work herself, so she was the last one to go out, so she left the door unlatched. But the more I argued, the madder she got. That is the way with a woman when they are wrong. They not only argue, but they get mad. So I just let her rave. When I did not say a word my wife got madder. In fact, Isabel got so mad that night she were shaking. When a woman shakes, you know you got her goat. So at that point, I said, 'Shut up!'

"Do you think she hushed? No, she just started all over again. It took the neighbors from both sides of the project to stop us. Folks wants to sleep and it were two o'clock in the morning.

"But the time that I won the argument, my wife were right, although I would not let her know it.

"Isabel said, 'Jess Semple, I saw you walking down the street with Della Mae Jones when I were passing on the Pennsylvania Avenue bus.'

"I said, 'You's a lie!'

"She said, 'Then my eyes must of deceived me.'

"I said, 'They did.'

"She said, 'I know you. I know her. I know the clothes you wear. I know the way you talk. It *were* you and it *were* she.'

"I said, 'Not me. It might of been she, but not me. Baby, you know I don't care nothing about that girl, not even enough to walk a block with.'

"I grabbed Isabel and kissed her, bam! On the mouth! Then I bit her on the left cheek. After which I kissed her on the ear, and before she could get loose I negotiated her mouth again. By that time, she had done throwed her arms around my neck and would not let me go. So I won that argument.

"The reason was that she was right. If I had argued with her, she would have won, because I do not have the patience to lie and then re-lie again. Lies show in my eyes, anyhow, so I just kept my face so close to her'n she could not see my eyes. Women do not use logic, they just use words. I didn't let her talk. That time I did not even speak. I just bit her on the cheek, hugged her, run my hand down her back, and said, 'Baby!' Which were enough.

"She knowed I had been out with Della Mae Jones, but she did not care after that. She had sense enough to know it would do no good to care nohow. A man is not like a woman. A man can love two, three, four womens at once and still go to work. If a woman loves *one* man, she does not want him out of her sight. She will quit her job and stay home to be sure he comes from work on time. She will miss her lodge meeting to be certain he does not go nowhere. When a woman is a fool about a man, *she is a fool*. But no matter how much she loves you she will *still* argue. Argument is something a woman never gives up, no matter how much she loves you. She still wants to win. If you are in no mood to argue, don't, daddy-o! Just don't! But when you do, do *not* expect to win, not once in a wife-time. If you don't give a wife the last word, she will take it anyhow. That I know! If Isabel says I deserted her in her divorce papers, let it be. Should I argue back, I might never get free. She put *me* out. *Thank God I went!*"

"Now you're about to get tangled up again," I said.

"I am—if the high cost of love don't get me down. Things has changed since I was courting Isabel. Love has done gone way up. It costs me more to take Joyce out now than it does to buy a summer suit or a pair of winter shoes."

"It's all according to where you take her," I said.

"Joyce won't go nowhere but to the Shalimar, Frank's, Mrs. Frazier's. And if she eats a steak, I'm out of a week's work! If she has a bottle of wine (and she won't drink plain old sherry) I am shook. Joyce don't drink nohow, but somebody told her wine goes with dinner when a gentleman takes a lady out to dine—so lately she must have wine—and it has to be some foreign kind like Beergindy or Sawturn, else Keyauntie.

"She says, 'You never take me nowhere, so when you do, I want nothing but the best.'

"I says, 'Baby, after you get the best, then there ain't no *rest*. Sorry! My money is gone.'

"She says, 'Let it go, and make some more.'

"I says, 'Joyce, I believe you is high. I never did hear you talk like that before. You have changed since first I met you. Besides, I don't *make* money. I earns it. I mean the hard way—work. I ain't no numbers man, neither a dope pusher. I ain't no politicianer with a licker store. I cannot afford to take you out more than once a year at this rate.'

" 'It has not been but *once* this year,' says Joyce. 'You are my only boy friend, you know that, so if you don't take me out, who will?'

"I said, 'Better not nobody else try.'

"Joyce says, 'Then if you want to keep your exclusive, buy! Baby, buy!'

" 'You know I've been saving up for my divorce,' I says as she called the waiter, but I could tell she had larceny in her heart. Somebody must of told her they saw me buying Zarita a beer.

" 'You should of had your divorce long ago,' says Joyce. 'I have nothing to do with your past. I am your future. You should be saving up now to take care of *me*. Don't you love me?'

" 'Sure, I love you, baby,' I says. 'But what makes the high cost of love so *high*? You are my heart throb. But every time my heart throbs in a restaurant these days, it's dollars. You are my all. But when you *take* all, what have I got left to put? I do not want to be embarrassed in the Shalimar, neither Frank's where just plain meat and potatoes costs more than turkey and dressing does in Virginia. Joyce, after all these years, is you trying to play me for a sucker? If you is, lemme tell you—I might look simple, but I definitely ain't no fool!'

" 'Jess, watch your grammar in public. Don't say, *is you,* and *you is.* That is not proper,' Joyce says.

" 'I begs your pardon,' I says. 'Forgive my down-home talk.'

" 'Down-home or up North,' says Joyce, 'such terms is not correct. You know it. You have been to school.'

" 'Colored school,' I said. 'Which is neither here nor there as long as you understand what I am saying. What I am saying is the high cost of living and the high cost of loving together is more than I can take. I don't mind dying for love, but I hate to be broke. I cannot pay my landlady with your affections. I cannot get my laundry out with heart throbs. Neither can I ride the subway with a kiss. I can't even buy a beer with love.'

" 'Beer, beer, beer! All you think about is beer! So go get yourself one of them girls what's satisfied with a hot dog and a bottle of beer. I do not call that going out myself, so I am going *in.* I will thank you to take me home.'

" 'Start walking then,' I said.

" 'Taxi!' she screamed no sooner than she got to the curb, and she wrapped her stole around her. So, daddy-o, I am broke this morning, broke this week, in fact, broke the rest of the month, just from one date. If I didn't love that girl, I would be mad.

"If I had kissed her before we started out, she might of said, 'Let's just stay home and play records.' Then I wouldn't of had to worry about the high cost of love. Love don't cost a thing in private. It's just when it's on display. When women get out they want Beergindy. I do not care nothing about love in public anyhow. I'm a house man, myself."

"Then it's about time you got married again and made a home."

"It is," said Simple, "because love is too high anywhere else. I should of kissed Joyce on the way to her house in that taxi. Now it will take a week to get her back to normal."

49

Whiter than Snow

Um-humm-mm-m! This morning there is snow. Must not be long on the ground because it is still white. Nothing stays white in Harlem except the mens that own the stores—and they was born that way. Um-hummm-m-m—snow! Good enough to eat, clean enough to advertise a laundry, cool enough to calm a hang-over. I wonder where is my galoshes?

"Yes, daddy-o, I woke up this morning and I saw all that snow down in the areaway and I thought to myself, 'My ancestors in Ethiopia was never so lucky as to be this unlucky because, beautiful as it is, I never really did like snow.' The best thing about winter is staying in a nice warm house, if you didn't have to go to work. Or better still, a nice warm bar full of people, with plenty of friends inside to set a man up to a drink, and Zarita to once in a while rub her cheek up against yours. Then I feel warm inside and out. Otherwise, winter is not for me."

"That's your African blood," I said.

"Ethiopian," replied Simple. "Anyhow, as soon as it starts getting cold, I start turning ashy. In the summer, I am a dark brown. But in the winter I am a light ash. I also have goose pimples when I go out in the street. Also my feets get wet."

"I gather you do not like winter," I said. "But I hate to think where the colored race would be if it were not for cold weather. Cold weather makes you get up and go, gives you life, vim, vigor, vitality."

"It does not give me anything but a cold," said Simple.

"You're an exception," I said. "It's a well-known fact that Northern races have more aggressiveness than Southern races, also that civilization has taken its greatest strides in the North. Look at Mother England on whose Empire the sun never sets."

"There's a mother for you!" said Simple. "It's setting now."

"Well, then look at Sweden," I said, "one of the happiest states in the world. Norway, one of the healthiest. Also France, modern culture's cradle. They are all cold countries."

"Which has what to do with me?" asked Simple.

"The American Negro, product of a cold climate, is leading the Negroes of the world in attainment," I said. "You are an American Negro."

"But I ain't nowhere myself," said Simple.

"I still say *you're* an exception. Take Joe Black, for example. What other country has a ballplayer like Joe Black? Has Africa? Has Jamaica? Has Brazil? No! Those countries have millions of Negroes. But have they a Lena Horne? No! A Marian Anderson? No! A Dr. Percy Julian? No! They are all hot countries. But here in the U.S.A. where it drops to zero in December, a Negro has to jump and go, do something, be somebody."

"Do you reckon I could jump up next December and be Rockefeller?"

"You're reaching for the moon."

"I ain't. I'm just reaching for a million," said Simple. "My grandma always told me to hitch my wagon to a star. She did not say no colored star. Besides, I want enough money to go to them warm countries when it gets cold up here. I told you I don't like cold weather."

"Ah, but it puts ambition into you," I said. "Suppose Paul Robeson had been born in a hot country like Brazil. Do you think he would be raising so much sand? Cold weather makes a man vociferous, aggressive, dynamic, ambitious. Take Joe Louis. After those cold Detroit winds off Lake Erie hit him in the face as a boy, he became the world's greatest heavy-weight champion. Do you think he would have been as great, had he stayed down in nice warm Alabama?"

"You know Joe couldn't fight no white boys in Alabama," said Simple, "so how could he be the champion? But I ain't built like Joe. And cold weather just drives me to drink."

"You're trifling," I said.

"Then don't trifle with me when I'm cold," said Simple. "Winter makes me evil. I do not love winter. I do not like snow. And I don't feel good when it is cold. I cannot keep my feet warm."

"Perhaps you have low blood pressure. Have you seen a doctor lately?"

"I have not seen a doctor for five years, and then only because Joyce drug me off to the hospital when I had pneumonia, like I told you, and them nurses would not let me get out. I believe they liked me. But I have been cold ever since I was born, except in the summertime, so it has nothing to do with my blood pressure. I do not think I was meant for winter nor winter for me."

"There could be something in what you say," I said. "Perhaps we are just not the right color for winter, being dark complexioned. In nature, you know, animals have protective coloration to go with their environment. Desert snakes are sand-colored. Tree lizards are green. Certain fur-bearing animals have coats the color of the environment in which they live so you can hardly tell them from the foliage or the forest leaves. Ermine, for example, is the color of the snow country in which it originates."

"Maybe that is why white folks is white, to go with the snow, since they come from the North. Which accounts for me not having no business wading around in snow, because it and my color do not match. I am only two shades lighter than dark. Saint Peter will have a hard time washing me white as snow."

"Now you are getting things of the body and things of the spirit mixed up," I said. "When you go to heaven that will be a spiritual change, not a physical one."

"I will have wings, won't I?"

"Wings of the spirit," I said.

"According to the song, they will be snow-white. But if I remain black, my wings will not match me—which must be why I am due to be washed whiter than snow. I never did see a Sunday school card with no dark angels with white wings on it."

"You know why, don't you? Sunday school cards are made by white folks."

"They have them in colored churches," said Simple. "Why don't the colored religions print some colored cards of their own? Every time I went to Sunday school when I was a little boy, they come handing me a card with white angels and a white Moses and white Adams and white Eves on it. I thought everybody in heaven was white. And we was always singing, 'You shall be whiter than snow.' I used to wonder about that— because I would not know my own mother if I went to heaven and she come running to meet me *white*. I would be forced to say, 'Mama, you certainly have changed!' "

"I keep telling you that you are looking at things with physical eyes, not spiritual ones. There are no colors in the other world. 'White' means purity. And being washed 'whiter than snow' refers to the shedding of your sins, not your color."

"I do not want no parts of snow," said Simple. "As I told you, I hate anything cold. And I sure would hate to be turned into a snowman, God forbid!"

"Have no fear," I said. "You are not likely to go to heaven anyhow. You are certainly no model of virtue on earth."

"I *could* turn over a new leaf just before I die," said Simple.

"Your end might come without warning, then there wouldn't be time."

"True. In which case, I reckon I'd be in the devil's rotisserie," said Simple. "But, at any rate, I would be warm."

50

Simple Santa

"Carlyle's wife is pregnant again," said Simple. "What do you reckon they are going to do with two babies in one room?"

"I imagine your landlady is worried about that, too."

"She is," said Simple. "She done swore she won't rent to no more *young* married couples. From now on they have to be settled folks that works hard—too tired and settled to raise a family in her house."

"Is your landlady really as hard-hearted as that toward children?" I asked.

"No," said Simple. "But she has her rules. Still and yet, she is really crazy about both them little old babies in the house, spite of the fact she objected to them being born. Every time she boils some beef for Trixie, she sends them babies up a cup of hot broth. And if one of them gets the colic, she is more worried than their mamas. Only thing she does not worry about is giving them heat. She says babies is due to stay wrapped up in blankets with bootsies on their feets. And if a house is too hot, they get overheated. So I asked her to give me an extra blanket since I do not have bootsies. Do you think she did?"

"Ha! Ha!" I said.

"She come giving me some kind of spiel about what makes men so cold-natured when women, she says, go around in zero weather in open-work shoes on the streets, yet do not catch pneumonia and die. Neither do they freeze. Which is true, I have never heard of a woman having chilblains yet. But if a man went out in his sox-feet in the winter, me for instant, I would be so full of cold the next day I could not draw a decent breath. Women can go low-necked and bare-footed in the snow in party shoes and do not even sneeze. In this New York zero weather, if men dressed like women we would develop galloping consumption and go into decline. Then where would the human race be without mens? For instant, without your father, you would not be here today."

"The same goes for your mother," I said.

"Cut it out," yelled Simple. "I'm not playing the dozens. Listen, I want to borrow a Dollar."

"For what?"

"To give a kid."

"What kid?"

"Not my kid, 'cause I ain't got none," said Simple. "But if you was to go across the street with me, you would see what kid. It is a kid who wants to buy his grandma a present for Christmas."

"Do you know his grandma?"

"No. Neither do I know the kid. But he made a mistake. He saw a present a week ago in the West Indian store window, and the sign was written wrong. It said, 'One—twenty-nine cents.' But it was written like this—see: O-N-E-and a dash—and a twenty-nine-cent sign. 1–29¢. The kid thought it meant one for twenty-nine cents. But what it really meant was One Dollar *and* Twenty-Nine Cents."

"For one what?" I asked.

"Dustpan," said Simple.

"What in the world does a kid want to give his grandmother a dustpan for?"

"Because that is what she wants for Christmas," said Simple. "So this kid had been saving up his pennies till he got twenty-nine cents. Now the man wants a *Dollar and Twenty-Nine Cents* for that dustpan."

"I never heard of such a price!" I said. "A Dollar and Twenty-Nine Cents for an ordinary dustpan?"

"It is made of genu-wine metal," said Simple, "and painted red with a white handle. It is a *fine* dustpan! So I want to borrow a dollar off of you to give that kid. He has got his heart set on giving his grandma that dustpan, so he is standing over there crying. See?

"He is only eight-nine years old—and he read that sign wrong. Some people do not know how to paint a sign. Besides, I remember when I was a little kid, I did not ever have any money but a nickel now and then, and I always wanted to buy something that costs more than I had. I have got no kids myself, but if I did have, I would want him to be happy on Christmas and give presents—so I am going to give that kid a dollar to get that there dustpan."

"You are a very sentimental Santa Claus," I said. "You haven't got a dollar and you do not even know the lad."

"No, I do not know that kid," said Simple, "but I know for a kid to save up Twenty-Nine Cents sometimes is hard. When he wants to give it away in a present to his grandma instead of eating it up in candy or going to see Humphrey Bogart, I admire that kid. Lend me a dollar!"

"Here! Pay me back Fifty Cents. I will also invest in an unseen dustpan for an unknown boy and his unknown grandmother."

"You are making fun of me and that kid," said Simple.

"I am not," I said. "It just strikes me as funny—a dustpan for a Christmas present! But hurry up across the street and give the youngster the dollar before he is gone."

"If he's gone, I'll be coming back—and we'll drink this dollar up."

"Oh, no!" I cried. "Either give it to the child, or give my money back to me."

"Then I will be broke," said Simple, "and I want to wish you a Merry Christmas ahead of time. How else can I wish you a Merry Christmas except to buy you a drink?"

"With my money?" I said.

"Don't be technical!" said Simple.

When he came back into the bar he was grinning.

"That kid thinks I'm Santa Claus," he said. "Right now I wish I was Santa Claus for just one day so I could open some of that mail he gets up yonder at the North Pole. I would particularly like to latch onto that mail from children down in Alabama, Mississippi, and Florida. I would answer them white kids down there in a way they would never forget."

"Race again, I'll bet! Those kids," I said, "have nothing to do with Jim Crow, and it would be a shame to intrude the race problem into their Christmas thoughts."

"A shame, nothing!" said Simple. "They are growing up to be a problem. And if I was a Santa Claus, being my color, I would teach them a lesson before they got too far gone. Suppose I was to open a letter from some little Johnnie Dixiecrat in Mississippi asking me to bring him a hunting rifle, for instant. I would dip my pen in ink and reply:

> *North Pole, Santa Claus Land*
> *December the so-and-so*
> *Year Now*

Johnnie:

　I would call you "Dear Johnnie," but I am a colored Santa Claus so I am afraid you might be insulted, because I fears as a white child in the South you have been reared wrong in regards to race. You say you are seven years old. Well, I hope you do not want that rifle you wrote me about to lend your cousin Talbot to shoot a Negro—because where you live lynchings is frequent, although they do not call them by that name now. I read in the paper the other day where eight white mens riddled one black man with bullets. Johnnie, the grown mens in your place do not act right. If you don't, I will not bring you a thing after you grow up. I will bring you this hunting rifle now, little as you are, because I believe you are still good.

But, listen, Johnnie! When you get up in your teens, don't let me catch you getting on the bus in front of some crippled old colored lady just because you are white and she is black. And don't let me catch you calling her by her first name, Sarah, and she is old enough to be your grandma, when you ought to be calling her Mrs. What-Ever-Her-Name-Is. If you do such, I will not bring you that bicycle you gonna want to ride to high school. And you sure won't get that television set if you go around using bad words about colored folks. As long as Santa Claus stays black, I will not stand for that!

Also, Johnnie Dixiecrat, sir, if you gets to be a salesman or a insurance man or a bill collector in Meridian or Jackson, Mississippi, show your manners and take off your hat when you go in a colored woman's house. If you don't, I will not put nothing in your sox on Christmas Eve, not a doggone thing! And if you get big enough to vote, see to it that colored folks can vote, too. If you don't, I'm liable to drop down your chimney a present you don't want—a copy of the United States Constitution. See how that would be for your constitution—since it says everybody is free and equal.

I am signing off now, dear Johnnie, since I have got one million letters more to answer from Alabama and Georgia, so I cannot take up too much time with you in Mississippi. If you see me on Christmas Eve, you will know me by my white beard and black face. Up North the F.E.P.C. has given a Negro the Santa Claus job this year. Dark as I am, though, I intend to treat you equal.

MERRIE CHRISTMAS! The rifle I will bring when I come. Don't be rowdy.

Cheerio!
Jess Simple Santa Claus"

51

Present for Joyce

"*Rowdy,* now that's a nice word. Sometimes I likes to be rowdy myself, but don't like to run with rowdies. Why is that? I like to drink, but I don't like drunks. I don't have the education to mingle myself with educated folks. I don't have a white-walled Cadillac to keep up with sports, numbers writers, and doctors. And not smoking reefers, I can't pal around with hep cats. So who are my buddies? You—and a couple of bartenders."

"The point of such a dissertation at this moment being what?" I asked.

"Nothing," said Simple, "except to offer you a small beer. And to tell you I am tired of working like a Negro all week in order to live like white folks on Saturday night. What I want is a part-time job with *full-time* pay, or else a position where you take a vacation all summer and rest all winter. But I am colored, so I know nothing like that is going to happen to me."

"Color, color, color!" I said. "It is so easy to blame all one's failures and difficulties on color. To whine *I can't do this, I can't do that* because I'm colored—which is one bad habit you have, friend—always bringing up race."

"I do," said Simple, "because that is what I am always coming face to face with—race. I look in the mirror in the morning to shave—and what do I see? *Me.* From birth to death my face—which is my race—stares me in the face."

"Don't you suppose race stared Ralph Bunche in the face, too? And Adam Powell? And Joe Louis? And Paul Williams? And Dr. Butts? But Ralph Bunche, Negro, became internationally famous. Adam Powell, Negro, went to Congress. Joe Louis, Negro, defeated the world's best fighters. Paul Williams designs houses for Hollywood stars. Dr. Butts writes articles for the leading papers, gets fellowships, speaks all over the country. Suppose they had all just stood at a beer bar like you and moaned about race, race, race!"

"I ain't as smart as Ralph Bunche," said Simple. "I can't holler like Adam Powell, having no microphone in my throat. And I ain't built like Joe Louis. I'm a light-weight. Paul Williams is colleged, and got mother wit, too. And I cannot write no articles like Dr. Butts. But every time Dr. Butts publishes something, Joyce buys it, or else asks me to buy it for her, so my money helps support him. Butts has got some of my money. I bought tickets to every one of Joe's fights in New York, so my money helped Joe get that championship belt. I put my dollars in the box office when I go to the movies which helps them movie stars pay Paul Williams to design them a house. And I vote for Adam Powell. So they all come right down to *me*. And where am I?"

"Through leaders like those we've just mentioned, you will get somewhere," I said. "You have to take the long view."

"It seems like to me this very last week were as *long* as a year. Sometimes I start work on Monday and by the time I get to Tuesday, it looks like I done worked seven days. By the time I get to Wednesday, it seems like a month. And when Saturday comes, I been slaving a year. Some weeks just naturally seems long, I mean, long! No week should seem like a year, but when you're working at something that don't get you nowhere, they do!"

"Some weeks do lengthen out to infinity," I said.

"I don't know infinitive," said Simple. "But there is something wrong somewhere with the way weeks are made. If I was to make a calendar, I would crowd a work-week into *one* day. But I would make a vacation-week stretch out over a month, particularly the week before Christmas on my calendar."

"Your calendar would be most confusing," I said. "Nobody but yourself would understand it—and I fear even you would get mixed up. You cannot change time around to suit your personal feelings. There is something inexorable about time. You cannot hold it off."

"You cannot hold off Christmas either," groaned Simple. "I know if Christmas came more than once a year I could not stand it."

"Don't you like the Christmas spirit?"

"I like any kind of spirits, provided they have alcohol in them. I love eggnog well spiked. What I mean is, if Christmas came *twice* a year, it would be more than a man could bear. Women like to shop. I do not."

"Has your shopping been so extensive this season that it has broken you down?" I demanded.

"It has near about done me in, and all I have got so far is one little old present—for Joyce. And there is no way of being sure she will like what I bought. Womens is funny about presents. Joyce is always yowling and howling over how I never give her nothing—so this time I thought I would spend Ten Dollars and get her something real good, and pick it out my own self, without advice from nobody. So I did. It strained my brain. It also strained my nerves, not to speak of my feet. But I did not want to shuff Joyce off with no easy present this time—since I really aim to marry that girl in June. So, beings as the downtown stores are open late on Thursday nights and, being a working man, I cannot get to *no* store in the day time, before I even et my supper Thursday I headed for Macy's to pick out Joyce's present.

"Don't you know that store were full, I mean jammed, even though everybody ought to have been home eating dinner! It took me one hour to get to the counter, one more hour to get waited on, another hour to pick out the present, and another hour to fight my way away from the counter. I did not want to get nothing too cheap, neither nothing beyond the cash I had in my pocket. As it was, it used up my carfare for a week after they added the tax onto it that the clerk did not tell me about. By that time it were eight P.M. Then it took me another hour to get the thing wrapped up in a gift box. By that hour I were so weak with hunger and my bunion hurt me so bad that, if I did not love Joyce, I would have said, 'To hell with it,' and give up. But I stuck it out. Now, if she do not like the present, I do not care."

"After all you went through to get it," I said, "she is bound to like it. Certainly I am curious to know what you bought for her."

"A purse," said Simple, "an evening purse, just big enough to hold her lipstick and handkerchief."

"Any purse is big enough to hold money also," I said, "so that is what your gift will remind her of."

"Doggone it!" said Simple. "You are right—money. I have made my first mistake for the coming year! But it is a beauti-fine purse, genuine imitation rhinestone studded with a silver lock. Do you reckon she will like it?"

"I am sure she will like it if you put a Ten Dollar bill inside."

"Daddy-o!" yelled Simple. "Must I give her my life? Besides, I will *never* open that gift-package to put nothing inside. I couldn't get it tied up again."

"You could put the Ten Dollar bill on the outside," I said.

"I could put the *store bill* on the outside," said Simple, "then she could take it back and get Ten on a refund."

"Joyce would not be so callous on Christmas," I said.

"She'd wait until after Christmas," said Simple.

52

Christmas Song

"Just like a Negro," said Simple, "I have waited till Christmas Eve to finish my shopping."

"You are walking rather fast," I said. "Be careful, don't slip on the ice. The way it's snowing, you can't always see it underneath the snow."

"Why do you reckon they don't clean off the sidewalks in Harlem nice like they do downtown?"

"Why do *you* reckon?" I asked. "But don't tell me! I don't wish to discuss race tonight, certainly not out here in the street, as cold as it is."

"Paddy's is right there in the next block," said Simple, heading steadily that way. "I am going down to 125th Street to get two rattles, one for Carlyle's baby, Third Floor Front, and one for that other cute little old baby downstairs in the Second Floor Rear. Also I aims to get a box of hard candy for my next-door neighbor that ain't got no teeth, poor Miss Amy, so she can suck it. And a green rubber bone for Trixie. Also some kind of game for Joyce to take her godchild from me during the holidays."

"It's eight o'clock already, fellow. If you've got all that to do, you'd better hurry before the stores close."

"I am hurrying. Joyce sent me out to get some sparklers for the tree. Her and her big old fat landlady and some of the other roomers in their house is putting up a Christmas tree down in the living room, and you are invited to come by and help trim it, else watch them trimming. Do you want to go?"

"When?"

"Long about midnight P.M. I'd say. Joyce is taking a nap now. When she wakes up she's promised to make some good old Christmas eggnog—if I promise not to spike it too strong. You might as well dip your cup in our bowl. Meanwhile, let's grab a quick beer here before I get on to the store. Come on inside. Man, I'm excited! I got another present for Joyce."

"What?"

"I'm not going to tell you until after Christmas. It's a surprise. But whilst I am drinking, look at this which I writ yesterday."

XMAS
I forgot to send
A card to Jennie—
But the truth about cousins is
There's too many.

I also forgot
My Uncle Joe,
But I believe I'll let
That old rascal go.

I done bought
Four boxes now.
I can't afford
No more, nohow.

So Merry Xmas,
Everybody!
Cards or no cards,
Here's HOWDY!

"That's for my Christmas card," said Simple. "Come on, let's go."

"Not bad. Even if it will be a little late, be sure you send me one," I said as we went out into the snow.

"Man, you know I can't afford to have no cards printed up. It's just jive. I likes to compose with a pencil sometimes. Truth is, come Christmas, I has feelings right up in my throat that if I was a composer, I would write me a song also, which I would sing myself. It would be a song about that black Wise Man who went to see the Baby in the Manger. I would put into it such another music as you never heard. It would be a baritone song."

"There are many songs about the Three Wise Men," I said. "Why would you single out the black one?"

"Because I am black," said Simple, "so my song would be about the black Wise Man."

"If you could write such a song, what would it say?"

"Just what the Bible says—that he saw a star, he came from the East, and he went with the other Wise Mens to Bethlehem in Judea, and bowed down before the Child in the Manger, and put his presents down there in the straw for that Baby—and it were the greatest Baby in the world, for it were Christ! That is what my song would say."

"You don't speak of the Bible very often," I said, "but when you do, you speak like a man who knew it as a child."

"My Aunt Lucy read the Bible to me all the time when I were knee high to a duck. I never will forget it. So if I wrote a Christmas song, I would write one right out of the Bible. But it would not be so much what words I would put in it as what my music would say—because I would also make up the music myself. Music explains things better than words and everybody in all kind of languages could understand it then. My music would say everything my words couldn't put over, because there wouldn't be many words anyhow.

"The words in my song would just say a black man saw a star and followed it till he came to a stable and put his presents down. But the music would say he also laid his heart down, too—which would be my heart. It would be *my* song I would be making up. But I would make it like as if I was there myself two thousand years ago, and *I* seen the star, and *I* followed it till I come to that Child. And when I riz up from bending over that Baby in the Manger I were strong and not afraid. The end of my song would be, *Be not afraid*. That would be the end of my song."

"It sounds like a good song," I said.

"It would be the kind of song everybody could sing, old folks and young folks. And when they sing it, some folks would laugh. It would be a happy song. Other folks would cry because—well, I don't know," Simple stopped quite still for a moment in the falling snow. "I don't know, but something about that black man and that little small Child— something about them two peoples—folks would cry."

53

Tied in a Bow

"When she took that present from the Christmas tree and untied it in front of all them other people, Joyce screamed, cried, danced, whirled around, run across the room, hauled off and kissed me, then cried, 'At last you have crossed the Ohio!'"

"What in God's name did she mean by that?"

"She were thinking about *Uncle Tom's Cabin*, Joyce explained to me later. And all she could say was, 'Free! Free! Free! Jess Semple, you're free!'"

"Do you mean to say you've been granted your divorce?"

"That is what I had hanging on the tree Christmas morning," said Simple, "my divorce. It were all tied up in a big red ribbon with a sprig of holly on it, also a bow. It were beautiful, rolled like a diploma. Did I ever show you my receipt? Look."

> *Baltimore, Maryland, 16th inst.*
> *For legal services rendered Mrs. Jesse B. Semple, received from her late husband, J. B. Semple, the sum of $133.34 re divorce.*
> *(signed) J. Harvey Scraggs*
> *Attorney-at-Law*

"See, I even paid the extra penny—the rest of them only paid One Hundred and Thirty-Three Dollars and Thirty-Three Cents. I put in the most—Thirty-*Four* Cents. But to see how happy Joyce was Christmas morning, it were worth it. Now we can have a wedding this June with a capital *W*—only a year late. Joyce is thinking about who she is going to invite to our wedding right now—fancy with a veil, graved invitations, and two receptions, one before and one after. Also a story writ up for the papers. She says we will call it: '*The Semple-Lane Nuptials,*' which is another name for wedding."

"That's going to run into money," I said, "so you'd better start saving again."

"Buddy, I have resolved to do nothing but save from now on in. With New Year's coming next week, and a wedding coming in June, my resolutions is already resolved, and I will not wait until New Year's Day to put them into force. Resolve No. 1: No whiskey and very little beer. For every glass of whiskey I can drink three or four beers. I will drink only four, no more."

"Economics, not morals, will keep you in a milder alcoholic groove," I said.

"So moved," said Simple. "Now, Resolve No. 2: This year I will not talk so much. I believe if I listen more, I will learn more. Also I will get in less arguments, and be more wise than I am. The Bible says, 'A wise man holdeth his tongue.' I will hold mine—especially with women and landladies."

"Excellent! When do you intend to start?"

"Shortly. Resolution No. 3: Whatever I do say, I will not try to get in the last word with a woman. I will let a chick have the last word from now on no matter what she says. A woman can be dead wrong, I will still let her have the last word. I won't let that worry me any more."

"You have turned diplomat in your old age," I said.

"Who's old? I am just tired of arguing with females. Now that I am going to be caged up with one come June, I wants no ruction in my cage."

"You and Joyce are going to make a nest together, not a cage."

"Whatever it is, I want no feathers flying. I want peace and calm, quiet and no arguments, that is, in my private life. There is also one more resolve I have resolved. Believe it or not, buddy-o, and that is this: To let the Race Problem roll off my mind like water off a duck's back— pay it no attention any more. I have been worrying as long as I have been black. Since I have to be black a long time yet, what is the sense of so much worriation? The next time I read where they have lynched or bombed a Negro, I will just shrug my shoulders and say, 'It warn't me.' The next time I hear tell of a colored singer barred out of Constitution Hall in Washington, I will say, 'I ain't no singer.' Next time I hear that colored folks can't eat in the Stork Club, I will say, 'Chitterlings is better than filet mignon anyhow.' "

"The New Year will completely change your character," I said. "You will no longer be yourself."

"I am already changed," said Simple. "Like the camel, I have been threaded through the eye of a needle and come out a new man. Like the sow's ear, I am a silk purse—only it is empty. Like the Liberty Bell, I ring for freedom. I've crossed the Ohio! Lend me a half, since it's a holiday week, and I will buy us both a bottle of Bud."

"That old habit of yours, buying drinks with borrowed money—after all those resolutions!"

"My resolutions don't cover other people's money," said Simple.

54

Sometimes I Wonder

"What's on your mind this evening?" I asked one cold January night when it was quiet at the bar, and Simple seemed depressed.

"I am trying to figure out how to stay alive until I die," he said. "The way things are happening to me, I might not live my time out. I got troubles. It makes me sick to think of them."

"You know what the preacher said, don't you? 'You might get too sick to eat. You might get too sick to sleep, too sick to work, too sick to talk—but you never get too sick to die.' "

"I know a man with all that sickness is liable to wake up some morning and find himself dead," said Simple. "But I blame all my troubles on talking. I did not want Joyce to know I took Zarita to the Bartenders Ball—but telephone, telegraph, tell-a-Negro—and the news is out. The last is fastest—a Negro. I told Joyce's girl friend's boy friend, and the boy friend told his girl friend. His girl friend told Joyce. Then the rumble were on! From here on in, I will never tell nobody nothing again."

"That is a safe rule," I observed.

"I also will not be caught in public with Zarita again. Some womens is all right in private. In fact fine. But in public they act like they are out of their minds. A crowd excites some folks and the show-off in them comes out, so they have to not only show-off but *show-out*. Zarita were the life of that ball. To tell the truth, she attracted attention."

"Do you mean to say she did not behave like a lady?"

"Less like a lady than usual," said Simple. "More like as if she was being paid to put on a show. She bawled and she brawled. She clowned. And she sounded out when I said, 'Baby, set down!' She got high and wanted to fly. Danced every set. Jived every man she met. That chick didn't miss a bet. Frantic! And me paying for her tickets. Keeping up with her nearly give me the rickets, man. Trying to get her home almost broke me. And if I was to tell you the rest, friend, well, words would choke me! When the musicianers started playing she started doing the mambo, the sambo, and the hambo. She danced twenty mens down, including me."

"You really had your hands full, fellow."

"That I did. Then at four-five A.M., Zarita wanted to stop in every after-hour spot on the Avenue when the ball were over. I thought I knew them all, but Zarita knowed some jook joints nobody I know ever knowed. With licker at Fifty Cents a shot, for the rest of the week what have I got? A big head, and a small purse. It were broad open daylight before we started home. By that time, it were time for me to go to work. Bartenders should have their balls on Saturday so a man can rest afterwards, especially when he goes out with Zarita."

"How could Zarita get an old night-owl like you down?"

"She did," said Simple. "But the worst of it was that news of all this balling got back to Joyce. She lit into me like a house afire. Then ended up telling me, 'I do not expect you to be a saint, Jess Semple, because they stopped making saints when they started putting M-r—period—Mr.—instead of St. in front of men's names. But I do know one thing, *if, when,* and *after* you marry me, you had better let Zarita alone. And, *just to get in practice,* you better start now. Don't let me hear tell of you running around with that woman again. Why, you liable to catch the seven-year itches. And from me you'll catch the kind of chastisement you read about only in the Bible. In fact, worse, because chastisements are up my sleeve you have never even read about. Mark my words.'

" 'They is marked,' I said. I could tell Joyce were not fooling. What is a chastisement, anyhow?"

"A castigation, a punishment."

"I do not want no more punishment from Joyce. Last night she were so mad she turned gray. In fact, she were *real* mad."

"Jealous, you mean."

"Joyce says she would not low-rate herself by being jealous of Zarita. But what made her so mad was that Joyce knowed I must have spent some money. She wondered where did I get it, when I had just borrowed Ten Dollars from her the night before. Joyce said if she thought I had spent *her* money on Zarita, she would annihilate me for life. Lucky I could show Joyce my receipt where I paid my rent. It's a good thing I had one from this time last year. My landlady do not put the year on them, just the month and the date. So Joyce thought it was a receipt for now. She don't know I didn't pay my rent this week."

"I call that deceit," I said.

"Better deceit than defeat. Now I have *really* got to figure out how to settle my rent. Can't you lend me Ten Dollars?"

"You know I cannot lend anybody Ten Dollars in the middle of the week."

"Then how on earth am I going to stay alive until I die? I cannot face my landlady."

"Borrow back from Zarita that Ten Dollars you spent taking her to the dance. Rob Peter to pay Paul."

"Zarita's name ain't Peter," said Simple, "and my landlady's sure ain't Paul. In so far as concerning Zarita, who just left out of here, sometimes I wonder why God made womens like her, because I don't understand her at all. I thought I did, but I do not believe I do. Zarita knows I go with Joyce. She knows I *love* Joyce. Zarita does not love me. Yet and still, Zarita is trying to make trouble between us—me and Joyce. Now why would she do that, as good as I am to that girl? I buy her a fifth of licker practically everytime I go to see her, treat her if I meet her, even take her out once in a while if I know Joyce is in bed and won't run into us. Nice as I been to Zarita, she comes telling me tonight she is 'thinking of telling Joyce how close we been.' She's done heard somewhere I'm planning to marry Joyce. Now, why would Zarita want to start some stuff?"

"Probably envious," I said, "because Joyce is going to have a happy home and she, Zarita, will still be on the loose."

"Loose as a goose," said Simple, "which is the way Zarita likes to live. She won't let no man tie her down, she says so herself. Plays the field, been playing it, and means to keep on playing it—no intention of being housebroke. Zarita will stick by a man only until the bottle is empty. Then she says, 'Don't you think we ought to run down to Paddy's before closing time and have a little drink?'

"Once back here in Paddy's, that's the end. Next thing you know she's found some other fellow who will take her to an after-hours spot. 'Bye, baby!' She's gone. Zarita likes to stay up and out all night long. She would exhaust a working man. When I first met her, she wore me down. Now I don't even see the chick more'n once or twice a month and nothing happens. So why does she want to come bringing up that she believes she'll tell Joyce all? There ain't no *all*! It's done, finished, over with."

"A man's past always lasts. In other words, 'Your sins will find you out.'"

"Truer words were never spoke," said Simple. "But I sure ain't gonna let Zarita come between me and Joyce!"

"Perhaps Zarita is just trying to blackmail you."

"I never will mail her a black cent! She's not much on money, nohow, just licker. That's one nice thing about Zarita, she's not a begging girl. In fact, she's free-hearted. She'll spend her money as fast as she will yours. I do not believe anything will shut Zarita's mouth but to scare her to death."

"Maybe she's only teasing you."

"I can tell when a woman's got larceny in her heart. When I told her I was getting engaged to Joyce formal this spring, I could see her ears go back like a cat looking cross-eyed at milk.

"Then she said, 'Oh, you is, is you?'"

"Any time anybody says, 'You is, is you?' they mean you no good, especially if they're smiling."

"Sometimes," I said, "even if a woman no longer wants you in her arms, she wants you in her heart."

"Dog-bite her heart! And she'll never get me in her arms any more. I wish I had never had her in mine."

"If wishes were horses beggars would ride."

"Zarita would ride, too," said Simple, "right out of my life. I would just like not to be worried by her any more."

"For once, race is not your main complaint. I am glad somebody has taken your mind off the color problem. In the past you have talked me to death on that score. Sometimes I wonder what made you so race-conscious."

"Sometimes I wonder what made me so black," said Simple.

55

Dear Dr. Butts

"Do you know what has happened to me?" said Simple.

"No."

"I'm out of a job."

"That's tough. How did that come about?"

"Laid off—they're converting again. And right now, just when I am planning to get married this spring, they have to go changing from civilian production to war contracts, installing new machinery. Manager says it might take two months, might take three or four. They'll send us mens notices. If it takes four months, that's up to June, which is no good for my plans. To get married a man needs money. To stay married he needs more money. And where am I? As usual, behind the eight-ball."

"You can find another job meanwhile, no doubt."

"That ain't easy. And if I do, they liable not to pay much. Jobs that pay good money nowadays are scarce as hen's teeth. But Joyce says she do not care. She is going to marry me, come June, anyhow—even if she has to pay for it herself. Joyce says since I paid for the divorce, she can pay for the wedding. But I do not want her to do that."

"Naturally not, but maybe you can curtail your plans somewhat and not have so big a wedding. Wedlock does not require an elaborate ceremony."

"I do not care if we don't have none, just so we get locked. But you know how womens is. Joyce has waited an extra year for her great day. Now here I am broke as a busted bank."

"How're you keeping up with your expenses?"

"I ain't. And I don't drop by Joyce's every night like I did when I was working. I'm embarrassed. Then she didn't have to ask me to eat. Now she does. In fact, she insists. She says, 'You got to eat somewheres. I enjoy your company. Eat with me.' I do, if I'm there when she extends the invitation. But I don't go looking for it. I just sets home and broods, man, and looks at my four walls, which gives me plenty of time to think. And do you know what I been thinking about lately?"

"Finding work, I presume."

"Besides that?"

"No. I don't know what you've been thinking about."

"Negro leaders, and how they're talking about how great democracy is—and me out of a job. Also how there is so many leaders I don't know that white folks know about, because they are always in the white papers. Yet *I'm* the one they are supposed to be leading. Now, you take that little short leader named Dr. Butts, I do not know him, except in name only. If he ever made a speech in Harlem it were not well advertised. From what I reads, he teaches at a white college in Massachusetts, stays at the Commodore when he's in New York, and ain't lived in Harlem for ten years. Yet he's leading me. He's an article writer, but he does not write in colored papers. But lately the colored papers taken to reprinting parts of what he writes—otherwise I would have never seen it. Anyhow, with all this time on my hands these days, I writ him a letter last night. Here, read it."

> *Harlem, U.S.A.*
> *One Cold February Day*

Dear Dr. Butts,

   I seen last week in the colored papers where you have writ an article for The New York Times *in which you say America is the greatest country in the world for the Negro race and Democracy the greatest kind of government for all,* but *it would be better if there was equal education for colored folks in the South, and if everybody could vote, and if there were not Jim Crow in the army, also if the churches was not divided up into white churches and colored churches, and if Negroes did not have to ride on the back seats of busses South of Washington.*

   Now, all this later part of your article is hanging onto your but. *You start off talking about how great American democracy is, then you* but *it all over the place. In fact, the* but *end of your see-saw is so far down on the ground, I do not believe the other end can ever pull it up. So me myself, I would not write no article for no* New York Times *if I had to put in so many* buts. *I reckon maybe you come by it naturally, though, that being your name, dear Dr. Butts.*

   I hear tell that you are a race leader, but I do not know who you lead because I have not heard tell of you before and I have not laid eyes on you. But if you are leading me, make me know it, *because I do not read the* New York Times *very often, less I happen to pick up a copy blowing around in the subway, so I did not know you were my leader. But since you are my leader, lead on, and see if I will follow behind your* but—*because there is more behind that* but *than there is in front of it.*

   Dr. Butts, I am glad to read that you writ an article in The New York Times, *but also sometime I wish you would write one in the colored papers and let me know how to get out from behind all these* buts *that are staring me in the face. I know America is a great country but—and it is that but that has been keeping me where I is all these years. I can't get over it, I can't get under it, and I can't get around it, so what am I supposed to do? If you are leading me, lemme see. Because we have too many colored leaders now that nobody knows until they get from the white papers to the colored papers and from the colored papers to me who has never seen hair nor hide of you. Dear Dr. Butts, are you hiding from me—and* leading *me, too?*

From the way you write, a man would think my race problem was made out of nothing but buts. *But* this, *but* that, *and, yes, there is Jim Crow in Georgia but—. America admits they bomb folks in Florida—but Hitler gassed the Jews. Mississippi is bad—but Russia is worse. Detroit slums are awful—but compared to the slums in India, Detroit's Paradise Valley is Paradise.*

Dear Dr. Butts, Hitler is dead. I don't live in Russia. India is across the Pacific Ocean. And I do not hope to see Paradise no time soon. I am nowhere near some of them foreign countries you are talking about being so bad. I am here! *And you know as well as I do, Mississippi is hell. There ain't no* but *in the world can make it out different. They tell me when Nazis gas you, you die slow. But when they put a bomb under you like in Florida, you don't have time to say your prayers. As for Detroit, there is as much difference between Paradise Valley and Paradise as there is between heaven and Harlem. I don't know nothing about India, but I been in Washington, D.C. If you think there ain't slums there, just take your* but *up Seventh Street late some night, and see if you still got it by the time you get to Howard University.*

I should not have to be telling you these things. You are colored just like me. To put a but *after all this Jim Crow fly-papering around our feet is just like telling a hungry man, "But Mr. Rockefeller has got plenty to eat." It's just like telling a joker with no overcoat in the winter time, "But you will be hot next summer." The fellow is liable to haul off and say, "I am hot now!" And bop you over your head.*

Are you in your right mind, dear Dr. Butts? Or are you just writing? Do you really think a new day is dawning? Do you really think Christians are having a change of heart? I can see you now taking your pen in hand to write, "But just last year the Southern Denominations of Hell-Fired Salvation resolved to work toward Brotherhood." In fact, that is what you already writ. Do you think Brotherhood means colored *to them Southerners?*

Do you reckon they will recognize you for a brother, Dr. Butts, since you done had your picture taken in the Grand Ballroom of the Waldorf-Astoria shaking hands at some kind of meeting with five hundred white big-shots and five *Negroes, all five of them Negro leaders, so it said underneath the picture? I did not know any of them Negro leaders by sight, neither by name, but since it says in the white papers that they are leaders, I reckon they are. Anyhow, I take my pen in hand to write you this letter to ask you to make*

yourself clear to me. When you answer me, do not write no "so-and-so-and-so but—." I will not take but *for an answer. Negroes have been looking at Democracy's* but *too long. What we want to know is how to get rid of that* but.
Do you dig me, dear Dr. Butts?

Sincerely very truly,
JESSE B. SEMPLE

56

Castles in the Sand

All-night cafeteria, one of the big ones. Glass-tiered sandwich counter, long steam table of tasteless foods. Puerto Rican countermen. Revolving door, marble-topped tables, people with trays. After the bars close at four A.M., full of characters. Rounders, professionals of the night, those who make their living after-hours, and the kind of people who never want to go home. And Simple. And me.

"It is cold in my little old small room, which is why I sets here, and them four walls looks like they squeezing in on me, squeezing in, squeezing. If I don't get some work soon, I will go nuts."

"Maybe I could lend you a little money," I said.

"I borrows only when I hope I can pay back. I'm O.K. anyhow. Last week I got a little old part-time job running lunches at noon time for a café near Radio City, taking trays up in the big office buildings to them pretty stenogs so busy with their bosses' mail they can't come out. It's too cold to come out anyhow these days, snow up to your knees. But all I got to warm my room when I get home is incense."

"Incense?"

"Aunt Pearl's stepson stopped by one night last week and gimme a dozen sticks he brought back from Korea on his furlough. Man, I lit one last night and it stunk up the joint so my old landlady thought I was smoking reefers. Scent drifted all the way downstairs, and she clumb all the way upstairs. Old landlady claims she's got rheumatatis so bad she can't walk, but if she thinks something wrong is going on, even on the top floor, she manages to get up there, nosy as she be. When she come sniffling at my door, I thought it were Trixie.

"*Bam! Bam! . . . Bam! Bam! Bam!* she knocked.

" 'Come in.' It were her.

" 'You know I don't allow no reefer smoking in my house,' says she.

" 'I allow none in my room either,' says I.

" 'Then what do I smell?'

" 'Chinese incense from Japan.'

" 'Is you running a fast house?'

" 'I would not try unless you was my partner. But, madam, you have give me an idea. Maybe we could make some money selling Sneaky Pete and renting out your alcove to transients.'

" 'I am not joking, Jess Semple. How come you burning that stuff in my house? Is it for bad luck or good?'

" 'I don't believe in no lucky scents. I am just burning this for fun because it were a present to me. Here, I will give you a stick to perfume up your part of the house. It also gives out heat.'

" 'I thank you. But next time you are going to fill my halls with heathenish smoke, let me know. I think I will keep my stick until the Canasta Club meets and try it on them ladies. Whee! It's right chilly up here.'

" 'You telling me. It's a deep freeze.'

" 'If you roomers would go to bed on time, I would not have to keep heat up until all hours of the night.'

" 'Has it been up tonight?'

" 'You know it were warm as toast in this house at seven P.M. It is now going on midnight. Go to bed, you'll get warm. What are you doing just setting up here doing nothing?'

" 'I'm thinking,' I said, 'and shivering.'

" 'That's funny where *your* heat disappears to. I fails to notice any change down in my Dutch basement.'

" 'Madam,' I says, 'science states that heat is tied in somewhatly with body temperatures.'

" '*Meaning* by that—?'

" 'Meaning you a bit fat, so naturally protected by your padding.'

"My old landlady puffed herself out to her full weight and said, 'Mr. Semple, I don't study ways of insulting roomers back. I considers that trifling. But there is one thing I got to say to you now, and that is this— you's lean, *that's* why you're so mean! I won't have you abusin' my form nor figger, and I'll thank you to regret your last remark.'

"Before I could say 'scat,' she swept her self out of that icebox, and left me setting there thinking—thinking about Joyce. I just set there in the cold thinking how that girl has waited all these years until I am free to marry her. Now here I am, got no job, and no money. Something always happens to keep a colored man from doing what he wants to do. Stormy weather! I been caught in some kind of riffle ever since I been black. If it ain't raining, it's blowing. If it ain't sleeting, it's snowing. I am just about to give up, jack, pack my bag, and start going! Yes, sir!"

"Migrate back South?" I asked.

"Whoever heard of a Negro in his right mind migrating back South?" said Simple. "I would not leave New York, not even to go to Brooklyn, not even the Bronx. They would be too far from Joyce. Married or not, I want to be near that girl. That girl is brave. You know, womens will not be downed. Last night she writ out her motto for me on a piece of paper and give it to me. See—

> *I do not know what life is,*
> *Nor what it may portend—*
> *But I think it will come out*
> *All right in the end.*

She said she got it out of a book when she was a kid. And Joyce is going right on planning her June wedding, putting down names on the guests' list, writing up the wording for the invitations, figuring out who is going to bake the cake and how high it's going to be, buying patterns for her bridal's dress. And I'm wondering where I'm gonna get the next payment on the engagement ring I give her New Year's Eve. I have to pay Ten Dollars a week on that, account of all them carats. Soon I'll have to start figuring out how to get a couple of wedding rings."

"One wedding ring, you mean, don't you?"

"We intends to have a double-ring ceremony with gold bands. She will give me one and I will give her one. But *I* got to pay for them both. I sure can't get no more credit without a job. This thing is getting serious, daddy-o, especially since I writ her father for her hand. She made me do it, so I got to put a gold band on her finger.

"Joyce's old man come writing back from Tampa, 'God bless you, son. I gives you my daughter with God's blessings for taking her off my hands. Joyce is one of the Lord's lambs, as I trust you is. I would thank you to send me the fare to come to New York and witness you and her united in holy wedlock with the blessings of the Almighty.'

"It seems like Joyce's father is very religious. Also that he is not working neither. I writ back and said, 'With God's blessings please pray that I get a job, because blessed if I ain't out of work myself, as you are also blessed by resting idle. Your lamb, Joyce, is the only one of us working this blessed winter. Pray for me and I will pray for you that *you* get the money to send for *us* to come down there on our honeymoon since we cannot send for you to come up here. Also we could use a rose-red 100% lamb's-wool blanket for a wedding present. Do not forget. Amen.'

"I thought I would ask him to send *us* something, too. There is nothing like laying down a counter-type to stymie the position—fare for fare. It's as far from Florida to New York as it is from New York to Florida. Anyhow, June is a long ways off, but it is not as far as it has been. And if I worked twenty-four hours a day from here on in, I could not catch up. It looks like it's fate for a dark man to see dark days:

> *White is right,*
> *Yellow is mellow,*
> *Black, get back!*

"I says, 'Joyce, what are we gonna do? I did not think this was going to happen to me. Soon as I gets one thing straight, another is out of whack. All these years I have not saved a thing. But I was intending to start saving with you. Now I have nothing to start saving with. Baby, have you figured up how much our wedding is going to cost?'

" 'I have,' said Joyce, 'but there is no need to worry you with that now, Jess. You got enough on your mind, darling. I just want you to know that I am behind you.'

" 'Joyce, honey,' I told her, 'I don't want you to be building castles in the sand.'

" 'I have built my castles in my heart,' said Joyce. 'No waves can beat them down. No wind can blow them apart. Nothing can scatter my castles. I tell you, nothing! Their bricks are love and their foundations are strong. And you, Jess Semple, you are the gate-keeper of my castle which is in my heart.'

"There was not anything I could say, so I just kissed her. It was like the end of a big act in a big show when the curtain comes down real quick and shuts out the old sceneries and cuts off whatever happened before, and you stop holding your breath and feel better. When the curtain goes up again, there's a new scene. The lights done changed to a brighter and better act—a brand-new act.

"Buddy, this is a new act for me. I disremembers the past. I disowns what I just now told you about going crazy in my little old small room. I will *not* go crazy. I will *not* let no wave beat me down, nor no wind smack me in the face no harder than I will smack it back. I will fight the wind, and the water—and come up swimming. I will say, 'Look here! World, here is me, still in there at bat!' Buddy, I see a whole lot of tomorrows— brand-new tomorrows—come what may!

" *What may* is me and Joyce together."

57

Four Rings

"I have not seen you for a few days," I said. "Where've you been?"

"Working," said Simple.

"Same place, your old job back?"

"Not yet—but the same place. I'm helping to reconvert. I went down there Monday and said, 'Look here, don't you need somebody to maintain while you converts?'

"The man said, 'I believe they are short-handed, but I don't believe they're employing any colored boys in the reconversion jobs.'

"I said, 'What makes you think I'm colored? They done took such words off of jobs in New York State by law.'

"I know he wanted to say, 'But they ain't took the black off of your face.'

"But he did not. He just looked kind of surprised when I said, 'What makes you think I'm colored?' Then he grinned. And I grinned. He is a right good-natured white man.

"He said, 'Go see the foreman.'

"I did. And I got took on. I got tired of waiting for them to reconvert that plant, so I am reconverting along with them. In six or eight weeks, they'll be ready to open up again. I will know a lots more about the new machines and things they are putting in because I'm watching every move they make and every screw they turn. Maybe I might even get a better job when the plant opens up. We got a good shop steward in my department. I believe he will look out for me."

"I hope so," I said. "You've been there long enough to deserve some upgrading."

"I'm on the up-and-up," said Simple. "I was so happy last night, I kissed Joyce all over the parlor. When we set down on the sofa she thought there was a bear next to her. I were so rambunctious, Joyce says, 'There's an end to this sofa—and you have got me right up against the end. Unhand me, Jess Semple. I'm going to make you something to drink.'

"Now that surprised me so that I let her go. Joyce had not ever made me a drink before—knowing how I drink in the street—except she's giving a party and serving guests and such, which must include me. Well, sir, Joyce went on back in the kitchen, and in a few minutes she comes out with two cups and a pot just steaming, something with a spicy smell.

" 'Whiskey toddy?'

" 'Guess again.'

" 'Hot rum punch?'

" 'No!' she says, 'Sassafras tea.'

" 'What?' I hollers. 'Sassafras tea?'

" 'To cool the blood,' she says. 'You remember down home, old folks used to give it to the young folks in the spring? Well, spring is on its way, dear. And I think you need this.'

"It did look right good, and smelled delicious, steaming pink and rosy as wine. I had not had no sassafras tea since I left Virginia when us kids used to strip the bark and bring it home to Grandma Arcie to dry. Trust Joyce to think up something different.

" 'You know we got to have our health tested before we can get married,' she said.

" 'I know it,' I says. 'Let's go tomorrow.' Not really meaning that, but don't you know that girl took time off from work and went. Me, too. And we'll have the certifications by the end of this week."

"This is only March," I said. "June is a long way off. Aren't you rushing matters a bit?"

"Them little details we wants to get out of the way," said Simple. "We is busy people. We got to start looking for an apartment. No more rooming from our wedding night on. Then soon as we can, we gonna start buying a house. Maybe next fall. Do you want to room with us in our house?"

"What my situation next fall will be, I cannot tell. So may I delay my answer?"

"You may, just so you're standing up there beside me at my wedding. You're supposed to hand me the rings. Ain't that what the best man does?"

"I think he does. But I'm rather backward about being your best man. After all, we are only bar acquaintances. A best man is usually a *close* friend, somebody with whom you grew up or with whom you went to college, somebody you know very well."

"I did not grow up with nobody, my folks moved so much. I stayed with fifty-eleven relatives in seven different towns. I did not go to college, and I do not know anybody very well but you. I bull-jive around with lots of cats in bars, and I sometimes cast an eye on different womens now and then. I drinks with anybody from Zarita to Watermelon Joe. But, excusing Zarita, I don't know none of them other folks very well. With them I just jives. Maybe I don't even know you, but with you at least I talk. No doubt, you got some friends you know better. But don't nobody know *me* better. So you be my best man."

"Then I'm supposed to give you a bachelor's party a night or two before the ceremony. Your wedding is going to cost me money, too, Jess! I'm certainly glad you're drinking less these days, so I won't have to stock up so heavy on liquors."

"Just a keg of beer," said Simple. "I mean one *private* one with my name on it. What you give the other jokers, I do not care. And the young folks will need some refreshments. F.D. is also getting married."

"At the same time as you and Joyce?"

"Yes," said Simple. "So he writ me to get him two rings just like ours. Him and Gloria wants everything to be just like me and Joyce's."

"Has that young boy gone and committed another Carlyle?" I asked.

"I asked him that, too," said Simple. "He said, 'No.' Him and Gloria do not want to have no children at all until he comes back from the army."

"From the army?"

"Didn't I tell you F.D. got his draft call? Soon as this college term is over, he has to go to his service. So them kids is gonna get married so F.D. can go with a clear conscience. F.D. and Gloria are marrying to separate—and me and Joyce are marrying to stay together. There's some advantage in being in a high age bracket after all."

"Love will find a way," I said, "whatever the age. God bless all of you—F.D. and Gloria, and you and—"

"Joyce—my honey in the evening!"

"Yes, all four of you."

58

Simply Love

Lent. Tentative sticking of heads out windows pushed up only to be pulled down. It is *not* warm yet, even if the sun is shining and the streets are dry. City Sanitation Trucks sprinkling pavements. Kids at stick ball competing with traffic. Marbles and tops, penny whistles, chalk on sidewalks, jumping ropes. Passersby duck and dodge handballs against stoops. Children think it's warmer than it is, running like they do.

Joyce is not the only one to brew sassafras tea, but it's hard to find sassafras bark in Harlem. You might have to have somebody mail you a bundle from home. Earliest breath of spring, when the sunrise is bright, landladies open their front doors first thing in the morning to air out the house, bright and early in the day, first thing. Joyce's big old fat landlady, still in her kimono, is sweeping out the vestibule and sweeping off the front stoop before breakfast when she almost drops her broom in amazement as she turns to see a man come running down the steps inside. Mr. Semple!

" 'What are you doing, coming out of *my* house at seven-eight o'clock A.M.?'

" 'Coming out is all,' I says.

" 'Mr. Semple, this is a decent house.' She pauses. 'Was you in there *all* night?'

" 'I were.'

" 'This is the first time! . . . Or is it? . . . I am surprised at you! And doubly surprised at Joyce Lane.'

" 'She is Joyce Lane no longer, madam.'

" 'What?'

" 'She is Mrs. Semple now. March has turned to June—we got married yesterday.'

" 'Ooh-ooo-oo-o!' she strangles.

"You could have knocked that old landlady down with a feather. She looked more surprised than you do."

"You can knock *me* down with a feather, too," I exclaimed. "Do you mean to tell me you jumped the gun and got married *before* the wedding—in March instead of June?"

"We did. Joyce and I did. And it feels like something I never done before."

"But I thought you were going to have a church wedding?"

"We were. But the feeling just overcome us early. So we went down to City Hall and rushed the season. We can get married again in a church any time we want to, when we get the dough."

"But what about the engraved invitations? What about the bridal gown she's having made? What about the relatives coming from down South for the ceremony? And what about the cake?"

"Man, that is where I was going this morning, to Cushman's to buy a cake when that big old fat landlady stopped me. Old landlady was so surprised she invited me right back in the house to call Joyce to come down and have hot cakes with her. She said, 'I'll make you your first cakes.'

"So the landlady fixed our wedding breakfast. It were *fine*. But she asked to see my license first just to be sure I were not there under false pretenses. Then she said it was O.K. that I had stayed upstairs last night."

"Well, friend, I still want to know, what about my dark-blue suit I was buying especially for the wedding, since you said I was going to be your best man?"

"You can wear it to our house to dinner. The invitations, the relatives, the cake, your suit, Joyce with a veil on—I asked her this morning, 'Baby, will you miss all them things? Are you mad or glad?'

"Joyce says, 'Glad, Jess, glad.'

"What happened was I took my first week's salary that I received back on the job and bought the license. I were not taking no chances of being laid off again before the wedding happened. Only thing is, buddy, I did not know where to find you yesterday morning to stand up with me, it being Saturday. We just picked out a couple of strangers who was down at City Hall getting married, too. They was our best people. And we was theirs. They were white. But we did not care, and they did not care. They stood up with us and we stood up with them. That white man were my best man, and I was his.

"We was all so happy when it was over that that white couple hauled off and kissed *my* bride, and I hauled off and kissed his. I did not think anything like that would ever happen—kissing white folks, and they kissing me. But it did—in New York—which is why I like this town where everybody is free, white, and twenty-one, including me."

"What about the wedding rings?"

"Me and Joyce is going to pick out the rings Monday."

"What about F.D. and Gloria, who were going to get married with you?"

"F.D. is grown. He can get married by his self. Joyce and me will stand up with him if he wants us to. But I will write that boy and tell him *I* could not wait. F.D. is young and got plenty of time. His memory don't go back no further than Sarah Vaughan—never heard of Ma Rainey. Besides he's on the baseball team, which will keep him busy pitching till June."

"Well, I did not have a chance to give that bachelor's party for you, which I regret."

"It would be no use to give it now because I have ceased from this day on to be a drinking man," said Simple, "so you'll save your money. Not that Joyce cares too much about me drinking, but I plans to respect what little objections she do have. She will never see me high again. And Zarita will never see me at all. Zarita has done cried, and wished me well, and is thinking about getting married herself—which is one more reason not to drink—with her off my mind."

"But can't I even buy you a beer in celebration of the occasion?"

"*One*—providing you got a stick of chlorophyll chewing gum about you."

"Hypocrite."

"Just kidding," said Simple. "But all kidding aside—and thanks for the beer—I *am* a new man. I intends to act like a new man, and therefore *be* a new man. I will only drink in moderation—which means small glasses—from now on. And this spring I will down as much sassafras tea as I will beer, if not more. What Joyce likes, I like. What she do, I do. Same as in the Bible—'Whether she goeth, I goeth'—even to concerts and teas."

"You are indeed a changed man," I said. "It's simply amazing."

"Simply heavenly," said Simple. "Love is as near heaven as a man gets on this earth."

Notes

Simple Speaks His Mind

1. Edward "Duke" Ellington.
2. Simple's own word for trickery, deception.
3. A vernacular or slang word for tricks, deceptions.
4. Rear end.
5. Jackie Robinson, the first black to play major league baseball, played with the Brooklyn Dodgers from 1947 to 1956.
6. A circus act, as discussed in "Nickel for the Phone," p. 116.
7. Dry skin needing lotion or vaseline to restore it to a healthy look.
8. Got upset.
9. "A Veteran Falls" first appeared in the *Defender* on December 7, 1946, as nonfiction narrated in Hughes's own voice. Simple was not mentioned. Hughes modified it for *Simple Speaks His Mind,* with Simple narrating the entire scene and the foil saying nothing.
10. As has been the case with many urban riots, the Harlem Riots of 1943 began after a black man was shot by a police officer. In this case, the black man was also a soldier in uniform, thereby exacerbating the frustration of the black community.

Simple Takes a Wife

1. Bootsie is a cartoon character developed by Ollie Harrington. Hughes wrote the introduction for *Bootsie and Others: A Selection of Cartoons by Ollie Harrington* (New York: Dodd, Mead and Company, 1958).

Index of Titles